MADRIGAL

MADRIGAL

A Jean-Louis St-Cyr and
Hermann Kohler Investigation

J. ROBERT JANES

VICTOR GOLLANCZ
LONDON

The right of J. Robert Janes to be identified as the author of
this work has been asserted by him in accordance with
the Copyright, Designs and Patents Act, 1988.

First published in Great Britain in 1999 by Victor Gollancz
An imprint of Orion Books Ltd,
Orion House, 5 Upper St Martin's Lane,
London WC2H 9EA

A CIP catalogue record for this book is
available from the British Library.

ISBN 0 575 06784 5

Typeset at The Spartan Press Ltd,
Lymington, Hants
Printed and bound in Great Britain by
Clays Ltd, St Ives plc

This is for Nancy Duncan
whose keen mind, quick wit and ready laugh
always cheered me on.

To the singer there is the song;
but to the truth, a very different tune.

Acknowledgements

All the novels in the St-Cyr–Kohler series incorporate a few words and brief passages of French or German, while *Madrigal* includes some Italian as well. Dr Dennis Essar of Brock University very kindly helped with the French, as did the artist Pierrette Laroche, while Ms Bodil Little, at Brock, helped with the German, and Carrado Federici with the Italian. Should there be any errors, they are my own and for these I apologize, but hope there are none.

Author's Note

Madrigal is a work of fiction. Though I have used actual places and times, I have treated these as I have seen fit, changing some as appropriate. Occasionally the name of a real person is also used for historical authenticity, but all are deceased and I have made of them what the story demands. I do not condone what happened during these times. Indeed, I abhor it. But during the Occupation of France the everyday crimes of murder and arson continued to be committed, and I merely ask, by whom and how were they solved?

I

As the sound of high and ancient iron wheels constantly hammered at him, Jean-Louis St-Cyr tried to find a moment's refuge to dwell on the murder investigation. But the coach's wooden benches were bolt upright, the buttocks numb, and there was hardly room to squirm. The Germans had taken over sixty per cent of France's rolling stock, thus pressing relics like this into service, even for the first-class carriages. And all around him, through the smoke-hazed, dim blue, fart-and-sweat-tainted air, the battered, dented steel helmets touched one another, and all around him there was the muffled sound of men not knowing what to expect.

Russia had taught these boys a lesson. The Battle for Stalingrad had been lost.

Hermann Kohler played *Skat* in the narrow corridor. Crowded around a Hindenburg Light, a stove that had been dredged from the trenches of that other war in 1914–18, he and two others held the cards. And the phalanx of silent men who were ranked on the nearby benches or stood or crouched, either stared at the guttering flame that brought no warmth but dreams of home, or at the cards, knowing only too well that after four hours of non-stop play, the *Vorhand* among them was a master.

He was not handsome, this partner of his, thought St-Cyr. He was a Fritz-haired, greying giant with a storm-trooper's lower jaw and chin, sagging jowls, and bags under pale blue eyes that seldom revealed anything when they didn't want to. A bullet graze, still too fresh to be forgotten, creased the heavy brow. The scar of a rawhide whip ran from below the left eye to the chin – the SS had done that to him for pointing the finger of truth. Another case.

1

There were shrapnel nicks from that other war and the years, particularly these past two and a half in France as partner to a Sûreté Chief Inspector, and as one of practically the only two honest cops left, had not been kind.

He was fifty-five years of age, a good three years older than himself. A *Detektiv Inspektor* from the Kripo, from that smallest and most insignificant branch of the Gestapo, but not like one of those, ah *grâce à Dieu*.

No, they fought common crime. Hermann was a citizen of the world and, yes, they had become friends. War does things like that, said St-Cyr to himself, but seeing Hermann sharing such a camaraderie made him think of that other war. Hermann had been in the artillery. Hermann had been taken prisoner in 1916 but not before the shells his battery had fired had come whistling over to bring the taste of mud, shit and rotten flesh or sour boot leather or mustard gas that would stick so fast in the gullet one could never forget it.

When a thin, cheap blue scrap of paper was passed from hand to hand, St-Cyr took it without a nod. Recognizing the PTT paper, the *Poste, Télégraphe et Téléphone* stationery, Kohler set his cards down, gave up the loot to be equally shared among the men, and got up to pick his way across the coach.

'Well, what's it this time, Chief?' he asked. Hermann had deliberately let the men know he was subordinate in rank to a Frenchman. He was like that sometimes.

'A love-note from an old friend.'

The flimsy tissue was proffered and quickly read.

Jean-Louis, though the circumstance is tragic, I welcome our working together again and recall the fisherman's wife. Everything has therefore been left exactly as you would wish it, and I have placed men on guard to ensure that nothing will be disturbed. May the Blessed Saviour keep you safe and bring you to us.

Alain de Passe,
*Commissaire de Police d'Avignon
et du Vaucluse*

2

The Sûreté's bushy, unclipped moustache was guiltily tidied with a pugilist's fist. The large and dark brown ox-eyes sought him out from beneath the brim of a battered brown fedora.

'He hates me, Hermann, so please read between the lines.'

These days everything was in code, even the day-to-day chatter between a husband and wife, or among other members of a family. No one knew who might hear and report or read and report. The SS, the Gestapo, a Pétainist, a Vichy 'inspector', a collaborator . . . it was the age of the anonymous letter or phone call, of old scores being settled, of the payoff and reward. A tragedy. It was 26 January 1943, a Tuesday.

'The fisherman's wife was a *petite lingère*,' confessed St-Cyr, still not taking his gaze from Hermann.

A seamstress – one who did sewing for others. 'You sure she wasn't someone's *petite amie*?'

Trust Hermann to think of it! Someone's 'little friend', someone's mistress. 'We could prove nothing. Her husband, a simple man, loved her as much as he did his fishing.'

'For the pleasure, eh?'

The blocky shoulders momentarily lifted. '*Mais certainement.* It's the only way to fish, *n'est-ce pas?* Doing it for a living would be far too hard.'

'I meant the other,' said Kohler.

Hermann's French was really very good. He had made a point of learning it in that prisoner-of-war camp.

'The other?' said St-Cyr. 'That, too. At forty years of age, and twenty-seven years younger than the husband, she was still possessed of a delectably eloquent figure, though when first seen on the beach at Cassis in the late summer of 1934 and then naked in the morgue, such things are always wanting. She'd been strangled and then for good measure her throat had been savagely opened with—'

'Okay, okay, spare me the details, eh? Why remember ancient history? Why not Avignon and the present?'

Patience was always necessary with Hermann. The Bavarian temperament often lacked it. 'Because, *mon vieux*, history is

3

inevitably involved in murder, and because the Church has power. Corrupt and otherwise.'

'The Church?'

The telegram was indicated. 'That crap about the Blessed Saviour keeping me safe. He's really saying, Let the warning be enough. Break glass and you will be cut. Tamper with the Host and the Blood of Christ and watch out.'

'And the *petite lingère*?'

'Maybe he's found another one.'

In the dim blue light of the railway station one man stood out beside the clock tower whose Roman numerals gave 11.59 p.m., all but an hour after the curfew in these parts. The doors had been locked. Most would have to spend the rest of the night in here and wouldn't be allowed to leave until 5.00 a.m. Berlin Time, which was 4.00 a.m. the old time in winter.

His face hidden by semi-darkness and by the cowl of a coarse grey woollen cloak, the man looked not at them when confronted but away.

'The carriage awaits,' he grunted in *langue d'oc*, the language of Old Provence. 'I am to take you to her.'

Merde, was he a monk? wondered Kohler. The ash-grey sackcloth was frayed at the cuffs and patched at the elbows. The bell-rope around the waist was old.

There were no sandals, only worn black leather boots, hobnailed and cleated like the thousands Louis and he had seen in use all over France.

Without another word from their guide, they passed on into a wind that took the breath away and caused the eyes to smart. The curse of Provence and the Rhône Valley, that wind of winds, the mistral, was in full force. '*Jésus*,' cried Kohler. 'Why us?'

'Why anyone?' lamented Louis.

The *calèche* was open, but unfortunately its only passenger seat faced forward into the wind. They threw up their suitcases themselves and as they and their driver mounted, his stick was used. Urging the tired old nag into the night, they left the kerbside.

4

The wind froze the cheeks and brought tears. There were no lights. The streets were empty. Muffled by the incessant racket, the sound of the hooves was hardly heard.

'The cours Jean Jaurès,' managed St-Cyr.

'Save it,' shot his partner. Impatiently Kohler tugged at the cloak. There was no response. He got up and tried to put a word into the driver's ear, but felt a grip of iron on his wrist. 'The Palais des Papes,' was all the man said.

And is this the way it's to be? wondered St-Cyr. The silent treatment?

'Nothing is colder than leather in the cold,' he grumbled. 'Not even a blanket has been provided.'

The nag took its time. Perhaps it was rebelling against being left behind when most of its fellows had been sent to Russia, perhaps it was simply old age which made it so uncooperative.

When the road began to climb, the stick was applied more rigorously. Ice soon caused trouble and their driver, thinking it would be better perhaps, took a slight turning on to a much narrower street where the cobbles were every bit as icy.

The darkness increased. Houses closed in on either side – many were substantial and had been built in Renaissance times and at the height of Avignon's power. From 1309 until 1377, the Papal Court had ruled from a city which had teemed with over 80,000 residents, by some reports, but had also had a 'floating' population of jugglers, minstrels, carnival dancers, thieves, con artists and prostitutes, thus earning it the sobriquet of the Second Babylon, or more politely where the popes were concerned, the 'Babylonian Captivity'.

At present there were perhaps no more than 50,000 residents and travellers were few, except for the Occupier and his minions. Yet the town was still very much a centre of wealth and power, of old money and old ideas.

'Louis, take a look behind us.'

Blinking, St-Cyr cleared his eyes. Faintly in the near distance, blue-shielded, slit-eyed headlamps were following.

'Three cars,' he mused.

'But whose?' demanded Kohler.

'The préfet, the bishop and the Kommandant – who else in these days of so few automobiles?'

It was an uncomfortable thought.

The Palais des Papes was as labyrinthian as he'd remembered it from years ago, thought St-Cyr. Brutally cold, insufferably dark, dank and fretted constantly by the wind, its many cavernous rooms and corridors seemed never to end and one had to ask, Why here, why now? And one had to answer, Was this not often a place of murder?

Hobnails ringing, their driver strode on ahead and at a turning, the shadow of him was flung upon a wall from whose thick and flaking, chipped and hammered plasterwork appeared the stark face of another age: 1343 perhaps.

From 1822 until 1906 the Palais had been a barracks, its wealth of early Renaissance frescoes plundered by soldiers so certain of profit they had even designed a tool to better cut and prise the paintings away.

A ruined scrollwork of grapevines gave the delicate green and brown of those time-faded days. 'She's in here,' grunted their guide impatiently, and tearing the shade from the lantern, flung light over a magnificent fresco of songbirds and swans, gardens and flowers, and a clearing from which a hare bolted before the threat of a pontiff's gloved hand on which was perched a hawk.

'*Mon Dieu*,' exclaimed St-Cyr, the breath escaping him.

'*La Chambre du cerf*,' grunted their guide dispassionately. The Stag Room.

She was lying on the floor, on her back but with her face turned away from them, and her long golden hair was bound by a tight headband of silver brocade in which there were insets of pale blue enamelled violets.

The right arm had been flung aside, its hand open, the beringed fingers now rigid.

Bent at the elbow, the left arm lay across her waist, its fist clenched tightly as if, in a last subconscious gesture of defiance, she would not give up its contents but would hide and hug them to herself even as her body collapsed.

Much blood had flowed from her to pool and darken on the glazed and soldier-ravaged tiles. Arterial blood had been pumped so hard, it had sprayed across the floor and over the wall to stain medieval fishermen and run down the long white neck of a swan that was about to be trapped for the table six hundred years ago.

Blood was spattered down her front – had she been on her knees and begging God to intervene? Had she fled to here? Had she run from her assailant? Why had she been in the Palais at all?

'Leave us. Leave the lantern,' breathed St-Cyr to their guide but not averting his gaze and aghast at what lay before them, for she was not dressed as she would have been today, but was in the finery of the very early Renaissance and as a maiden of substance, a petitioner to the Papal Court perhaps.

Time clashed – the present, the past, those intervening epochs when the palace had been a prison during the Revolution and then a barracks.

Time folded in on itself, he seeing the victim against the faded frescoes and broken tiles but seeing, too, in the imagination, the furnishings that once would have decorated the Palais, the tapestries, the velvet of its carpets – triple pile, it had been reported – the gold, the silver.

Faintly Kohler said, 'Our boy has already buggered off.'

'Good.'

'What the hell's that supposed to mean?'

'Merely that, like those who made a point of following us, he was meant to be unsettling at a time when we can least afford it. Now go and find him. Pry what you can from him.'

Leave me alone with her.

'You'll need me here.'

'Then please don't vomit all over the place. If you have to throw up, head for the Latrines Tower. It's near the far corner of the old palace. It's where the Revolutionaries dumped the bodies of the sixty Royalists they had imprisoned here and then murdered in a moment of passionate fervour in 1791. If you think this is blood . . .'

'Look, I won't be sick. Not this time.'

St-Cyr had heard it all before. It wasn't just the bodies they had had to examine. It was the roll call of them right back to 1914 and that other war. Hermann had recently lost his two sons at Stalingrad. He'd had a breakdown during their last investigation, had been on Benzedrine for far too long.

Always it was blitzkrieg for them, and almost always there were things like this to confront them.

'Please hold the lantern up. Let us see her as completely as possible.'

Her throat had been savagely opened. 'The windpipe, Hermann. The gullet and main arteries, muscles and nerves – the wound must continue to the cervical vertebrae. A little more and she would have been decapitated. She wouldn't have moved after this. Her assailant had to lower her to the floor.'

Kohler crouched to point out a few short strands of hair that had been cut and left clinging to the blood. For a moment he couldn't say anything, then at last he blurted, '*Un sadique? Jésus*, Louis, why us? Why here? Why now?'

He was referring to a previous case and another sadist, but it was odd that her killer – if it had been the killer – had found it necessary to take a sample of her hair. 'Nineteen years old, I think,' said St-Cyr to calm his partner.

'Nineteen it is.'

The lantern was brought closer to the body, Louis removing his fedora so that it wouldn't shade her as he went to work. He loved the challenge, could stomach anything, thought Kohler. Not short, not tall, but blocky and, even with the starvation rations of the Occupation, still somewhat corpulent, the Sûreté's detective crouched and began to get to know their victim. He'd be 'talking' to her soon. He always did that and always it seemed to help.

'Ah *merde*, Hermann, it's as if she had stepped right out of the pages of history. The dark green woollen cloak is trimmed with white ermine tails. The gown is of saffron silk and decorated with a faint design, but over this kirtle, whose tight sleeves, collar and hem are visible, she wears a cote-hardie of cocoa-brown velvet whose bodice is of gold brocade and laced up the front from the waist to the softly curving, now much blood-spattered neckline.'

The cote-hardie had sleeves that came only to above the elbows and were piped with gold brocade. At the hem, it was cut jaggedly so that upwardly-narrowing wedges of the saffron underdress would show through to a height of about thirty centimetres.

The shoes were as no others Kohler had seen except in museum collections. They had no heels, no laces either, and were like modestly pointed slippers of fine black kid, and they fitted perfectly, as did the rest of her costume.

'It isn't right, Louis. It's too weird for me. Her belt—'

'The girdle, yes.'

Of exceedingly fine suede, the belt was studded with silver and gold, with brooches and pins of emerald, lapis lazuli, amber and moonstone. And this comet's tail of trinkets began high on the left hip, falling to well below the right hip, in the fashion of the times.

'There are tiny silver bells,' managed Kohler, forcing himself to ignore the wound. 'There are little silver and gold buttons. There's a—'

'The "buttons" are *enseignes* – signs. But among them there are also talismans which were to ward off evil and disease. The bells were to frighten away the devil.'

'The purse wasn't taken.'

'Her *aumônière sarrasine*. It probably contains the alms she would willingly have handed to the beggars in the streets had she lived back then.'

Everything was as it once must have been. The purse was richly embroidered with silver thread . . .

'The wound is from the left to the right,' muttered Jean-Louis and, losing himself in that moment, said, 'Excuse me, mademoiselle, but I must bring the light closer now just for a little.'

Concern and sympathy moistened Louis's brown eyes. The Sûreté used a pair of tweezers to gently prise the edge of the cloak away from where it had become stuck. 'Strength,' he grimaced.

'The one who did this has slaughtered sheep, Hermann. A ruthless cut and done continuously. One motion . . . and held against the assailant, her back suddenly arched. Something wide, something curved. Ah *merde*, could it be? Please look for the cork from an old wine bottle. It's just a thought.'

Please leave me to talk to her.

Rigor would have set in from perhaps two to four hours afterwards, thought St-Cyr, but if she had been running through this empty place, her muscles would have been under extensive exertion and it could then have come on immediately.

The wretched frost of one of the coldest winters on record would prolong it.

Rigor there was. The fingers which clasped her little treasure would have to be broken.

'There's a wine cork, Louis. Maybe he flung it aside and didn't give a damn if we found it.'

'I'm not so sure it was a he, are you?'

'Not really, but with a wound like that . . .'

'There are bits of dried lavender on the floor, Hermann. Whoever did this also forgot to remove them.'

'Lavender?'

'Not from her person. Also winter grass and thyme.'

'A shepherd?'

'Or one who has to daily gather feed for rabbits and chickens.'

'A sickle, then, with a cork to protect its tip when not in use,' sighed Kohler. Louis had made a point of doing comparative studies of wounds in his early days as a detective. 'Dead how long, Chief?'

'At least twenty-four hours. The coroner can, perhaps, be more positive about it and the weapon. We'll have to ask for Peretti. I want none of the préfet's interfering, none of the bishop's and certainly none of the Kommandant's.'

Killed Monday night, the twenty-fifth. 'Then you'd better speak to them,' came the faltering words. 'We've company.'

The Sûreté didn't even take his eyes from the victim. 'Please escort them to the entrance, Hermann. We will question each of them individually as necessary.'

'A moment,' said someone – the Kommandant, by the atrocious accent.

'No moments, Herr Oberst,' said St-Cyr. 'This is a matter for the Sûreté and the Kripo. If in doubt, please consult Gestapo Boemelburg and Maître Pharand. You will find both at 11 rue des Saussaies in Paris.'

Formerly the Headquarters of the Sûreté Nationale and now that of the Gestapo in France *and* of the Sûreté. 'It was myself who asked specifically for you both.'

'Then please leave us to do what you asked.'

'*Verdammt!* How dare you?'

There was a sigh and then, still not pausing in his work, the admonition of, 'Herr Oberst, you of all people must be accustomed to delegating authority and to placing trust in those so chosen. Are you then also mindful of Orlando Gibbons, the English madrigal composer of the late sixteenth century and the first quarter of the seventeenth?'

'Don't talk nonsense.'

'Fortunately, before leaving Paris I was able to find something on madrigals, since that word was mentioned in Gestapo Boemelburg's directive to us. The book hadn't been banned and burned by the List Otto.* I'll give it to you then, shall I, in *deutsch*, this little quotation I discovered on the train?, and will ask you to listen to the question it forces us to consider, since the three of you are so anxious about this killing you would wait for us to arrive and would stay up more than half the night.

' "The silver swan, who living had no note. / When death approached unlocked her silent throat:" did she have something to say, Herr Oberst, and is that why she was killed?'

There was no answer.

'Now please leave, as I have asked. Find Peretti, Hermann. Maître de Passe, get me your best photographer and fingerprint

---

*The works of Thomas Mann and 841 others, including those of all British authors except for the classics. Spy novels were considered a particular threat, as were histories and novels of WW1.

artist, and we'll want the Palais sealed and placed off-limits to everyone but those we wish to consult.'

They didn't like it. They huffed and farted about but obeyed. And when he had them at the ancient door and under its Gothic arch, Kohler said, 'He's like that. Get used to it. We're here to find out who did it, and we will, no matter what.'

Alone with her at last, St-Cyr apologized for the disturbance. 'Murder invariably attracts the concerned and the curious,' he said, his voice gentle. 'But sometimes the killer is among the first to appear and is most anxious to assist for reasons of his or her own. Tell me why you are here, dressed as you are? Did you come to meet someone?'

Her eyes, though glazed, were of the softest shade of amber. They couldn't blink or appear to be evasive, of course, yet he swore the question had upset her.

Ancient keys of beautifully but simply worked iron hung from her belt. There'd be those for the linen boxes – closets and *armoires* were all but unheard of in those days – others for the pantry and storehouses. Keys for the money box, too. Keys for this and that. In total there were eight of them, and one was both longer by five centimetres than the longest of the others, and stouter. But these were the keys to a house or villa, not a Palais, and the original lock could no longer be in place here in any case.

Had she had a key to the present entrance, or had someone left the door open for her?

'And if the former, then who gave it to you?' he asked. 'A lover? Were you to meet in the Palais, and if so, why? To sing?' he hazarded.

Madrigals were part songs, the popular music of the day, and she . . . what would her voice have been? 'A contralto?' he asked. 'A soprano?' Had it been a lover who had killed her? A boy, a young man, a former shepherd, former altar boy, a baritone now, a tenor or bass among the madrigal singers?

'You were dressed for your part,' he said. 'There were four, five or six of you in the group. Together you sang so well the préfet, the Kommandant and the bishop must have known of you and had their reasons for coming.'

There were so many things that needed looking into. Her belt, the cabochons, they'd tell a story with the *enseignes* and talismans. There were pewter scissors hanging from the girdle. There was a dirk in its richly tooled sheath of silver and leather. There was also a plain soft brown velvet pouch – needles and thread, no doubt. Did she carry the tools of her trade as well? he wondered.

Easing his back, he stood a moment. 'You are begging us to become detectives of those times. For myself that may be possible, but for my partner, let me tell you he is definitely of the present. He lives with two women and enjoys them both but rarely, and never at the same time, or so I am given to understand. It's curious, isn't it, seeing as the one is almost twice the age of the other? Both are *très gentilles, très belles, très differentes*, yet are fast friends. War does things like that.'

He knew she would have been shocked – intrigued, but so modest her eyes would have ducked away. She was young – perhaps two years younger than Hermann's Giselle – and pretty. Not beautiful, but lovely – *très charmante*. One could tell she'd been decent, honest, diligent, steadfast and true, but the detective in him had to say, 'I mustn't be a sentimental fool.'

No matter how hard he tried, he couldn't avoid the gaping throat. Had she the voice of an angel? Just what had she known and had her killing really been to silence her?

Hatred, rage – so many things were evident in her murder, a total lack of conscience, a ruthless arrogance that frightened. She'd have been alone, must have been terrified. Had sex been denied? One always had to ask, and where, please, was the murder weapon?

Caught in the flesh there was another bit of winter-grey lavender. Bending closer, he teased it away, said, 'This clung to the haft of the sickle, if that really was the weapon.' And furious with himself for not having any envelopes – the constant shortages these days – found a scrap of paper in a pocket, another of the leaflets the Allies were dropping to encourage resistance.

Carefully he gathered the bits from the floor, then used yet another leaflet to hold the hairs that had fallen when her assailant or someone else had cut off a sample.

Though faint, there was the scent of coriander and cloves.

'A toilet water,' he said. 'Did you make it yourself, according to a recipe from those times?'

Mon Dieu, but she was so of the past, her skin had even been anointed with one of the unguents of those days. 'You're a puzzle,' he said, and then, 'Forgive me.'

Abruptly he broke the fingers of her left hand. Her little treasure rolled away, and for a moment he was too preoccupied to say a thing.

'A pomander,' he managed at last. 'Of gold and in the shape of a medieval tower with battlements, whose lid is hinged and with a fine gold chain and clasp.'

There were second- and third-storey windows in the walls, and embrasures for firing arrows – openings from which the scent could constantly escape in those times of plague to momentarily purge the stench of raw sewage and rotting refuse in the streets. But there were few of these openings and he had the thought that the pomander must have been modelled after an actual tower in the Palais.

The pomander was filled with half-centimetre-sized spheres of grey, polished ambergris. Though hard to define, its scent was musty, earthy and still quite strong, though he had the thought the ambergris wasn't recent.

All over the walls there was the finely engraved design of an alternating upright lute, separated by a downwardly pointing needle, beneath which was an upended thimble to catch a single droplet of blood.

The pomander was very old and, in keeping with the riddles of those times, he wondered if in its design there wasn't a rebus, a puzzle with which she would tease others to discover its true meaning?

When he opened the purse, he found gold double dinars, base-silver dineros and silver pennies, gold écus and agnels, salutos, ducats and a Cretan coin, an exquisite piece, dating perhaps from

14

the first century BC. Cast with all its imperfections of roundness, it held the beautifully executed, raised design of a maze.

'*Le fil d'Ariane*,' he sighed. 'Is this why you carried it?' Ariadne's clue. The thread Theseus used to escape the labyrinth after slaying the Minotaur. 'Were you trying to indicate that should something happen to you, that others must find the thread and follow it?'

Among the hoard at the bottom of the purse there was a tin of sardines that had definitely *not* come from the very early Renaissance or from such a far distant time as the maze.

'Hermann,' he said. 'Hermann, what is this?' But his partner was busy elsewhere.

The corridor was dark except for the faint flickering of an 'Occupation' fire in the room ahead. Kohler waited. Drawn by the smell of smoke that the mistral had driven down the chimney and throughout the palace's ground floor, he had at last found them.

Their voices were muted, the patois not easily understood and soon silenced, they sensing an intruder.

The monk, still with hood covering his head, sat to the left on a three-legged stool that must have been rescued from a medieval cowshed; the boy was to his right, sitting on the hearthstone, all but hidden under a filthy horse blanket and no doubt freezing.

'Okay,' sighed Kohler. 'Let's start by your telling me who the hell you are and why the kid's here, and don't tell me he's taken the vow of silence.'

Such impatience befitted Gestapo Paris-Central. 'My name is Brother Matthieu. I am envoy to His Eminence, the Bishop. I do odd jobs.'

'In sackcloth?'

'It's my mistral coat. You'd be surprised how effective are the clothes of our departed brethren. Six hundred years ago the mistral was every bit as much of a curse. Now, please, Inspector, I must send Xavier back to the kitchens and to his bed. The boy knows nothing of the matter here.'

Neither of them had turned from the fire. Too afraid perhaps. The room was barren except for the stool, a wooden soup bowl, a wooden spoon and a small cast-iron stew pot whose lid had been set aside.

A thin litter of reeds barely raised the threat of a fire.

'Xavier is a ward of the Church, Inspector, and was given into God's Holy Service by his parents as was I myself. We share much in common, and out of the great goodness of his heart he has brought me a modest repast for which I am truly grateful.'

'*Un civet de lièvre*, eh?' snorted the Kripo. A hare stew. Both continued to stare at the tender flames. 'Hey, *mon fin*, trapping hare and rabbit is illegal, and so is eating meat on Wednesdays, Thursdays and Fridays, and it *is* Wednesday now.'

All spoils to the victor, even small game. 'Are you threatening me with three years in prison, Inspector, or with forced labour in the Reich?'

The official and much-touted penalty.

The face that had turned to look up at him was in shadow but darker still and fierce, the nose prominent and scarred.

'Pull the hood back. Go on, do it!'

'If it pleases you,' came the mild rebuke. The harshness of a perpetual smile registered in once broad lips, the lower of which had been tightly folded up and in by the surgeons of twenty-five years ago. The rugged, scarred cheeks, with the grey-black bristles of a thin and closely clipped beard, hid nothing. Not the terrible shrapnel wounds of that other war; not the fear, the pain of knowing one had been about to die – that never left a person; not the reprieve and the disfigurement. *Une gueule cassée*, one of the Broken Mugs.

There were pouches under the dark grey eyes, one of which was permanently half closed, but the intensity of the gaze had mellowed a little as sympathy had registered starkly in the face of the detective.

Without a word, Kohler dragged out the apology of cigarettes and, offering each of them a smoke, reached into the fire to take up a light.

'Inspector,' said Brother Matthieu, 'you must forgive my

16

recent absence, but you see, I was worried. Xavier is my responsibility and I was certain you might think his presence untoward when the préfet and the bishop had ordered that no others were to enter the Palais. The repast also had to be shared. It's our custom, and I knew the stew would not keep hot and he'd be hungry.'

Ravenous, no doubt, and probably fresh in from trapping game in the countryside, and with a corpse up there on the first floor neither of them seemed to care to mention.

The remains of a salad of Belgian endive, marinated green beans, sweet red peppers and chopped chives lay on a soiled napkin before the boy, as did a half-eaten round of goat's cheese that had been wrapped in a grape leaf, marinated in olive oil and dusted with herbs.

The kid had tried to hide the cheese. Oil glistened on the slender fingers. He was nearly thirteen years old, tall for his age, old beyond mention, willow-shoot thin and with blue eyes that, though stunningly wide, held a peasant's watchfulness and were otherwise empty of all feeling.

He smoked his cigarette like a pro. He'd flick the butt away when done. He had that insolent look about him.

The dark brown hair was parted in the middle, cut in a pageboy style and bobbed about the ears. The lips were wide and sensuous, the cheeks thin, the bone structure fine, the brush of the eyebrows full and wide. A pretty boy, one might have said, if his clothes hadn't been so worn and filthy. The lashes were long and curved upwards, the nose was aquiline and of some passing nobility deep in his family's ancestry, the skin that soft shade of brown so typical of the Midi.

'*Ihre Papiere*,' breathed Kohler, hating himself for getting Gestapo-like, but somehow he had to get through to them. 'Your *Ausweis*, too. *Bitte*, eh? *Schnell!*' Hurry! He snapped his fingers.

The monk threw the boy a warning glance and blurted, 'Inspector, is this necessary?'

'It is, if we're ever to find out where he's been, Father, why he's really here, and what connection if any he has to the murder. Oh by the way, what was her name? You haven't forgotten it, have you?'

'Mireille de Sinéty. That . . . that is all I am permitted to tell you for the moment.'

'The bishop's got your tongue, has he? Hey, *mon fin*, refusing to give information is a criminal offence.'

With vegetable slowness, the boy hauled out a dog-eared ID, a residence permit and ration booklet from which, since it was close to the end of the fortnight, virtually all of the tickets had been removed. One thousand one hundred and fifty calories a day *if* one could get them.

Kohler held the ID photos to the light. An altar boy's white surplice had been worn for the head-and-shoulders and profile shots. The kid had been scrubbed clean and looked like an angel without its wings.

'They made me bathe,' he taunted insolently.

'Who?'

The boy indicated his mentor. '*Les pères de Jésus. Mon père.*'

'Inspector . . .' began Brother Matthieu only to hear the Kripo shriek, 'Silence! Let him do the talking. So, empty your pockets, Xavier. Let's see what you're carrying.'

'Inspector . . .'

'*Sei still, Priester!* Look, don't force me to get rough. I simply want the truth. Neither of you appears to be shedding a tear over the dearly departed.'

'Our tears are already dry,' muttered Brother Matthieu sadly. 'She was God's gift, an example to us all.'

Tears fell and there were plenty of them as the broken lips quivered in silent prayer and the fingers trembled, but at memory's touch of what? wondered Kohler uneasily.

As if on cue, the boy suddenly turned out his pockets. A *mégot* tin held a connoisseur's pick of cigarette and cigar butts that had obviously been gleaned from the courts of the high and mighty. There were a dozen dried apricots, some almonds and cloves of garlic to stave off hunger.

A flat, brown, hip-pocket-sized bottle from prewar days was half-filled with home-distilled brandy, the fierce grappa of the hills.

18

'For the toothache, Herr Detektiv,' offered the boy, with no feeling in his gaze or voice.

Two 9mm Parabellum rounds were confiscated. 'We'll get to these. Now tell me where you got the goat's cheese?'

'From home, from les Baux.'

A village some twenty-three kilometres to the south.

'Inspector, he ran away,' confessed Brother Matthieu lamely. 'When he heard of what had happened here, Xavier left us and has only just returned by way of our kitchens and at the bishop's command.'

'Afraid, was he? The boy, that is.'

'Upset, yes. All of us were and are.'

Kohler gave the brother a curt nod. Towering over them, he said, 'Is that why he hasn't quite emptied his pockets, Father?'

The monk silently cursed this Bavarian from the Kripo as a small brass bell, *une clochette*, fell to the hearth to ring and roll into the ashes.

'The boy sleeps with the dogs for warmth, Inspector. They are a modest duty he undertakes.'

'For whom?'

May God forgive me, said Brother Matthieu to himself. 'His Holiness, the Bishop.'

Each dog, when out hunting, would wear a bell whose sound was different from those of all the others. And when the dogs drove game towards their master, he would know exactly where each of them was.

The tin of sardines had come from the firm of D'Amelio et fils in Marseille and it would have cost a fortune on the black market, thought St-Cyr. At least 1200 francs, the equivalent of a kilo of butter or five kilos of potatoes, if one could find them, and half a month's wages for a department store clerk or minor government official. Its presence was so incongruous he drew in an impatient breath. Always there were questions, and always under the Germans virtually no time was allowed to sort such things out.

The label carried an artist's romantic view of the Vieux Port with the slumbering industry of beached and anchored trawlers whose burnt ochre sails held their inverted triangles to the intense blue of the sky. Twin sardines, swimming away from each other, were superimposed on the label in a softer, greyer blue but he thought no more of them.

Not two weeks ago, from 13 to 15 January, the Germans had destroyed the warren of slum housing that had occupied the whole of the first arrondissement of Marseille. Hitler had been in a rage. On the third of the month German security forces had attacked a brothel hoping to arrest *résistants* in hiding, and several of the Occupier had been killed.

Avignon could not help but have shuddered at the news, and this one must certainly have been aware of it.

There were several rings on each of her fingers – one of plain gold had round projections, others were of polished cabochons: a superb jasper of deep red was thinly banded by silvery-grey magnetite; there was a sapphire . . .

Three spare rings hung around her neck on a fine gold chain. There was a zodiacal ring on the fourth finger of her right hand, with garnet rings placed before and after it. This fourth fingernail had been broken, a painful tear she had not had a chance to attend to. What had she torn it on?

'I don't even know your name,' he said apologetically. 'Forgive me.' And lifting the hem of the cote-hardie, the gown and sheath, examined her hose for tears, for pulled-down garters, for bruises and scratches.

There were none, and the hose, which came to just above her knees, was also of the very early Renaissance, of a soft, crocheted wool and white in colour – grey had been preferred for practicality but this one had spared no expense. She had come to the Palais, to a rendezvous perhaps, and had worn nothing but the finest of raiment.

But how had she come by such clothes in these times of extreme shortages, and who had she really been?

'You lived in your imagination,' he said. 'You were a creature of it. You must have been.'

'Her name was Mireille de Sinéty, Louis.'

'Ah! Hermann. You took your time.'

'It's nearly five a.m. The photographer and fingerprint artist is waiting. The *flics* have brought a van with two of the sisters to guard her virtue.'

'*Bon.* I'm staying with this one. I'm not letting her out of my sight until I'm satisfied we have a record of the trinkets she wears and where they are located. Each item may have meaning.'

'And you don't trust others, not even the sisters?'

'Avignon is like Lyon, a city of the hidden, Hermann. They play games here and we must never forget this. Petrarch wrote of it in his secret letters to Rôme in 1346 or thereabouts, but it is Victor Hugo we have to thank for the statement, "In Paris one quarrels; in Avignon one kills." '

The Latin temperament. 'Any sign of a dog?'

'Why?' Louis had been startled by the question.

'Because, *mein lieber französischer Oberdetektiv*, there could well have been one.'

A dog . . . 'Is there a priest with the sisters?'

'The bishop himself, who else?'

'Then he has had a long night and is very stubborn.'

'I'll show the photographer in first, shall I, Chief, and then the others when he's finished?'

Their voices were rebounding from the walls and would be heard. 'You do that. You tell His Eminence we will allow the Sacrament of the Death but his anointing the body with oil is definitely out until after Peretti has seen her, unless, of course, Extreme Unction has already been given and we have not been informed of it.'

'To not anoint the body is a sacrilege, Inspector. What harm can it possibly do?' came a voice, firm and determined, the traces of *langue d'oc* as old and stubborn as the hills.

He stood alone, this Bishop of Avignon. He wasn't tall but was as if cut from stone, the nose so fiercely prominent it would dominate his every expression. The dark brown, steely eyes were hooded and empty of all else beneath bushy iron-grey brows that feathered thickly to the sides. The forehead was blunt, a stern and unyielding prelate whose grimly set lips were turned down at their corners.

'Bishop, why is there secrecy with this one?' asked St-Cyr.

'There is no such thing.'

'Then please be good enough to tell us who found her and when?'

'Salvatore awaits your pleasure in the guardroom near the entrance. He'll tell you what you need to know. Now if you don't mind, I must give this poor child the release you spoke of. Her soul has already been forced to wait too long.'

The bishop removed a black woollen overcoat and a grey scarf, and thrust these at Hermann. Dressed simply as a humble priest in a black cassock, he found his kit and opened its little leather case as he knelt beside the victim.

St-Cyr brought the lantern close, recording distress in the bishop's questioning gaze at the affront of such an intrusion, the slight trembling, too, of short, thickset fingers whose nails were closely trimmed.

'Inspector, have you no conscience? This is a matter between Mireille and her God.'

Not 'Mademoiselle de Sinéty', or even simply, 'the mademoiselle', but Mireille. 'Murder is never private, *mon père*. God is as aware of this as He is of her needs.'

'How dare you?'

He wore no ecclesiastical rings, this bishop, not even a wristwatch. The Cross he used was of black iron. 'My child,' he said, turning to the victim, 'God forgives your sins as He forgives the one who did this and the one who intrudes upon our sacred moment.'

He closed her eyes but couldn't stop his fingers from lingering. Tender . . . did he think this of the touch of her skin? wondered St-Cyr. Seen from above, the bishop's hair was thick and grey, cut short and unruly below and around a tonsure which hid neither blemish nor birthmark but was in need of a razor.

Bishop Henri-Baptiste Rivaille anointed her body with the oil, made certain her soul was consigned to Heaven. He would take an hour at least to do it if necessary! he swore to himself. The rings were there on her fingers, the decade with its ten projecting knobs so that she could privately say an *Ave* as she touched each of them and then a *Pater Noster* at the bezel. Had she done so in her darkest moment? he wondered.

A gimmel ring was there too – a pair of circlets and bezels that interlocked when worn together as now, but which could be separated so that each half of a couple could wear one as a sign of true affection, but would the Sûreté who was watching him so closely understand its meaning?

The fleurs-de-lis of twin brooches were on either side of her wounded neck and mounted high on her chest to clasp the mantle she wore beneath her over-cloak. The brooches were of *champlevé*, with polished cabochons of ruby, emerald and sapphire which were set in collets or mounted *à jour* with claws to let the light shine through them.

On a gold chain, fastened to her girdle, there was a pendant box, of two foiled crystals mounted in silver gilt, and Rivaille knew he mustn't let his eyes dwell on the box, knew precisely what it contained.

A jasper ring drew him as he continued, his lips so familiar with the sacrament that his eyes and mind could search undisturbed for the slightest detail of her person.

The dark red jasper was banded with silvery-grey magnetite and he knew it was a type of loadstone and associated with earthly love, the stone worn so as to attract another.

But would the one from the Sûreté discover this?

Her kirtle was of Venetian silk, the colour of the finest La Mancha saffron. Her belt was of the softest suede but he mustn't examine it too closely, mustn't tremble at the sight of it.

From high on her left hip a trail of gold and silver, of precious and semiprecious stones fell to lead buttons and pearls but began with her own sign. And he knew then beyond question that she had defied God and the Church and had left a rebus among the *enseignes* and talismans, the cabochons and zodiacal signs. But would the detectives be able to decipher it?

Making the sign of the Cross over her, he gave a sigh whose

sadness he hoped would not be misinterpreted. He touched her hair, her lovely hair . . . 'My work here is done, Inspector. The sisters are to stay with her until she is released for burial.'

'They may have a long wait,' said St-Cyr.

'That does not matter. This one was special.'

2

In the guardroom just inside the entrance to the Palais, the smell of roasting garlic was mingled with that of smoking kerosene. Bent over the lantern, the concierge had pushed up the globe to warm a tiny repast but was still unaware of company. '*Putain de bordel*,' he hissed at the lantern. 'Behave yourself!'

The skewered garlic was withdrawn, smoke continuing to pour through the lantern's vents. Brushing away the soot as best he could, he cut the clove in half and took to rubbing it into a twenty-five-gram slice of the National bread.

With great deliberation he finally gave up and began to finely slice the garlic with an ancient, wooden-handled knife. The bread would be grey and full of sweepings best not eaten but when one is hungry enough to eat lunch a good six hours before noon, what could be said?

'It helps, doesn't it?' Kohler indicated the garlic, startling him. 'It stays with you longer than most things and gives the illusion of a stomach at work.'

The chewing stopped. The mouse-brown, unblinkered eye began to moisten.

Salvatore Biron dragged off his beret, the garlic chips tumbling from the bread to lie sweating their juice under the flickering light. 'Forgive me,' he said and ducked his good eye down.

Immediately he began to tidy things, the left hand busy, the hook that served as the right hand unoccupied. One of the *anciens combattants* from the last war, like Brother Matthieu, he was, in addition, a *grand mutilé*, an amputee. 'Verdun,' he muttered, not looking up. 'Your side's machine-gun nest. In the carelessness of my grenade attack the bunker was removed but so was my forearm, and fortunately for me, but a portion of my *parties sensibles.* One testicle, not the member.'

'A fag?' said Kohler, hauling them out only to see Biron shake his head and hear him mumble, 'I have my own and because tobacco is so severely rationed, must limit myself lest the desire become too great.'

'*Nicht deutschfreundlich,* eh?'

Not friendly to Germans. 'Should I be?' he asked, looking up at last but not defiantly. 'They removed my right leg below the knee. Another mistake of mine, but no matter.'

The face was pinched, the hair dyed jet black, as were the eyebrows to match the layers of cloth that had been glued to the inside of the right lens of his specs.

'And yet you're here, guiding "tourists" through the Palais, seven days a week at their command.'

'One has to live, and since the pension is small, we Avignonnais tend to take care of one another. The bishop has a kind heart.'

Had Biron turned grey overnight during the war? wondered Kohler. Many of the boys had. 'So, okay then, start telling me about the girl.'

'I found the child on Monday night at about ten minutes before the curfew started.'

At 10.50 p.m. on the twenty-fifth. The wire summoning Louis and himself to Avignon had arrived in Paris at about 8.00 a.m. on the twenty-sixth. 'What made you go up there at that hour?'

'The bishop always requires that I go through the Palais to make certain all is well and no one has remained behind to make mischief.'

'But someone did.'

'Our "tourists" often throw stones at the statues or yell so as to hear the echoes of their voices.'

'Soldier boys will be boys. When do you usually check through?'

Salaud! Son of a bitch! 'After closing. At . . . at five thirty in the afternoon, unless, of course, there is one of the concerts. The madrigal singers perform here and when they do, *la chambre de la grande audience* is always full. A crowd, some of whom like to wander off, especially in summer when it's warm outside, but cool in the darkness here.' If the Inspector thought anything of this, he gave no indication.

'What detained you from five thirty until ten minutes before the curfew?' he asked.

Jésus, merde alors, why must he persist? 'A film. It's not often I get to see one but . . .'

'But on Monday evening you just had to go to the cinema,' snorted Kohler. 'Which one, eh? The film, I mean, and then, the cinema.'

'The . . . *The Grapes of Wrath.*'

'Pardon?'

'An American film left over from the evacuation.'

The Occupier had moved into the Free Zone to occupy the whole of France on 11 November 1942. On the 8th the Allies, the Americans, having joined them, had landed en masse in Algeria and Morocco. On 27 November the French had scuttled the French fleet in Toulon Harbour – over seventy ships – and on 17 December General Niehoff, now based in Lyon, had been appointed Commander-in-Chief of the *France-Sud* military region.

'The cinema?' asked Kohler, a breath held.

The detective would find out anyway – he had that look about him. '*L'Odyssée de la grande illusion.* It's one of your *Soldatenkino* but Monsieur Simondi, the owner, turns a blind eye sometimes.'

'*Nur für Deutsche,* eh?'

Only for Germans. 'Yes.'

'So you spent the evening watching *The Grapes of Wrath.*'

'It's . . . it's supposed to show your soldiers what things are really like in America. Such poverty, Inspector. Such dust. Do they have the mistral there too?'

Had there even been subtitles to tell the boys what was being said? 'I'll ask my partner to check into it. He's a film buff. Simondi, did you say?'

'César Simondi.'

'Any connection to the victim?'

'She was one of his singing students in addition to her being the group's *costumière*. Still, for her there were the auditions, the constant need to prove herself when she . . . she was ten times better than any of the others.'

'A golden voice?'

'That of an angel.'

This time the offer of a cigarette was accepted. The concierge's fingers trembled. He coughed twice, shook some more, and finally got to inhaling the smoke.

'When I found her, Inspector, there was no one with her – I swear it – but the blood was still hot. It was running down the wall and from that terrible gash in her slender throat, a throat I . . .'

'You what?'

Ah *Jésus*! 'I admired as much as did many others. It's no sin, is it, for a broken man to admire a pretty girl?' The detective would file the remark away. He had that look about him constantly.

'Did you touch anything – apart from dipping a finger?'

'Touch . . . ? I heard a sigh but it couldn't have come from Mireille, this I know, for I've seen death often enough.'

A sigh . . . 'At ten fifty p.m., or very close to it.'

'Yes. I . . . I went at once to inform Brother Matthieu but couldn't find him. I then went to see the bishop.'

'Hang on a minute. Was there any sign of the murder weapon?'

'The weapon? No, I . . . I didn't look closely, though.'

'But you definitely heard someone?'

'Yes.'

'A man or a woman?'

'I . . . All right, I didn't hang around to find out who it was.'

'You went to inform the bishop. Where was he?'

The eyeglasses were removed and the good eye wiped with a handkerchief. 'Bishop Rivaille was out – that is what his house-keeper told me when I woke her. A dinner engagement, things to discuss. The concert on the thirtieth. The singers. This new tour they are planning – Aix, Marseille, Toulon, Arles also, I think. The bishop takes a very special interest in the madrigal singers because they also sing the Masses, the Magnificat and other canticles. Simondi is choirmaster and director of music at the Cathédrale de Notre-Dame-des-Doms.'

Right next door to the Palais. 'Either that girl had a key to the front entrance here or someone left the door open for her. Who has keys?'

'Only the bishop, myself and Brother Matthieu. The door wouldn't have been left open, Inspector. How could it have been? Are you certain she had a key?'

'Not certain, but why doesn't Simondi have one? If the group sings here, they must practise here.'

'All right, he has one too.'

'Good. Now tell me a little about our victim.'

'There isn't much to tell. She made the costumes as well as doing sewing for others. Right from when she started working for Maître Simondi, and it's some years now, I think she had it in mind to join the singers, but theirs is a tight little group, you understand. They're very possessive of their positions and guard them well. Jealous of one another, oh *bien sûr*, but fiercely united too. Simondi is very particular who he lets in and they know this and govern themselves accordingly. She had a very high voice, clear and sweet, but the Italians are fussy when it comes to Monteverdi and others of their composers, and the six-part singing places terrible demands on its participators, or so I am often told.'

'Six parts.'

'Three young men, two girls, and the boy, Xavier. Mademoiselle Mireille would fill in when the soprano or the shepherd boy was ill or away. She could also play the lute beautifully and sometimes was allowed to accompany them.'

'And Brother Matthieu . . . does he have any part in looking after the group?'

Biron's head was tossed as if struck.

'Him? Why should he have?'

'I'm simply asking.'

'Then the answer is he has *nothing* to do with the singers. Hah!

He sings his own tune and makes a big noise of it, but he ran, you know. His God deserted him on the battlefield and ever since then he has been trying to find Him.'

'And the shepherd boy?'

'Xavier is trouble, but has a voice that enraptures the bishop.'

'Just like our victim's.'

Biron fussed with the lantern. He clucked his tongue and muttered impatiently, 'I really wouldn't know, Inspector. The grenade left me deaf in one ear.'

And blinded in that eye. 'Come on. Let's take a little walk. Show me through the palace. I want to get the feel of it.'

As she must have had – was this what the detective was implying? 'What are you looking for, Inspector?'

'Reasons as to why she was here at that hour and obviously not alone.'

The morgue was across town, near the Porte Saint-Lazare, deep in the cellars of the hospital and adjacent to ramparts that had been built in the fourteenth century. It wasn't pleasant, thought St-Cyr. Hearing that the exemption for students was soon to be annulled and that all Frenchmen born between 1 January 1912 and 31 December 1921 would have to register for the *Service de Travail Obligatoire* – the forced labour in Germany – medical students had spent the night dissecting corpses to fulfil assignments before they escaped to join a *maquis* or resigned themselves to fate. Preservative jars yet to be removed held every imaginable organ. The younger of the sisters vomited repeatedly into a deep stone basin which had, unfortunately, been used for other things.

'Sister Marie-Madeleine, I really must insist. Please get a hold of yourself!' scolded the elder of the two.

'I can't! Sister, what is this place? Hades?'

'Now listen, she's dead, do you understand? *Dead.* Take two deep breaths and hold them until your stomach settles.'

'Sister Agnès . . .' hazarded St-Cyr.

'Well, what is it?'

'Why not take her upstairs? A tisane of linden blossoms or of camomile?'

The Chief Inspector was simply trying to get rid of them. 'That is impossible. The Holy Father told us to remain with the child.'

Could nothing turn her stomach or her mind? 'But surely not when Coroner Peretti cuts into her?'

'Cuts? But . . . but why should he do such a thing?'

'The stomach contents, Sister. The large intestine. What she last ate and drank. Such things can tell us much.'

In tears, Sister Marie-Madeleine rushed to the nearest drain to empty whatever remained in her own stomach. Wrenching on the tap, she splashed her face. Pale and shaking, she turned to confront them but steadied herself against the stone pallet. 'Sister, you're used to the slaughterhouse but me . . . Mireille was *not* an animal!'

She wept. She clenched her fists in rage at herself, and begged the sister to release her from her duty.

Finely boned, her face thin, the large dark brown eyes revealing the depths of her despair, she was only twenty-one, if that, thought St-Cyr. The elder sister, in her mid-sixties, stepped up to her charge and let her have it across the face, once, twice and . . .

'*Doucement!*' he exclaimed. Now just a moment.

The last slap resounded. It knocked the tears from the young one, causing her to grip her cheek. 'Forgive me,' she blurted. 'I needed that, didn't I, Sister?'

They faced each other, these two who were married to God. Her dark eyes livid, the older sister's jowls quivered at the retort. An attendant in a filthy, bloodstained smock snickered joyously through the silence from across the room.

'She has nerves of steel,' said the younger one bitterly.

'Sister Agnès, let's all go upstairs,' cautioned St-Cyr. 'No one will touch the body, but if you wish, I'll have the attendant put her into one of the lockers and will personally present you with the key.'

Touché, was that it? wondered Sister Agnès, folding her arms across her ample bosom and drawing herself up. 'Leave if you wish. For myself, I will remain and so will she.'

The bare hands with their bony knuckles were thickly calloused and raw from constant work in the kitchens and fields.

'Very well,' sighed St-Cyr. 'Perhaps you would be good enough to tell me what you know of the victim.'

It was Sister Marie-Madeleine who, finding an inner strength that was admirable, answered, 'She was of the lesser nobility from the provinces – what the Parisian nobility used to derogatively call *les hobereaux* after the little falcon that is satisfied with small prey – but her family had fallen on hard times.'

'When?'

A fleeting smile revealed the stomach, not the grief, had been conquered. 'Six hundred years ago. De Sinéty was a name to be proud of in the Avignon of those days, Inspector, but there were some who were jealous of such wealth and position and took steps to remove it.'

'The girl was from the hills,' spat the older nun.

'She was *not*, Sister, and you know it. She was very well brought up and, as a result, was an elegant seamstress who could work wonders with very little. Oh *bien sûr* her mother fell on hard times and had to move out to a *mas* to try to eke out an existence by buying a flock of sheep others would then have to tend, but Mireille . . . She came to live and work in Avignon, Inspector, for Maître Simondi, and took home every sou she could.'

'And this farmhouse and farm, where are they?' he asked.

'In the hills behind Saint-Michel-de-Frigolet,' said Sister Agnès, glaring defiantly at her companion who gazed right back at her with the sympathy of one who was trying to understand and to forgive such venom.

'Fifteen or so kilometres to the south of Avignon, Inspector,' said Sister Marie-Madeleine. 'Mireille lived here in the Balance Quartier which is just below the Palais.'

'A place of slums and gypsy hovels,' seethed the older nun.

'Rooms of her own, Sister,' entreated the younger of them, 'whose rent was paid each week and always on time.'

'You know it was sinful of her to live in that house. You know the Holy Father wanted her to move out of that *quartier* and had arranged far better lodgings.'

'But she had refused his offer?' hazarded the Sûreté, startling them both and causing the younger one to blurt, 'Forgive me, Sister,' and to silence her tongue.

'There are no more gypsies. It's all over with those people,' said Sister Agnès. 'They've been sent away just like the Jews.'

To camps in Eastern Europe and in the Reich, said St-Cyr sadly to himself, he, too, falling into silence but adding, Hermann, I don't like this. The younger one knows too much, and the older one is now only too aware of it and will be certain to inform the bishop.

Kohler let the concierge continue ahead of him. They were upstairs again, on the first floor, and had passed through and beyond the room where the girl had been killed. The chamber they were now in, the Grand Tinel, was huge. Light from the still-smoking lantern made a feeble pool about Biron but seldom touched the walls and not the vault of the ceiling above.

'What is it?' asked the concierge uneasily as he sensed he was no longer being followed and turned to look back.

'Just keep going. Don't stop until you get to the end.'

'A fire here in 1413 destroyed the magnificent frescoes with which Giovanetti decorated the walls. The ceiling also.'

'I'm not interested in the past, not yet.'

Had the detective cared nothing for the palace's history he'd been given? Nothing for the painstaking details of the restorations whose work had ceased because of the Occupation? 'We are now once again in the "old palace" Inspector. By "old" I mean the Palais of Bénédict the Twelfth, which was built between 1334 and 1342 and well illustrates the austerity of the Cistercians, whereas in the "new palace" there are the pointed arches of the Renaissance Gothic, the splendid frescoes and magnificence of Clément the Sixth, who was a Bénédictine and therefore far more worldly.'

'He built his palace on to the other one between 1342 and 1352. Keep talking.'

Their voices easily filled the hall – superb acoustics, an ideal setting for a concert . . . The grey overcoat and black beret of the *grand mutilé* receded, the concierge lopsidedly rocking as his weight fell on the prosthesis that had replaced his right fore-leg.

When he reached a canopied fireplace at the far end of the hall, Biron, dwarfed by the size of the room, held the lantern above himself as he turned to face the Inspector who had remained at the other end. 'It is forty-eight metres long by ten and a quarter wide but is not nearly so wide as *la chambre de la grande audience.*'

The Great Audience Chamber was on the ground floor of the new palace, recalled Kohler, and, to let Biron know he'd been paying attention, said, 'That one's length is about the same as this but the width is nearly fifty-two metres and it has fantastic arches in the ceiling. Can you sing?'

'With the voice of an *étourneau*?' A starling. 'Inspector, what is it you really want of me?'

'Answers, *mon fin*. Answers.'

It would have to be said. 'The madrigal singers use this chamber as their practice hall.'

'For auditions too?' hazarded Kohler, the rich baritone of his voice filling the hall and startling the concierge who uneasily muttered, 'Those also but . . . but none was scheduled. I would have been informed.'

'So she wasn't here to audition and yet was dressed like that?'

No answer was forthcoming. 'Who judges the auditions?'

Biron hesitated. 'The singing master, Monsieur Simondi and . . .'

'The bishop?'

'Yes.'

'Who else?'

Ah *merde alors*! 'One other. Always there are three, and always the third person's identity is kept secret so as to make the audition entirely fair.'

'Kept secret by whom?'

'The bishop and Monsieur Simondi. Well before each audition

34

they always discuss this and then . . . then agree upon who to ask.'

'If she *had* come here for an audition . . .'

'She couldn't have.'

'But if she had . . .'

'She *didn't*! I'm always informed of them beforehand. The candles, the black-out curtains over the windows, the chairs . . .'

Finally they were getting somewhere. 'Where would the chairs have been placed?'

Must the Inspector pry into everything? 'Two metres from the wall nearest yourself. The singer then enters from the doorway in the far left corner here behind me and comes to stand an equal distance from this wall. Here the floor is marked with a cross for just such a purpose.'

She'd have been all keyed up. 'Would she have recognized the third judge if there had been an audition?'

Biron gave an exasperated sigh. 'Avignon is a large town, Inspector. Some who fled here during the Defeat have been allowed to remain. The contestant might realize the judge was new to us citizens but wouldn't likely know who he was.'

'Or her – could it have been a woman?'

Ah damn this one and his questions! 'Sometimes but . . . but not often and then only after a first refusal.'

'Stay there. I might need you to.' Switching on his torch, Kohler shone it along the wall but, search as he did, he couldn't find the chairs.

'Inspector, they are kept in the stairwell to my right. This area by the fireplace was once a pantry and separated from the hall to hide the *dressoir* upon which the Pontiff's meals, brought from the Kitchens Tower to my left, were placed so that after rewarming them at the fire, they could be properly served on the finest pewter and then taken to his table and to those of his distinguished guests, the lords and ladies of the . . .'

'*Ja, ja,* skip the details, will you?' Was Biron always such a windbag? If so, it was no wonder the troops threw stones at the statues and yelled their lungs out during his guided tours. 'Get the chairs. Bring them out here and set them up.'

'Of course. But please forgive the wounds I received at the hand of my own grenade. They will cause me to drag the chairs across the floor.'

Kohler let him be and shone his torch up over the outer wall. There were windows inset into tall, arched alcoves. The leaded glass wore the Occupation's coat of laundry blueing. Heavy black curtains had been installed but had been flung open here and there, the irregularity of their openings causing him to wonder if the girl had waited in any of the alcoves, listening for the slightest sound. Ah yes, after the rustling of her skirts had first been silenced and the sounds of the tiny silver bells, the trinkets, the scissors and the coins had been finally quietened by her.

Right in the middle of the outer wall there was the entrance to a square stone tower with a staircase. Perfect ease of access and departure, then, and with heavy curtains to seal it off.

'That is the Saint John's Tower,' sang out Biron. 'There are two lovely chapels. The one you're facing is above the other. Giovanetti painted the frescoes. If you would care to . . .'

Ignored, or so it seemed, Biron carried on with the chairs. They were old, of darkly stained wood, and they folded outwards to form gracefully curved Xs with no backs, but with plain, straight armrests.

He lined them up. Under the light from the lantern they threw the shadows of their slats on the floor behind.

Three chairs, side by side and sitting as if in judgement in the flickering light of a smoky lantern, thought Kohler. Had they been there on the night of the murder? Had they been used during the Renaissance – were they that old?

The thought was eerie and unpleasant, for the length and size of the hall made one automatically focus on them. Brutally Kohler rang the *clochette*. Instantly Biron was alerted and never mind his having a deaf ear.

'Inspector, where did you get that?' he shrilled.

It was rung again and then again – clear, sharp, musical tinkles – and when they were back in the *Chambre du cerf*, light from Herr Kohler's torch fled over the frescoed wall down which her blood had run. The hare they'd seen before must have been

36

chased by hounds towards the monk, the Pontiff Clément VI, some said, upon whose gloved fist a hawk waited to make the kill but—

'Inspector, what is it you wish me to see?'

'The monk . . . He's distracted and is looking the other way, even though the hounds are driving that hare towards him and he has yet to release the hawk.'

Six hundred years ago each of the hounds would have worn a *clochette* similar to the one the Inspector was holding but why had he to notice this? wondered Biron. It could only mean trouble.

'The monk, the pontiff or whatever, should have heard those dogs,' breathed Kohler.

One would have to try to divert him. 'Perhaps he did. Perhaps one of his hounds had wandered off and he heard its *clochette* against those of the others and wondered what it was driving towards him.'

'A hound that likes to wander, eh, and a wild boar after truffles and disturbed at its repast?'

'Inspector, the *maquis* of our hills, the *garrigue*, is very rough. The little bells make it possible for the hunters to know where each of their dogs is as the game is driven towards them.'

'But this hound couldn't have been running with the pack, could it?'

'I . . . I wouldn't really know. I'm just a simple man.'

'Then tell me, *mon fin*, if the girl knew the dog that wore this bell and if that dog would have come to her as a friend?'

Ah *merde alors*! 'I have nothing to do with the bishop's dogs, Inspector, and couldn't even keep one as a pet. Indeed, they are each served more meat in a day than I, or most of my fellow citizens, taste in six months.'

Apart from the meatless days, the adult ration, if one could get it, had been pared from 184 grams per week in September 1940 to 100 grams with bones, 75 without.

'Then the dog wouldn't have been hungry?'

'Inspector, dogs are always hungry, some more than others,

and the bishop always oversees their feeding so as to make certain nothing is wasted or inadvertently taken, but they are kept in the stables at his residence. They don't come here.'

'Then you tell me why there's a bird's nest over in the window alcove closest to that fireplace?'

Ah *nom de Jésus-Christ*, what was this? 'The mistral, Inspector. From time to time things are blown in from the battlements. There are pigeons . . . Traps have been set. The birds are always causing a problem. The Kommandant has seen the need and . . . and allows them to be taken.'

There, he had said it, thought Biron, and the detective knew he was sweating.

'Tasty are they? Hey, that's no pigeon's nest, *mon fin*. It's a reed warbler's, and you're talking to an ex-farm boy who loved dogs and always had one or two.'

They went to look at it and all the *grand mutilé* could find to say was, 'So it is.'

'Then if the mistral didn't carry it in here through closed windows, what did?'

A bird's nest . . . who would have thought of such a thing happening? 'I can't possibly say, Inspector. One of your soldiers perhaps. They often go for walks along the river. They are always exploring the countryside and picking things up they then tire of.'

'But you just said you couldn't possibly say?'

Sainte Mère, what have I done but make matters worse, thought Biron ruefully. 'You must ask Xavier or Brother Matthieu. Reed warblers . . . pigeons . . . I have nothing to do with the dogs. *Nothing*, do you understand?'

Piece by piece, garment by garment, the body of Mireille de Sinéty had been stripped of its finery in the morgue and each item noted, tagged and described as to its nature and position, once by Jean-Louis and once by himself, thought Ovid Peretti. He let his sad grey eyes pass down over her. The breasts sagged sideways, the skin had begun to blotch and discolour. She'd soon begin to stink. A waste, a tragedy – a danger. Why had he been so stupid as to have agreed to take on this task? Was he bent on self-destruction? he asked himself.

The elder of the two nuns stood grimly on guard at the head of the corpse, refusing to budge.

'Sister,' he said, 'I won't molest her. I'll be as kind and gentle as possible.'

'With forceps?' shrilled the younger nun. 'With bone-cutters?'

'Jean-Louis, get those two out of here at once!'

'Sister Agnès, it's illegal for you and Sister Marie-Madeleine to be here,' said St-Cyr. 'With the clothing, the jewellery and other things we could make allowances, but with what's about to happen you will understand Coroner Peretti can't possibly continue in your presence. Now come away.'

'The clothes . . . We must dress her in them after it's done.'

'For burial?'

'Yes! The casket is to be open.'

'With a neck wound like that?' stormed Peretti, towering over the corpse.

She gave him a cold look. 'Such things can be hidden. There are ways and we will use them.'

'Then leave us, Sister,' said St-Cyr gently. 'I'll join you shortly for a quiet word. A few small questions, nothing difficult, I assure you. The preliminary autopsy will take several hours and I can't remain here either as I've other things I must do. You can come back after the midday meal.'

'We don't eat lunch. Not in these troubled times.'

'*Merde alors, foutez-moi la paix!*' shouted Peretti. Bugger off.

He turned the body over and, shaking a thermometer to get its mercury down, eased it into the girl's rectum. 'Sister, I told you to leave. I might break the glass.'

The nuns fled, with the Sûreté driving them, and when Jean-Louis returned, his cheeks blown out in exasperation, he, too, swore, then said, 'The bishop . . .'

Peretti recorded the body's temperature. 'You want to watch your back with him, Jean-Louis. There are whispers.'

'Whispers?'

Bon, the point had been taken. 'Power. The bishop yearns for the old days, covets the Palais and thinks our friends from beyond the Rhine can be convinced to give it to him if Il Duce fails and Italy falls to the invader when that one makes up his mind to invade.'

Ah *nom de Dieu* . . . 'The Papacy?'

'He dreams of its return to Avignon and is convinced of the possibility. The Kommandant lets him since it costs nothing, except, perhaps, the life of this one.'

They were alone, thank God. 'How sure are you of this? The Papacy . . . ?'

There was a shrug. The thermometer was cleaned off and sterilized. 'There are always whispers, some more prevalent than others. Here in Avignon is God not held in contempt while everything breathes a lie?'

Petrarch had said as much. 'But the Vatican . . . ? Surely they must have something to say in the matter?'

'Rivaille keeps up a continuous correspondence which His Holiness answers, of course, for, like the Kommandant, what is there to lose? The Church always dabbles and hedges its bets, so why not with this?'

'But . . .'

'Look, all I'm saying is let's not fool ourselves. Let's find out the truth but keep as much of it as we can to ourselves. Oh by the way, she was still a virgin.'

'A virgin . . . The Papacy? Does he *want* to become the Pope?'

'A cardinal perhaps. I really don't know, but you're in Avignon, remember? Six hundred years ago or today, it's exactly the same. Whereas the Occupier uses guns, the citizens still prefer poison, the garrotting wire or the knife.'

'It was a sickle. I'm all but certain of it.'

'Bend, gather, pull and then reap, eh? We shall see.'

Still upstairs in the Palais, Kohler was lost in thought. A chamber separated the Grand Tinel from the Kitchens Tower and in it the girl could have waited out of sight until the judges had been seated. But had she taken off her overcoat, her winter boots, hat and mittens? 'She couldn't have walked through the streets dressed in costume, not even after dark,' he said to the concierge. 'There'd have been the chance of a spot check or control – a *rafle*, maybe.' A raid, a house-to-house search or roundup. 'She'd have had a handbag.'

Her identity papers . . . 'There was nothing here, Inspector. Nothing in the Palais to suggest . . .'

'Nothing but a bird's nest.'

Kohler shone his torch around the barren floor and up over walls that had once held frescoes whose patchy remains revealed the faint grid lines in reddish ochre that had allowed the artist to easily transfer his drawings. Together, he and Biron went into the Kitchens Tower. It, too, was barren.

'The chimney is huge, Inspector. A pyramid in the octagonal shape.'

Nothing remained of the bake ovens and yet one could sense the constant comings and goings. Well over four hundred retainers, cooks, scullions, guards and porters – thirty chaplains alone and all of their servants – would have occupied the Palais, in addition to the guests and the family of the pontiff. The spongers.

'There are pantries and storerooms in this tower,' said Biron. 'Other kitchens below us, all of whose flues go up and into the central chimney, which is unique for these parts and for such times.'

Again Kohler used his torch. The mistral played fitfully with the flame of the lantern. The downdraught carried a trail of smoke towards the open entrance where tall wooden doors would once have stood.

'The Revolution destroyed them,' said Biron of the doors. 'The pots, pans and stone or clay crocks – everything was smashed, burned or stolen. One can but regret the loss, the pages of history which are gone from us for ever, the . . .'

'Just cut the travelogue, eh?, and show me where they dumped the bodies of the Royalists that were imprisoned and then murdered in 1791.'

The *Glacière Massacre* of that October. 'The Latrines Tower is just through here. On each floor of the Palais, latrines gave relief and refuge to servant, dignitary, guard and pontiff alike. Rainwater and kitchen slops joined the waste, and the refuse fell to a large pit that had been sunk into the rocks far below. A drain then carried this waste to the Sorgue which soon joined the Rhône.'

The torchlight didn't shine down the shaft nearly far enough. Biron went on about how, during a siege, invaders had entered the drain, waded across the cesspool and then had climbed into the Palais to surprise the guards.

'What happened to the bodies of the Royalists?'

'Quicklime was dumped on top of them. When the stench became too great, they were removed through an opening.'

'Is that opening still there?'

'An iron grille keeps all but the smallest of animals from entering.'

'Then you'd better show it to me, hadn't you, especially as some son of a bitch must have tidied up and dumped her things down there.'

Ah *merde*, did this one miss nothing? 'We will need a hammer and cold chisel.'

'Then get them. Bring help if necessary.'

Though an hour had passed, the body of Mireille de Sinéty had still not been cut into. 'I thought you were going to question the sisters?' asked Peretti, not looking up from her hair.

'I lied,' murmured St-Cyr. 'Avignon has already tainted me.'

Nothing more was said. Peretti was in his late fifties. The face was angular and often sad, for he'd seen death many times, both in such places and on the field of battle. But the hands that could break bones if necessary could also be gentle. Something was teased from her hair and carefully mounted on to a microscope slide. Without pausing, he pulled the instrument from its case and set to work.

St-Cyr turned back to the trinkets which had been carefully arranged on a nearby pallet. The girl had carried no papers, but to walk the streets without them was to invite arrest, interrogation and possible deportation to one of the camps. Had her killer relieved her of them? he wondered, cursing the Renaissance's lack of pockets. Had she parked them on a ledge or tucked them into a crack?

You were a Libra and of the House of Balance, he said silently. Among the zodiacal signs is the oft-repeated hand-held weighing scale, but did you then seek rooms in the Balance Quartier for good luck perhaps, or for some deeper reason?

Superstition had played such a part in the daily life of the Renaissance. Her gimmel ring set lapis lazuli side by side with a saffron-yellow topaz which matched exactly the colour of her gown. Yet the pattern on the gown, in a faint and delicate shade of brown, was of oak leaves and branches that were entwined with grapevines. Had this, too, had meaning for her and for others to puzzle over? And wasn't the background pattern in the frescoes of Clément VI's bedchamber of spiralling vines and oak branches and the deeper blue of lapis lazuli?

On the soft leather of her girdle he found, among so many other things, the sign of the Archer in gold. A tiny medallion. The Centaur's arrow was pointed away from a silver House of Balance and towards a Goat that had been cast in lead.

The House of Balance weighed a tiny lapis lazuli cabochon against that of a saffron-yellow topaz, the two stones of equal weight.

She would tease and she would dare but had such things led to her death?

The little silver bells were very old, and he wondered how she had come by them, by all of this, for the trinkets and jewels dated from the Renaissance, whereas the clothing had been cut and sewn by herself.

'Lapis is the stone of fertility,' grunted Peretti impatiently. 'What I've found in her hair isn't much, I admit, but perhaps it'll be enough.'

Down through the ocular of the microscope, and at thirty times magnification, the image of a tiny clot of coarse black wool rushed at the eye. 'A cassock . . .' breathed St-Cyr.

'Or cloak, overcoat or sweater.'

'The bishop . . .'

Back came the Commissaire de Police's warning. Break glass and you'll be cut. Tamper with the Host and the Blood of Christ and watch out.

'Be careful,' sighed Peretti. 'I meant what I said.'

'We will.'

'How sure are you of that partner of yours?'

'Hermann? We are like two perpetually crossed fingers. God's honest cops trying to stop themselves from drowning in a torrent of officially sanctioned crime.'

Everyone was only too aware of what the *Boches*, the Germans, and those who would collaborate with them were stealing. 'Then leave me with her, Jean-Louis. Go and warn him to be very careful. I'll lock everything up. No one will touch a thing.'

'Just let me go over it once more. I must see if something, other than her papers, is missing. I must find what the bishop was looking for when he gave her Extreme Unction.'

And sent two of his nuns to police the corpse and have a look themselves or to thieve an item or two! thought Peretti. 'He's one of the Black Penitents, as is de Passe.'

'Hence his wearing a simple black cassock when giving her the last rites?'

Peretti indicated the microscope slide. 'Unless he was trying to tell you any one of them could have killed her, including himself.'

Several brotherhoods, including *les Pénitents Noirs*, dated back to the Baylonian Captivity when there were no fewer than sixty churches and thirty-five monasteries and Rabelais had described Avignon as the bell-ringing city, while Petrarch had called the Palais 'the habitation of demons'.

'Some of them practise flagellation,' snorted Peretti. 'Our bishop happens to be one of them and regularly scourges himself, or so it is rumoured.'

'With a *martinet*?'

A small but many-thonged whip that some parents used to discipline delinquent children . . . 'Two of his fellow "brothers" hold him while he thrashes himself, Jean-Louis, but to purge himself of what sins, I know not.'

'The Black Penitents also were and are men dedicated to good works,' countered St-Cyr.

'But for whom, Jean-Louis. For whom?'

The bishop, the préfet and others of the establishment were implied. 'There's a tiny silver *martinet* among her jewels.'

'Then perhaps you have your answer.'

Dawn broke, and from the battlements of the Trouillas Tower some fifty-two metres above ground and next to the Latrines Tower, the view was of those ancient times. Eerie, steeped in mystery and deceit, damned cold and utterly heartless.

Kohler tugged the collar of his greatcoat up and crammed bare hands into its pockets. He was dying for a fag but the wind put paid to any such notion.

'Inspector . . .'

The word, though shouted, was ripped away and pelted southward.

'In a moment, Préfet. I have to get the lie of the land.'

Bâtard! cursed de Passe silently. 'You find things at the base of the Latrines Tower. You do not immediately inform me in the proper manner. Instead, you demand my presence here in this wind? What is it you want? I haven't all day.'

'Nor have I.'

The gun-metal grey of a thickly layered ice-fog was being swept down the Rhône Valley and from distant hollows among the hills. Faint touches of pastel pink were beginning to intrude but offered no promise. The bitterly hard air took the breath away.

Would it have been like this in Russia? wondered Kohler. Would the boys have watched the fog lift or hug the ground to remain as they waited for the battle to begin again?

Everyone said the mistral had its origins in Russia. 'My sons were within a year of her in age,' he shouted.

'Could we not go inside?'

Ah damn you, eh? 'This wind makes people edgy, doesn't it?'

'What is it you want of me?'

'A word, that's all.'

45

The coal-black eyebrows arched under the grey snap-brim fedora. The cleanly shaven chin and wind-burned cheeks stiffened as the grey eyes swiftly narrowed. 'Get to it, Inspector.'

'Answers. That kid lived right down there in a slum next to the ramparts and by that four-legged bridge that looks as if it still might like to cross the river but can't quite make up its mind.'

'You've found her papers.'

De Passe was of medium height and build and immaculately dressed in a grey overcoat whose thin and perfect collar wasn't turned up to ward off the wind. The blue silk of a Royalist's tie showed from between the arms of a grey cashmere scarf. Arrogant and of the *bourgeoisie*, he was not quite of the *bourgeoisie aisée*, the really well off, but would have aspirations, especially these days when anything was possible for the chosen few.

A civil servant, an administrator, he would consider himself far above such a lowly station as a cop.

'Start by telling me why that girl was here and then, Préfet, what the hell she might have known that someone didn't want her saying.'

This was Kohler of the Kripo, a conscientious doubter of Germanic invincibility who was disloyal to his peers, reviled and often hated by many at Gestapo Paris-Central, yet kept on by Sturmbannführer Boemelburg because he and that infernal partner of his gave some semblance of law and order to the ordinary citizen. They were Boemelburg's flying squad, dealing with the difficult, thus opiating public outcry. They still couldn't seem to learn that policemen were never dismissed for doing too little.

'She had a lover. A boy who fled to the hills to join the *Banditen*.' The 'terrorists', the *Résistance*, the *maquis*. 'This matter was known to the bishop who, Herr Kohler, prevailed upon me to let him try to convince the girl to give up such a foolishness and agree to help us take the boy into custody before he did anything untoward.'

Anything that might damage the status quo, namely that of those in power. But good of him to have agreed to let the bishop

46

have a try, though there must have been a little something offered in exchange for such a consideration.

'And you think she was here to meet that boy?'

'It's possible. She would dress as if to cover herself for the lie of an audition, should the authorities stop her in the streets.'

'But she wore her overcoat and beret, Préfet, a scarf and boots, too, and carried a handbag?'

Further discoveries had been made in the Latrines Pit, thought de Passe, and Kohler had seen fit to tease his ears with the information so that he would now fret over what else had been found. 'I'm only suggesting a possibility. You and Jean-Louis are in charge of the investigation.'

'Why'd they choose to meet here?'

'Her place of residence was being watched. Quite obviously she must have realized this and found a way to arrange a meeting no one would suspect or question.'

But someone had. 'Patriotic, was she?'

'Misguided, Inspector, as so many of our young seem to be.'

'Then there was some urgency to what she had to impart?'

'Inspector, could we not go inside? There's a window in this tower from which the view is almost as good.'

'But then I couldn't see the hills behind us. Those ones. That big one to the northeast. Right out there, Préfet. Yes, there.'

Mont Ventoux and the plateau de Vaucluse, home to some of the *maquis*.

'What else did you find in the Latrines Pit?'

'Anxious, are you?'

'Why should I be?'

'Because maybe I found something you didn't expect. Maybe whoever tidied up and dumped those things of hers should first have taken a damned good look through her handbag.'

'What, damn you? Tell me. I have a right to know.'

'Nothing, then. Absolutely nothing.'

'*Maudit salaud! Cochon*, how dare you defy me?'

Livid, de Passe turned abruptly away and headed for the exit rather than embarrass himself further. Left to the rooks which would haunt the battlements after a siege, Kohler thought again of his two sons. He thought of Giselle and Oona in Paris, the two loves of his life. And he thought of Louis who had lost his wife and little son to a Resistance bomb not so long ago, a mistake if ever there was one – that bomb had been meant for Louis who was not and could never be a collaborator – and he thought of Avignon and of men like de Passe.

'Ah *merde*,' he croaked, 'have I gone too far this time?'

The lady's wrist-watch he had found in her handbag was from Cartier's and, though it was tastefully modest and had but a plain brown leather strap, the watch would have cost from 30,000 to 50,000 francs in 1938, the year it must have been purchased.

Ovid Peretti gently stroked the girl's breasts using a swab of cotton wool. He did her hips and arms, the inner thighs. He wasn't going to miss a thing and that was good. Because I have, thought St-Cyr, cursing himself. There had been three rings on the fine gold chain that had hung about her neck – he was positive of this and had reread his notes – and now, unfortunately, there were only two of them.

Search as he had, no sign of the third ring had been uncovered. 'The sisters,' he said. 'One of them made off with a trinket.'

The cotton swab was added to others in a labelled glass vial. '*Le bijou par excellence*, eh?' snorted Peretti. 'Are you still certain the youngest of the sisters was vomiting only because of this place, or are you now wondering if God's servant, in all of her innocence, also did it to distract you?'

'That was no act. The younger sister was suffering deeply from grief as well as a queasy stomach, but the older one must have used these against me. The ring had a ruby cabochon of at least four carats.'

'Pigeon's blood and free from flaws?'

'Why did they take it?'

Had Jean-Louis now realized that, at the very least, the younger sister must also have known what they had been told to retrieve?

'Was it the bishop's?' hazarded St-Cyr.

'And on loan? You're asking the wrong person, *mon ami*.'

'Then what about this?'

At least six hundred years old, the pendant box that was attached to her girdle next to the sewing kit was ovoid in shape, and not more than six centimetres long by about three in width, and one-and-a-half in thickness. Foiled crystals, in silver gilt, threw back a golden light when the box was opened to reveal a thorn.

'Christ wore a crown of thorns,' murmured Peretti, 'but this one bathed herself before going to her death. After the bath, an oil of some kind was used.'

'One that she had made herself?'

'Perhaps.'

In the pendant box, in translucent enamel, Christ was depicted on the Cross, and being lifted gently down from it. The tiny figures wore vivid colours of blue, green, red and saffron yellow. The clothing of the Virgin Mary and of Mary Magdalene and the Disciples was medieval and of a style probably worn fifty to one hundred years earlier than the Babylonian Captivity.

'Louis the Ninth led the Seventh Crusade,' muttered St-Cyr, his mind lost to the relic. 'In 1250 he was defeated at El Mansura and held for ransom, after which he remained in the Holy Land until 1254. He died of the plague in Tunis in 1270, soon after landing at the head of another crusade. History has it that he purchased the Crown of Thorns from the Emperor of Constantinople.'

'Even canonized kings can be conned,' said Peretti dryly.

'Ah yes, but did the bishop lend it to her? The fastener was loose as though an attempt had been made to take it back.'

And hidden away among the folds of a black habit. 'Then you'd better ask him in the presence of those two sisters.'

'I'll attempt to, but first I must catch up with my partner.'

'Then before you go, please take a look at this. It was caught in that broken fingernail.'

The image of a single hair rushed up the ocular to meet the eye – short, stiff and tan-coloured, and most probably from a dog.

'I'll need to make microscopic comparisons, and of sections

too,' said Peretti, 'and for this I must have samples. But I leave the matter in your good hands lest the bishop question my sudden interest in his hounds.'

'Be careful.'

'You too.'

3

Mullioned windows, punished by hoarfrost, overlooked the place de Horloge in the centre of town. St-Cyr didn't remove his overcoat, scarf and fedora. One seldom did these days due to the lack of heat and threat of theft. 'A tisane of rose hips, madame,' he called out.

'At this hour?' she shot back from behind the brass scrollwork of her cage. It was not yet eleven in the morning.

'At any hour,' he said.

Ah! A Parisian as well as a Sûreté – the blind could have sensed it; for herself, it was written all over him, but to his credit, he didn't attempt to hide it. 'The girl . . .' began Madame Emphoux, indicating the headlines of the Occupation's thin and tightly controlled *Provençal*. ' "*Découverte du cadavre d'une jeune fille au Palais*," ' she read the headline aloud as if for the first time. 'Is it true, Inspector?'

She would have heard plenty by now but he met the gaze she gave, one of brutal assessment, given from under fiercely knitted brows, as if she had heard nothing. 'True,' he said warily.

'Violated?' asked the woman, leaning closely so that unclipped nasal hairs and florid cheeks unbrushed by rouge or powder were more than evident beyond the scrollwork. There was butter on the double chin. *Butter!* He was certain of it. The hair was frizzy, a mop of tired auburn curls that hung over the blunt fore-head. The cardigan, of wine-purple wool, had frayed holes at the elbows and was too small for her. Tightly buttoned, it gave glimpses of a turquoise blouse and a flannel shirt. 'Violated?' she prodded.

'That I cannot say,' came the still wary response, the Sûreté not budging unless . . . unless, perhaps, the offer of something useful was made. 'They come here,' she confided, her voice still low but her hard brown eyes flicking over the clientele who, disinterested or otherwise, appeared to keep entirely to themselves.

These days such a manner was mandatory. 'They?' he asked, giving his head a slight upward lift.

Her pudgy, ringless fingers moved things aside. '*Les chanteurs de Monsieur Simondi*. The madrigal singers are *habitués* of *Le Café de la mule blanche affolée*.' The café of the panic-stricken white mule.

As proof, she found a greasy, sweat-stained bit of cardboard on which had been written a list of six names. Beside each one, the latest credit extended was shown next to all other additions and cancellations. Two hundred and seven francs . . . four hundred and thirty . . . 'Mademoiselle de Sinéty's name isn't on your list,' he said.

'That one seldom had the time, or the money. Nor would she beg for credit like the others. Too proud, if you ask me. She only came here if in need of one of them.'

'And Monsieur Simondi?'

Had the Sûreté smelled trouble already? 'Sometimes he joined them. Sometimes he took one of them away with him, or two, or three as the need demanded, the others always letting their eyes and thoughts hunger after those who were departing. He has, of course, a wife.'

The taint of trouble with that wife was all too clear. Swiftly Madame Emphoux watched him to see if her *confidence* had registered and when he returned nothing, she let escape, 'An absinthe drinker.'

'That's impossible. It was outlawed in 1915.'

Her rounded shoulders lifted with an uncaring shrug. 'So it was,' she said, fingering her left cheek as if in thought, 'but one cannot help but overhear students. Absinthe was often discussed.'

'In relation to Madame Simondi?'

And to the students themselves? She could see him thinking this, but said simply, 'Yes.'

Jules Pernod had had an absinthe factory at Montfavet not six kilometres to the east of Avignon . . . St-Cyr indicated the card with its accountings. 'Was Madame Simondi known to all of them?'

'Including Mademoiselle de Sinéty?' fluted the *patronne*, her eyebrows knitted fiercely again.

This one was deep, thought St-Cyr, but no well should ever be overdrawn lest there no longer be water to drink. 'Including her.'

'Then, yes. The girl did sewing for Madame Simondi as well as for the Kommandant's wife and others.'

A small token would have to be offered in expectation of more information later. 'She wasn't violated but I am curious as to why you should think she might have been.'

Now she had his ear, and now he wouldn't give up trying to get her to whisper little things into it! 'Because she was pretty and full of *joie de vivre* when so many these days are not, and because . . . Ah! What can one such as I say, Inspector?'

He waited. Again he held his breath – was this a sign with him, she wondered. Every muscle was tense, so, *bon; oui, bon*, she had him hooked. 'Because I have seen the way others have looked at her. The singers, especially the two girls among them. Monsieur Simondi *aussi* – ah! One can see such a thing in a married man's eyes, is it not possible? Brother Matthieu also, but only when she and others couldn't see him doing so and then the eyes quickly averted.'

She compressed her lips, grunted firmly and nodded tersely.

'And Bishop Rivaille?' he asked, wincing at the possibility of being totally out of his depth with her.

'That one also. From time to time in the dark of night, even the Bugatti Royale of a bishop can draw up to a café such as this and its owner enter to enquire of where he might find a young girl to mend a robe, sew on a button he has somehow misplaced, or sing a little to soothe a soul in torment. God forgives all such thoughts, is that not so, Inspector?'

The table was at the left side of the café, and halfway to the back. It was surprising how intuitively one sought such seating but, like the *réfractaires*, the draft dodgers of the Forced Labour, and

53

others in trouble with or simply avoiding the Occupier and the Vichy police, one tended automatically to sit where one could observe and yet blend into the crowd. It was never customary for a *patron* or *patronne* to give credit to students and seldom if ever to others, so there had to be a little something on the side, but one didn't ask of such things. One sat quietly minding one's business and, in between one's thoughts, observed.

Madame la patronne had realized that to take too evident an interest in him would only draw further attention to herself. Satisfied he'd be left alone, St-Cyr took out his pipe. Letting his mind drift back to the largest of the keys that had hung from the girl's belt, he recalled that it had been all but free of decoration, as was typical of fourteenth-century keys. But, of course, the lock to the entrance of the Palais couldn't possibly have survived. Yet had this ancient key and the others been worn to indicate that she had a key to that door, or to something else? Did everything about her person present a riddle, or had the door been left unlocked in expectation of her arrival?

Finding the tin of sardines and the pomander, he took them out as he drew on his pipe and asked, Why had she carried the sardines in her purse, if not to give it to the person she had come to meet, if indeed that had been why she was there?

Why had she gripped the pomander so tightly if not to keep it from her assailant?

Suddenly the entrance door to the café was violently sucked shut by the mistral. Few could not help but look up. Some briefly sought out the newcomer whose back was thrown against the etched glass. '*Mon Dieu!*' exclaimed *Madame la patronne*. 'Be more careful. And *don't* come in here unless you are prepared to pay your bill. Enough is enough!'

Shock registered. Flashing dark eyes under finely arched jet black brows rapidly searched the faces of the clientele, the warning taken. 'Forgive me, madame. I . . . I only wanted to ask if . . . if the others had been in.'

A lie if ever there was one, thought St-Cyr. The charcoal corduroy overcoat was of the thirties and trim, the jet black cloche matched the protruding curls.

Clutching a small parcel that was wrapped in newspaper and tied with old bits of string, she hesitantly approached the *caisse*. A girl of more than medium height and light on her feet. '*Enfant*, I have told you,' seethed *Madame la patronne* under her breath. 'Don't be an *imbécile!*' She jerked her head to one side to indicate the company from Paris.

Outside on the place, the local detachment's brass band began to sound the noon hour. As the belfry's clock rang it out, strains of *Preussens Gloria* faltered in the mistral. The swastika above the entrance to the Hôtel de ville and Kommandantur was nearly being ripped to shreds by the wind. None of the pedestrians took any notice. Why should they?

The fullness of the girl's gaze left him. 'Just let me leave a message for them,' she said demurely to the *patronne*.

'I'm not the PTT!' shrilled Madame Emphoux.

The package was placed on the counter. 'A pencil, if you have one, and a scrap of paper,' and when these were reluctantly slid under the scrollwork, the girl quickly wrote a few words, then, tossing her pretty head at the clientele, made her exit but deliberately held the door open so that all would hold their breath and she could then ease it shut without a sound.

When confronted, Madame Emphoux knew there was little sense in arguing, for already the Sûreté was unwrapping the parcel. 'That was Christiane Bissert, one of the singers,' she said tartly.

'Age?'

'Twenty, I think.'

'Let's not think about it. My partner and I already have too many questions and are being given no time to consider them.'

'Twenty, then.'

The parcel contained four paperback detective novels from the thirties. On the cover of one, a cigarette wastefully smouldered its life away in an ashtray full of butts Hermann or anyone else would have given their eyeteeth for. On another, a semiautomatic Colt .45 lay next to a pool of blood and a purse which had been torn open and dumped in a mad search for whatever the killer had been after.

An interrupted *petite infidélité*, no doubt, but had the killer been a woman wronged?

Feeling foolish at being so easily sucked in by a jacket illustration, he said, 'Does Mademoiselle Bissert understand English?'

'No. These have been offered in exchange for some of her debt.'

'How much?'

Madame Emphoux teased the books away from him. 'What, then, does this one say?'

'That's *The Maltese Falcon*. It's one of Dashiell Hammett's very tough, no-nonsense pieces. Bang, bang.'

'And this one?' she asked.

She was being coy, thought St-Cyr, and said, 'An Erle Stanley Gardner, a Perry Mason, *The Case of the Caretaker's Cat.*'

'Four hundred francs for the lot.'

This sum was well below the trade in such things – detective novels were avidly sought, but in English would they not command less? he wondered.

'For the Kommandant,' she confessed. 'And . . . and others.'

He'd have to let it be but wondered if the girl had deliberately left the parcel so as to distract him. 'Where did she get these?' In addition to British nationals who had sought refuge in 1940, there had been plenty of Americans in the Free Zone before 11 November of last year. Many had come to Provence from Paris when the Führer had declared war on the United States on 11 December 1941 and they had had to leave for the south.

'How could I possibly know where they came from, Inspector?'

No questions were ever asked in the black market. One didn't haggle or complain lest one never get another chance to deal. But it was interesting that credit was extended in exchange for such things since this implied there had to have been other deals.

'The note,' he said firmly, and she knew that the Sûreté, like a cobra in its little basket, would let the matter lie only until ready to strike.

Inspector, please find me at the *hôtel particulier* called the Villa Marenzio. It is on the rue Banasterie where I await your questions with a heart that is open.

Hermann . . . where the hell was Hermann?

The Oberst Kurt von Mahler hadn't come in with the tide on 11 November 1942 when the whole country had been occupied. He'd been here since the blitzkrieg in the West, had been in Avignon since the Defeat and partition of 1940, both as head of the Reich's legation and as the Wehrmacht's liaison officer with the Occupied North. But now the Allies were on his doorstep, a constant worry.

'I'm telling you, Kohler, I want no trouble with this matter. The girl was like family. My wife and children adored her.'

Yet how was it von Mahler's family had been allowed to join him? That wasn't official Wehrmacht policy. Wives and kids were to be left at home.

'She's young,' said von Mahler, having anticipated the question. 'She's not well. The rape of Köln was too much for her.'

Nearly 60,000 had been left homeless by the RAF raid on the night of 30/31 May of last year. Hundreds had died, thousands had been injured, many of them horribly. Incendiaries – the resulting firestorms – had consumed twelfth- and thirteenth-century half-timbered houses. Over 20,000 buildings, the very heart of the historic city, had gone up in flames. 'Colonel, my partner and I will do everything we can to apprehend the girl's killer. We do need help. Transport, for one thing.'

'A Renault has been arranged.'

'Food and lodging . . .'

'Sixteen rue des Trois-Pilats. It's near the villa Simondi uses for his students. If the meals aren't to your taste, try La Fourchette in the rue Racine or the Auberge Julius Pallière on the place de l'Horloge. Acclimatize yourselves. Get to know the city and get to the bottom of this thing. The faster the better.'

Von Mahler was in his early forties, but was the expression always so severe, the frown so constant? The dark brown hair was crinkly and cut short. The wide-set eyes under knitted brows were iron-grey, the lips firm in resolve and slightly turned down at their corners as if to silently cry out, Don't you dare involve me.

He'd probably been an academic in civilian life, an economist in the military until the war had torn him from his desk. Good at polo and the steeplechase – he had that look about him. He'd have got to know the powers that be among the French in Avignon and the Vaucluse. He'd have made a point of that. 'Herr Oberst, what can you tell me about the night of the murder?'

'What have the others told you?'

No cigarettes were in evidence, no ashtrays either. 'The others?' asked Kohler.

'Rivaille, de Passe and Simondi.'

'Very little, and I've yet to speak to the singing master.'

'Then you'd better. It was Simondi's idea to hold yet another of his infernal auditions. I refused to sit in on it. I'm not competent to judge such things. To me Mireille was an absolutely beautiful musician. Pure magic. A natural.'

'This audition, Colonel. If you refused . . .'

'I did.'

'Then who took your place?'

'I've no idea. Simondi may, for all I'm aware, have cancelled it yet failed to notify Mireille.'

There it was again. Not Mademoiselle de Sinéty or even the girl, but Mireille, one of the family. 'The concierge says no audition was planned.'

'Then it had been cancelled.'

'Could she have gone there to meet someone?'

'I'd spoken to her about the boy she was infatuated with. I'd told her it was foolish of her to even think of him and that she had best, for all our sakes and particularly that of herself, keep her distance.'

One of the *maquis*, then, as de Passe had said. 'And how did she greet this advice?'

'With fortitude and with that inherent practicality both my wife and I found so engaging. She wasn't ordinary, Inspector. She was extraordinarily gifted and, in another age, would have been the daughter of a nobleman, the wife of a king.'

Subconsciously a fist had been clenched. Irritably a hand was now passed over the crinkly hair to hide the fact, thought Kohler wryly.

'She was extremely well versed in the city's past and very much

58

wanted others to see it as she did. Heroic in spite of the pit of sin, the "sewer" of Petrarch.'

Von Mahler hadn't demanded to know if he and Louis had discovered anything. Instead, he had avoided asking. 'Colonel, in the course of our enquiries might we talk to your wife?'

Verdammt! The insolence of the police. Could Kohler not take the hint? 'Absolutely not. There's no need. You'd only upset her and I can't have that.'

'But an independent view? A German view? The girl may have confided things or let something slip.'

'Ingrid sees no one but the staff and myself, and that, my dear *Hauptmann Detektiv Inspektor*, is an order.'

Okay, okay. 'Then can you tell us anything you think might be useful, apart, that is, from questioning Bishop Rivaille, the préfet and the singing master?'

Would Kohler now leave things well enough alone? 'Just start with Simondi. He's a superb musician in his own right.'

'He owns a cinema.'

The concierge of the Palais must have informed Kohler of this. 'He owns several – both here and in Orange, Arles and Aix. In smaller centres too. He operates theatres as well and has additional properties either under option or outright ownership. He's a very astute businessman, Inspector, but music, not money, is the guiding passion of his life.'

'A hobby,' muttered Kohler. And among the *petite bourgeoisie*? *Merde*, did the Colonel take this Kripo for an idiot?

A faint grin wouldn't be remiss, thought von Mahler. 'Far more than a hobby. He's extremely gifted and therefore intense when it comes to his music. Mireille was very loyal to her teacher and grateful for his help. "He believes in me," she would say to my wife. "He says I'm almost there."'

And kept on the hook, was that it, eh, but for what purpose? 'So, an audition was planned for the night of Monday 25 January. You were asked to sit in as the third judge but refused. Concierge Biron attended your *soldaten-kino* to take in a screening of *The Grapes of Wrath* and didn't check through the Palais, as the bishop always insisted, until well after twenty-two hundred hours, after which, Colonel, he went to notify Brother Matthieu and then Bishop Rivaille but could locate neither of them.'

'And why was that?'

A coldness had entered von Mahler's voice, a stiffness. Had it been a warning to push this particular part of the matter no further? wondered Kohler, not liking the thought. 'No reasons were given, Herr Oberst.' This was a lie, of course. Rivaille had been at a dinner party to discuss the concert the madrigal singers were to give, and then the tour. Aix, Marseille, Toulon and Arles had been mentioned by Salvatore Biron. But a dinner party with whom? The Colonel and his wife – was that it, eh?

'Then is there anything else I can do for you at present?' asked von Mahler. 'I've a busy afternoon ahead and must check in on my wife and children before we head out into the hills.'

After *Banditen*? *Un ratissage*? wondered Kohler. A 'raking' of the countryside – Kommandants didn't usually do such things, but he had mentioned the boy the victim had been infatuated with. 'I can't think of anything, Herr Oberst. Both my partner and I appreciate the help.'

A hand was extended, the typical salute, Heil Hitler and the crashing of jackbooted heels, not given, the lie of not thinking of anything to ask accepted.

The Balance Quartier, lying between the Palais and the river, was desperately in need of renovation. Shoulder-to-shoulder slum houses of two and three storeys surrounded once lovely inner courtyards. The years of siege, the visitations of the plague – wars, fires and utter poverty – had left many of them ramshackle and ready to be torn down.

Though Sister Agnès had roundly condemned it, Number 63 rue du Rempart du Rhône was better than most and had, at the rear of the house, a square tower that rose a storey above the other two so that its windows overlooked both the river to the west and the courtyard and the Palais to the east.

'Our victim chose well, Hermann,' said St-Cyr. 'Plaster over the holes, replace the shutters, fix the chimneys and roof tiles and *voilà*, you will have the fourteenth-century villa of a merchant, the scant remains of whose coat of arms suggest an importer of cloth.'

Carriage entrances were to the left and right – great, solid, weathered oaken doors with rusty driftpins. All windows at ground level were tightly shuttered, though some of the slats had disappeared. On the floor above, some windows had closed curtains. In others, these had been drawn aside. In one, there were pots of herbs and green onions the frost had killed. In another, a caged rabbit was trying not to think of things as it awaited the stew pot.

The concierge, grey and toothless, her hair pinned in a tight chignon, was in tears. 'Inspectors!' she wailed. 'Who would do such a thing?'

A tattered black lace shawl was pulled tightly about the tiny shoulders. More tears fell and then she said accusingly, 'What is Thérèse to do?'

'Thérèse?'

'*Oui.* Her assistant. The girl can't sew without her fingers being guided. *Mon Dieu*, how could she carry on such work? A girl with a dead mother and a father who has fortunately been absent all her life except for the moment of conception? Mademoiselle Mireille was teaching her. Painstakingly, I must add!'

Tears were abruptly wiped away but then, of a sudden, the woman turned aside and broke down completely. 'Forgive me,' she blurted. 'The child was like a daughter. Her throat slashed! Ah let me get my hands on *his* filthy throat. I will wring his neck like a chicken's!'

A doubter of all such outbursts, Kohler looked up at the ceiling to where flaking paint and ancient wallpaper threatened to join the plaster as it caved. 'The key, Louis. Ask her for it.'

'Thérèse is up there waiting for her to return, *monsieur*! Always I've seen the way he has secretly watched the tower room from the ramparts. Always he has stood clothed in darkness while he planned to steal her little capital.'

Ah *nom de Dieu*. 'Who, madame?' asked Louis.

She raked them with a savage look. 'He took it, didn't he?'

Her virginity. 'No. No, she remained pure to the last.'

'Ah *grâce à Dieu.*' The bosom was hastily crossed, the fingertips kissed and then the black beads of an ancient rosary were sought and also kissed.

'Who?' repeated St-Cyr.

They had both crowded into her *loge*. 'I . . .' She threw them a tortured look. 'I . . . I don't know. I spoke out of grief. You . . . you can see how distressed I am.'

Kohler sighed and then said, 'Withholding information is a criminal offence. We'll have to see that she's charged, Louis. Otherwise she'll only set a bad example.'

'Dédou Favre. The one who is wanted by the authorities so much that Monsieur le Préfet has the house watched constantly.'

'Her lover, Louis. The boy the bishop was trying to get her to give up. The Kommandant spoke of him. De Passe told me he had agreed to look the other way while Rivaille worked on her.'

A 'terrorist'. One of the *maquis*. 'And you think he killed her, madame?' asked Louis pleasantly.

'She said he would misunderstand and that for him, it would be enough.'

'Misunderstand what?' asked St-Cyr.

'The attentions of others. Those of the madrigal singers of Monsieur Simondi, and of that one *aussi*. What they want, they take. A girl's virtue is nothing to such as them, and she was totally aware of this. "Dédou will be insanely jealous," she said. "He will think that in joining the group I've succumbed, that even I can be led astray in order to advance my career."'

And in Avignon such jealousy was cause enough for murder. History was replete with the evidence.

'Inspector, that was one of the reasons she wouldn't leave this house to take up the lodgings Bishop Rivaille had arranged for her. She also said, "Here I keep my independence. Here I can stand on the side of what is right as I reach out to clasp the true hand of God." Every day, on waking, she would make that little vow to herself as she gazed up at the Palais. A saint.'

The German lit a cigarette for her and left her two others for later. 'Thérèse?' he asked. His voice was gentle for one so formidable and with the mark of a terrible scar down the left cheek – how had he got it? she wondered.

'Barbed wire,' lied Kohler. 'The Great War. My partner and I were enemies then, but we're friends now.'

The other scars from that war were much older, except for the graze across his brow which was still very fresh. 'Thérèse hasn't eaten, hasn't slept, nor will she listen to me, messieurs. Please do what you can for her. Mademoiselle de Sinéty would wish this of us all.'

'Won't the sisters take her in?' asked St-Cyr, only to see the woman's expression tighten and to hear her rasp, 'The sisters? You mustn't ask them to do that. Not until you've brought the one who did this terrible thing to justice.'

'But . . . but you've just told us Dédou Favre must have killed her in a jealous rage.'

She gave him a piercing look. 'One can still be wrong, is that not so, Inspector? And if I am wrong, why then it would have to have been someone else.'

Pure logic. 'But the sisters?' snorted Kohler in disbelief.

'Have among them, messieurs, the disease of those who are capable, especially if they believe it is God's work.'

'Did Sister Marie-Madeleine come here often?' asked St-Cyr.

Had this one from the Sûreté seen it too, the bond between Mireille and her friend? 'Often enough and not always with one of the other sisters, though it is their rule to go two by two when escaping the tight embrace of their walls.'

Thérèse Godard was about fifteen years old – thin, frail, not healthy-looking at all. 'Tuberculosis . . . ?' breathed Kohler – the door had been left open.

'The flu . . .' cautioned Louis, perturbed that God should do such a thing to them at a time like this.

She was shivering, was sitting at a cutting table, staring emptily at an upturned pair of dove-grey woollen gloves whose fingers, especially in these days of so little fuel, had been cut away at the first joint.

Gently Kohler spoke her name. She tossed her head.

'Mireille . . . ?' she managed, only to see the two of them and to turn swiftly away.

The auburn hair, once curled, was unkempt. 'I'll take her downstairs to madame, Louis. See what you can make of this clutter.'

'It is not clutter!' blurted the girl angrily. 'Everything is in its place just as we kept it. They came. They searched. They did that to her privacy but I . . . I have put things back exactly as we kept them.'

Ah *merde* . . . 'De Passe, Louis?'

'The police,' she managed.

Kohler dug into a pocket and dragged out the wrist-watch he had found in the victim's purse. 'Was this hers?'

The girl buried her face in her employer's gloves and wept.

'Sorry . . . Look, I'm sorry,' he said gently. 'Please forgive me.'

'Xavier gave that to her. She needed a watch and he . . . he said he could get her one.'

The shepherd boy.

The rooms – there were two of them – opened into each other through double doors that had been permanently flung wide. In a far corner, a spiral staircase led up to the tower.

Rescued, pieced together, were the stone fragments of letters which had once been a part of the coat of arms. 'De Sinéty . . .' exhaled St-Cyr. The time, the diligence needed to gather and fit the artefacts together said much about the victim. A scattered collection of pieces, obviously uncovered from courtyard and cellar excavations, yielded a bent and much corroded ducat, the remains of an ancient pair of shears, those also of fourteenth-century clothing pins and clasps, and those of what must have been the original keys to the house.

Two silver thimbles, one crushed flat, the other crumpled, had been cleaned but were still black.

The pattern on them matched that of the thimbles in the motif on the sides of the pomander.

There was cloth in plenty, either folded neatly on the workroom shelves or in bolts and remnants, and he had to ask, How had she come by it? and had to answer, 'The Church, the

bishop and the nuns – wealth that has been stored for centuries.'
And then, fingering satin, silk and velvet, 'The drapes, bed linens
and clothing from abandoned villas. Wrist-watches, too, no
doubt.'

Those of the wealthy who could get out before the Free Zone
had been occupied had had to leave virtually everything behind.
Now most of these places had been taken over by the Occupier
and his friends, if in convenient locations and 'suitable'; if not,
they had remained empty. A ready source of fabrics especially for
a group of singers to collect when on tour.

The cutting table yielded patterns, fabric shears, scissors,
thread, thimbles, needles and detailed sketches of the costumes
she was making. There were hundreds of notations with arrows to
each seam and tuck. A collection of volumes on Renaissance
painting offered ready comparisons.

An order book would hold the dates, customers, projects and
fees charged. Alain de Passe would have looked through it but in
search of what? he asked himself.

A recent page had been torn out. A fragment remained, and
from this, there were two letters in pencil. *Ai* . . . Aix? he asked
himself. The tour the group were to make? Had Simondi
demanded different costumes for every tour? Had the girl written
down his needs? Then why tear the page out?

Unfortunately several other pages had been removed and these
went right back to the beginning, nearly four years ago. But why
hadn't de Passe simply taken the book and destroyed it? Thérèse
Godard would have told them of it, yes, of course, but had it been
left as a warning to watch out and tread lightly?

'Ah *merde*, Avignon,' muttered St-Cyr, not liking things at all.

A narrow cabinet held spools of thread, including that of gold
and silver. There were buttons, ribbons, bodice laces, boxes of
pins, rolls of basting tape, et cetera.

When he went up into the tower, he saw at once that the
pomander was a replica of the Palais's Bell Tower, that it must,
indeed, date from the mid-fourteenth century, and he had to ask,
How had she come by such a valuable thing?

Her lute was a treasure, too, not nearly so old as to have come from those times, but old and beautifully kept. A relative? he wondered. A legacy?

There were letters that had been written in Latin, in the French of the North, and in the *langue d'oc* of those days. Treasures, too, and many of them bore the signatures of the de Sinéty family and of another Mireille. Her namesake.

On the table she had used as a desk, there were recipes for beauty oils and creams, and these had been noted down from references no longer in evidence but attributed to this other Mireille.

Stanzas, verses and lines were from poems and madrigals.

> My love for my mistress is so gentle,
> I serve her so timidly, am so humble,
> I do not even tell her of my longing,

Bernard de Ventadour had been among the leading troubadors of the third quarter of the twelfth century. The passage, more of which appeared, was from *The Timid Wooing*. 'His style of poetry,' she had noted, 'is very firmly elemental and of *les provençaux*.'

De Ventadour had been a baker's son who had risen to sing at the court of Eleanor of Aquitaine. After the age of the troubadors had come that of the motet, and then the madrigal.

A leather-bound volume, the *Musica Transalpina*, of 1588 and borrowed from whom, he wondered, held a collection of madrigals, written in Italian but with their English translations, too, and many of these pieces had been composed by Luca Marenzio. Unbidden, the face of Christiane Bissert as she had entered the café this morning came to him. The Villa Marenzio. *I await your questions,* she had written, *with a heart that is open.*

'Louis, de Passe went through her things all by himself. There was no one else with him.'

'Then let us find what he missed.'

Two tins of sardines were from Marseille and they matched, exactly, the one Louis had taken from the victim.

Kohler reached well into the hidey-hole he had found under

the floorboards beneath a wooden box that was full of fabric remnants. A corked, dark green wine bottle was next. 'Extra *Vierge*,' he breathed.

There were freshly harvested black olives as big as small plums. Dried figs and apricots had been threaded on to braided lengths of straw for ease of carrying to and from market or hanging up in the kitchen, but few would have done so these days for fear of a visit from Vichy's hated *Service d'ordre,* soon to become the *Milice,* who, among other tasks, hunted for hoarders and the lesser black-marketeers, the little men, the *lampistes.* Never the big ones. Never! It was only the little ones who couldn't buy their way out of trouble.

A beating and arrest were guaranteed; theft, too, of the offending items and anything else that might appear appealing.

The braiding of the straw and style of tying matched that of the recently acquired ropes of garlic and sun-dried tomatoes that hung freely in sight above the tiny basin she had used as a sink.

A cake of homemade olive-oil soap smelled of honey, too, and lavender, not of ground horse chestnuts, sand and slaked lime as did the infamous 'National' soap, which was always served up in grey, pasty two-centimetre-sized cubes and rationed. Nor would this soap have burned her skin and scratched it as the National's did Giselle's and Oona's. Not used until recently, the soap had to have come with the olives and the oil. None of these items was ever seen in Paris by ordinary people. And as sure as that God of Louis's had made olives to ripen like that near les Baux, the shepherd boy had some answering to do.

A small round of *chèvre de crottin* had been dusted with herbs. Three slices of honey-drenched, fried bread were golden in colour and lying under a cover on a plate – the *tranches dorées* the peasant would take at his mid-afternoon *goûter,* his little 'tea break' among the groves or vineyards and fortified by at least four litres of red wine. Had the shepherd boy been bribing the victim or just trying to encourage her favour?

A last item was harder to retrieve and it caused consternation for it couldn't have come from a similar source.

'Hédiard,' he muttered. 'Kumquats. *Merde alors*, she's full of surprises!'

The pale green glass jar, with its gold lettered and embossed label, spoke of luxuries not seen by most since before the war and then only from the street side of a shop window.

There was dust on the lid; the seal was intact, a puzzle these days.

From behind the false backing of the small cupboard that served as her kitchen counter and drainboard, he took a jar of English marmalade, one of candied ginger, a tin of litchi nuts and another of crystallized, unrefined sugar from Barbados. Again, all the items had come from Hédiard's. Again there was dust on all of the lids and this was thickest on the jar of marmalade. From there through to the kumquats it varied, indicating the items hadn't come in all at once but had been given to her in payment perhaps, and at intervals. But why had she partaken of none of them?

Everyone knew or had heard of Hédiard. One of Paris's venerable institutions, and much revered not just for its delicatessen but for its upstairs tearoom, the shop had occupied premises at 21 place de la Madeleine since 1851. And oh *bien sûr*, had they closed it in protest at the Defeat of June 1940, they would have lost the business to a friend or friends of the Occupier. That had been one of the many ordinances of the time, and had been obeyed or else.

Among other things, she had been working on an order for six replacement surplices for the Cathedral's choir, a donation of her already overstressed time, no doubt, since there was no mention of the order in her ledger.

But then, of course, Alain de Passe, that warner of Don't mess with the Host and the Blood of Christ, had torn out page after page.

When he found a false panel beneath the top of her main worktable, his fingers trembled and he had to calm them. Infrequent sleep and meals hadn't helped the nerves, nor had the pace of things. Always it was blitzkrieg for them, and always of late those little dove-grey pills of Benzedrine the fighter pilots took to stay awake and alive had been necessary.

The ledger she had hidden was complete. Greatly humbled by the thoroughness of this *petite lingère*, he began to peruse it. 'Aix-en-Provence, Marseille, Toulon and Arles . . . The tour after the concert on the thirtieth.'

Beneath each of these place names she had noted the costume changes the singing master had demanded. Detail after detail followed in columns and sketches so orderly he had to recall the Kommandant's admiration of her practicality. She had even used a code – in glyphs – to denote the singers' names and those of others, and nowhere here did the actual names appear. A kind of shorthand, he supposed, but another rebus for them to sort out.

Beneath the glyphs and the details there were notations of payment: for the costumes at Aix, a mere 205 francs; for those at Marseille, 103; for Arles only 63 francs.

The singing master must have had her modify existing costumes, but even so it was far too little, far too parsimonious.

At the bottom of the page she had written: *Maître Simondi's cheque for 876 francs has been postdated to 25 April* – three months, no less! – *and given on the Arles branch of the Banque des Pays du Sud this time.*

Two things were immediately clear: the singing master was a demanding, cheap son of a bitch – an astute businessman, the Kommandant had said. And Mireille de Sinéty had felt it necessary to keep hidden a far more detailed copy of her ledger.

They'd been watching her, and she had damned well known it.

Xavier had brought her gifts from his father's farm, and things he had stolen when the group had broken into abandoned villas. Someone else – he didn't think it could have been the shepherd boy – had paid her in, or given her, the tins of sardines. And yet again, someone had done so with the items from Hédiard's, but at intervals.

Up in the tower, Louis was lost in thought, puzzling over something on the girl's dressing table and sucking on a pipe he had forgotten to light.

Fingering a cheap, ersatz pewter crucifix and a rosary of black Bakelite beads, the Sûreté said, 'This medallion, Hermann. The image of the Holy Mother has been so poorly stamped, the second impression blurs the first.'

Yet their victim had been a perfectionist, a lover of the past, her family once of the lesser nobility.

The items were next to her hairbrush and comb as if, in a final gesture, it had been they to which she had turned before leaving for the Palais. A pair of scissors lay on top of a four-centimetre-long lock of her hair . . .

'A label provides the source of the religious bric-a-brac, which has only just recently been purchased from Les Fleurs du Petit Enfant,' said St-Cyr. 'It's on the rue de Mons not far from the Palais and the Cathedral, but what does a shop which sells religious motifs of the worst kind have to do with *this*?'

Of postcard size, but definitely *not* a postcard, the black-and-white photographic print was of a young woman's naked breasts. No shoulders, arms or waist were visible, no name either. Instead, one end of a curl of their owner's hair had been glued to the lower right corner of the card so that the hair could be fingered while gazing raptly at the breasts.

The card had been hidden behind the backing of a gaudily framed sketch of the *Petit Jésus*, complete with phosphorescent halo and angels in the sky.

The hair was distinctly reddish, a pronounced strawberry blonde and soft, but with a sheen like burnished copper in strong sunlight. There were scattered freckles on the breasts. The skin was very white – 'creamy', a *fétichiste de cheveux* might have whispered during his orgy of gawking and self-masturbation. The nipples had been stiffened, probably at the photographer's insistence and simply by their owner having first wetted her fingers. Chorus girls did this as a matter of routine at the Lido and other such places, so much so that in winter they were always bitching about their being chapped.

'The Silver Swan . . .' hazarded Kohler, indicating the post-card.

' "When death approached unlocked her silent throat," ' said Louis, comparing the hair with the loose strands Mireille de Sinéty had cut from herself and had left for them or others to find.

'De Passe must have seen the hair she left but not the photograph, Louis.'

'But did he leave it for us to find as a warning to us, or not think it important?'

Kohler indicated the card. 'Is this the reason she was silenced? Is the *fétichiste* the bishop?'

It had to be faced. 'He practises flagellation, Hermann. He's one of the *Pénitents Noirs*. I'm not sure that such a practice is common to them now, but there was also the *enseigne* of a *martinet* on her belt.'

'And wouldn't you know it, eh? The sins of the flesh needing to be scourged.'

'Whoever tidied up after the murder took the time to cut off a lock of our victim's hair.'

'To go with a photograph of her breasts – is that it, eh? Is that why she cut this off herself?'

'Calm down. We must think as she would have had us think.'

'The Church, you idiot! The préfet and his warning!'

Early in the afternoon long shadows were cast by the Palais, and the town, with its ramparts seen from the tower room, held narrow streets, some of which already appeared as if at dusk, such was the flatness of the sun's trajectory in winter.

The clouds had vanished; the mistral still blew every bit as fiercely.

'Monsieur le Préfet said I was to keep silent,' confessed Thérèse Godard faintly. 'He told me that if I did not wish to embarrass myself, I should remember that silence protected a girl's honour.'

The son of a bitch!

'We'll protect you,' said the one called Kohler but she knew this could never be and said, 'You don't know what it's like here! They have their ways. People like me are nothing to them. *Nothing*, do you understand?'

'Who do you mean?' urged St-Cyr.

'Them! I . . .' The girl shrugged and wiped her eyes with her fingertips.

'Listen to me, mademoiselle . . .'

71

'Go easy, Louis. She's really upset.'

'And so will we be, *mon ami*, if there are more killings!'

'More killings . . . ?' shrilled Thérèse. 'Myself and Sister Marie-Madeleine, perhaps?'

Louis calmed his voice. 'Please, mademoiselle, you are our closest link. You owe it to her to tell us everything you know of what happened.'

'So as to empty my head before I am drowned in the river, monsieur? Drowned in an *accabussade*?'

Ah *nom de Dieu*, what the hell was this? wondered St-Cyr. Six hundred years ago husbands, masters and fathers could deal with recalcitrant and errant females in their charge by locking them into a wooden cage which was then repeatedly and publicly dunked in the river like a crayfish trap.

'An *accabussade*?' he asked.

'I . . . I didn't mean to say that. It . . . it was only because of Mireille's telling me what had happened to the other Mireille, the one she was named after.'

There, she had told them, but they would never understand. How could they?

In a whisper, she said, 'Sister Marie-Madeleine knows far more about it than I do. She . . . she came here late on the night before Mireille was murdered. They spoke quietly. I know they must have talked of this other Mireille, of what it must mean, but I . . . I do not know what they said up here in the tower – how could I? I sleep downstairs under one of the tables. Mireille let me do that. Mireille was my friend, my best friend!'

It was Louis who asked of Xavier. Still choked up, she blurted, 'Before the sister left, and still well before dawn, he . . . he brought us things from the farm. He'd been away for the harvest. He always goes home for it. A week, ten days . . .' She ran a hand through her hair in anguish and wiped her nose on a sleeve. 'The bishop . . . he has to let him. It's part of the agreement the Church made with Xavier's father. In return, the *monseigneur* sends a car to . . . to collect the olive oil and . . . and other things.'

'*Verdammt*, Louis, that little son of a bitch was here in Avignon before the murder. He's been here since then and didn't run away at news of it!'

Thérèse wanted to ask who had lied to him but knew she was too afraid, and to hide her fear, tried to straighten her dress. 'Mireille was "special" to Xavier. He was always dropping in, often using the excuse of things he and the others had found. Cloth, fabulous dresses, skirts and silk blouses, waistcoats of gold lamé, buttons and thread – we had to take these things for the costumes. We had to! This time more food from les Baux, but fish he had caught in the river, hares and rabbits too, sometimes. Once a *grive* – did you find it, messieurs?' she asked and hastily wiped her eyes with the hem of her dress.

'Tell us,' urged Kohler gently.

He had such nice eyes, this detective, but such terrible scars. 'Let me go downstairs and get it,' she said.

Louis nodded and Kohler went with her. The cigar box, one among several that were used to store buttons, held a mummified thrush.

Hastily the girl crossed herself and said, 'It was shot by the *monseigneur*. Xavier was positive of this and laughed when he presented it to Mireille last year in late November, but by then it had been dead for about a month. Yes, a month at least.'

Thrushes were tasty, thought St-Cyr. Not gutted, they were hung and allowed to rot and then were roasted on a spit so that the juices from their entrails could rain on to the backs of their fellows. Before the war, those who could hunt them had taken hundreds in a single day's shooting. The best time was in the autumn and at dawn, just as the birds were feeding and preoccupied. 'But why would she have wanted this in the first place?' he asked.

He was genuinely puzzled. Dear God forgive and protect her, then, for telling him. 'She . . . she said she had to see what His Eminence could kill with such impunity no remorse was felt, only joy. She . . .'

They waited for her to continue. Finally the one called Kohler asked, 'Who accompanies the bishop when he's out hunting?'

Her heart sank, and she could feel it doing so. 'The

Kommandant, the préfet, Maître Simondi and . . . and others. The Chief Magistrate. Lots of others, for the bishop and Maître Simondi, they . . . they know many important people. All are friends and business associates. Isn't that the way of things among such people?'

'What about Xavier?' asked the one from the Sûreté.

'Xavier?' she squeaked. 'The dogs are in his care. He's very good with them and . . . and knows exactly where each one is at . . . at all times.'

Kohler resisted the temptation to show her the *clochette*. There'd be time enough to settle that little matter. 'After Xavier left the house on Monday well before dawn, what did your friend and mistress do?'

There had been two of the hooded, ankle-length cassocks to finish. Hideous things they had hated having to make, but Préfet de Passe had warned her not to mention them . . . 'She worked all day on her costume. Everything had to be absolutely perfect. Late in the afternoon she must have gone to the *bains-douches municipaux*, at the other end of the street.'

The public bathhouse. 'She didn't practise?' asked Kohler gently.

'I . . . I don't think so. I was away and didn't get back from the *mas* near Saint-Michel-de-Frigolet until well after dark. By then Mireille was . . . was all but ready.'

'You went to see her mother?' asked the one from the Sûreté.

'Who issued your *laissez-passer*?' asked the other one.

The two of them were crowding her again and she wanted to cry out, Please leave before it's too late for me! She wanted to weep in despair and clench her fists. 'The Kommandant himself, and yes, I went to see Madame de Sinéty. Mireille . . . Mireille wanted me to take a letter to a friend.'

'What friend?' breathed the Sûreté softly.

They wouldn't leave things alone now! 'Dédou Favre, the boy she loved.'

'And did he love her in return?' asked the Sûreté.

Would they arrest her for delivering the letter? 'He doubted her. He always felt she might give him up to . . . to the authorities.'

'In order to advance her career?' asked Kohler. 'Hey, don't worry about your having broken the law.'

'Then yes, but you . . . you have to know Dédou to understand. He's terribly afraid of what they'll do to him if he's caught. It's only natural because he's on the run and in hiding.' There, she had told them. That, too.

'And did you deliver this letter to him personally?' asked St-Cyr.

'No! I . . . I couldn't find him so I left it in the mill, in a special place he would know of. He and Mireille had used it lots of times. The stones . . . a crack between the stones.'

When the detectives were gone from the house, she went down into the workrooms to search for the hooded shrouds – she could call those hateful things nothing else. They were not grey or black. They were of coarse white woollen cloth and when, at last, she had found them – rolled up with her mattress, her *paillasse*! – their empty eyesockets stared accusingly up at her, she realizing then that Monsieur le Préfet hadn't taken them as he should have but had left them here for her as a further warning.

'*La Cagoule*,' she wept and, flinging them from her, stood among the silks and satins, the patterns of the past, with head bowed.

It was Madame Guillaumet, the concierge, who, coming upon her like this and seeing the hooded shrouds on the floor at the girl's feet, said, 'Thérèse, what have you to do with those?'

They sat in the Renault, staring bleakly out at the wind-ravaged rue du Rempart du Rhône. Each waited for the other to speak, until Kohler could stand it no longer. '*La Cagoule*, Louis. Two of their outfits were rolled up in that kid's straw mattress but I didn't let on I'd found them.'

'De Passe?' asked St-Cyr emptily.

'It has to have been him. No wonder she was afraid.'

'She spoke of being put into an *accabussade* . . .'

'That little bit of history can't apply to the present, can it?'

Hermann was really worried, but it had to be said, 'Our victim must have been aware of those cassocks.'

'An order, Louis, but it's not even mentioned in the book she kept to herself.'

'Ah *mon Dieu*, Hermann, what had she discovered?'

Unbidden, Kohler hauled out his cigarettes and offered one, only to see Louis shake his head and find pipe and tobacco pouch.

Not until the pipe was going to his satisfaction did the Sûreté say, 'De Passe agrees to turn aside while Rivaille works on our victim to see if he can't convince her to betray her boyfriend – let us put it no other way.'

'The bishop lends her things and sends the sisters to watch over her corpse in an attempt to retrieve at least two of the items before we take too great an interest in them.'

'A ruby ring,' said Louis, 'and a pendant box. One of the thorns supposedly from Christ's crown.'

'The elder of the nuns succeeds with the ring, but not with the box. The younger one is marked down by her as knowing too much.'

'That sister was a close friend of our victim. They spoke in private on the night before the murder.'

'Did Sister Agnès realize this at the morgue, Louis?'

'I'm certain of it, but . . . ah *merde alors*, we must think as Mademoiselle de Sinéty would have had us think!'

'Then start by telling me are you certain it was the bishop himself who loaned her all those trinkets?'

'Simondi?'

'We'll have to ask him.'

'But must proceed carefully, since the *Cagoule* may well be involved,' mused St-Cyr.

'Both Rivaille and de Passe are members of the Black Penitents.'

'Our singing master may also be one of them.'

'But is Simondi the leader of the local *Cagoule*, Louis? Is de Passe or Bishop Rivaille?'

The Hooded Ones. The action squads of the *Comité secret d'action révolutionnaire*, a fanatical far-right political organization of the 1930s that had dedicated itself to the overthrow of the Third Republic by any means. In Nice, in 1938, *cagoulards* had murdered the Rosselli brothers, two prominent anti-fascists Mussolini had wanted eliminated.

In return for the favour, a substantial shipment of small arms had crossed into France from Italy only to be intercepted by agents of the Deuxième Bureau.

The leaders of the CSAR had been arrested. They'd been brought to trial in July of '38 but the war had soon intervened.

'End of story,' said Kohler, picking up the thread of Louis's thoughts, 'but sadly not so, eh?'

'No, not.'

On the night of 2/3 October 1941, perhaps as Bishop Rivaille was looking forward to a morning's shooting courtesy of the Kommandant's ignoring the ordinance against hunting and possessing guns of any kind, *cagoulards* in Paris had dynamited seven synagogues in a show of solidarity with Nazi policies against the Jews.

'And now?' asked Louis, lost to it and still staring at the street. 'Now Ovid Peretti has twice made a point of warning me to watch our backs, and the bishop dreams of returning the Papacy to Avignon.'

'It all has to mean she was killed because she damn well knew too much,' swore Kohler.

'But what, Hermann? That is the question.'

They began to look through the order books, comparing the one she had kept privately with that from which de Passe had torn so many pages. 'All references to Simondi's post-dated cheques have been removed,' said Louis. 'Some of these have even put payment off by as much as six months and yet all are for the most insignificant of sums.'

'Overextended, is he?' snorted Kohler. 'He owns several cinemas and theatres but loves music more than money, or so von Mahler took pains to claim.'

'But is Simondi alone in owning them or merely the front man?'

In several places where the pages had been removed, the complete copy revealed she had used alchemical glyphs for the signs of the zodiac as a shorthand for the names of her customers and had paired these with measurements and other notations for each costume. Where more than one customer had been born under the same sign, she had used a vertical line, placed on one side of the glyph or on the other, to distinguish them. 'But again, Hermann, why would the préfet remove such pages unless he had been warned by Bishop Rivaille that she had left the riddle of it all on her belt?'

A rebus . . . the talismans, *enseignes* and cabochons, the signs of the zodiac themselves . . . 'Salvatore Biron is adamant there wasn't an audition, Louis, but there was one. He was delayed and claims to have come upon the body seconds after the killing, only to hear a sigh that clearly couldn't have been hers.'

'But was it the killer's or that of someone else – a witness perhaps?'

'And why didn't he run into whoever had tidied up?'

'A lock of her hair was cut off and that would have taken time . . .'

'And now we have similar locks from her dressing table and from a strawberry blonde, and this last is glued to a photo.'

'Mireille de Sinéty wears ancient keys that can't have been of any use to her, Hermann. She takes rooms in the ancestral home, gathers artefacts from the same, clasps a pomander that is as old as the Palais and modelled after its Bell Tower.'

'Has a namesake from those times.'

'Has recipes and letters that can be attributed to this other Mireille. *Merde, mon vieux*, why can I not recall more of the very early Renaissance? Did my professors at the *lycée* freeze their minds into accepting rigid dates – Early, Middle and Late, and never mind that such dates are normally far from perfect, and that the Renaissance began much earlier here and in Italy?'

'But we have her record book, Louis, and we now know how she used the glyphs. Hey, that's progress. Cheer up.'

'We still don't know which glyph represents which name.'

'Was Dédou the Archer?' asked Kohler.

'Was the bishop the Goat, the Scorpion or the Cancer?'

'Xavier must have tidied up, Louis. I'm certain of it.'

One of the bishop's hounds had been with the boy and must

have come into the Palais with him, said St-Cyr to himself. She had known the dog and had removed its little bell so as to prevent its sound from giving away her position, but had broken a fingernail in the process . . .

'Rivaille wanted her to move into the Villa Marenzio with the other singers,' said Kohler.

'Then let us hear what they have to say. Let us listen to the madrigal of them.'

'You're forgetting the sardines. You can't do that. Three tins, one of which she took with her.'

'Along with a wealth of old coins, one of which held a maze, *mon ami*. A maze!'

4

The Villa Marenzio could not help but engender admiration, thought St-Cyr. Seventeenth-century diamond leading and stained-glass armorial shields faced the rue Banasterie with a quiet calm that belied the centuries.

Kept in excellent condition – worked on even now when materials were so hard to come by – the villa was to the northeast of the Palais. A delightful bas-relief of pomegranates, grapes, eagles and grinning, hollow-eyed masks surrounded the family crest above the carriage entrance, while matching life-sized statues of the Virgin flanked it. A superb pentagonal stone staircase was directly across a large inner courtyard where ancient plane trees were partially sheltered from the mistral. At the north of the courtyard, sunlight glowed from the soft, buff-grey of the walls.

'Hermann. It's magnificent.'

'But a bugger to heat.'

'*Merde alors*, must you always look on the bad side of such things?'

'*Wenn der Führer wusste*, eh, *mein lieber Oberdetektiv*? That's woodsmoke *and* coal smoke coming from the chimneys.'

If only the Führer knew . . . People had taken to saying this in Paris when such privilege was witnessed. Twenty-five kilos a month was the coal ration – enough to heat one small room for a few brief hours, *if* one could get it. 'Unless I'm mistaken, *mon vieux*, that is Mademoiselle Bissert who has been watching for us from one of the second-floor windows.'

Though distant, and seen but fleetingly, for she soon ducked away, the girl looked like a moth trapped behind leaded glass, and must have been anxiously awaiting their arrival for hours.

There were two storeys. An open balcony and its ground floor arcade looked out on to formal gardens in the centre of which, drained for the winter and bleached by the half-light of partial shade, stood a fountain. But such a one. In summer, in the midday heat especially, and under moonlight too, stone carp would piss their streams on to the heads of cavorting naked nymphs as cicadas sang.

'An addition an eighteenth-century owner must have felt necessary,' commented the Sûreté drolly. 'Our Monsieur Simondi has an eye for value, Hermann; our bishop, one for accommodations.'

The concierge, his wife and fourteen-year-old daughter had braved the wind and cold to dutifully stand outside their *loge*, which was near the staircase and next to what had, until the advent of the motor car, been both stables and storage sheds.

None of them was tall, but the daughter had awkwardly shot up past her parents, leaving her ankle socks to lose their elastics above well-worn, laceless black boots. The man's beret was crumpled into a tight fist. The wife's dark brown eyes were impassive; those of the daughter, modestly averted.

With a guarded tongue, this grizzled patriarch in brown cords, boots and a flannel shirt, his skin the colour of tannin, said in manageable *langue d'oc*, 'Maître Simondi wishes us to bid you welcome, messieurs, and to assist your enquiries. Please, he has put us completely at your disposal. I am Octave Leporatti and this is my wife, Mila, and daughter. The house, it is big, but most of it was made into flats some time ago and now only the north wing is reserved for the students.'

At the far end of the courtyard, where Christiane Bissert had watched for them, the brick-red tiles so common to the south climbed to the line of the roof beyond which rose a two-storeyed square tower. The wind plucked at the concierge's close-cropped grey hair and brought water to his watchful eyes – he'd seen the girl too. And forget about that crap of their being at our disposal, thought Kohler. This one's family, and that of his wife, had hailed from Sicily two hundred years ago, but always the code of silence had governed life. *Omertà*.

'I'm to take you to the singers, messieurs. As it is the afternoon, you will find them at practice in the salon where there is a fire.'

'They never use the tower for their music and . . . and other things in winter,' chimed in the daughter only to receive the sharp sting of, '*Gina!*' Nothing else.

At least thirty-five years separated the father from the mother. The daughter burst into tears but wept silently. She'd have had to, poor kid, thought Kohler, not liking it.

'Come on, Louis. Let's see what the singers have to say.'

It was the Sûreté who cautioned the father. 'We may want to question your daughter, monsieur. Please be certain she isn't punished for anything she might wish to confide in private or anything you might think she has said even though she denies it.'

They fell behind the bastard so as to have a quiet word as they went up the spiral staircase to the first floor. 'You'll get a knife in the guts one of these days if you're not careful,' hissed Kohler softly. '*Tout doux*, eh?, and that's an order!'

Take it easy . . . '*Bon*, then I'll let you miss what you should have seen.'

Startled, Kohler stopped him. '*What?*'

St-Cyr gave a nod towards the concierge's retreating boots. 'Rabbit dung and hairs. Bits of winter grass too, and lavender.'

'Ah Christ . . .'

Genoese velvet, silk and wool; damask from the north. Cotton, muslin, quilted muslin, linen with a plain weave, a twill weave, block-printed cloth, plain cloth, fine cloth, ivory silk and gold brocade, silver, too, the silk so fine it was as if transparent, the colours so striking they clashed, they harmonized, they leapt at one. Emerald green, matt red, sky blue, sea blue, dove blue, orange, a fiery orange, burnt umber, a beige, a cocoa-brown, a soft yellow, saffron yellow, purple . . . wine purple flowing, melding as the part song raced to fill the ears, its background, '*ch'i . . . ch'i . . . ch'i . . . rom-, rom-, rom-,*' the melody and words leaping away in, '*So-spi-ra Dolce-men . . . te et s'a di-ra Con pa ro – le ch'i sas –*'.*

* From *Io piango* (1581), by Luca Marenzio (1553–99), after a poem by Petrarch.

She sigh-eth oh so gent–ly, then fli-eth in a ra–ging with words . . .

The six of them sat to one side and with their backs to a magnificently carved Renaissance fireplace. A blonde girl was on a dais, with an exquisite lute in her hands and outspread lap. Christiane Bissert sat below her and to the left, a recorder ready; Xavier the same but to her right, while the young men, the boys – everyone still called them that these days – flanked him, voice following voice, the part song light and full of laughter, yet sad, too.

They didn't hesitate. They carried right on into the *Silver Swan* which they sang in French with evident delight and then . . . then a long madrigal in which occurred the line, '*Tue! à mort*'.*

Kill! To the death!

The fire was of olive logs, the salon hung with tapestries and filled with far more recent fine antique furniture and sunlight, so that one saw the group bathed in soft gold, while across the blonde's hair and the shoulders of the crimson cloak she wore the firelight flickered. Stunning blue eyes there, but dark brown eyes, too, grey eyes, greeny-brown eyes . . . None of the singers wore jewellery of any kind, noticed St-Cyr, but they sang so perfectly each was completely at ease with the others.

The introduction over, their response to the killing, given each in his or her own words, was also as one.

'Mireille didn't work out.'

'We tried, but with some, no matter how great the desire, they simply do not have what it takes.'

'The intonation.'

'The tenuosity.'

'The ability to hear all other parts while singing precisely as directed.'

'With a full voice.'

'From the heart.'

'Or not at all.'

* From *La Guerre* (The War), by Clément Janequin (1485–1558).

'From the soul.'

'With love.'

'Desire.'

'Hatred too.'

'*Merde!* What're we to do with them?' blurted the Sûreté.

'Use the scissors and cut each one off from all the others,' said Kohler firmly.

'Find the music, read the part and let us each audition for you.'

Christiane Bissert had said this and, swiftly exchanging a knowing glance with the lute player, bid the Sûreté to follow. '*Ma chambre à coucher*, Inspector,' she said. 'It's very private and will allow me to strip the soul bare without the distraction of other voices.'

Kohler chose the blonde who, having swiftly turned her back on her fellow musicians, and having carefully set her lute aside, warmed her hands while gazing raptly into the flames.

The men, the boys, drifted off as males will do when uneasy, with the cops around.

She was almost as tall as he was, she thought. 'Name?' he said, and he was formidable. A scar . . . but such a scar. Could he bed a woman with that? What sort of woman? she wondered.

'Genèvieve Ravier, *Canto Primus.*'

'Pardon?'

The smile she gave was frail and disconcerting.

'*Primo Soprano, Ispettore.* First Soprano. Xavier is the other but his voice . . .' she said hesitantly and left the thought hanging but the detective didn't ask further. 'Shall we sit, Inspector, or do you always prefer to stand when questioning a suspect?'

'No one said you were suspected of anything.'

'*Merci,*' she said so softly he could hardly have heard her, and turning her back to the fire, added, 'That is good to know. We all thought . . . I mean, she *was* one of us. Well, almost. We *were* with her that afternoon. She came here – were you not aware of this? We sang together for two hours, at least. Over and over again. The works of Landini, Marenzio and Monteverdi. Lots of others, too, for none ever know what the judges will demand. Xavier hadn't returned from the harvest – at least, I don't think he

84

had – so Mireille sang his part but . . .' She shrugged. 'But what can I say?'

'No good, eh?'

She faced him silently for a moment, her expression candid and searching.

'We are a unit and complete, Inspector. It's like two lovers engaged in the act of giving themselves to each other. The energy of each, the will, the striving to *le grand frisson* – *l'orgasme* – is shared equally if success is to be guaranteed, but with us, you understand, there are six.'

A regular *partouse*, an orgy, was that it, eh? 'Let's sit down, then.'

'Let's.'

Not dyed, her hair was parted in the middle and fell almost to her shoulders, but two tresses at the front had been shortened and these framed the soft oval of her face, half hiding her eyes, which were widely set and of clear conscience, perhaps. The skin was smooth and creamy, but definitely not that of the postcard. 'Your age?' he asked.

'You like pretty girls, Inspector, but I am, I fear, making you nervous.'

'It's the costume, the six hundred years that separate us. I don't want to see another murder like that. The throat . . .'

'Me?' she cried, startled.

'Your age?' he demanded.

His little black notebook was pressed open on the left knee of his trousers. Involuntarily a shiver passed through her and she cursed herself for having let it escape. 'Twenty-three. I've been a student of César's for the past five years, one of his singers now for three and a half.'

'Since well before the Defeat.'

'Yes. It's been good. Secure, if you know what I mean. My parents live in the north, in Beauvais. I'd no one. César, he . . . he gave me both a family and a purpose to my life.'

'A sense of order, a regimen and a job, eh? A good roof over your head, three square meals and a fire. The clothes on your back, especially those.'

Does he take them off me – is this what you're wondering? she wanted to ask but calmly said, 'A sense of being. A place, a profession. We're all professionals, Inspector. Please don't think otherwise. What we do, we do as one because that's the way it has to be.'

Genèvieve Ravier's expressions could be hawkish, warm, coy, intensely interested, concerned, flirtatious or tender and innocent of all wrongdoing.

'You wear no jewellery . . .' he hazarded, and she could see that the closeness of her was disturbing him in more ways than one.

'Why don't you have a cigarette?' she asked softly. 'It will help, I think.'

Verdammt! The girl was electric. 'Please just answer.'

He fidgeted. He looked her up and down and then fully met the frankness of her gaze. 'Did Mireille wear lots of little things?' she asked.

He waited. She would have to tell him and would therefore be firm about it. 'To be complete, we should each have worn such things during every concert but you see, the Church, though its collections are very good, no longer possesses enough, and even the private collection of His Eminence Bishop Rivaille is . . .' She shrugged. 'Insufficient. Mireille was a perfectionist, Inspector. That was a part of her problem. Always she would insist; always the *monseigneur* or César would say it just wasn't possible and she would "sigheth oh so gently, then . . ."'

'Okay, okay, I get the point. Bishop Rivaille was the source of the trinkets your *costumière* wore to her death.'

'The rings and . . . and other things but . . ' Again he would have to be told. 'But not all of them.'

Herr Kohler's sigh was one of exasperation and she could see that he was distressed at the thought of others having loaned Mireille things. 'She knew people who were well versed in the past, Inspector. Some she could count as friends; others still as enemies but only because of what had happened to her family during the Babylonian Captivity. Once tainted, always tainted, is this not so? And there are whispers even in a little place like

Avignon and especially under *les Allemands*, though they do not encourage such things as whispers, do they?'

Merde, but she was really something. 'Would one of these other custodians of bric-a-brac have sat in judgement of her on Monday night?'

Herr Kohler's eyes had emptied themselves of all feeling. Suddenly she wanted to get up, to stretch her legs, but knew his knees were deliberately touching hers for just such a signal. 'I really wouldn't know, Inspector. Mireille kept things to herself – that was a part of our problem with her. She had secrets she shared with no one, whereas we of the singers have none any more.'

'Where were you on Monday night?'

'Here with the others. Ask any of them. All will tell you the same thing. We are our own alibi, Inspector, or had you not thought of this? Christiane will only echo my words, as she often does in part song.'

The cote-hardie was of an emerald green velvet whose sheen rippled softly as Christiane Bissert moved about her bedroom. The bodice was of white silk with gold piping and brocade, and was crisscrossed by lacing that extended from the belted slender waist to the gently curving neckline.

Beneath the cote-hardie, the gown was of burnt sienna with the faint imprints of halved pomegranates, and as with the victim, thought St-Cyr, jagged cuts from the hem upwards for about thirty centimetres revealed tantalizing triangular wedges of the gown.

With the raven curls and the dark, now uncertain eyes, the girl was an enigma. She had said so little since coming to her room it was as though, once its door had been closed behind her, she had lost all confidence and had become another person.

He said how lovely the room was.

'A fire? Would you like one?' she asked hesitantly.

The bed was that of a Provençal bride, its coverlet white and trimmed with white lace. A simple wooden crucifix was attached to the wall above the ornately carved headboard. A small, stiff leather suitcase lay under carefully folded slips, silk stockings and underwear. There were three perfume vials as well, and he wondered if she had just received the largesse.

'Gina looks after us. Gina picks up,' she said, searching desperately for the right words. 'That suitcase is mine. She uses it to keep our laundry separate.'

And the perfume? he wanted to ask but let the matter rest – she could see him thinking this and cursed herself for not having put the things away and stuffed the suitcase under the bed.

On a round, marble-topped table by the windows, there was a vase of dried flowers and a half-empty bottle of Campari amid a clutter of books, some of which were still tied in their bundles.

He picked up the bottle, and with a sinking feeling in her heart, she knew he would miss nothing.

'César loves his apéritif. Would you like some?' she asked and saw those priest's eyes of his looking at her.

'That would be nice,' he said. 'Please. Allow me.'

He gave her time. He let her take a sip to recall the café this morning. Then he said, 'I understand his wife is an absinthe drinker.'

Ah *maudit*, Madame Emphoux, that bitch! 'It's only talk. Absinthe is no longer legal so how, please, could this be possible?'

Among the books were several of Simenon's train novels, inexpensive paperbacks, but also hardbound first editions of *Gone With the Wind* and *The Sun Also Rises*.

Her dressing table doubled as a writing desk, and on this, among the tidy clutter, were a Parker fountain pen with a verd antique finish, and monogrammed notepaper that didn't bear her initials.

Next to these items there was a beautifully engraved gold compact with the linked gold chain of the *belle époque*, complete with diamonds and the enamelled portrait of a reclining nude on a bed of flowers amid a deep blue background.

'Tiffany and Company,' he said of the compact, completely ignoring the matter of the absinthe. '1900 or thereabouts. It even has a little compartment to hold a lady's dance cards.'

'I love it.'

'Whose was it, please?'

Ah damn him! 'My grandmother's.'

A lie. '*Bon*, so . . .' He tossed off his Campari and said, 'A few small questions. Nothing difficult, I assure you.'

She, too, tossed off her drink, grimaced at its bitterness and, sitting on the edge of her bed, glanced briefly at the light of day and waited. 'I'm ready, Inspector.'

She looked so fragile. A classic Midi beauty. 'Let's begin with Xavier,' he said, coming to stand next to those same windows and to gaze out of them as she had.

'Xavier?' she asked.

'He was in Avignon well before dawn on Monday.'

Her voice must sound innocent of all wrongdoing and with just a touch of apprehension. 'The *monseigneur* sent the car for him, as . . . as he does every year at the close of each harvest. The oil, the wine and olives – garlic, too, and honey. Many things are loaded into the car. Perhaps . . . perhaps there wasn't room for Xavier and that . . . that's why he came back early.'

Thérèse Godard had said as much, but would this one now begin to tell him the truth? wondered St-Cyr.

The Inspector had taken out his pipe and tobacco – he sensed that she was really apprehensive at this activity, for it signified hours of questions and that he had all the necessary time to spare.

'You don't mind, do you?' he asked.

'No. César doesn't wish us to smoke – the voice, you understand – but he doesn't prevent us from allowing others to do so in . . . in our presence.'

'What time was her audition set for?'

'Ten o'clock, I think.'

'Why so late?'

'Other commitments, perhaps. Really, Inspector, I couldn't possibly know – none of us could. Bishop Rivaille dined with César and the Kommandant, and that one's wife. I . . . Ah! Forgive me. That sounds as if we *did* know.'

She forced a faint smile he ignored. Damn him . . .

'Who, then, was the third judge? The Kommandant has told us he had refused.'

So *don't* try to suggest him – was that it? 'Why not ask César?'

'I'm asking you.'

'I really couldn't say.'

Her tone of voice had been desperate. 'Try,' he breathed.

'Monsieur le Préfet or . . . or Madame Simondi. Others, too. I . . . I wouldn't know, Inspector.'

'Who let the victim into the Palais?'

Merde, why must he be so difficult? 'She had a key. Didn't your partner find it when he discovered her things in the Latrines Pit?'

'Who told you he'd discovered anything there?'

'I . . .' She felt herself blanching, and swallowed hard. 'I can't remember. Monsieur Biron, perhaps. Yes. Yes, it must have been him.'

The concierge. 'Who gave her that key?'

'Brother Matthieu, I think. Yes . . . Yes, I'm sure it was him.'

'Tell me what you know of the boy Mademoiselle de Sinéty was in love with.'

Like the absinthe, he had abruptly left the matter of the key so as to unsettle her. 'Dédou? I hardly knew him. He . . . he was of the age of the troubadors, I think. A throwback, you understand, and fiercely so. He was her mother's shepherd among . . . among other things but . . . but had joined the . . .'

Again her head was bowed, this time as if she'd known she had said too much and was truly shaken. 'The . . . ?' he asked gently.

'The *maquis*. Mireille always said he was very possessive of her and insanely jealous.'

A killer, then, was that it, eh? He scoffed inwardly but asked, 'Would she have planned to meet him in the Palais after her audition?'

Now she must look up at him and her answer must come softly. 'Yes. Yes, she could well have planned this. Dédou, he . . . he didn't want her to join our little group, nor did he like Bishop Rivaille's having arranged for her to live in this house with the rest of us. Marius is very handsome and . . . and so is Guy.'

Two of the male singers.

The detective turned abruptly away from the windows and,

walking over to her dressing table, sat down before its mirror to look at her reflection in it.

She met his gaze. He didn't ask more of Dédou. Instead he asked, 'Have there been others who aspired to join your little group?'

'Others since when?' she heard herself bleating.

'Within the past year, perhaps.'

Ah no, how had he learned of it? 'One,' she said faintly.

'Only one?'

'Yes! She . . . she didn't work out either.'

He removed his pipe and, searching for an ashtray, found none. 'What happened to her, Mademoiselle Bissert?'

His tone of voice had been *très insistant* and he'd come to stand in front of her, looking down at the crown of her head. 'I . . . I don't know, Inspector.'

'Look at me when you say that.'

Ah *Jésus, sweet Jésus* . . . 'She died. She was . . .'

'Murdered?' he asked, dropping his voice.

Vehemently she shook her head. 'She drowned in the river. She couldn't swim.'

He waited. He forced her to gaze up at him through her tears and when he asked, 'What colour was her hair?', she blanched and said, 'Her hair? Why, please, do you ask?'

'Just tell me.'

'Red . . . it was distinctly reddish. A . . . a strawberry blonde.'

The men, the boys, were in the wardrobe room, unseen as yet among the maze of hanging cloaks and capes and headless mannequins that wore the brightly coloured costumes of six hundred years ago. Kohler could hear them softly calling out to him, presumably as they put away the clothes they had worn to change into others. Everything in the room Mireille de Sinéty had made and he couldn't help but note the sacrifice, her utter dedication to reawakening the past.

'You took a *clochette* from Xavier,' said one.

'That boy sleeps with the dogs,' said another.

'Is of the dogs.'

'His voice departs.'

'Oh futile love!'

'He dreads its absence.'

'Longs for its return.'

'Kisses the bishop's ring.'

'Prays for his life here with us.'

'With us.'

'With us.'

There was silence. And when Kohler found the shepherd boy's costume for that day, he knew Xavier wasn't present. Letting his fingers trail down over the shimmering sky blue of a satin cape that was edged with gold embroidery, he saw that there were six coal black cassocks nestled beside it. Any of them could have been worn to the Palais on the night of the murder, and so much for the clot of black wool Peretti had found in the victim's hair.

'A bird's nest was found,' sang out one of the three.

'Her locks were cut,' sang out another.

'Her boots cast down.'

'Her overcoat.'

'Her purse.'

'A key . . . had she a key?'

'Who let her in?'

'A key.'

'A key.'

More silence followed, while softly now, the scent of musk, of clary sage and verbena came to him. Other things too . . . Scents Louis could easily have identified, but Louis wasn't here. He was still upstairs with Christiane Bissert.

'Extreme Unction was called for,' sang out one – the bass.

'Two sisters accompanied the corpse,' sang out another – the tenor.

'To the morgue,' gave the baritone.

'She was undressed.'

'Has no modesty now.'

'Is of the thorn.'

'A thorn was found.'

'The thorn of Christ.'

'But not the hair.'

'The Virgin's hair.'

'The hair.'

'The hair . . .'

An unlaced bodice revealed an underdress whose rose-coloured silk was as of lingerie.

It was being fondled by fingers as calloused and sure as those of a fourteenth-century stonemason who had made mischief with the count's wife. The jet black hair was thick and wavy and fell to broad shoulders. The eyes were a dark olive brown, the gaze level.

'Inspector, I'm Marius Spaggiari.'

'And I'm Norman Galiteau,' sang out another well to Kohler's left.

'I, Guy Rochon,' came from far to the right and still unseen.

Two faces only, thought Kohler, and this one still fingering the bodice as if to now seduce the lady-in-waiting.

'*Basso Continuo*,' said Spaggiari.

'*Baritono*,' said Galiteau, his chin resting on pale white hands atop a mannequin's wooden neck-knob and wearing wire-rimmed spectacles that made his cherubic face appear rounder, the inquisitive smile even more mischievous.

'*E io sono il Tenore*,' said Guy Rochon, the third and youngest of the three, suddenly appearing.

'Look, let's just find us a place to talk.'

'But we are of this?' hazarded Spaggiari.

'And this is what you must understand,' said Galiteau.

'Slaves to the past, we can never leave it.'

St-Cyr resisted the urge to show the postcard to Christiane Bissert. He let her worry over how he and Hermann had found out about the strawberry blonde, would leave her now.

'Inspector . . . ?' she blurted as he reached the door to her bedroom. 'Don't you want to know the girl's name?'

The white, laced bodice of the cote-hardie rose a little as she took a deep breath and held it.

'Very well,' he said. 'If you must.'

She cringed at the put-down. 'Adrienne de Langlade. Like

Genèvieve, her family lived in the north but not in Beauvais, in Paris. They still do, I guess. She and Madame Simondi used to talk about the city for hours. Fouquet's, Maxim's, the rue Royale . . .'

'Hédiard's?' he asked.

The delicatessen. 'Yes.'

A wary answer . . .

The Inspector stepped out into the corridor and softly closed the door behind him, suddenly leaving her alone and feeling abandoned. Long after he had gone she stood uncertainly before the windows. Fog clouded the bevelled diamond glass whose leading was so old it made her think of the Catacombs and of Adrienne's descriptions of them as given to the devouring ears of Madame Simondi who yearned constantly for news of Paris, her Paris . . . Hédiard's, ah damn.

'They know about Adrienne,' she said when Genèvieve came into the room to stand behind her. 'They'll soon find out everything.'

'Not if we're careful.'

'She shouldn't have had to drown.'

'It was the only way.'

'It was cold. It was foggy. The river was swollen. There'd been heavy rains in the Cévennes. The Ardèche had become a raging torrent. Everyone had been warned. A flood . . .'

'*Calme-toi, chérie. Calme-toi.* Here, let me help you out of those things.'

'He saw the books, Genèvieve. He knows I took some of them to Madame Emphoux. That bitch told him about César's wife.'

Arms encircled her waist and drew her tightly. Lips brushed a cheek, then embraced it firmly, the two of them looking down into the courtyard, brocade upon brocade, velvet upon velvet. '*Courage*,' whispered Genèvieve. '*Courage.* You know we have to put up with a lot, the two of us. You know how much we mean to each other and exactly how much we might lose.'

'Everything,' managed Christiane. 'Just everything.'

When Brother Matthieu, in grey sackcloth with hood up and wearing black trousers and boots, hurried across the courtyard through the wind, they knew exactly what he was after. Xavier had missed an audition before the bishop.

'In the Cathedral,' said Genèvieve, her arms still encircling Christiane's waist.

'The Requiem for Mireille.'

'His voice is changing to that of a cicada and the matter can no longer be hidden. Even God has refused to intervene.'

'The tonsils could be removed,' quipped Christiane, feeling a little better, a little more secure.

'The testicles, I think, but Monsieur le Maréchal would never allow such a thing.'

Not with over 500,000 dead so far in this war, 1,500,000 locked up in POW camps in the Reich and still others away with the British or in Africa. So many had died in the Great War of 1914–18, the birthrate had remained disastrously low, and as a result, Maréchal Pétain and his government in Vichy preached the code of the family, rewarding fruitful mothers, frowning on birth control and denying abortion on pain of imprisonment and even death.

'Today women need servicing, no matter how young the sperm,' offered Genèvieve.

'But will the widow's basket take his head before a harvest has been sown that lasts?' asked Christiane softly.

The guillotine . . .

They looked at one another steadily and each reached out with a forefinger to tenderly silence the lips of the other.

'Xavier!' came the thunderous shout. 'Xavier, you little bastard, don't you dare defy me!'

'Be quiet,' said St-Cyr. 'Sit down, shut up and let the rook crow.'

'*Maudit salaud!*' hissed the boy. 'If that cocksucker lays another hand on me I'll kill him!'

'*Doucement!* To admit to such a desire in front of a detective is foolish.'

The blue eyes narrowed, the sensuous lips compressed. 'Foolish or not, I mean it! I've taken all the crap I'll ever take from him.'

Xavier yanked off the white surplice he had been wearing when

95

found rooting around in the props room. Crumpling it into a ball, he defiantly waited for his mentor to kick the door in.

They heard Brother Matthieu encountering Hermann upstairs, heard Christiane Bissert and Geneviève Ravier laughingly calling out, 'But he left us ages ago, Father.' 'To the Cathedral, I think.'

When the double doors finally opened, it was a subdued but still distrustful brother who entered, searched among the props, and finally confronted them in a far corner. 'Xavier, the bishop is angry. You know how important this funeral is to him. The Kommandant has to see the full strength of the Church, its magnificence, its power.'

'Forgive me, *mon père*. The detective detained me. I . . . I couldn't leave.'

Liar! hissed St-Cyr silently, we had only just met.

A nod passed from brother to boy. Sadness filled the elder's dark grey eyes. The rugged cheeks and chin, with all their scars and grey-black bristles, were gripped in thought, a decision soon made. 'Go now. Apologize as only you know how. Tell His Eminence you'll sing your heart out for him tonight, no matter what happens to your voice, and that you and I have spoken. Beg him to choose whatever time is most convenient.'

The surplice was dutifully untangled by the boy. Clucking his tongue, and automatically sucking at his twisted, wounded lips to stop himself from slobbering – a constant problem so many of the Broken Mugs had to face – the brother tugged the garment down, smoothed it over the boy's shoulders and sadly shook his head. 'How many times must I tell you your future is with God? Xavier, your voice will return as that of a man, and will be perfect in every way. A tenor, I have it in my prayers and God listens, believe me.'

'You should've come earlier,' said the boy softly.

The *gueule cassée*'s head was tossed as if struck. 'I was detained. An errand, idiot! Now don't defy me any more!'

'A moment, Brother,' cautioned the Sûreté. 'A few small questions.'

'Must you?' leapt the priest.

'Unfortunately, yes. You lied to my partner. You told him Xavier had run off home at news of the murder when, really, he

96

had returned to the city well before dawn on the very day she was killed. Was it a week or ten days at the harvest, Xavier?'

Warning glances passed between the two. 'Ten days.'

The boy would offer little; the brother even less. 'You stopped in to see the victim,' said St-Cyr.

'I took her some things.'

Must he always be so insolent? 'Olives, a bottle of oil, a rope of garlic, another of sun-dried tomatoes. She was "special", Xavier, but in what way, please?'

'She made me nice outfits. One always massages the neck of those who make one look good.'

The little bastard, thought St-Cyr.

'Inspector, is this necessary?' asked Brother Matthieu.

'You know it is.'

'Then can't it wait?'

Folding screens, their paint flaked and ancient, crowded closely. Fourteenth-century scenes of gardens, villas, turtledoves and bathing nymphs appeared – trysts under moonlight along the river with lutes and shawms, the Palais in the background or the Pont Saint-Bénézet. Carved fruitwood panels were festooned with carnival masks, banners and ribbons, heraldic shields and crossed horns, a cittern . . .

'We're like *marchands forains*,' spat the boy on noticing how sharply the Sûreté had stepped over to the wooden-tined rakes, flails, scythes, hoes, shovels, butter-churns and cartwheels supposedly from a *mas* of some six hundred years or less ago.

Like travelling stall-keepers . . . 'Your sickle's missing,' said the Sûreté flatly. 'Where is it, please?'

Ah dear *Jésus* . . . 'The sickle?' blurted Brother Matthieu.

'It was stolen in Aix on our last tour,' said Xavier, only to see the Sûreté look away through the maze of props past the andirons of a Renaissance farm kitchen to the shoulder-high candlesticks of a sixteenth-century villa and a mirrored trumeau. Sheaves of wheat and barley, dried lavender, sage, thyme and winter grass met the detective's eye until at last that one said coldly, 'Does your God excuse lying? Must an examining magistrate decide?'

'Inspector . . .'

'Brother, let the boy answer. You may, however, remind him that my partner found him with two nine-millimetre rounds in his pockets. Sufficient, as you and I both well know, for the Kommandant or the District Gestapo to send him into deportation.'

'The killer must've taken our sickle, Inspector,' said Xavier blandly. 'Wasn't it found with the other things in the Latrines Pit?'

The page-boy styled dark brown hair had been smoothed in place by the brother, but the boy had shrugged off the hands and had moved aside.

'Did you tidy up after the killing,' asked the Sûreté, 'or did your mentor?'

'Inspector . . .'

'*Silence*, Brother!'

The boy found his *mégot* tin and, selecting three choice butts, crumbled them into a palm and proceeded to deftly roll himself a forbidden cigarette.

'I "tidied" nothing. Why not ask Salvatore, since he was the one who found her a moment after the killing when he could so easily have found her a moment before?'

'Now listen, you . . .'

'Xavier, tell him.'

A drag was taken and held until exhaled through the nostrils, the boy sizing the two of them up as if they were already old men whose time had passed.

'The rounds were for Dédou Favre who was to have met her in the Palais that night. Dédou had a stolen Luger but no bullets, so Mireille took a couple from the Kommandant's house when he wasn't looking. When I got to her place on the rue du Rempart du Rhône, it was well before dawn and freezing, but Dédou never showed up. Mireille was worried about him coming to the Palais to meet her after her audition as they'd planned. She felt the préfet might somehow have found out about the meeting. She wanted me to give Dédou the rounds and to tell him not to come if he felt it best, but I couldn't find him.'

A member of the *maquis* . . . The 100,000-franc reward for all such betrayals would have had to be forgone, thought St-Cyr, so too praise from the préfet, the bishop and the Kommandant. It just didn't seem possible. The urge to accuse the boy of lying was very strong but it would be best to draw in an impatient breath and leave the matter for now. Brother Matthieu looked as if searching the Sûreté to see if the lie had taken hold.

'You arrived at her flat at about what time?'

'Five-thirty, the new time.'

Berlin Time. 4.30 a.m., the old, and after walking all night from les Baux, lugging a heavy rucksack.

'She was really pleased to get the soap,' hazarded the boy. 'She'd asked for it especially.'

He was grinning now at the thought of her naked, no doubt, but Brother Matthieu looked as if ready to smack his charge's face for being so cheeky. 'How long did you stay with her?' asked St-Cyr.

'Not long. I had to find Dédou, remember? There's a hollow along the ramparts not far from the Porte du Rhône – I'll show it to you if you like. I knew he'd be waiting there because that's where she said he'd be.'

'And when you didn't find him?'

'She was most distressed and said, "I have to go through with it anyway. I must."'

'With what, apart from the audition?'

The Sûreté was like a dog after a scent. Well this one would cock its leg, thought Xavier.

Cigarette ash was insolently flicked aside.

'I've no idea. She had her little secrets. One didn't press.'

I'll bet! scoffed St-Cyr inwardly. 'You took her a grive last autumn, in November.'

One must match tone with tone. 'Nino had brought it to me instead of to His Holiness, so by rights it was mine. One less would not have mattered.'

The memory was savoured, a touch of softness entering until asked who Nino was.

'One of the hounds. A beagle bitch with the name of a male.'

'A friend?' asked the Sûreté softly.

99

'They're all "friends". Each one of the pack is special. They'd only get jealous of one another otherwise. Don't you know *anything* about dogs?'

Nino. 'When was the *grive* taken?'

'In October. The first week, I think. I can't remember.'

'But you kept it for a while?'

'Yes.'

'Then that's all for now. You're free to leave. Get out, the two of you.' But when they had reached the door, he called to them from well within the room and barely in sight. 'A moment. I almost forgot. Who gave her a key to the Palais or left the entrance door open for her since the concierge was attending a film?'

Brother Matthieu swore.

Xavier hesitated and then said calmly, 'César. He didn't want her to be late.'

Christiane Bissert had said Brother Matthieu had given the victim the key. 'And Monsieur Simondi told you this?' asked St-Cyr.

The boy shook his head. 'Mireille did. She wondered if the third judge would be Madame Simondi since Avignon's *petite pomme frite* had told her the Kommandant was certain to refuse.'

Avignon's little French fried potato . . . Frau von Mahler. How cruel of the boy to have called the woman that, a victim of Köln's firestorms. 'And was Madame Simondi that third judge?'

The urge to ask, What do you think?, was there but unwise. 'That little matter was always kept secret, Inspector. How could I possibly know?'

'There was also Monsieur Renaud, Inspector. A notary,' interjected Brother Matthieu. 'An old friend of Monsieur Simondi and of the girl's family. Mademoiselle de Sinéty often went to see him when in search of information or to borrow things.'

'*Enseignes*, jewels and coins?' asked the Sureté and waited for the brother to oblige.

'The rue des Teinturiers, near the fourth waterwheel, or is it the fifth?'

The street of the dye-workers.

The door was closed, the storeroom soon quiet. For a moment St-Cyr argued with himself. Should he have Xavier taken into custody, or could he leave things for the present?

When he found, under folded tapestries in an old trunk, a wine-purple, gold-embroidered ecclesiastical pouch, he sighed.

There were wrist-watches, diamond rings, necklaces, brooches, cufflinks, several pairs of ear-rings, a gold lipstick, gold compact, a cigarette lighter and two cigarette cases, both of which were engraved with the names, no doubt, of the owners of the abandoned villas from which they'd been taken.

Xavier's little hoard had been laid by for a rainy day, and from this, quite obviously, had come the wrist-watch Hermann had found in the victim's handbag. But there was more, much more.

There was a thick twist of reddish blonde hair.

'Herr Kohler, why do you ask about a girl we hardly knew?' Marius Spaggiari, the bass, looked to the others for support.

'Students come and go all the time,' offered Norman Galiteau, the baritone.

'Few succeed, no matter their discipline, be it the violin, piano or voice,' hazarded Guy Rochon.

They'd made damned certain he wouldn't talk to them one at a time. 'Something's come to light. My partner will be expecting me to see if I can't find out a little more.'

'But . . . but what's there to tell? A strawberry blonde . . . ?' blurted Galiteau.

'We get a few of those,' countered Spaggiari.

Fixed up by the students as a lounge, the lower of the tower rooms was furnished with sagging armchairs, chaise longues and sofas from the twenties. The carpet was worn and stained by booze, vomit and food. The flea-market lamp shades were yellowed and unravelling. Above a marble mantelpiece, a gilded Venetian mirror, with streaked and stained backing, was being held by the outstretched arms of sumptuous, avant-garde nudes who licentiously defied the viewer not to look at them while gazing in the mirror.

The room wasn't used for 'their music and . . . and other things in winter', the girl Gina had said and been censored. It had been Galiteau who had led the way, hoping, no doubt, to soon freeze him out, but they'd been getting nowhere until he'd mentioned the girl – not the postcard, never that until needed.

'Her name was Adrienne de Langlade,' said Guy Rochon. The boy was twenty-two years old, very fit, tall, good-looking and with wavy, auburn hair and the finely boned features of the French aristocracy. The eyes were a greeny brown, the brows wide and curved, the smile engaging, open and honest if one wanted to believe this.

I don't, said Kohler to himself. 'How old was she?'

Rochon shrugged. Galiteau answered. 'Twenty . . . the same age as Christiane.'

They were just too wary, and oh *bien sûr* they had a lot to lose if their little group should be broken up – years of forced labour for them. They were ripe for it. 'Let me question this one first, eh? Then I'll get to the two of you.'

They didn't like it. Spaggiari drifted off to the windows. 'Monique is returning,' he announced. 'She's talking to one of our German tenants who's asking her what's in her string bag. "Some carrots, Herr Freisler. A cabbage," ' he fluted. 'Freisler's suspicious of her violin case and wants her to open it, Inspector, but knows she'll refuse unless ordered to. Drugs, alcohol, condoms . . . who knows what students will try to hide? Our Otto is with the Ministry of Trade, an exporter of olive oil, among other things, and a closet pornographer.'

'His wife attends our concerts,' offered Galiteau, whose beatific expression suggested mischief, only to hear Kohler saying, 'I thought I told you two to be quiet?

'Now where were we?' he said, flipping open his little black notebook to look over the pages of answers with nothing in them so far.

'She drowned. An accident, we were told,' offered Rochon.

There was a seven-centimetre scar on the back of his left hand. 'A cut I received last autumn from a broken bottle.'

'Drunk were you?'

'A little. It . . . it was really nothing. An accident.'

'Just like this drowning you were telling me about.'

'Inspector, we've already told you, students come and go,' insisted Spaggiari, not turning from the windows. 'At times we have fifteen or so living here in addition to our group, at present only five others. All girls. The boys . . .'

'Have thought better of hanging around, eh?'

Kohler was referring to the forced labour call-ups. A shrug would be best. 'We're "essential" workers and must remain in France, or hadn't you noticed?'

Very much of the Midi, the *Basso Continuo*'s strongly boned face wore an expression that seemed always to be grave. In his mid-thirties, a professional singer for years and probably exceptional, thought Kohler, one thing was clear. He knew exactly what had happened to this other girl but wasn't about to say a damned thing. A leader, and what was it Louis had muttered on the train south from Paris? 'Everything in a madrigal is built from the bass up.'

The baritone sat on the couch with cushions pulled tightly in on either side of him, for security perhaps – did he need that? He was rotund, cherubic behind those specs of his, very musical no doubt but did he always delight in mischief and in showing up dumb-assed detectives from Bavaria?

Something would have to be done to break the impasse. Never one to sit still for long, Kohler got up and took out his cigarettes but was forced to set his notebook and pencil on the mantelpiece.

Verdammt! Now what was this? he wondered. 'Hey, *mes fins*, it's the little things in life that matter, isn't it?' he quipped, not looking at any of them but rather into the mirror. 'These days the chance happening can so easily change everything. One moment the street is calm and everyone is going about their business, the next you accidentally trip and draw attention to yourself. They rush you. They grab you. "I've done nothing!" you cry. "Nothing!"'

He hesitated. He had their attention now. 'But then those bastards question you for hours, eh? And maybe they beat the shit out of you and make you swear to anything.'

The Gestapo or the Vichy goons, the *Service d'Ordre*, too, and others. The French Gestapo . . . 'Inspector, what have you found?' asked Rochon who was still standing closest to him.

'A photograph. It's slipped down behind the mantelpiece but once must have rested on it.'

Taking out the pocket-knife the Kaiser had given to him and countless others in those early days before the Great War, Kohler began to prise the photo from its depths. Smoke from the hearth had darkened the upper half a little, the photo having turned itself around as it had slipped. But it was still clear, still good enough . . .

The girl was leaning against the stone wall of a windmill or *mas*.

'Inspector . . .' began Spaggiari, only to hear the Kripo caution him with, 'Why not use your head and keep your mouth shut for now?'

She was wearing a one-piece bathing suit and espadrilles. Her hands were behind her back and she was smiling demurely at the camera. Moisture beaded her skin. Her hair was pinned in a tight chignon that was very wet. She had only just come out of the water.

'Was she a good swimmer?' he asked, 'seeing as she "accidentally" drowned?'

They didn't answer. It was so damned dry in summer in the hills, the pond or whatever would have to have been deep enough for bathing. Later, or beforehand, she had bared her breasts and had let someone photograph them, but this one showed every sign of being modest.

'Okay, so we've got her name and now a snapshot of her, and one of you – I don't give a damn which one since you're all in the same bucket of shit as far as I'm concerned – stated clearly that you hardly knew her.'

'She was of the Parisian *beau monde*,' offered the cherub, nervously darting little looks at his confrères. Did he like to feel a girl's hair when looking at a photograph only of her uncovered breasts? wondered Kohler.

'Her family sent her to Avignon to get her away from an affair they didn't want to happen,' said Guy Rochon.

'A mezzo-soprano,' interjected Spaggiari with an exasperated sigh. 'She had passed her final audition and was to have joined our little group. César had written in a part for her halfway between those of Christiane and Genèvieve.'

'Or Xavier. We mustn't forget him,' offered the cherub hesitantly. 'Xavier's voice . . .'

'What Norman means to say, Inspector, is that Xavier and Genèvieve often sing the same part. Their voices are equally pitched, though hers is fuller and far more mature.'

Like wine, eh?, Kohler wanted to snort, but said, 'So why was this photo up here if you hardly knew the girl?'

'A Requiem of our own,' said the cherub softly, the mischief all too clear.

'A drunken orgy, was that it, eh?'

Again Spaggiari sighed heavily. 'Her drowning has nothing to do with what happened to Mireille, Inspector.'

'And she was a good swimmer?'

'We swam in a cistern, Inspector. A cave, but our feet could touch bottom if desired.'

'So, when and where was this taken?'

He'd have to be told. There was no way of avoiding it – Kohler would stick to the matter until satisfied. 'Early last June, at the *mas* Madame de Sinéty leases from César. The windmill is no longer in use. It's on a hill behind what remains of a small retreat that was once used by the monks at Saint-Michel-de-Frigolet. The cistern is a little farther into the hills, but is easy to find.'

A ready source of water in a normally parched and thirsty land. 'And Simondi owns the place?'

'As he owns many places. After all, there are lots of bargains these days and even six hundred hectares of good farmland in several choice parcels will bring only 30,000 francs if one is lucky.'

'Could she swim?'

'Why not?'

They sat in the car, letting the engine warm while knowing they were being watched through more than one of the Villa Marenzio's windows.

'Spaggiari made a point of telling me his boss could buy farmland for a song, Louis. Hell, everyone knows the farmers can't get their produce to market and the Occupier steals it anyway, so the price of land has plummeted. And sure, what few tractors they had before the war have long since been taken and the Russian Campaign has left so few horses, pulling a plough is now damned hard on the wife's shoulders, but did our *Basso Continuo* tell me that about Simondi to take the heat off himself and the others?'

'The *accabussade* . . .' muttered St-Cyr. 'For Thérèse Godard the threat of being locked into one was real enough.'

'And drowned?'

'Perhaps.'

'Spaggiari indicated Adrienne de Langlade could swim.'

'Whereas Christiane Bissert stated positively that the girl couldn't.'

Kohler waited. After nearly two and a half years of working together, he knew Louis hadn't finished.

'A sickle is missing from among the stage props. Xavier tried to lie about it and in the process convinced me he had done the tidying up.'

Again Kohler waited.

'The boy hides a thick twist of Adrienne de Langlade's hair, Hermann. Dried twigs, waterweeds, sand grains and fragments of snail shells were caught in it, so the hair was taken *after* she had drowned. I took only sufficient for Peretti to match with the curl on our postcard, but visually there is absolutely no doubt in my mind.'

'Did the boy kill her?'

'Or find her body under the water?'

'What now, then, Chief?'

'The Préfecture and a file others may hope remains closed.'

Police photographers, lacking in sensitivity, welcomed the thought of lesser beings vomiting on seeing their photos; detectives especially.

Hermann was using a waste-paper basket as a receptacle. Once, twice . . . *ah mon Dieu*, couldn't someone give him a brandy?

Buried up to the waist in the bottom muds, the girl had obviously been in the water a good two or three weeks before the floods of last November 11 to 18 had dislodged her corpse. Swept along, tumbled, dragged, her skin pierced by sticks, rusty bits of metal, broken glass, pebbles and sand, she'd been jammed among the debris – caught against an abutment of the Pont Saint-Bénézet.

Her seat was up, her legs spread at odd angles among the timbers, the rest of her half hidden. A frayed bit of rope was still tied around her right ankle but the boulder that had anchored her to the bottom was now missing.

'Hermann . . . Hermann, wait in the car. Go on, please.'

There was no answer, not even the lifting of a feeble hand. 'He absolutely has to be allowed a damned good rest,' swore St-Cyr to the clerk. 'Go with him. Be gentle or I'll deal with you. I'm worried about him.'

'You can't take any of that file away.'

'I won't. The memory will be sufficient, eh? Now beat it. And *don't* let de Passe know we're here.'

No one had expected them to look for this file. No one.

She'd been a pretty girl with a figure she'd have been proud of, but after such a time under water, her hair had slipped completely away. Like gloves, the skin of her hands had been peeled off to cling at the last by the nails.

Fish, worms, eels, parasites, all manner of underwater creatures had been at the torso and head whereas the rest of her, buried beneath the mud, had been somewhat protected. The face, un-recognizable to any, would have been livid to flaccid grey and blotched by bluish green. Even in black-and-white photos there were sufficient differences of shading to indicate this. Tatters of flesh had all but been parted from the bones. The lips and nose were gone, the ears, the eyes, the eyelids also.

He bowed his head and said grimly, 'Where? Where were you drowned and when, exactly, you poor thing?'

There was no mention of any of this in the file. Others would have drowned in the flooding. Animals . . . Overtaxed, the rescue crews would have had her taken to a temporary morgue.

'Unidentified Caucasian female,' had been crossed out later and her name entered above it.

There was no mention of who had identified her. Peretti had not examined the corpse. No coroner had. 'And yes,' said St-Cyr coldly to himself and the photos, 'Xavier must have found you along the bank a good two or three weeks before the flooding. Your hair was still intact. You'd been in the water but a short time. Did he then tie the boulder to your feet and remain silent, or was it already there and yet he'd known exactly where to find you?'

Back in the car, himself behind the wheel and Hermann looking like death, he went through the order book Mireille de Sinéty had kept privately.

' "Sunday, 25 October, 1942", Hermann. She has used a glyph to represent the name – an alchemist's symbol, an *m* against and with whose tail there is an *l*, but I'm sure it must mean the girl. "Adrienne has missed her final fitting. I can't understand this because she knows how terribly important it is and that only I can help her hide what has happened to her.

' "Tuesday, 27 October". There's another glyph that looks like two Grecian columns with a flat roof and floor. Yes, it must be one of the singers. This person "says Adrienne went home to Paris to tell her parents the good news about joining the group." *Merde*, there's yet another glyph! This one has asked – ah! it's Madame Simondi – "Adrienne to go to Hédiard's with a request she has written out.

' "Friday, 30 October. Adrienne has still not returned and we are to leave tomorrow. Nice, Cannes and then Fréjus. Will she catch up with us, I ask but am afraid for her. Something isn't right. There has been no word from her. César . . ." *Grâce à Dieu,* she gave us a name! "César is very angry and swears she is finished and that he will have nothing more to do with her for leaving him in the lurch like this.

' "I am to take her costumes along just in case he can bring himself to forgive her." '

'Louis, for Christ's sake don't tell anyone we may have another murder on our hands. Not yet. Giselle and Oona need me. You know they won't be able to make it through this lousy war without me.'

'The Kommandant, Hermann. We have no other choice but to go to him.'

'But he's not here! He's out in the hills. He's probably hunting down our *petite lingère*'s boyfriend.'

The Kommandant was one of Simondi's and the bishop's hunting partners, but was he also a business associate? wondered St-Cyr. He had been evasive when interviewed and had refused to let them question his wife . . . 'Mireille de Sinéty must have known about the death of this one, Hermann, and was about to confront her judges with the truth. She went to her audition hoping Dédou Favre would be there to back her up.'

'Favre wasn't waiting on the ramparts.'

'But Xavier lies, as do all the others.'

'Then was Dédou there, Louis, and did our altar boy of the cracked voice and the thieving hands tell her differently?'

'She took a tin of sardines with her just in case he should come . . .'

'Had prepared herself for every eventuality.'

'Was found by a dog, Hermann . . .'

'A dog named Nino, with a penchant for wandering and collecting last year's birds' nests.'

'There was a *clochette* . . .'

'The *clochette* of one of the bishop's hounds, Louis . . .'

'A bell that rings . . .'

'When a *grive* has been shot, a young girl drowned, or a throat opened with a sickle.'

They sat a moment in silence. Then Kohler said, 'I didn't know you could part sing.'

'Nor I you, but you're better.'

Louis deserved to have the last word, but it had to be said, 'Let's go to the dogs, eh?, and see what they have to tell us.'

5

The study was huge and hugely cluttered, and it showed at once a side to Bishop Henry-Baptiste Rivaille that was totally unexpected. It was not a room in which to officially greet people. It was very private and tucked away in a far corner of the Cloister of the Pilgrims' Well, *le Cloitre du puit des pèlerins*, which dated from the fourteenth century and was on the rue Sainte-Catherine within a few minutes' walk of the Palais.

'You find me at home, Inspectors, and busy at my researches,' he said, taken aback at the intrusion but valiantly trying to hide the discomfort. 'What can I do for you? A glass of anisette, some coffee . . . ? It's not often detectives from Paris visit the Bishop of Avignon and the Vaucluse unannounced.'

The cook, who had, under the threat of Sûreté duress, escorted them from a side entrance, and who had been with the house for centuries, was going to get a tongue-lashing later. 'The anisette, *merci*,' said St-Cyr.

Ah not that *Quatsch* again, swore Kohler silently as he grimaced at the thought of liquorice's cloying taste. 'Some coffee?' he asked and swallowed.

'Both, then. I'm honoured. Please . . . please find a seat. Move things . . . ah!, be sure to put them back exactly in the same order. One grows old. One tends to forget in the heat of one's thoughts.'

Rivaille turned to the cook. 'Bénédictine, *ma chère*, our visitors look hungry. A little of the bread and *chèvre*, some of the *prosciutto affumicato* César so kindly brought us – he smokes it himself, Inspectors, with juniper and fir from the hills. It's perfect.

A dish of the olives, Bénédictine – they must try them, of course. All who seek succour at the hand of God must be given sustenance.'

And warned, was that it, eh? wondered Kohler, realizing that word of their not having eaten must have reached here some time ago. No longer used as a cloister, the villa's seemingly endless corridors, salons and staircases had been hung with Old Masters, tapestries, crossed swords, heraldic shields and armour. There'd been bronzes, too, and marble statues, and a wealth of carpets and furnishings. But here there was none of that. Here there was at heart a simple man but one who was dedicated absolutely to an ideal, a dream.

'The return of the Papacy to our fair city,' breathed Rivaille, hesitantly watching them, for he must have sensed they would peel back the ancient manuscripts, thought Kohler, searching through their blotting paper flags if necessary until they damned well had what they wanted.

'Please, I'm a consummate student and collector of our past. The bas-reliefs on the walls are pieces from the days of the Romans. Naked Gauls being taken to the coliseum to be torn to shreds – one can still hear their cries, can't one? Maidens being debauched in the streets and then slaughtered mercilessly, their tresses caught in bestial hands, Christ unknown to them, poor innocents; God but in waiting.'

There were bits and pieces from more recent centuries, Renaissance floor tiles, plans of the Palais with each of its periods of construction, terracotta pottery, and hundreds of books and manuscripts, many in Latin. These last were arranged around the simple table-cum-desk in phalanxes with their spines facing upwards so that flags could extend from both the top and bottom of each book.

'I learned to read while still a shepherd,' he said. 'Everything you see here I owe to the Church, especially the freedom to pursue independent lines of thought. The carpentry is, of course, my own and deliberately functional.'

Among flanking stacks of papers was the discourse Rivaille had been working on when interrupted. Dark, horn-rimmed glasses lay on top of pages where an irritated pen had released droplets of ink as it had been set down.

'Bishop, a few . . ' began the Sûreté only to hear Rivaille mildly chide, 'Paris has informed me of this habit of yours. "A few small questions, nothing difficult." Ah *bon*, let us get down to it. Sister Agnès removed a ring and this has understandably provoked you. A ruby, the stone blood-red and perfect.'

They waited. Chairs not being available, they sat, like he did, on the same side of the 'desk', on the small and simple benches of another age.

Rivaille unlocked a drawer. 'This ring . . . These days one can't tell who to trust and so trusts no one, am I not correct?'

The song of their times . . . well, one of them, thought Kohler wryly. Louis took the ring. Light from the desk lamp made the stone appear as if warm. A good four carats.

'Open it,' said Rivaille, his voice hushed by reverence.

'You do it, then,' said St-Cyr.

'There's a secret compartment in the bezel,' confided the bishop. 'Such things were very common in the Early Renaissance but this . . .' The detectives would wonder now about his tone of voice and no doubt would think it motivated by thoughts other than holy when they realized what the compartment held, but God would judge. Only God.

He slid the compartment open and handed the ring back. For a moment the Sûreté was speechless. 'It's . . . it's a coiled human hair. Bishop, what is the meaning of this, please?'

Ah Christ, thought Kohler.

Rivaille's unrelenting gaze fell on each of them. 'That,' he said, 'is from the head of the Virgin herself. Down through the ages the great masters have invariably depicted her hair as being auburn or very fair, but among them some such as Pontormo accurately revealed it to be a distinctly reddish strawberry blonde.'

Adrienne de Langlade, swore Kohler silently.

'A thorn from Christ's crown,' interjected Louis, meeting the believer's gaze with suitable awe. 'Had I not seen these relics, Bishop, I might never have known they existed.'

Liar! thought Kohler. You don't believe it any more than I do!

'Irreplaceable,' breathed Rivaille. 'So you see why I absolutely had to have it returned and yet . . . and yet maintain that element of secrecy all such priceless relics demand.'

'And the pendant box?' asked Louis warily.

'Coroner Peretti is, unfortunately, far too stubborn. He could never have guaranteed the safety of the thorn and when presented with Maître de Passe's ultimatum, quickly found he had no other choice but to return it.'

'What ultimatum?' croaked the Sûreté.

It would be best to give the two of them a magnanimous shrug. 'These things, they are understood without their being said.'

A little trip then, in a railway cattle truck to an unspecified destination in the east, or simply a case of what the Gestapo and the SS were fond of calling *Herzlähmung*. Cardiac arrest.

They went on to other matters. There was a small round stool between them, and on this, a game of *jacquet* whose marquetry gleamed. This board was removed and the tray of food set down. Somehow the coffee and cakes, the thick sandwiches of crusty bread and a small pewter pitcher of anisette, with matching cups, could never taste as well as had they been served before the threat that had just been made.

'To the Babylonian Captivity, Inspectors, and to its return in this new and even brighter Renaissance,' said Rivaille, lifting his cup. 'These,' he indicated the pewter, 'are all that remain in Avignon of the personal effects of his Holiness Clément the Sixth. Each time I drink from one, I tremble at the thought of what must once have been and must return.'

Yet another warning they understood only too clearly, so *bon*, that was as it should be, thought Rivaille. He gave them a moment to satisfy hunger. The olives they would recognize as similar to those they had found in the girl's rooms, the *chèvre aussi*. Each would realize they were eating like kings in these troubled times, and perhaps there were twinges of guilt, but both would make no mention of this, nor of the black-market origins of the bread, the ham and coffee. Neither of these two men could ever be bought and that, he told himself, could well be their downfall.

But one must always reveal enough to satiate curiosity and dull inquisitiveness, thus keeping hidden that which must never be exposed.

'Brother Matthieu apologizes for misleading you about Xavier, Inspector,' he said to Kohler. 'The boy, as I'm sure you have discovered, didn't run away but had returned to us on Monday at dawn.'

Did Rivaille know everything they'd discovered, wondered Kohler, uncomfortable at the thought of their being constantly watched.

'You found a reed warbler's nest in an alcove of the Grand Tinel, Inspector. Please don't look so dismayed at my knowing. Salvatore is a most dutiful and loyal servant.'

'The *clochette* . . .' blurted Kohler.

'I have Xavier's absolute loyalty too, and that of Brother Matthieu. My Nino is such a trouble. Always she runs off by herself – it's in a beagle's nature to stray, is that not so?, but she's such a wanderer. Repeatedly I tell myself I must put her down, but . . . ah!, we're all mortal. She and Xavier are inseparable. When he first came to me at the age of five, I gave him to her as a puppy and let him name her. The boy hadn't even realized her sex. Another of our little secrets.'

He had, you *dummkopf,* thought Kohler, and you've just contradicted yourself by saying you have their loyalty in an age when none can be trusted. But I'm an idiot, aren't I? You've led me right to the trough and now I have to eat the swill by saying it. 'Might I see the dogs, Bishop?'

Isn't that why you've come? challenged Rivaille silently. 'But of course. That door will lead you to them. Keep always to the left until you reach the bell, then pull its chain.'

The stone staircase was steep and of another time. The air was dank and held the smell of long-cut hay, of sage, sawn lumber, fermenting wine, horse piss, old harness and dogs. There was dust . . . the ever-present dust of a stables, and this filtered through the winter's light from an iron-grilled window.

Kohler couldn't help but think of the frightened little boy who would have had to climb these stairs in those first few weeks of his new life. The iron grille would have brought a meagre moment of relief but could the kid have even reached it on tiptoes to stare out into a courtyard no peasant could ever understand but only marvel at? The night sky too.

Then Xavier would have had to continue timidly on up the stairs to knock, wait and enter into what? Benevolence or rape? And never mind fingering the hair of some young girl while staring at a photograph of her breasts and dreaming of the Virgin Mary!

Rivaille didn't look the type to bugger about with little boys, but then, priest or layman, they seldom did.

The cloister must at one time have housed a hundred or so. Now most of the storerooms were empty. Barrels of Côtes du Rhône were patiently waiting to be bottled, aged, kept, and the years of the bishop's cellar went back. A fortune.

Rivaille had trusted Xavier. He must have for there was no lock on the wine cellar. Brother Matthieu, too, had been trusted.

Long before he reached the dogs, they barked, but the musical tinkle of their *clochettes* was silent, for they would only wear these when on the hunt.

A corridor off to the right led to the street. Easy access, then, and no one the wiser if you slept with the dogs. Trust again. Unwavering loyalty.

The boy didn't appear, and there was no sign of the beagle, only of harriers whose kennels and run were clean and laid with freshly cut dried reeds, not winter grass or lavender or any of those things.

'Bishop . . .'

It was now or never, thought Rivaille, and one must gradually raise the voice to shouting and give the Sûreté the look of one who is about to crush a scorpion. 'No, you listen, *mon cher détective*. I know everything about you.'

'Divide and conquer, is that how it's to be, Bishop? Hermann to look in on the dogs, myself to face the music of the Church? That black woollen cassock you wear may be of the hills and centuries, and doubtless it is warm, but frankly what you say is out of place.'

'*Bâtard*, do you think you can trifle with me? You, a cuckold? A man whose second wife fornicated repeatedly with a German officer and moved in with him? In, *mon fin*. Taking your little son with her.'

Ah *merde*, he was serious. 'The couple were secretly filmed by Gestapo Paris-Central, Bishop, but only last week my partner saw to the destruction of those films. Now she rests in peace and that is how it is to be.'

'She was naked! They copulated! The films were seen by many! She begged for more, St-Cyr. More! In . . . in with the thrusting. The child was witness to it!'

Nom de Jésus-Christ! How had he come by this? A courier from Paris? Oberg, Head of the SS in France . . . Gestapo Boemelburg, Hermann's boss, or simply through Alain de Passe? And certainly too many knew of it but . . .

Rivaille was watching him closely, the hatchet of condemnation fierce. 'Bishop, let us calm down and set the matter straight. First, Philippe was in a nursemaid's care at all times and had found in the Hauptmann Steiner the friend I couldn't be due to the constant and lengthy absences both common crime and the Occupier demand. Second, as a Breton living in Paris, Marianne was terribly lonely, the depths of which, I readily confess, I didn't realize until it was too late. Third, she knew I would forgive her and that I loved her far too deeply not to have understood. When Steiner was sent to Russia—'

'By his uncle, the Kommandant von Gross Paris!'

'Who is a prude and a stickler for the morals of his family and its honour, Bishop, which, incidentally, was why the Gestapo's Watchers took interest in the couple. Their interest had really very little to do with our battles with crime, but stemmed from their constant need to get the better of the Wehrmacht's High Command.'

'Steiner was killed in action.'

'My wife was coming home—'

'Home, yes, and to a Resistance bomb that, though you are no collaborator and loud about it, was meant for you. Oh *bien sûr*, it was a mistake, but—'

'A tripwire. I—'

'Get down on your knees, my son. Beg God's forgiveness before it is too late.'

'You hypocrite! I won't! I can't! Gestapo Paris-Central, though they knew of that wire, had deliberately left it in place for me, Bishop. For me!'

'And?' asked Rivaille softly.

'I . . . I hadn't been able to warn her. I was too late in returning to Paris, damn you.'

There were tears. Overwhelmed by what he had failed to do a good two and a half months ago, St-Cyr was trembling and couldn't hide his outrage at being so savagely driven into a corner. Both he and his partner were still reviled by many in Gestapo Paris-Central, and this one was still hated by some of the Resistance whose internal communications were, at best, paltry. 'Ah *bon*, we understand each other perfectly. You and Kohler had defied the SS. Someone had to pay.'

And was that the crux of it? For pointing the finger of truth at them, the SS had used a rawhide whip on Hermann and had left a bomb in place.

'That partner of yours lives in sin with two women, one of whom is a Dutch alien without proper papers.'

Hermann should have been here. 'Bishop, the threat is understood. Oona Van der Lynn, the woman of whom you speak, lost her two children during the blitzkrieg to Messerschmitts that were clearing the roads of refugees. Her husband was then taken in Paris two months ago by the French Gestapo of the rue Lauriston and murdered.'

'A Jew . . . She was married to a Jew she had kept hidden.'

Hermann had taken her in for her own safety. 'You don't fool around, do you, Bishop?'

'I can't afford to. There's far too much at stake.'

Crumbs had fallen on the Sûreté's waistcoat, he looking old and defeated, but had the message finally registered? Would he now be very careful not to touch the Church?

'Bishop, why not state what you have in mind?'

Rivaille helped himself to more of the anisette. Without asking, he refilled the Sûreté's cup. 'This girl, this murder in our Palais . . . oh *bien sûr* it's a tragedy, a terrible loss and one I could ill afford. She was to be my assistant here, in addition to her other duties – trusted implicitly – but we can't let her death cloud negotiations with the Holy See and the Reich. Go carefully. Steal eggs if you must but do not awaken the hens.'

Or the rooster. Had Hermann been here, he would have had the son of a bitch up against the wall or down on his knees with a Walther P38 jammed against the back of that tonsured head. But Hermann was of the Occupier, and when in Avignon, all others had best do as the Avignonnais.

'Begin, then, by telling me where and with whom you were on Monday evening between six p.m. and curfew.'

'I could refuse.'

'You won't. Not if you want to keep the hens quiet. I would simply go to the District Magistrate for an order making you comply, and though he's no doubt a good friend of yours, it still would be difficult for him to say no.'

'I could then ask the Kommandant to rescind it.'

'A request, I'm certain, he would ignore, given that he and his wife much admired the victim.'

Having been suitably prepared, St-Cyr would now begin to scrape the mould from the bread, but would he eat from the loaf? wondered Rivaille. Would he accept what he would be allowed to discover? And what of Kohler? Had that one stepped in the shit he was supposed to find?

The photograph, one of several Kohler had found in Xavier's trunk, was of Adrienne de Langlade and there was no mistaking that the girl had been at least four months pregnant at the time. Her breasts were beginning to swell, her bellybutton to protrude. The pulled-up white cotton underpants emphasized her state. A pleasing young girl with good, square shoulders, good legs, her head cocked to one side, the shoulder-length hair thick and worn with an almost eyebrow-length fringe, looking at herself in an unseen mirror with a quizzical expression.

The right hand grasped the leg of the tripod which came between her slightly parted legs and on which was mounted a bellows camera whose black headdress, like that of a nun, was thrown back to keep the film from the light, framing the lens and box.

She had taken the photo herself in front of what must have been a full-length mirror, the snapshot revealing all but her ankles and feet. Her left hand rested on her tummy, as if she was asking, How could this be?

All of the other photographs had been taken near the *mas* of Mireille de Sinéty's mother in early June of last year. He was certain of it, certain, too, that the girl definitely hadn't looked pregnant in any of them. There'd been no shots of the *petite lingère* and he had the thought that she hadn't been invited along for the picnic and the swim.

Naked, Adrienne de Langlade lay fast asleep on a bed of lavender that had been freshly cut in swaths which had fallen all around and under her. Time and again she'd been photographed that way. Bits of lavender clung to her hair. Her skin was very fair and, with the strong sunlight, fairer still. The left leg was crooked. Her arms were extended languidly above her head which was turned on its side away from the sun as if by instinct.

The mouth was slack, the hair caught the light and, even in the photos, he could see that it would have had a coppery sheen.

That of her underarms and pubes was darker. A pretty girl Xavier might well have lingered over, ogling the photos night after night in secret. But that couldn't have been, he told himself, and wished Louis was with him. Louis had an eye for things detectives weren't supposed to see.

The prints had been cared for. Yet he'd found them loose between a rumpled old sweater and a pair of sweat-stained trousers.

Twelve-by-fifteen-centimetre prints, a dozen of them, including the most recent.

They had rolled her over and had photographed her backside,

and likely she'd got more than a sunburn out of it, for there were the shadows of at least two of those who had stood over her. An initiation into the singers, had that been it, eh? Spaggiari, Galiteau and Rochon, with Genèvieve Ravier and Christiane Bissert as witnesses?

Had the girl been dead drunk or drugged? Had the singers, or one among them, then given the photos to the bishop? They must have, but why would they have done so?

To torment him? To show him what the girl was really like – was that it, eh?

And why had Rivaille then put them here for this *Schweinebulle* to find? To take the heat off himself and throw suspicion on to the boy and the rest of the singers?

Xavier didn't have much. His rucksack was years old. Kohler took it down and emptied it out. Wire snares, a much used slingshot, fishing lines, lead weights and hooks, dried apricots, garlic too . . .

The empty medicine bottle the boy had drained of its grappa, 'for the toothache, Inspector'.

When he found beneath the *paillasse*, and under the floor-boards, the boy's private little hidey-hole, Kohler discovered what he felt could not have been left by the bishop for him to find.

'A hundred thousand francs,' he said, sadly looking at four bundles of used banknotes, in five-hundreds, one-hundreds and fifties. 'Xavier is trouble,' Salvatore Biron had said.

Had the choirboy with the broken voice sold Mireille de Sinéty's boyfriend to the préfet?

'He must have, and so much for Dédou not having been waiting on the ramparts last Monday before dawn.'

What had it been that Xavier had claimed she had said on hearing Dédou hadn't come as promised? 'I have to go through with it anyway. I must.' But of course the little bastard could well have been lying about that too.

Instinct said otherwise.

The Parabellum rounds had been for the Luger Dédou was supposed to have had. Thérèse Godard had been sent to the *mas* on Monday with a letter, but hadn't been able to give it to Dédou and had left it in the mill.

The couple had used that letter box before, but had Xavier learned of it? The *petite lingère* had been 'special' to him. 'The costumes,' he had said.

The 100,000 franc reward.

Xavier hadn't slept with the dogs. He had slept with his pal Nino up here. There were dog hairs in plenty, and Kohler took several for Ovid Peretti to compare with the one that had been caught in the girl's fingernail.

Some of Nino's treasures lay in a far corner. Pig bones, beef bones, duck eggs now in the half-shell and in bits and pieces, a bit of driftwood, a strap of leather . . . Rubbish all of it.

Crammed into the toe of a tennis shoe was one of the high heels from a pair of dress shoes. Jade green to go with the strawberry blonde hair and sea-green, smashing eyes, no doubt. Prewar and Italian-made by the look but purchased in Paris, for that's where Adrienne de Langlade had come from. Very classy, very expensive and overlooked by the bishop. Ah yes!

Again he turned to the photos and only then noticed what Louis would have seen straightaway, that in three of them the girl's nipples had been stiffened. 'Wetted with alcohol?' he wondered, she so out of it otherwise. 'Absinthe?' he asked. Drinking it had excited the central nervous system – in the addict, it had often caused fits of delirium, violent fist-fights and generally highly antisocial behaviour; in others, a blissful contentment, a numbness, a passivity.

If drunk on it, she wouldn't have felt a thing or remembered much. And as sure as he was standing here, someone had taken close-ups of her breasts and had cut off a few curls of her hair. Enough for how many postcards? he wondered, and decided Louis and he had better find out. But Louis was still busy.

Drawing on his pipe, St-Cyr took out the little black notebook that had always served him well, both for the apprehension it induced in a suspect – and Rivaille was most certainly that! – and for the record that would be made.

'Bishop, pardon a simple detective, but could you state absolutely for me that there was an audition on Monday evening, 25 January 1943?'

So it was to be like this after all, the pedantic, cleat-booted mind of the Paris *flic* St-Cyr had once been. 'Even such as yourself can rise up through the ranks to attend the Police Academy and earn laurels as a *pugiliste.*'

A *boxeur* who had won acceptance not just for the fists. 'Bishop, please answer the question.'

'Then, yes, at ten o'clock that evening.'

'Wasn't that a . . .'

'A little late? It was the earliest that could be arranged.'

'You dined out, I gather?'

'With the Kommandant and Maître Simondi.'

Offer nothing more than asked – was that it, eh? 'You had details to discuss about an upcoming concert and a tour the singers were to make.'

'Schedules, *laissez-passers, sauf-conduits* only the Kommandant could issue. The singers don't just entertain our citizens, Inspector. We have to think of our friends as well.'

The Occupier. The troops, their officers, and yet another warning . . . 'Was Frau von Mahler present?'

'During the meal or before it?'

'Both, and just afterwards. Let's get things straight so as to save time.'

'Then, yes. For this occasion only. It . . . ah, *mais certainement* it wasn't that dear lady's custom to dine with others than her immediate family, or to show her face in public. The burns, the terrible scars most of which are not those of the skin but of the . . .'

Rivaille hauled himself to a stop.

'But of *what*, Bishop?'

'Must you write down everything I say?'

'Forgive me. It's a habit from the old days. It's in a shorthand few but myself could ever read. My partner constantly complains. Please don't concern yourself a moment longer.'

Touché, was that it, eh? Ah! It would be best to give the Sûreté an impatient sigh and admit defeat so that the *coup de filet*, the knife stroke, could come later when most unexpected. 'Frau von Mahler is still extremely terrified of fire – in the mind, you understand. She had nothing but praise for Mireille and was deeply concerned that the girl should at last succeed and be allowed to join the singers. Therefore that good lady set aside her own difficulties to put forth Mademoiselle de Sinéty's case.'

'And the third judge?'

'Both César and I wanted the Kommandant to join us – it would've swung things the girl's way, but von Mahler is a man of principle and claimed rightly that he wasn't musically qualified.'

The Sûreté sucked on that pipe of his, seemingly to pass the hours in contemplation, thought Rivaille, a habit Paris had emphasized since it could also be used by the questioned to plan ahead.

'The audition, Bishop. Could it not have been cancelled?'

Maudit! He was a nuisance. 'The girl was fully prepared. Everything that she wore, apart from her clothing, had been patiently assembled from a variety of sources. Each piece was authentic and most were of considerable value. To turn the clock back, to deny her the weeks of preparation, would not have been right.'

One should choose an olive now, thought St-Cyr, to savour its taste as well as that of the Dutch pipe tobacco Hermann had been good enough to find in Paris. 'The identity, then, of the third judge.'

'Albert Renaud, the *notaire public*.'

'The rue des Teinturiers . . .'

Good for Matthieu. 'Yes.'

'An old friend of her family. One of Simondi's and yourself also, I gather.'

And a fellow *Pénitent Noir*, was that what this one was thinking? 'A friend, yes.' And a believer, then, in the dream of returning the Papacy to Avignon – he could see St-Cyr thinking this.

'Was it usual for the singers to wear scissors, bells,

enseignes . . . irreplaceable rings with a hair from the head of the Virgin?'

'*Maudit salaud!* How dare you doubt me? No! Such things would only detract from the music and cause jealousy amongst the singers, and since we do not have sufficient nor could we risk their loss or damage.'

'*Bon.* Then tell me, please, why Mireille de Sinéty insisted on wearing them to this audition?'

Had she not worn them before? was in the Sûreté's expression and the bastard gave a satisfied nod to indicate as much. 'Mireille . . . to understand her is to understand a commitment second only to that of her belief in God and the Church. The girl had tried everything, Inspector. It was her tenth audition – the eleventh perhaps. I can't remember but will have it written down. She thought that this time, if she appeared exactly as one from the past, we, her judges, would have no other option but to admit her.'

'Then the audition was unique in this regard?'

'Yes.'

'And did you admit her?'

'No.'

'A brief answer, Bishop, for one who had prepared so diligently and had then been murdered. Did she take that to her death?'

'I had nothing to do with her killing.'

'I didn't say you had.'

But it's interesting I should state that I hadn't, eh? thought Rivaille. Well, listen then! 'The girl was too nervous. Her voice quavered. One can't have that, can one? It's the supreme test. To sing alone in the Grand Tinel or in the Cathedral itself, with only God to guide the voice and strengthen the heart, is not easy. All of us are aware of this. But the test quickly separates those who can overcome their fears and distrust from those who can't. She also, on hearing the result, abruptly turned her back on us and left the hall which was, I must say, unforgivable of her.'

' "Distrust", Bishop? Please explain this.'

'Ah! It was nothing. A matter from the past. The Avignon of those days wasn't the Avignon of today. Young girls . . . the one she was named after. Recently married, loved dearly – treasured, but desired by another . . .'

'Ordered to do what, Bishop?'

'Summoned to the Papal Court to take up but a temporary residence. An honour . . . a great honour.'

'Under duress.'

'It was a foolishness our Mireille wouldn't leave alone. Repeatedly I counselled compassion. The differences in our ways then, the forgiveness that is necessary if one is ever to come to grips with the past.'

Six hundred years ago . . . 'The girl's husband and the de Sinéty family tried to get her back, didn't they?'

'And fell into disgrace, their lives in ruins, their properties confiscated even as she threw herself from the battlements of the Bell Tower.'

'Was she murdered, Bishop?'

'Why do you ask?'

'Because I must.'

'Then understand that nothing I could say or find in the manuscripts, court documents and letters of the time would satisfy our Mireille but the truth is, this girl from the past of her family simply jumped out of despair.'

A typical Provençal tale from the age of the troubadours, Hermann would have said, and snorted at the folly of such a waste. 'Why couldn't Mademoiselle de Sinéty be convinced, Bishop?'

Was there something else, then, something far more recent and equally sinister? Ah *bon*! St-Cyr and his partner hadn't believed for a moment that Adrienne de Langlade had accidentally drowned. An *accabussade* . . . was that what he was thinking, the girl stripped naked and then given repeated dunkings in the river? Her piercing cries for mercy silenced only after Absolution as those who judged stood round with mud on their boots, the rain beating harder on her pale white skin, harder, the dappled light from the lanterns falling over her kneeling frame, the girl terrified and shivering uncontrollably even when in prayer, the cage ready. Her hair . . . her lovely hair . . . 'This interview is concluded, Inspector. I have duties I must attend to and unfortunately they cannot wait.'

Christ walked through lavender wearing clothing from the fourteenth century. Mary stood in the attitude of prayer wearing the same, her straw-coloured hair not the black or dark brown it might well have been. Her eyes were very blue, the plaster 'sculptures' garish and unforgivable.

'It's the Italian influence,' Louis would have muttered, but was still probably with the bishop or wondering where the hell his partner had got to. 'Fair hair was prized so much, Hermann, the women who could would spend hours in the sun to bleach it and tried all manner of rinses, even mule's urine. They bleached their skins too, but covered up when attending to the hair, and wore white lead as a base to their cosmetics but couldn't change the shade of their eyes.'

An encyclopaedia of the times, snorted Kohler silently at the thought of his partner. From floor to ceiling, wall to wall, and on table, counter and shelf, the rat hole of *Les Fleurs du Petit Enfant* was a carnival of objects of piety. Bits of mirror and picture glass threw back the light. Candles burned in these hard times, perfuming the air with ersatz cinnamon behind tightly drawn black-out curtains. But still there was no sign of what he'd come looking for. Portraits of the Christ Child, in violent shades, clashed with those of the Virgin who held Him but was never seen here to suckle her babe like a normal mother. And in a stable, no less!

Crucifixes of zinc had been painted silver for those foolish enough to part with ten times the price of those that had been dipped in black. Madonna-and-Child medallions were so poorly stamped they echoed the one Louis had found on Mireille de Sinéty's dressing table.

Kohler picked up a framed portrait. Did some of them have postcards hidden behind their backings – bare breasts and curls, other things too, or was the switch made while taking the cash?

'I can't decide,' he said, giving a helpless shrug to the *patron* who was in his late forties, short, rotund, and wearing gold-rimmed specs and a rumpled dark brown business suit. A failed novice, was that it? Life in the seminary too confining? The peach-down covered cheeks were pink and fair and had never seen the touch of a razor. Moles sprouted unclipped dark brown hairs. The greeny brown eyes had begun to water.

'The wife's very religious,' said Kohler. 'I promised to send her a little something.'

That wife of too many neglected years back home on the farm near Wasserburg had just recently got herself a divorce and had married an indentured farm labourer from France but no matter. This was Avignon where lies counted.

Dangling a Bakelite rosary in front of the *patron*, he grinned and asked, 'How much?'

'Two hundred francs.'

'Hey, it's a bargain. I'll take it. Here, I've got lots in this canvas sack. I just came into a fortune.'

There were at least 25,000 francs in the bundle that was taken out. Armand Corbeau furtively looked over the rest of the clientele, all of whom had paused in their infernal pawing to listen as he gave up and sighed, 'Inspector, one can't but recognize a policeman no matter his country of origin. What can I do for you?'

A wise man. 'A few small words into the shell of your ear, *mon fin*. Nothing difficult, I assure you.'

The shop emptied. In one minute, two nuns, a priest, three soldier boys with their girlfriends and a couple of ordinary citizens looking as if they were after other things had fled.

'*Papiere bitte. Schnell!* I haven't got all night.'

The residence listed on the *carte d'identité* was the shop, but where did he eat and sleep?

Kohler tapped the identity card with evident uncertainty before pocketing it only to hear the expected gasp of, 'Monsieur . . . ?'

The Kripo's representative leaned on the counter, pushing trash aside. 'Hey, you'd already decided it was Inspector. Use some respect. It's *Herr* Kohler, Gestapo Paris-Central.'

The fleshy lips quivered. Pudgy fingers hesitated but moved

secretively along the back of the cash counter to a hidden push-bell.

'*Don't!* It wouldn't be wise, now would it?'

The Gestapo . . . Corbeau sucked in a breath and fought with himself not to let his eyes stray from the detective's empty gaze but the temptation was too great.

He darted a glance to the back of the shop, then waited.

'So, we understand each other,' breathed Kohler, enjoying getting the jump on such leeches. 'Now you're not to lock the front door and hang up the *fermé* sign. That wouldn't be fair. You're to leave that door open to all comers while we have ourselves a little chat.'

Darkness had come quickly. The bishop's courtyard was pitch black, the mistral fierce and icy.

Hermann had departed with the car.

'Ah *mon Dieu* . . .' muttered St-Cyr uneasily to himself. No stranger to the dark, he had to admit he was afraid. Adrienne de Langlade must have been murdered – he was all but certain of this now but as yet had no final proof.

Mireille de Sinéty must have been about to confront Rivaille and the other judges with the girl's murder or perhaps had done so.

'And this is Avignon,' he softly breathed. 'An Avignon which still hungers for and exudes its past.'

He started out. It could have been six hundred years ago. The smell and sound of the dogs were there on the air. Had Hermann found Nino dead? Had Xavier taken that dog up river a piece to make certain it wouldn't be found? Was that why Hermann had left his partner all alone?

The branches of the bishop's plane trees were in torment. The scent of burning olive logs and coal mingled with those of sage and thyme and ah! so many things that grew wild on Mount Ventoux and elsewhere to the north. The smell of the river was there too, that of decay, of cold black mud and dead reeds, and why had that girl been drowned?

Oh *bien sûr*, the singers were a closed group and very protective of their positions and Adrienne had been the newcomer. And, perhaps, even last autumn Xavier's voice would have shown signs of changing and the boy would have become increasingly desperate at the thought of losing everything.

But to kill her over something like that didn't make sense, did it?

Reaching the courtyard gates at last, he clung to them to steady himself. By continuing to the left up the rue Sainte Catherine, he could then keep to the right and hopefully reach the Palais. Once in its shadow, there would be some relief from this infernal wind.

And from there he could strike south along the rue de Mons to that religious shop, if he could find it.

The sound of steps behind him didn't come easily and it was some time before he realized he was being followed. Brother Matthieu, he wondered, or had the bishop or Alain de Passe sent someone else? A hired assassin?

Hermann, as keeper of their guns, had this Sûreté's treasured Lebel hidden under the driver's seat of the Renault. It was Hermann's responsibility to look after the weapon and to assign it to his partner only when needed.

There were no lights. God had even seen fit to shut out the stars and moon, perhaps to emphasize that at any moment an *alerte aérienne* could sound and drive everyone underground.

Everyone.

The steps had ceased. He was certain of it but their sound had come so tenderly on the wind he had to wait a little longer. Reaching deeply into his overcoat pocket, St-Cyr found and held the pomander. He thought of that other Mireille. Rivaille had said she'd thrown herself from the Bell Tower but had that been the truth? Had there not, perhaps, been far more to it and sufficient, yes, for the present Mireille to insist on appearing before her judges dressed *exactly* as this first Mireille might well have been?

Though partially covered under opened manuscripts and letters from the past in the bishop's study, there'd been recent newspapers. *L'Oeuvre*, the mouthpiece of Marcel Déat's pro-Nazi party, *L'Oeuvre rassemblement national populaire*, also the weekly, *Je suis partout*, that of *L'Action Française* since 1930. Monarchist, violently anti-Semitic, anti-Communist and profascist, *Je suis* had promoted outright hatred and fear of the foreigners who had increasingly sought refuge in France.

A new and far brighter Renaissance, Rivaille had called life under the Nazis. Fascist and ultrafascist sentiments had always been present, a little stronger in the south perhaps, but one had to be fair. Equally there were, and had been in the past, strongly opposing views.

But what of *La Cagoule*, he asked himself. The 'action' squads of the *Comité secret d'action révolutionnaire* – were the bishop and the others leaders of Avignon's branch of that organization?

In the thirties there'd been so many far-right splinter parties. The *Croix de feu* (the Cross of Fire), the *Camelots du Roi*, and the *Voluntaires nationaux*. All in some manner had looked forward to the downfall of the Third Republic and the rise of a new era.

A new Renaissance.

When the steps started up again, he moved into the deeper darkness of a nearby house and waited.

Les Fleurs du Petit Enfant was full of surprises, thought Kohler. Right at the back of the shop, and hidden completely from all but the closest scrutiny, was a curtained doorway to a tiny alcove.

Knitting needles stopped. A woollen scarf began to settle into a copious lap. Dark brown, narrowly spaced eyes under heavily kohled lids looked up at him and blinked in alarm.

In row after row, and on thin shelves that climbed on either side of the alcove and ran to the sheet-iron comfort of an oil-drum sawdust burner, were postcards of naked breasts.

Other things too.

Curls of female hair – black, brown, blonde, reddish blonde and red – male erections, scrotums, small clutches of pubic hair, peephole views of unmentionable female parts. Close-ups of copulating couples, of bare asses, of girls on their hands and knees and grinning as they looked over a shoulder, the fellows too, and often not with the girls. 'Hey, I think I get the picture,' he quipped. 'If there is no sin, what is there to confess?'

'It's all quite legal,' shot the woman fiercely.

'Inspector, Dénise and I share the duties of the shop.'

'And the profits?'

Her expression emptied. 'I am my brother's keeper, Inspector. As for these,' she indicated the merchandise. 'Even God must make a living in such hard times.'

Sainte Mère! They were a pair, thought Kohler. Corbeau was sweating; the sister, as cold as ice.

He took out the postcard of Adrienne de Langlade's breasts and said flatly, 'Who sold this photo to you?'

Dénise Corbeau didn't even bother to throw a warning glance at her brother. She just started up, all gestures and spittle. '*Quelle folie!* How could we possibly know? Who shouts the name for the few sous that are paid? We buy from those who sell and no names are given.'

'What a pity,' he breathed. 'You see, the Kommandant isn't aware of this little service his soldier boys have been frequenting along with your other customers. Oh *bien sûr*, the man who has needs must go to where they can be satisfied best, the woman also, but—'

'Armand, pay him off and get the fucker out of here. You people. You cows. You think you can constantly put the squeeze on us? *Pour l'amour du ciel*, we pay off the préfet, idiot! Now *fous-moi la paix!*' Bugger off! She tossed a hand.

Her ample bosom heaved. A knitting needle fell and as it hit the floor, the bell above the shop entrance rang.

'*Mort aux vaches*, eh?' breathed Kohler. Death to cows, the cops.

'Dénise, he's Gestapo,' blurted the brother.

'*Couillon, ferme-la!*' Asshole, shut your trap!

They listened to the shop, these two. 'Hey, it's probably my partner,' said Kohler. 'Now there's more than one of us and he's the religious one. A fanatic. His sisters are both Mother Superiors.' Louis had been an only child, but what the hell.

'Armand, go and see who it is. *Don't* stand there looking as if I had caught you with your trousers down. *Do it!*

'Monsieur . . .' she crooned and snapped her fingers. 'The card, if you please.'

Kohler handed it over and watched as she fondled the curl and studied the breasts before drawing in a breath. 'A musician brought us the negative and some samples of the hair. He said she was a student and needed the money but was too embarrassed to come herself.'

'You can do better.'

'His name?' she asked, frowning now as he waited. 'That I don't know and didn't ask but I think he was a singer.'

'You're lying. I think you know exactly who sold that negative to you and when. You'd seen and heard that person singing often enough in the Cathedral. Even such as yourself must go to Mass.'

'The baritone, Norman Galiteau.'

'Ah *bon*. Now was more than one copy made?'

'One only.'

'That's not true. How come I've got one?'

'Ten . . . no, twenty.'

'Fifty.'

'Perhaps. Some were sent to . . . to other shops.'

'Where?'

Maudit salaud! 'Marseille . . . Aix . . . We often swap so as to meet demand.'

'Okay, now who bought this one from you and for whom?' Each card carried a number and he had noticed this.

'It was stolen.'

'When?'

She shrugged. Her painted lips opened up with a torrent of *langue d'oc*, the last of which suggested the theft might quite possibly have taken place during the first week of December. 'After the flooding. Yes. Yes, I am positive.'

'By whom?'

She had him now but wouldn't rejoice. 'Two girls, one of whom was a nun.'

Sister Marie-Madeleine . . .

'Armand had gone out, Inspector, so I was tending the shop myself, you understand. So many customers, Christmas approaching . . . Those little thoughtfulnesses that mean so much. The—'

'*Ja, ja*, get to the point.'

'She was with a girl of about her age. Twenty, I think.'

'The *petite lingère* who was murdered?'

'The one who was married to God purchased some things, while . . . while the other one entered here to steal. To *steal*!'

But took only what she must have known exactly to look for.

Kohler found a cigarette and paused to light it before placing it between her lips. 'Now I'm going to ask you once, and then it's up against the post for you.'

The firing squad . . .

He gave her a moment. 'Who did you sell copies of this to?'

'A priest. *Une gueule cassée*. No others. I swear it.'

She was lying again – several had been sold – but he had what he wanted. 'Brother Matthieu, when?'

'Late last June. He was very excited when he first saw it and trembled at the touch.'

'Okay, I believe you, but let's cement our bargain. Was he a frequent buyer?'

May God forgive her and keep the knife from her back. 'Yes, but . . . but only of the bosoms, never of the others which shamed him. He was not like most of the holy fathers who make their way to us, the sisters also, some of them. When he would come, I . . . I would have to cover everything else up before he would dare to enter *la caverne de joie* to . . . to make his selection.'

A collector, and not the bishop. Not Rivaille.

St-Cyr held his breath. Subtle differences of darkness gave silhouettes. The one who had been following him hesitated. The urge to cry out, *Sûreté, you're under arrest!*, was there but suppressed. Uncertain if the quarry had been lost, the man moved off, the darkness of the street swallowing him.

Two minutes later, the Sûreté began to follow him. Hermann was better at this sort of thing. No one could touch Hermann when being followed by him, or being allowed to follow him. It was uncanny how such a giant could walk so lightly. The poacher in him, perhaps.

The man hesitated. St-Cyr hesitated. Here and there, but at

some distance, were tiny, furtive, blue-shaded lights – other pedestrians – and then, its wheels squeaking as it fought the wind, a *vélo-taxi*.

The bicycle-rickshaw, one of the Occupation's greatest indignities, trundled past, its driver cursing the mistral as the couple in the back giggled and laughed. A German soldier or officer and his Avignonnaise, his *petite amie*.

Silence overcame all sounds save those of the wind, but then the droning, muffler-banging, incessant throb of a motorcycle patrol plundered the silence. Four bikes with sidecars, their headlamps squinting blue-shaded slit-eyes into the darkness, roared up the narrow street, the sound of their engines crashing from the walls until . . .

The sound had faded and he realized again – how often had it been since the fall of 1940? – that for Hermann and himself it was only a matter of time.

We have survived so far, but no one else really cares about common crime, not any more, he said to himself. And those who get in the way only get removed.

Far to the west, along the whole of the Spanish Frontier, the Wehrmacht had stationed some of its finest alpine troops. Whereas in 1940, '41 and even in '42, night crossings to freedom had always been difficult, now they were exceedingly hazardous. Gone were the days of a 12,000-franc *passeur*, a guide. Now it was 1,000,000 francs. Hermann knew it, too, but kept talking about taking Giselle and Oona to safety before it was too late. A bar, a tobacco shop . . . the retirement options were always well off on the horizon and always golden.

'Inspector, is that you?'

'Ah *merde*!' he cried. 'Madame . . .'

'Sister. It's Sister Marie-Madeleine. Forgive me for following you but . . . but I had to see you before it was too late and this . . . this was the only way.'

Armand Corbeau stood on tiptoes clasping the bell above the door, but he hadn't been quick enough. Some of the sound had escaped to reach the back of the shop.

Kohler reminded him of this. The shop bell was hesitantly released, Corbeau warily looking over a shoulder and down the long, narrow tunnel of the shop to where they stood as if in judgement of him.

Dénise Corbeau hesitantly wet a hairy upper lip and let a breath escape. 'You fool,' she softly exhaled.

The customer who had entered earlier had just departed.

'De Passe,' blurted Corbeau. 'The préfet has said we are to keep silent and to destroy immediately our stock of . . . of photographs, even though he knows you have just seen them.'

'And Brother Matthieu?' asked Kohler.

'Wasn't with him. I swear it.'

'But de Passe asked you if the brother had been in?'

'He said he wished to speak to him. He . . . he was worried, I think, about him.'

'Worried?'

'A little. Inspector, Brother Matthieu had a terrible time in the Great War. Everyone is aware of this. We . . . we all must make allowances for *la gueule cassée*. The constant doubts about God, the . . .'

'Desires?' asked Kohler.

'You fool,' said the sister again to her brother. '*Idiot!* Why can't you keep your mouth shut?'

'What desires?' demanded the Kripo.

'Desires to touch and to explore,' she said, tossing the words aside at him. 'Those are nothing, Inspector. Always there is the desire; always the fear. Both are in balance before God with such a one, and therefore left undone. Well, almost.'

'The hair,' said Kohler.

'He just touches it,' blurted Corbeau from the other end of the shop. 'He doesn't touch the Virgin's breasts. He wouldn't dare to do that.'

'The Virgin . . . You said, the Virgin.'

'That's what he called her,' said the sister tartly.

Adrienne de Langlade . . .

Darkness was complete, the sound of the wind total as St-Cyr and

Sister Marie-Madeleine fought their way along a street that, by the funnelling force of the wind, could only be narrow.

A shutter flew off. An iron gate swung shut. Then the wind let up and the sound of it dropped off so suddenly that the steps behind them were momentarily heard before they, too, had ceased.

St-Cyr swore and, pulling the sister with him, took refuge against the gate.

The steps didn't start up again. Straining to hear them, he felt the trembling in her and knew at once that she'd been the quarry all along.

The damned gate was stuck fast. Yanking on it, he tried to open it and silently cursed as her breath moistened his cheek. 'Forgive me for bringing him to you,' she whispered.

'Who?' he asked so softly she understood the word only by feeling it on his lips.

'One of them,' she whispered. Nothing else.

La Cagoule? he silently demanded of himself and, putting her behind him, faced the street and the darkness.

A bicycle passed by, its lonely blue-shaded light a faint welcome that all too soon departed. An ancient carriage sounded in the distance. On and on it came, but the bastard who had been following them was now very close. And what will it be, eh, shouted St-Cyr into the silence of his thoughts. The knife? The wire garrotte?

The scent of black tobacco came harshly with that of the aniseed that was being chewed since no cigarette could be alight.

Through the darkness, the hooded silhouette grew until, at last, he was able to see the man. Even in a good light, the face would have been all but hidden.

The steps departed quietly. He and the sister were suddenly alone and he felt her tears hot against the fiercely cold air as she kissed his cheek and held him tightly. 'Forgive me,' she said again but now . . . 'I . . . I forget myself.'

'You've left the convent, Sister. You no longer wear your wedding ring.' Her hands were freezing.

'I had to. I couldn't stay there a moment longer.'

'Where were you leading me?'

'To the Kommandant's house on place des Carmes. To Frau von Mahler, my only hope of refuge.'

6

Two Wehrmacht sentries, wearing goggles and armed with Schmeissers, barred the entrance to von Mahler's house. On the shrieking of the wind came the Oberfeldwebel's grunt in broken, brutalized French. 'That one stays, Sister. The Colonel was positive about it.'

'But the Chief Inspector's with me. Frau von Mahler has to hear what we each have to say.' The torch beam indicated the flagstone path she was to take. 'Wait here,' she said in dismay.

'He will,' came the savage rejoinder.

His back to the tall iron gates that had shut him out. St-Cyr pulled up his overcoat collar and gripped his fedora more fiercely. One couldn't lose one's hat, not these days. And damn Boemelburg for sending them on this investigation. To be followed like that, to have the former sister targeted, was not nice – but had Walter known such things would happen? As Head of Section IV in France, Hermann's boss hadn't liked what had gone on during their last investigation . . . a safe-cracker, a Resistance thing that had struck too close to home. And what better way to get rid of two disloyal detectives than to send them into the arms of the *Cagoule*?

Only the sound of the wind came to him but was he being watched from out there in the ink? There was, he knew, a fourteenth-century cloister across the square. The Barefoot Carmelites had established a monastery there. At the far end of the square the remains of the bell tower were all that was left of the convent they had established in 1261.

And, yes, the square would still exude that same sense of calm. And, yes, with a young wife who had been badly scarred by the incendiary fires of Köln, von Mahler had chosen the house wisely. But did that wife of his never go out? And why, having told them not to question her, had von Mahler then thought it necessary to make absolutely certain they didn't?

Hungry and tired – exhausted – he waited. It was now about 8.00 p.m. on Wednesday. Since arriving at midnight yesterday, he and Hermann had been constantly watched, and those who made certain of this had taken the trouble to find out everything they could about them. Not every item Mireille de Sinéty had worn would have its story, but many of them must have.

Longing for a quiet moment to go over things, he turned to face the wind and force himself to remain alert.

Kohler hit the door to the Café of the Panic-Stricken White Mule or whatever. Madame Emphoux, the *patronne*, let out a screech of anguish. Newspapers fluttered in hands that froze.

'Ah! Now that this Gestapo *Schweinebulle* has everyone's attention, madame, where's our little group?' he demanded.

The frizzy mop of tired auburn curls jerked towards the rear of the café. No one moved. A tableau of terror was registered in faces caught. Old, young, not so young . . .

'Ah, *merde*,' he muttered in defeat. 'I'm an idiot, *mes amis*. Relax.'

He'd seen it too, thought Madame Emphoux. At a table next to the black-out curtains, the woman with the little boy had burst into tears and now Herr Kohler couldn't seem to move. He had realized what he'd stumbled into.

'The . . . the ones you want, monsieur, are over there,' she said and heard her voice breaking. 'Please, I . . . I will take you to them.'

Kohler let his eyes drift over the assembled, most of whom might or might not have suspected a thing until he had barged in. Oh *bien sûr* he could pick out the madrigal singers but so, too, could he not fail to notice those who had been watching a middle-aged woman and her 'son', a kid of about eight years of age.

'I'm a fool,' he said softly as he passed the woman's table en route to the two plain-clothed sons of bitches who had been waiting to nail the *passeur* who would take the boy to another safe house. They'd have nailed the woman also, and the kid.

These things happen, he said sadly to himself, for he couldn't know where they would lead. And reaching the table at last, grabbed a chair and sat down.

They were both French Gestapo – gangsters; members of the *pègre* rescued from jail and put to work on, among other tasks, hunting down Jewish children to send to the camps.

'Look, let's not argue,' he said. 'My partner and I are on to something big and can't have you two messing things up. Forget you ever saw her and the boy. Let it go.'

This was heresy of him. They said nothing. They didn't even move and that could only mean they were dangerous. Kohler raised both hands and spread his fingers. 'Hey, *mes amis*, I'm not going for my gun, but for a little present. I just came into my inheritance and would like to share it with you. Okay?'

Not even the briefest nod was given.

First twenty-five thousand francs brushed the table, disappearing immediately, and then another twenty-five. 'You go after her and I'll hear about it and come after you. Right?' he said. And offering cigarettes no one would refuse these days, sat there for about five minutes, never once taking his eyes from them.

Again, they said nothing, but when he got up to leave the table still wishing Louis was behind him, the woman and the boy had left the café.

Now it was Madame Emphoux who, the tears streaming from her, nodded ever so slightly. 'It's okay,' she said under her breath. 'May God be thanked.'

Bass, baritone, tenor, alto and soprano sat still bundled up in their overcoats and hats like most everyone else in the unheated café. With a forefinger, Christiane Bissert coyly traced the rim of a glass that held one of the Occupation's ersatz apéritifs, since the *Pas d'alcool* sign was out. Wednesdays, Thursdays and Fridays now, and a lime-green, godawful, cloudy concoction that had been sweetened with saccharin. A 'liqueur'.

'That was impressive,' she said and thought to heave a mothering sigh. 'Here, sit beside me. Join us, please.'

Herr Kohler was still trembling from his little encounter. He took out a glass vial and, uncorking it, shook two grey-white pills into his giant's hand.

'For the digestion,' he said.

A near-beer, one of the 'approximate' drinks for such days, was set before him. Looking up, and suddenly subdued, he thanked *Madame la patronne* who said, 'Please, it is on the house.'

'My partner, madame. Has he been in?'

He was so anxious, so much a man, a real man, she hated to shake her head but would have to. 'Drink. You will need to with . . . with your tablets.'

The near-beer was half brandy! The tablets were Benzedrine. 'Now where were we?' he said, and hauling out his little black notebook, gave the five of them a moment. 'Ah yes, a picnic, I think it was. A mezzo-soprano who had just passed her final audition and was to have joined your little group. Early June, wasn't it? – the picnic, that is. At the *mas* Mireille de Sinéty's mother leases from your boss. One of you said Adrienne de Langlade couldn't swim, and one of you indicated she damned well could.'

The townhouse, overlooking place des Carmes, had been remodelled in the late eighteen hundreds. An eloquent staircase curved gracefully upwards from the tiled foyer to a landing before whose leaded windows and black-out curtains hung a magnificent Beauvais tapestry.

Leaving hat, overcoat and scarf with a very disgruntled *Haushälterin* who hadn't liked his being admitted, St-Cyr followed Marie-Madeleine. There were Old Masters, some very good pieces of sculpture, exquisite porcelains and figurines in vitrines. Swans, pastoral scenes . . . Everything had, apparently, been carefully chosen so as to offer peace of mind.

There were no candles in evidence for when the electricity would go off, as it surely must these days and did in every town and city in France. There were no lanterns, no ashtrays, no sign of any matches. Only cold fireplaces. Not even the lingering smell of tobacco smoke apart from that of himself. Simply sachets and bowls of dried, fragrant petals or chopped leaves and stems. Lavender, verbena, wild rose and sage – pomanders of a sort to calm a frightened mind that must be constantly terrified of the firestorms.

Mireille de Sinéty had placed each bowl or sachet at convenient and frequent intervals so that Frau von Mahler could reach out to touch sanity and pull herself back from terror.

They entered a salon and passed by a Louis XIV *bergère* where quiet little *tête-à-têtes* must once have been held. In the adjoining *salon de musique* there was an eighteenth-century harpsichord, one of Blanchet le Vieux's masterpieces. A lute equalled that of the *petite lingère* and he had the thought the girl must have been given hers by the Kommandant's wife.

Reams of patiently hand-copied sheet music were scattered on the floor. The music stand had been knocked over and had broken. An embroidered Louis XV *canapé* was all but threadbare but still held the needles and thimbles of a patient restoration that had been suddenly left off, never, by the look, to be taken up again.

Marie-Madeleine didn't hesitate. Her mind long since made up, she led the way down a corridor. In the near distance there was a narrow anteroom whose mahogany bureau drawers, to one side, were half or partially open and in disarray. Beyond the anteroom there was an oval dressing mirror on a moveable stand, positioned so as to give warning of visitors.

In its reflection, and past the girl's shoulder, he caught a glimpse of the richly carved blanket box that sat at the foot of a canopied bed. A nightdress was spilled over the box. Lace and fine white silk . . .

'Inspector, please stay here.'

Concern filled her dark brown eyes. Marie-Madeleine indicated a visitor's chair on the other side of the anteroom. 'Frau von Mahler will have seen you in the mirror. Promise me you won't come nearer.'

From somewhere distant came the muted sounds of children. Their *nounou* was trying to cheer them up. And surely this household needed laughter.

When two little girls raced down the hall, dragging their towels and dripping, the *Kindermädchen*, of about seventeen, tore after them with an upraised bath-brush, and the excited howls of the chase echoed. The children darted past him. The nanny stopped abruptly and blanched.

Her chest rose and fell. St-Cyr indicated that the girl should collect the children. 'It's their bedtime,' she said sheepishly in *deutsch*. 'I . . . I would never hurt them, *mein Herr*. It's . . . it's only a game we play. They've been so sad. I had to . . .'

She couldn't say it. Things quietened down. Wearing their towels and frowning, not daring to look at him, the girls trooped by and were soon gone from sight.

Time and again Frau von Mahler had been at the bureau. Slips, half-slips and silk stockings had been yanked aside or half out. Sweaters and blouses . . .

When he saw the butt of the pistol she had repeatedly taken out and put back, his fist held the crumpled négligés it had been under.

The gun was a Belgian FN semiautomatic. There was a box of cartridges and this had been broken open and spilled, but some time ago, he thought, for there were 9mm Parabellum rounds under many of the things.

Mireille de Sinéty hadn't taken the two rounds Hermann had found in Xavier's pockets from the Kommandant, to give to Dédou Favre before dawn on Monday. She had taken them from here.

The gun was fully loaded. A thirteen-shot Browning *Modèle à Grande Puissance* (High Power). Many of such weapons were being made in Belgium for the Wehrmacht now and most of them, this one included, had deliberately had the safety catch removed. But Frau von Mahler had understood enough to leave the firing chamber empty and that could only mean she knew well how to use the gun.

Ah nom de Dieu, he silently cursed, what was he to do? Had she been about to kill herself? Had the murder put a temporary stop to it?

With uncertainty, his mind so obviously in a turmoil, the Chief

Inspector held the gun, and when he looked at her, thought Frau von Mahler, he too, like all others at first sight, sucked in a breath.

'Inspector, it's good of you to come but my husband doesn't know about that. I'd be grateful if you would put it back and say nothing of it to him.'

'Might I ask, please, how you came by it?'

Tough . . . he must really be so, for he gave no further hint of dismay or alarm at the sight of her. 'You might, but I, like so many these days, wouldn't tell you unless tortured.'

The black market then, and perhaps a good 10,000 francs.

'Forty thousand,' she said and turned to lead him into her room. 'It's better we meet face to face, then you can judge for yourself if the answers I give are lies.'

In the café, Genèvieve Ravier let the fullness of her stunning blue eyes fill with concern as she sought Herr Kohler out to hold him fast with her gaze. 'The girl could swim a little,' she said of Adrienne de Langlade whose photograph, found behind the mantelpiece in their common room, he had set on the table before them.

'A little,' echoed Kohler.

The soprano unbuttoned her overcoat and pulled her scarf aside to bare a soft and slender throat. 'Christiane was positive the girl couldn't. I was not so sure.'

I'll bet, thought Kohler.

'Inspector, we helped her,' insisted Christiane. 'She was very shy and ashamed of her fear of the water. A childhood mishap. A near drowning . . .' *Maudit!* Why had she mentioned *drowning?* 'One of the lakes in the Bois de Boulogne. Yes . . . yes, it happened there. Madame Simondi would often force the girl to recount the incident.'

'César's wife was always pumping her for news of Paris, even such old news,' offered Marius Spaggiari.

'The girl wanted us to hold her under the water for a moment. She trusted us,' said Guy Rochon.

'And exactly where did this "holding under" happen?' asked Kohler.

Rochon threw the *Basso Continuo* a questioning glance. 'Why, at the *mas*, Inspector. The cave. The picnic.'

'Inspector,' said Spaggiari, 'the girl couldn't swim from here to Madame *la patronne* without one of us holding her about the waist.'

'And exactly *what* happened at that picnic?' he asked.

'The picnic? Why nothing much,' said Norman Galiteau.

'She got a little drunk, didn't she?'

Genèvieve nonchalantly shrugged and handed the photograph back to him. 'After the swim we had our lunch and then . . . then we cycled home.'

And even girls can lie, especially the pretty ones! 'The Kommandant issued your *laissez-passers*,' said Kohler, flipping through his notebook. 'Your reason for the visit . . . Now where did I put it down? Ah, yes, here it is.'

They waited. He gave them time to digest this, then flipped the page over, letting them think a little more of what von Mahler might or might not have told him.

Then he let them have it. A lie if ever there was one, but to all good lies must come a solid element of truth. 'The Feldwebel in charge of the control on the bridge recorded that one of your group failed to show up. That one had been left behind. She was . . .' He paused. 'Too ill to return.'

There was nothing in Herr Kohler's pale blue eyes but emptiness. 'She was badly sunburned, Inspector,' said Spaggiari levelly. 'We did what we could but had to leave her with Madame de Sinéty.'

'Goat's milk and butter . . .' blurted Galiteau, his gold-rimmed glasses framing a nervousness that couldn't be hidden.

It had to be asked. 'Where was Xavier?'

'Xavier?' blurted Christiane. 'Why he—'

'He had had to remain in Avignon, Inspector,' said Spaggiari. 'A small matter Brother Matthieu was upset about.'

'A penance,' swallowed Galiteau. 'Xavier had to scrub out the dog run.'

'Okay, so the boy was with you – that's what Feldwebel Jacob Dorst wrote down.'

'Xavier . . . Inspector, if you're so certain he was with us, why don't you ask him?' said Spaggiari.

'I already have.'

'That boy lies . . . You can't trust him,' said Christiane earnestly.

The ersatz lime-green apéritif hadn't been touched but when he laid the photographs of that picnic on the table before her, she reached for it only to suddenly withdraw her hand.

'You lot got her drunk,' said Kohler. 'Was it on absinthe?'

None of them answered. All were panicking and wondering how the hell he'd come by the photos. 'In these you can see that her knees are stained by lavender and soil, as are the palms of her hands and her seat,' he said and pointed this out to them.

The day had been very hot. Round and round they had spun her, each of them looking up into the sun, recalled Christiane. They had all laughed. Adrienne had done so, too, and had stumbled when they had let go of her. She really *had* fallen several times, and then . . . then had passed out.

Herr Kohler set something in front of her, and when Christiane looked down at it, she saw that it was the postcard that had been made from the negative Norman had sold to the *Petit Enfant*. Clamping her eyes shut at the thought of what must now happen to them, she felt the detective take her by the hand. He pressed her fingers against the hair . . . the hair . . . It had been so soft – hot in the midday sun. Guy had laughed. Genèvieve had urged them all to help. They had turned the girl over but how had the Inspector come by the photographs? Norman had kept them. Norman . . .

'Who raped her?' asked Kohler gently. 'Please don't lie to me, Mademoiselle Bissert. That girl was at least four months pregnant when she drowned in October of last year, a good two or three weeks before November's flooding freed up her body.'

The singer and the song . . . A life so suddenly gone. 'Xavier. We . . . we didn't know what he was doing to her. I swear it!'

'Until it was too late,' said the tenor.

'Too late,' echoed the baritone.

'We had gone up to the *mas*,' said Spaggiari.

'The *mas*,' said someone.

'The sun,' said someone else.

'Hot . . . it was so hot,' said Christiane in despair.

'Absinthe isn't very kind, Inspector,' said Genèvieve. 'It can make some crazy, others numb to what is happening to them.'

Rose madder, saffron yellow, thought St-Cyr. Dark forest green and cocoa brown, the white of crocheted stockings and the undersheath a well-bred girl of nineteen would have worn six hundred years ago. The fine, soft suede of her belt, the girdle that had been worn low off the hip and had held so many things. Tiny silver bells, a dirk, a purse, a pair of scissors, a sewing kit. The *enseignes*, cabochons and talismans . . . the rebus, the riddle she had presented.

'Venetian velvet, Flemish linen. Silk that is so soft and supple it's cool to the touch but once radiated the warmth of her body, Inspector,' said Frau von Mahler earnestly, her dark blue eyes never leaving him. 'Go on, take up a handful of the remnants she gave me. *Bitte, mein lieber französischer Oberdetektiv.* Breathe in the scent of her, of me! A soothing lotion, a balm she made for my skin, from an ancient recipe.'

Shredded strips of fabric, all of them taken from those the girl had used in her costume, filled the large white porcelain bowl the woman held. They'd been sprinkled liberally with honey water. The Greeks had favoured its use, and the ancient Egyptians before them, probably. Honey, coriander, nutmeg and cloves, gum benzoin, vanilla pods, storax and dried lemon rind – all had been mixed and ground in a mortar, after which, in the early Renaissance, a litre or so of fine cognac or brandy had been added. Two or three days, the mixture had been allowed to steep. Then rosewater and orange blossom water had been joined with ground musk and ambergris and the whole concoction placed in a matrass, a glass flask with a long neck, and heated gently for three days and nights before cooling and bottling.

'Frau von Mahler,' said St-Cyr, still holding the fistful of remnants he had brought to his nose.

'*Please!* Let us speak *en français.* Let me show you how well she was teaching me. So many things. All gone now. *Gone*, do you understand?'

He waited for her to set the bowl aside but she refused to relinquish it to Marie-Madeleine and remained sitting with it in her lap. A woman of perhaps twenty-seven. It was so hard to tell. Once tall and flaxen-haired, now thin and stooped and . . .

'Forgive me,' she said. 'You see, I . . . I've very few friends and she became my dearest one. Ah! it's strange, I know. A foreigner, a *Boche*, one of the Occupier, but you see, Inspector, Mireille was above all that. She knew I needed help and that my children shouldn't suffer from the loneliness their mother had imposed upon them because of . . . because of this.'

The reddened scars that were threaded, stippled and bulged with newly grown and still-growing whitish tissue on her neck and her face, the skin grafts that had been painfully undergone and still would have to be. The terrible loss of so much of her lovely hair.

'My chest. My thighs. These arms of mine,' she said. 'When you're engulfed in flames, Inspector, you can never forget your screams. I think I must have rolled about in the street but have no memory of it. Someone – I still don't know who – threw a blanket over me and smothered my little fire. But by then, of course, I'd torn off my clothes, and perhaps that one act saved me from being even more severely burned but, again, this I can't recall doing.'

Avignon's *petite pomme frite*. Had she learned of Xavier's having called her that, and the others too, he wondered. How hateful of them, if so.

'Mireille knew things, Inspector. Things someone couldn't have her saying.'

'Bishop Rivaille?' he asked, only to see her draw in a breath.

She plucked at the remnants. 'Rivaille . . . He proclaims we're at the dawn of a new Renaissance and says the past must be purged, the slate wiped clean. But I wonder which slate he means. That of the Babylonian Captivity, or that of last Monday night at ten fifty.'

There were no tears. These had all been shed, or perhaps it was that she could no longer physically cry. Grief was registered in once fair cheeks.

'Did he tell you that the first Mireille fell to her death of her own accord from the Bell Tower of the Palais where she had been taken as seamstress to his Holiness? Did he tell you how they had taken her from the Palais to the Pont Saint Bénézet, there to publicly strip her naked and lock her into an *accabussade*? The Pontiff, the cardinals, magistrates, captains and Papal Guard?'

The Chief Inspector St-Cyr waited for more of the truth. 'Most of the city turned out for the spectacle,' she said. 'You see, the girl was being punished for harlotry, it was falsely claimed, and once back in the Palais, having been nearly drowned, she then clothed herself again in all her finery. And in despair of what they had done to her good name and to that of her family and her husband, threw herself to her death, or was pushed.'

Marie-Madeleine hastily crossed herself and, not taking her gaze from him, said softly, 'She had refused absolutely to consort with the cardinal who had wanted her, and for this, was put on trial first and then . . . then punished.'

'The pomander,' said St-Cyr and, taking it out, held it in a fist. 'Gripped just as she must have done and then again by our Mireille last Monday night.'

'It's filled with ambergris that is very old,' said Frau von Mahler. 'The *notaire public*, Albert Renaud, loaned it to her. He has extensive collections, and among the artefacts are many that once belonged to this other Mireille and to the de Sinéty family.'

'The third judge,' said St-Cyr. 'Brother Matthieu suggested the possibility; Bishop Rivaille confirmed it.'

The Inspector looked at Marie-Madeleine when he said this. Suddenly the girl blurted, 'The postcards, the hair. The shop of the Petit Enfant . . .'

'And another girl, madame. Another murder.'

'Adrienne de Langlade. Is it true?'

'Very, I'm afraid.'

'Marie-Madeleine, please go to the kitchen and bring the Inspector some refreshment. I . . . I have something I must say to him in private.'

'Absinthe . . . The singers, they—'
'Marie, *please*! I . . . I must insist.'

As the wind embraced the place de l'Horloge, Kohler stood still. Tiny blue lights would wink and duck and run but stop. Dark silhouettes would fight. Angry shouts would be tossed into the frigid air to be ripped away.

The citizens of Avignon were fighting over the branches that had been torn from their beloved plane trees. One man had a handsaw which he brandished when approached. 'Back off! I'm warning you!' he screamed.

'Hey, I only want to find the cinema, *L'Odyssée de la grande illusion*.'

'*Idiot!* Who has time for that?'

'Couldn't you just tell me?'

'That way. Downwind. The far end of the *place*.'

'*Merci.*'

'Who asked you to be polite? *Piss off!*'

The fuel hunters were freezing at home and he couldn't blame them for not being happy about it. People burned everything they could these days. Sawdust was like gold. Libraries were sacrificed to the papier-mâché balls everyone made and dried. Tarmac, that was found loose and not so loose around the potholes of *les routes nationales*, was torn up, bagged and carted off in the dead of night. Furniture: chairs, tables, the bookshelves that were no longer needed.

When he reached the Kommandantur and Hôtel de ville, the sounds of madly flapping canvas tarpaulins all but drowned out those of the diesel engines that told him four Fiat lorries had just come in. Von Mahler's tourer was in front of them. Had the *ratissage* been successful? Had they bagged their quota of *maquisards*?

The troops were huddled inside their lorries, von Mahler's driver was scraping frost from the windscreen. 'Kohler, Gestapo Paris-Central, my friend. How did it go?'

'*Go?*' shouted the driver. 'The boy wasn't with them but the tip was good. Four of the bastards. Run . . . *mein Gott* but they ran.

Here, there, like rabbits. All dead. One screamed at us that the boy had got away, but that one died before we could question him further.'

'What boy?'

'Dédou Favre. The Kommandant insists Favre must have killed the girl.'

'But . . . but the boy was taken well before dawn on Monday. Two days ago.'

'*Taken?* Are you crazy? Hey, *mein lieber Schweinebulle*, we've been out in the fucking hills hunting that son of a bitch!'

'What tip?'

'The préfet's *Spitzel*, who else?'

De Passe's informer. Xavier . . . The reward had been paid. Then had it been the torture of the coal shovel for Dédou, wondered Kohler. Through broken lips and shattered teeth, had he coughed up the whereabouts of his friends? He must have, but de Passe had failed to let the Kommandant know of the arrest and interrogation.

'Where . . . where were you today?' The news had unsettled the detective.

'In the hills of the Montagnette, well to the south of a monastery.'

'The one at Saint-Michel-de-Frigolet?'

'*Ja, ja*, that's the one, but like I said, the boy wasn't with them.'

De Passe must have wanted von Mahler out of the way and had found a good enough reason.

'When you have to hide something, you soon find you have to hide a lot more,' muttered Kohler sadly to himself as he walked off into the night. 'Especially when you've two *Schälingen* who won't leave things alone until they find the truth.' Two irritating pests. 'Two thorns, I think,' he snorted, and wondered where Louis was. 'Christ, we haven't eaten yet, haven't slept! I'm dying for a cigarette, dying for a little warmth.'

L'Odyssée de la grande illusion was just that. Hot, the air was ripe with the smell of farts, boot grease, stale sweat and tobacco smoke. In row after row, seat after seat and up in the balcony, too, the troops sat stolidly mesmerized by the dust storms of

Oklahoma. And wouldn't you know it, the bankers had sent in giant caterpillar tractors to flatten some poor sharecropper's house!

The Great Depression of the 1930s. Every last one of these boys had memories of it, himself as well. Every one of them had been raised on the dream of *Wie Gott im Frankreich*, to live like God in France where the food was always so good and plentiful. There were tears. Cigarettes had been forgotten, yet few of the eight hundred or so could understand a word of English. And all around them in the smoke-filled dusk, bas-reliefs of warring Roman foot soldiers led captured slaves to the lions or dragged away half-naked females, while high above everything, cove lights threw a pale glow towards a sun that was at full eclipse, since the show was on.

'Monsieur?'

'Oh, sorry. Maître Simondi. I've come to see him.'

'Is he expecting you?' asked the usherette.

'Sort of, I think.'

The boys didn't pay any attention to her tightly fitted blouse and skirt, nor did they to any of the others, so mesmerized were they. Sitting among the men were a few of the grey mice, the Blitzmädels from home who had rushed to help their Führer in his hour of need. One had her tunic open and sweater and throat supporter up, but her breasts and lips had been forgotten. A few others among the men were just as forgetful. When presented with the dust storms of Oklahoma and life in the United States of America, nothing else seemed to matter.

'The lobby and the stairs,' said the usherette. 'César's office is next to the projectionist's booth, his flat is just down the hall.'

'You sure know the way, don't you?' quipped Kohler.

Her smile must be soft even though there was a terrible scar on his cheek and, when seen under the light from the projector, he was formidable. 'César is in a meeting with Monsieur Renaud.'

'*Bon*. That's exactly what I want, but do you know something? My partner would really like to see this film.'

'Then you must ask César, who is the giver of all things.'

*

'Inspector, I hardly know where to begin,' said Frau von Mahler. 'César . . . his grandiose schemes, his friends and business associates. The consortium they never mention but to themselves. Oh *bien sûr* my husband is certain Alain de Passe is one of them. So, too, is Albert Renaud, the writer of mortgage agreements which suit only the buyer. Themselves! Derelict monasteries, *maisons de maître*, *hôtels particuliers*, the *livrées* that were built in the fourteenth century in Villeneuve-les-Avignon by the cardinals – César has a magnificent one. It's where he keeps that wife of his. She seldom leaves the house, is nearly always "not well", but spins a web of her own, we're certain.'

Frau von Mahler paused but couldn't let discretion interfere. 'Farms, *théâtres*, *cinémas*, *châteaux*, even a gambling casino in Nice, and all of it legally bought for next to nothing and yet still on a shoestring the bishop tugs since he, too, is among them. They're very powerful and they secretly rejoice in the power they hold over others. Of course it's all very self-righteous, but what one does for the good of another is done for the good of all.'

A cover-up, then, was that what she was trying to say? 'And this other girl?' hazarded St-Cyr.

Adrienne de Langlade. 'Even though greatly distressed by her death, my husband insisted the matter be left up to the French. Kurt claimed it was an internal affair and he'd no right to interfere. My husband believes in letting well enough alone, Inspector. It makes life easier for him. Adrienne was the protégée César desperately wanted the others to accept. Everyone knew this, herself especially, I suspect. He has the eye and ear for them, hasn't he? Young and tractable. Cultured, well-educated and well-bred, a marvellous voice . . . a truly gifted girl with a beautiful body. In many regards, the equal of Mireille who would never have agreed to be tractable and thus could never be accepted because hers would have been the one voice of dissent in an otherwise sweet harmony. But then Adrienne de Langlade went away to Paris, it was said, to see her family.'

'Who said she had done so?'

'Who indeed? These things are simply said in Avignon and then passed around so much that no one knows who first said them. Haven't you sensed it too? The secrecy. The feeling that things are about to happen and yet you have no control over them. You try to appease wherever possible but these people are far more powerful than you. They're so set in their ways, in their judgement, nothing you can do or say will ever have the slightest effect. And please let's not forget that the Occupier couldn't occupy without their help and sanction.'

Again she paused. 'Forgive me,' she said. 'I . . . I let my feelings show. Adrienne . . . you were saying?'

'She was drowned between two and three weeks before her body was recovered.'

'In an *accabussade*? As punishment for what, please? For refusing to have sex with someone? César . . . was it César? He possesses Christiane Bissert and Genèvieve Ravier, holds the lives of them and the other singers in his hands at all times. Kurt is certain of it, but . . .' She shrugged. 'It's a French matter, *n'est-ce pas*? *Les culs des jeunes filles sont à elles.*'

The asses of young girls are their own. 'We don't know yet how she came to drown.'

'But Mireille felt it had been done in the old way, didn't she?'

'This, also, we really don't know yet.'

'Bishop Rivaille thought very highly of Adrienne, Inspector. To him she was perfection, and her hair exactly the shade and texture of Christ's Mother. Still a virgin, too. He was positive of this and who's to say, since no coroner was ever allowed to examine her corpse.'

When he didn't respond but only waited for more, she said, 'Mireille was going to confront the judges with hiding the truth about the girl's death. I'm sure of it now.'

The woman watched him with an intensity that demanded utter honesty. 'I really don't know that yet, but I think it too.'

'Then you had best have this, hadn't you?'

Frau von Mahler dug a hand into the remnants and, finding what she wanted, took it out. 'The Cross of Lorraine,' she said, looking at a small enamelled brooch in the palm of her withered hand. 'The symbol of the Resistance. I . . . I found this under the lapel of Mireille's overcoat about two weeks after Adrienne's body had come to light. Mireille and the singers had only just returned from their tour to learn what had happened. I removed it, of course. Perhaps she came to believe I had taken it. No doubt she searched everywhere and worried desperately, for that, too, was in her nature. But I never told her what I'd done, nor have I told my husband. That death hardened her attitude, Inspector, and firmed her resolve.'

Was there more to it, then, he wondered, and tucked the pin out of sight. 'Dédou Favre was to have met her well before dawn on Monday but failed to show up, or so we've been told. She sent Thérèse Godard to the *mas* of Madame de Sinéty with a note for him.'

'And even now, at this hour, my husband hasn't returned from searching the countryside for Dédou. Another tip of the préfet's he couldn't refuse to act upon. Tell me something, Inspector. Will we lose the war? Please, you can speak freely. Although it's forbidden, I listen to the BBC news broadcasts, to those of the Free French in Britain and to both wavebands of the Voice of America.'

'And what do you think, madame?'

How cautious of him. 'It was I who asked you.'

She was begging him. Hermann and he needed desperately to gain her confidence if they were ever to solve this thing, but Hermann wasn't here to preach caution.

The Inspector cited Napoleon's defeat in Russia and then said, 'Stalingrad.'

The whole of the Sixth Army had been lost there, over 150,000 men had been taken prisoner to say nothing of the almost equal number who had perished or been terribly wounded. 'And the Allies, now that the Americans have joined them?' she asked.

'Will invade when they judge it best. The Côte d'Azur or the toe of the boot.'

The truth, then, and no lies from him. 'I . . . I couldn't face being a refugee. Everyone would see me.'

'How did you acquire that pistol?'

'I've ways.'

He had to reach out to her with a comforting thought. 'Please believe that before it's too late, your husband will see that you and the children are safely returned to your family.'

'To Köln? Ah! It's true our girls were fortunately with my parents at their estate when this . . . this happened to me. But they will have everything taken from them if the Russians are the first to enter what is left of the city. And if I was to be with my parents by then, I would have to face the Communists too. My skin . . . I . . . I can't be touched, not yet. You do understand?'

Rape . . . they'll rape the women. The *Propagandastaffel* had certainly done their work in the Reich.

When he nodded grimly to indicate he understood, she bowed her head and said, 'My husband was very fond of Mireille. He enjoyed seeing her with our two little girls. A wife notices such things, Inspector. I had planned to leave him with her. It would have taken a little time for them to have grown together, but my Kurt desperately needs someone like her. So, you see, that little pin she so foolishly and bravely wore was a very great worry to me, as was Dédou Favre.'

'Frau von Mahler . . .'

'Madame, please.'

'Madame, what are you trying to tell me?'

'She came to see me at about five o'clock on Monday afternoon, after having endured hours of practice with the other singers at the Villa Marenzio. She was very worried and upset – harried, and not herself at all.'

'And?' he asked.

He could be so gentle, this detective, so sincere, but would he really understand? 'You must have seen that my music stand lies broken. When that happened, Mireille burst into tears. She was exhausted. They had hammered at her incessantly all through practice. To the singers she was never right, always wrong – terrible, awful. She had been up night after night preparing for that damned audition. I insisted she confide in me. They didn't want her joining them. She was certain of it. "They don't want me with them," she said. "I know they don't."'

'And?' he asked again. How cautious of him.

'Dédou was to have been with her at the Palais. He was to have waited, hidden from those who were to judge her, but as you've said, he failed to show up.'

It was coming now, and to give him credit, the Chief Inspector had some inkling of it, for he again waited for her to continue. 'Dédou didn't want her joining the group, Inspector. He was very possessive of her, very jealous . . . but also there was this other business of his belonging to the Resistance, the "terrorists". To them she must have presented a grave and constant danger that could not have been overlooked any more and would have to be dealt with. His comrades, his chief, would have insisted. A collaborator, a friend of the *Boches*? Had he not agreed to do something about it, they would have banished him. You know it as well as I.'

The boy had killed her – was this what the woman believed? 'At dinner that evening, madame, you made what for you must have been an extreme sacrifice. You dined with Maître Simondi, Bishop Rivaille and your husband.'

'I wanted Kurt to be that third judge in case Dédou should show up. I was afraid Préfet de Passe might have planned to take the boy. With Kurt there, things would go easier for the couple, but my husband refused to do what the husk of his wife begged. Oh *bien sûr* he had his reasons. Perhaps he felt he shouldn't interfere any more. Berlin . . . who knows what ears Berlin have or what they will think? I knew Mireille was very afraid and not just of their decision – ah no, that was nothing new, really. She had failed many times before, but this other matter was something else. What I didn't know at the time.'

'Her intention to accuse them of the murder of Adrienne de Langlade or of its cover-up.'

'To her it must have been a repetition of what had happened six hundred years ago. That's why she dressed the way she did. I'm certain of it. The unmitigated arrogance of those – the Church especially – who, for whatever reason, would take the law into their own hands. But how could she possibly have known who did it?'

'We don't know yet. My partner may have something. I . . .' He shrugged.

'Bishop Rivaille suggested they ask Monsieur Renaud to be the third judge, and a call was put through to his house but . . .'

'But what, madame?'

'But I was certain César had anticipated my husband's refusal and had already taken steps to fill that post.'

'With Madame Simondi?'

How quick to suspicion the Inspector was. 'He said nothing of it. Monsieur Renaud agreed to be there. The time was given, and still César said nothing of that wife of his. I worried. The woman would have been drunk – "not well", as César is so fond of saying, but if not drunk, what then, I asked myself. Kurt had to return to the Kommandantur. He often works late. The telexes and coded messages from Berlin, from General Niehoff in Lyon. I—'

'A moment, please,' interjected St-Cyr. 'This Madame Simondi . . . why were you so concerned about her being there?'

'*Why?* She knew Adrienne well, knew that girl inside out, I think, for she forced her to visit with her constantly. Paris . . . always they talked of Paris, but secretly Marceline Simondi is a very jealous, very conniving woman, or so I'm given to understand, and César . . . César was entranced with the girl. He wanted her, Inspector.'

The *marmite perpétuelle,* the constant soup that simmers on the backs of all stoves in the provinces, was getting thicker.

'She knew Mireille, too, Inspector – of course she did – and had presented her with little gifts in payment for work done. Gifts Mireille swore she couldn't bring herself to touch, so repugnant did she find the woman. You see, Marceline eggs the singers on. Mischief . . . wild parties. She insists they do her bidding or face dismissal and they, in turn, are afraid of her.'

'You forced yourself to go to the Palais.'

'I felt I had to.'

The *salon* of César Simondi's *pied-à-terre* was like the sun seen at its setting beyond the dust storms of Oklahoma. It was fiery red in plush, velvety carpets and armchairs with footstools where triflings of gilding flamed to long vertical shafts of saffron yellow on the walls beyond them. Gold was everywhere in draperies and hangings that rose to an expansively timbered, carved ceiling and let the night come down with visions of loveliness. Forest nymphs playing lutes, flutes and recorders. Satyrs leering at mischief among the undergrowth while a well-hung Bacchus bathed with several voluptuous things in a secreted pool and lifted a delighted young creature out of the water by the hips.

There were marble statues, bronze busts, amphorae . . . islands of privacy among the furnishings. And oh *mein Gott*, what a place, breathed Kohler as the usherette, her shoes left at the door, finally brought them to a halt.

'César . . .' she hazarded, for the two men had been caught closeted over their wine glasses and papers. 'César, forgive me, please, but I have had to bring you a visitor who would not take no for an answer.'

'*Figlio di puttana!*' Son of a bitch! '*Ispettore,*' boomed Simondi. 'What a pleasant surprise. *Buona sera, amico mio.* You are just the man we want to see.

'*Merda*, Renée. *Proprio a me dovevi fare questo?*' Did you have to do this to me? 'Bring another glass and quickly, eh? Then leave us. Vanish. *É finito per te*, do you understand? *Finito!*' It's finished for you. Finished! 'We must let the Inspector taste the milk of Provence.

'*Entrate, prego, Ispettore.* Come in, please. Alberto . . .' He indicated his companion. 'You know of Avignon's premier *notaire public*? You don't? Ah, how can this be? Alberto, this is the Detective Inspector Hermann Kohler from Munich first, Berlin second, and Paris at present and for the past two and a half years. A man who lives with two exquisitely beautiful women, I am told.'

Simondi settled back to hook a thumb into the left armhole of the soft cream waistcoat he wore. The black suit jacket was open, the white dress shirt had been freshly laundered. The polka-dot bow tie was of another age, one of refinement, culture and the *belle époque*, if one cut out the swearing. A throwback, wondered Kohler. A showman certainly. A man in his mid-fifties. Shrewd, tough, ambitious, a schemer and dreamer, a manipulator, the look Simondi gave him was one of penetrating assessment. The face was wide and strong, the brow high. A cigarette, forbidden to his singers, held a good centimetre of forgotten ash. The lips were wide, the moustache dark brown and bushy, the nose Roman and pronounced, the greeny-brown eyes swift to sense trouble, the hair well-groomed, unparted, pomaded and without a wave.

'Herr Kohler, before you jump to conclusions, let me say how upset we both are at the loss of our beloved Mireille. Frankly, I don't know how I'm to replace her. She took care of everything. A brilliant girl, so talented, so conscientious.' He clenched a raised fist. 'A tower of strength. You know, of course, that costume is half of great theatre; *la voce, la musica*, it's equal.'

'A few small questions, Maître. Nothing difficult.'

It was the line Paris had said would begin each interview. 'Ah! Renée, how thoughtful of you. A glass of the Châteauneuf-du-Pape, Inspector, the 1940. Still in the barrel where it will stay, God willing, for at least another four years before bottling.'

While the girl, nearly in tears now, poured, Simondi's gaze never left her nor did the tenor of his mute condemnation alter. Albert Renaud was far more the professorial-looking type. A grey-haired, pipe-smoking man in a rumpled beige tweed suit of the early 1930s, a green plaid tie, wire-rimmed spectacles, dark blue eyes and with the perpetual expression of having just delivered a profound question or answer.

The hair was silky and thinning rapidly, the brow deeply furrowed, the moustache full, the mouth small. 'The wine is from the Clos du Clément Sixth, Inspector,' he said, as if this Kripo should know how important that was.

'It's on its way to surpassing the 1934 and the 1926,' acknowledged Simondi. 'Renée, *angelo mio*, you're forgiven. Take a little sip and tell us what you think. Ah! *C'est bon, n'est-ce pas? Nettare puro* from the breast of mother nature herself.' He kissed his fingertips.

Pure nectar. Well, maybe, thought Kohler. The girl said what was expected of her and was allowed to leave without a farewell glance from her boss.

'I trust her judgement,' confided Simondi with a flick of his cigarette to clear it of ash.

A jade green, velvet-covered double sofa was flanked by Carrara marble damsels that held gilded candelabra above their heads. Home turf, was it? wondered Kohler. The cushions were plump and soft, and when he sat down in the sofa, he sank deeply into it.

'This terrible murder. Please tell us how the investigation is progressing. Spare nothing. Alberto and myself are here to help.'

Like vultures over carrion, was that it, eh, snorted Kohler to himself as he took out his little black notebook and flipped it open to a blank page they couldn't get a look at. 'Let's see what we've got. Three judges. The two of you and Bishop Rivaille. Time: ten p.m. Location: the Grand Tinel and one young lady singing her heart out from the far end of an otherwise empty hall.'

He let them think about this, then said, 'One dog that answers to the name of Nino but is a beagle bitch that wanders and brings home little treasures she finds so that her friends, male and female, can share the joy of them. A girl's tennis shoe . . . The jade green heel from a pair of expensive dress shoes that were bought in Paris, I think.'

'*Ispettore* . . .'

'Got your attention, have I? I want the truth, Maître. The wine's okay, by the way. A bit heavy, but of a nice deep colour. Maybe it suffers from being too inexperienced. *Ja, meine lieben Herren*, it's like a young virgin. Slow to develop, but given the fullness of time, will come into its own.'

They waited. Simondi had returned to surveying him with that thumb of his still hooked into his waistcoat. Renaud was calm.

'I take it those are the deeds to the vineyard?' said Kohler.

'And the mortgages,' offered Renaud eagerly. 'Bishop Rivaille has always expressed an interest . . .'

'A passion, Alberto.'

'A passion, yes, for returning the Mother Church to her former glory in Avignon. We try to assist in whatever ways we can.'

'The vineyards lie on land that is immediately below the ruins

162

of the papal summer palace, Inspector,' said Simondi, taking up the unlabelled bottle to refill Kohler's glass. 'Keep the memory of this with you while I get us a bottle of the 1926. It's no trouble. Alberto and I were about to share one anyway.'

'Forget the wine. Suppose you start by telling me why Salvatore Biron, the concierge, wasn't told of the audition.'

'But he was! I'm certain of it,' exclaimed Simondi. 'Didn't Bishop Rivaille tell you this?'

'Biron claims he didn't know there was to be one.'

'Then he lies for reasons of his own. Strike only for the truth, Inspector, as you've stated yourself.'

Again, Simondi, adopting the same pose, settled back to study him.

'Salvatore loves the cinema,' offered Renaud apologetically. 'César is too kind. It's not the first time our *grand mutilé* has lied, nor is it the first time he has been absent from his duties. When I couldn't find him, I simply drew the black-out curtains myself and set up the chairs.'

'I found the candles,' said Simondi. 'The bishop and I lighted and placed them about the hall. The girl entered. She was obviously extremely nervous. I asked her if she wished to put off the audition until another time.'

'You begged her to do so, César. I heard you. Why not say it?'

'*Scusate, Ispettore*. Forgive me. Yes, I was, I must tell you, uneasy. Mireille . . . Ah! She had the voice, the manner, the bearing. Her costume was perfect.'

'Perfect!' said Renaud softly. 'Magnificent!'

'Evocative. The past personified in every detail, yet I knew in my heart, Inspector, things would not go well for her.'

'Who else was present?'

'Only the three of us and herself. Why, please, do you ask?'

'What about the singers?'

'Them? Most certainly not. Each understands totally that such an interference would lose them their position. When one does what I do, Inspector, one has to insist on absolute obedience. A commitment that is total. Auditions are always private and, as much as possible, held in confidence.'

'It was too close to curfew in any case, Inspector,' said Renaud. 'None of them would have had *laissez-passers*.'

'What about Brother Matthieu?'

'That one?' exclaimed Renaud. 'Ah no, Inspector. By that time of night, our *gueule cassée* would have been alone in his cell with his God and his thoughts.'

'He has a small problem, Inspector,' confessed Simondi, reaching for his glass. 'It's harmless, I assure you. When one has suffered so much, others must make allowances, isn't that so?'

'What problem?'

They looked at each other. 'A fondness for hair,' said Renaud.

'A girl's hair?'

'And her breasts, but only to look at, never to touch,' conceded Simondi. 'Photographs, I believe.'

'Entirely innocent,' interjected Renaud with a nod.

'And you're certain no one else was present?'

'No one,' said Simondi.

'Then that has to mean one of you killed her.'

'*Ispettore* . . .'

'No, you listen, *amico mio*. Find paper and pen and each of you set out exactly what you did and where you were between dinner and after the murder was discovered and you were "notified". My partner will expect me to get this from you both. He's the boss. Sign and date it too.'

'*Merda!* Can't this wait, *Ispettore*? My wife is the one I think you should question. Earlier on Monday I asked her to join us as the third judge but later understood her to be unwell and called upon Alberto here. But she . . . she may mistakenly have gone to the Palais at the last minute.'

'There *was* someone else,' said Renaud. 'César, I was certain of it and still am. You see, the chairs are hidden out of the way, Inspector. When I went to get them I felt strongly that someone was there, but when I shone my light around the stairwell, there was no one.'

'Didn't the three of you lock the main door behind you?'

'I'm sure Henri-Baptiste did, Inspector. We went in together using his key,' said Renaud.

'Before or after Mademoiselle de Sinéty?'

'Why, before her, of course. She had my key,' said Simondi.

'Then it was Mireille who, in her agitation, César, must have left the door unlocked.'

'I'll get us the 1926, Inspector. *Scusatemi un momento.* Alberto, find him a cigarette, or perhaps he would prefer one of my cigars.'

And *il profumo del successo*? wondered Kohler. The sweet smell of success. One targeted wife, was that it, eh, and one distracted, baffled detective? 'You do that. A *marc*, though. Wine always seems to give me gas even when one's hosts have just bought a six-hundred-year-old vineyard.'

7

The curfew had come down, the city was like a tomb. High above the river and the Palais, the clouds had parted to reveal the sickle of a waning moon.

Kohler drew on his cigarette and hunched his shoulders against the cold as he waited for Louis to join him on the bridge. A Wehrmacht motorcycle courier had come to the cinema with a note calling him away at once. Von Mahler had insisted on the meeting place and hadn't been happy. Louis had gone against the Kommandant's express wishes and had spoken to his wife.

'And now, suddenly, von Mahler doesn't want anyone else to know of it.'

The stars were very bright, the wind had dropped to almost nothing. Mireille de Sinéty hadn't just been murdered. She'd been savagely silenced. But had there been something else? Had that savagery been used to set an example to others? Had the *Cagoule* done it?

And what of Adrienne de Langlade? Xavier had been accused of raping her. He had known of the girl's drowning, had removed a thick twist of hair from her corpse and kept it.

'To blackmail Brother Matthieu?' he asked. Every cop who was worth his salt knew that schoolboys often garnered pocket money by blackmailing illicit lovers, homosexuals and perverts. Some of the little buggers had paid dearly for it.

'Xavier, what the hell did you do to Nino? Did you take her up river to where she had come upon that girl's clothing and had led you to her corpse? Did you kill that hound?'

Only the sound of the river came to him, roiling softly. When the blue cat's-eyes of the Colonel's tourer slowly approached, he asked, 'And you, *mein lieber Kamerad*? What of you?'

Von Mahler gripped the steering wheel. Louis sat beside him. Kohler got quickly into the back.

'Gentlemen, this meeting never took place. Neither of you has at any time spoken to my wife, nor had any verbal or written communication from her. Is that understood?'

'But she was at the Palais on the night of the murder,' objected Louis.

Verdammt, would they not listen? 'She wasn't. She never leaves the house and everyone knows this. Psychologically she is incapable of doing so.'

'But—'

'No buts. Berlin still have deep reservations about your loyalties. Gestapo Boemelburg made a point of telling me this. If you want it verbatim, he said he'd be very glad to be rid of you both.'

It was Louis who asked if the *Cagoule* had been mentioned. Kohler snorted and said, '*Idiot*, of course it was! What better way of taking care of a problem than feeding it to assassins?'

No cigarettes could be allowed lest the smell of the smoke cling to him. Von Mahler regretted this, for shared tobacco was often a facilitator. 'Officially I must tolerate and even be seen to get along with de Passe, Rivaille and Renaud – Simondi, too, for that matter and the games they play, their constant acquisitions. The existing power structures are so useful to us. Without them, how could we possibly maintain control?'

'*La Cagoule*, then, Colonel?' asked Louis, a reminder.

'I have no proof and officially must look the other way.'

'And did you do that with Adrienne de Langlade's death?' asked Kohler.

'I had no other choice but to leave the matter in de Passe's hands. Privately I felt, and still do, that the girl met an unfortunate end. At the least, Simondi and the others know what happened to her; at the most, they were responsible.'

It was Hermann who rolled down a side window to bring in a breath of fresh air.

'Gentlemen, I should have seen that Mireille was putting herself in grave danger. Officially I told myself it was a French matter; privately I knew from talking to my wife and to the girl that things were far from right.'

'And with Dédou Favre, Colonel?' asked Louis.

In irritation von Mahler pulled off his gloves. 'Officially I stated the boy must be guilty of her murder. Privately I knew he could never have harmed her even if ordered to by his *maquis* chief. I wanted to talk to Dédou, to reason with him. Do you think Kommandants have the time to comb the hills for *Banditen*? That is always left to others. But I didn't and *don't* want him killed. You see, he alone must know what Mireille had planned to say to those who judged her.'

'The killing of Adrienne,' said Louis.

'But was there something else?' hazarded von Mahler. 'Was there something the terrorists needed that only the establishment and the Church could give in exchange for her silence?'

'Blackmail . . .' managed Kohler. 'Herr Oberst, are you saying she was about to—'

'Call it what you will, but the terrorists are desperate. Many are no more than bandits and live like them, stealing from the peasants and everyone else. Extorting money, clothing, food, cigarettes and drink. They're poorly armed, badly disorganized, ill-trained, lawless most of them, and cowardly. But if allowed sanctuary from the bitterest winter in years? If allowed sleep, full bellies and proper training, what then? As Kommandant I have to look beyond the obvious. As detectives you must do the same in spite of your patriotic leanings, St-Cyr, and your acquired love of the French, Kohler. In short, gentlemen, I want that boy taken alive and kept safely so that I can talk to him. I want the truth, nothing else. And that I will relay to Gestapo Boemelburg if and when you conclude this affair. Have I made myself clear?'

He still hadn't been told that Dédou had been arrested, thought Kohler.

'Well?' demanded von Mahler.

'*Bestimmt*, Herr Oberst. *Bestimmt*,' muttered Louis. Definitely.

*

168

Alone with his partner in the Renault, St-Cyr hunted for words to express what Hermann would know only too well he felt. The threat Boemelburg posed was far deeper than the Kommandant had let on.

In Paris, Gabrielle Arcuri, a chanteuse and the new love of this Sûreté's life, had been a suspect in their last investigation. Now she'd be considered a hostage until the present matter was concluded to suit the Gestapo, the SS and the Führer.

But Bishop Rivaille had said nothing about her. Instead, he had let him know only too clearly that Gestapo Paris-Central looked askance at Hermann's living with a former prostitute and Oona Van der Lynn, a Dutch alien without proper papers. Blackmail again.

Things would have to be absolutely out in the open between them. 'The *Résistance*, Hermann. About two weeks after the flood waters of mid-November released Adrienne de Langlade's body, Frau von Mahler took this from under the lapel of Mireille de Sinéty's overcoat.'

The Cross of Lorraine . . . Abruptly Hermann rolled down his side window to fling the pin into the river.

'*Don't!* Please don't. Not yet.'

'Are you crazy? Boemelburg, Louis. Gestapo Mueller . . . If anyone should find this on us . . .'

'Idiot! That pin is the key to Frau von Mahler. The Colonel unfortunately came upon us just as she was about to tell me who she had seen in the Palais on the night of the murder.'

'He insists she never goes out.'

'Then ask yourself, as I have, how many trips to Paris she has had to make for skin grafts. Berlin is too dangerous, too terrifying – the nightly bombings, *n'est-ce pas*? Ask also how it is she came by a Belgian FN at a price of forty thousand francs if not purchased on the black market in Paris where it would be both safer and easier for her to have acquired such a thing without her husband knowing.'

Everyone knew the troops sold things they shouldn't. 'De Passe took Dédou Favre well before dawn on Monday, Louis, but failed to tell von Mahler.'

'And sent the Kommandant out on a wild-goose chase?'

'Not quite. He bagged four *maquis*.'

'Xavier . . . A traitor. Ah! Why must God do this to France?'

It had been a cry of despair. 'The hundred thousand francs was paid in four nice bundles, two of which have already gone for expenses.'

Kohler told him about the photographs and what must have happened at the 'picnic' early last June. 'That little member of the *pègre* is old enough to want to try it with a girl even if she's out like a light, but did he really do that to her or is it but another of their lies?'

'Absinthe . . . Was he told to do so by Madame Simondi? Apparently she eggs the singers on, Hermann. Frau von Mahler made a point of telling me this and that Mireille de Sinéty found the woman repugnant. The singers do as she asks or face dismissal.'

'And the car is pointed in the right direction, eh? *Verdammt*, I'm tired. I want to go to bed!'

'Then trust me, *mon vieux*. If Simondi's Villa Marenzio is any indication, his house in Villeneuve-les-Avignon should have plenty of room.'

A pedal-pushing *garde champêtre* challenged them, and when asked, led them to the villa. *Il palazzo della mia pastorella divina* (the villa of my divine shepherdess) was on the rue de la République, about halfway between the cemetery and the Fort Saint-André whose ramparts rose above the promontory from which they had commanded the terrain since the latter half of the fourteenth century.

Hermann yanked on the bell.

'Messieurs, madame is asleep and not well,' came a strict female voice from out of the darkness of the foyer.

'It's okay. We're doctors. We've come all the way from Paris just to look after her.'

'Paris? The detectives. You—'

Nobody could close a door on Hermann if he didn't want it to be closed. Nobody. Especially if he had help and was agitated.

*

The four-poster was richly carved. Deep in a cocoon of sleep and wearing nothing but a coverlet rich with antique gold brocade, Christiane Bissert and Geneviève Ravier lay wrapped in each other's arms exactly where they'd fallen.

'Absinthe,' muttered Louis, lifting the bottle from a table.

They didn't stir. The *Primo Soprano*'s blonde hair was laced with dried lavender. The *Alto*'s skin glistened with a fragrant unguent; her jet black curls and long lashes were still damp with perspiration.

'The tapestry,' breathed Hermann, not turning away to look at it. 'A horn player . . .'

'A shawm. It's like an oboe, but with a flared bell.'

Tambourines and tabors joined recorders and citterns in medieval accompaniment among dancing country folk at a wedding. 'The rites of spring,' snorted Kohler. 'So, where is Madame Simondi?' he asked the housekeeper who hadn't stopped glaring at them.

'On . . . on the other side of the stove room. She is . . . is with another of them.'

'Which one?'

'The *Basso Continuo*. They . . . they keep her company from time to time when she demands it or Maître Simondi thinks it is needed.'

'And who demanded it this time?'

'The maître.'

'*Bon!* Louis, find yourself a chair. There isn't room.'

Shoes were prised off, overcoat, fedora, scarf and suit jacket dropped on the floor. The Walther P38 was removed to be tucked under one of the pillows as the coverlet was flung back. 'Sweet dreams, *mon vieux*. I've had it.'

Hermann dragged up the covers and was instantly asleep, warm in his own cocoon.

'My partner always considers he has the right to take over, madame. He's had a hard two days and must be excused,' yawned St-Cyr. 'Please introduce me to Madame Simondi, then find me a distant room whose door is tight when shut. This one snores but refuses to admit it. They will tell him, I'm sure.'

Beneath a life-sized poster of a dancer of a far different sort, Marceline Simondi lay on a divan among scattered cushions and little treasures, next to a headless classical nude that was wrapped in chains.

There was no sign of Marius Spaggiari.

'The baths,' warned the housekeeper. 'He may have fallen asleep. Please, I must go to him at once. Avail yourself . . .' She indicated a deep and shabby *fauteuil* from the thirties. 'Use it. She will not even be aware of your presence and will sleep now until noon if not longer.'

'Cover her.'

'You do it. I must hurry.'

Gaunt, her wiry, raven hair unpinned and all over the place, the former dancer from the Cabaret Pigalle, the Narcisse and the Alhambra had lost her charms. A false eyelash had come loose. The once alluring mouth was slack. The cheeks were pinched as, deep in the recesses of her mind, another nightmare had begun to build.

She frowned. She twitched. Self-inflicted scratches marred the bony buttocks and thighs.

'Were you there at the Palais?' asked St-Cyr, but had to answer, 'How could you have been, since your present state shows every sign of being your usual?' Yet Simondi had made a point of suggesting to Hermann that she might well have mistakenly gone to the Palais on the night of the murder.

A long strand of crimson chorus-girl beads had been broken and she lay among them as if, in her struggle to piece the necklace together, she had fallen into a stupor, her body absolutely numb.

The absinthe drip glass was in two parts. Into its thick-stemmed bottom he poured a jigger, not bothering to measure with the *dosette.*

Into the top, he placed a lump of sugar over the drip hole, then, there being no longer any cracked ice, added water only.

Drop by drop, the deep emerald green of the absinthe became cloudy and he remembered vividly his first sight of this magic and how, as a boy, he had seen *grandmaman* St-Cyr compress her thin lips in anticipation as she silently steeled herself to be patient. 'It is, when taken, like ascending to the gods,' she had said, hardly conscious of him. 'One is free of all cares and casts aside the weight of these frightful garments a widow must constantly wear.'

Apart from the classical nude, the ogive vaults in the ceiling and the tiles of an early Renaissance floor, the room was totally what one would have expected of a Parisian chorus girl who had depended for much of her life on the flea markets of Saint-Ouen.

'Ah! I must correct myself,' he said on examining another of the posters. 'By sheer force of will, and talent, too, you rose to become the *vedette* at the Alhambra.' The top of the bill.

Removing the dripper, he stood with glass in hand looking down at the shell of what had, in the early twenties, been the toast of the rue de Malte and the quartier Folie-Méricourt. Though now in her forties, she looked much older. The legs that would have commanded avid attention, lust, too, were mere sticks. The stomach, whose navel would have drawn the eye for more reasons than a thumb-sized sequin, was wrinkled with excess skin. The breasts whose nipples had once been tassled or bare, were shrunken and withered.

'*À Paris et à votre santé*, madame,' he said, 'and to the far more recent past. For the first time since arriving in Avignon, this humble servant of justice senses that here, at last, we have come upon an element of unquestionable truth.'

Tossing off his drink, he prepared another and then, having downed that, yet another. But was it wise to have done so, he wondered, as she began to dance from the posters.

The water was hot, and as Geneviève eased herself into it, the bath sheath she wore drifted outwards like a slowly settling cloud, its fine white gossamer mingling with the steam. She swam a little, using gentle breaststrokes. Her blonde hair was pinned up, exposing the graceful slenderness of her neck. Always when seeing her like this, a reassurance came to Christiane. 'Your eyes are very clear this morning, *chérie*. Their blue is perfect.'

'Don't worry so much,' said Geneviève, her voice soft beneath floor-to-ceiling frescoes of women bathing with their children during the Babylonian Captivity. Of couples, too, and men and boys and girls. 'Don't do anything foolish. Trust me, *petite*.'

They came together in the centre of the bath, where all around their little ocean the marble of six hundred years ago was grey and wet and variegated. They held one another. Lips brushed those that were nervous. Geneviève's fingers lingered to trap the tears that were falling and to brush them away. 'What are we going to do?' blurted Christiane. 'The detectives will find out everything. They'll destroy what we have. They won't stop. Where will we go; how will we live?'

Hands gripped her by the shoulders and, forcing her under, legs entangled hers until . . . until, arms thrashing, lungs bursting, she was released and rose suddenly to the surface. 'I'm sorry,' she gasped.

'Then understand that what we do must always be done together.'

'We keep silent,' blurted Christiane.

'We know nothing,' said Geneviève.

'The one was drowned, an accident.'

'The other thought she knew things about her.'

'But wouldn't tell us.'

'We were together on the night she died.'

'We were at the Villa Marenzio.'

They swam a little, these two gorgeous creatures with gossamer sheaths clinging to them. Christiane Bissert stood on the lowest step to brush water from her face and clear her eyes. Geneviève Ravier looked up at her. *Primo Soprano* and *Alto*.

The black-haired one brushed water from her breasts and flicked it at her friend.

They laughed now, and the sound of this echoed musically.

When they began to soap each other as they stood on the steps Kohler hated to disturb them but, what the hell, he needed a bath. Louis should have been with him to enjoy the scenery, but the Sûreté had still been snoring on the floor of Madame Simondi's room with tumbled glass next to hand and had only himself to blame.

174

Unaware of the visitor, Christiane asked, 'Where's Marius?' of Geneviève who smiled and touched the tip of the girl's nose with the soap, then said, 'In César's little cinema where he went last night after we were finished with her.'

'A duty done,' confessed the *Alto*.

'As it always must be.'

'If we are to continue.'

'As we have.'

'Secure.'

'And warm.'

'Content.'

'Our voices chasing one another's.'

'Throughout the song.'

'The madrigal.'

The film had long since wound itself on to the take-up reel. The screen was blank, the projector beam focused down the length of the corridor between flanking suits of armour.

Shields, swords, pikes and lances lined the walls right up to a second-storey vaulted, ogived, ornamented gallery. There were helmets, too, and in the silence of the corridor, the muted clicks the projector made were constant.

Wrapped in slumber and in the colours of Avignon's Papal Guard, Marius Spaggiari was slumped into a folding Renaissance armchair. His mouth was open, his legs were too. The stone-sculptor-like chest, groin and thighs were dark and hairy, the flaccid penis was uncircumsized.

Both glass and bottle lay on their sides on the chequered, black-and-white tiles of the floor.

Simondi had written the name of the film in Italian on the canister. *L'informatore*, The Informer.

'An American film,' softly mused St-Cyr, dredging it up from prewar memories. 'The Irish Troubles well before the partition, a truly diabolic tale of betrayal. If I remember it correctly, the informant gave away a boy who was then arrested by the British and made to talk.'

But why had the film been on the projector? Spaggiari would

have been far too inebriated to have fed its leader through the sprocket. Simondi must have had it out earlier.

When he switched off the machine, the *Basso Continuo* instantly awoke but immediately stilled himself in alarm. 'Inspector . . .'

There was only one way to get the truth and that was to put the run on him. 'Where were you on Monday night between the hours of eight and midnight?'

'Water . . . I'd better have a little. That stuff is hellishly bitter.'

'So is this Sûreté when perturbed.'

'I was at the Villa Marenzio.'

'And Madame Simondi? Where would she have been?'

'Where else but here? You've seen how she is, haven't you?'

'How often does she get like that?'

'Constantly.'

'But if the supply should run out?'

'Why should it?'

'Please, let's not kid ourselves, monsieur. There may well have been French absinthe in the cellars at one time, but that bottle and the ones I saw in her room were from Spain.'

'Where it's still legal to make it.'

'So, if the supply should temporarily run out?'

'Pastis, then.'

'But it never satisfies, does it?'

'She becomes highly agitated, yes.'

'Unmanageable?'

This one wanted everything. 'She's tied down until the doctor comes to give her a shot of morphia. Inspector, she craves absinthe. Surely, having lived through the days when it was freely available, you must have seen its addicts?'

A nod would suffice. 'The physician, Legrand, stated in his papers that there were two types of *absinthisme*. Those who repeatedly drank to violent excess, and those who constantly tippled. Which is she?'

'What do you think?'

'I'm not here to reveal to you my thoughts, monsieur.'

'The latter, then.'

'How often does Simondi illegally have the supply replenished? Come, come, you had best answer.'

'Often enough.'

'And recently?'

'A shipment came in a week ago.'

'*Bon!* For now that is all I want from you. Please be ready to make yourself available when requested.'

'That's the story of our existence, Inspector. Ours is but to sing at the command of others.'

'And to have sex with her, eh?'

A gigolo . . .

The faint smile on Spaggiari's lips lingered only to fade suddenly under Sûreté scrutiny as St-Cyr said, 'You were told to give her absinthe last night, weren't you?'

Maudit salaud, cursed Spaggiari silently. 'I thought, Inspector, that was just what I said.'

'Then prepare yourself, *mon fin*, for our next interview. Practise the part you must sing but always have the truth on those vocal cords of yours. My partner and I are singing masters of a far different sort from Maître Simondi, yet our ears are equally keen.'

'All our parts must be memorized, Inspector,' said Genèvieve Ravier, coyly laughing at him, for Herr Kohler had come upon them suddenly as they stood on the steps of the bath and had blithely asked if they used sheet music during auditions and concerts. 'Music stands and part-books would only get in the way.'

'I thought as much,' he said, nodding sagely. He seemed oblivious to bath sheaths that hid nothing, and to his own nakedness.

Her fingers were prised open and the soap taken, she to gaze questioningly into faded blue and empty eyes, he – to see what in her, she wondered. Lies, deceit, intrigue and murder . . . Could it be murder?

'Such things as part-books would simply detract from the illusion César wishes to create,' interjected Christiane, coming to the rescue, she standing close . . . so close to him, a girl could not help but notice the scar that crossed his chest. It ran from the right shoulder to the left hip through curly greying hairs. A livid wound and much longer than the one on the left side of his face. A few centimetres lower and it would have deflowered him. A giant. A rawhide whip, César had said. The SS had done it.

'The illusion . . .' he said, she self-consciously averting her gaze from the scar but not daring to meet his eyes, and saying diffidently, 'That of grandeur and of the past.'

'When singing, we are sometimes not positioned together,' interjected Genèvieve, 'but are placed apart and often separated by considerable distances.'

Again he nodded sagely. 'All the more reason, then, for you to have memorized things,' he said, letting his eyes seek out Genèvieve whose gaze was frank and calm . . . so calm, thought Christiane, and said earnestly, her dark eyes meeting his at last, 'It's the way part songs were often sung. A *château*, a villa such as this, a great hall, cathedral or *théâtre de l'opéra*. Only one or two of us will be in front of the audience.'

'Another will be at the back of the hall,' said Genèvieve, not smiling, just looking steadily into those eyes of his. Meeting challenge with challenge. 'Another will be positioned up in a gallery or balcony. Maybe two of us, each to a side or together in the centre, but, again, at the back.'

'Another and another will be placed in far corners, but downstairs,' said Christiane, trembling a little at the look he gave her.

'Our voices constantly move, Inspector,' hastened Genèvieve. 'Note chases note but as each voice sounds, another has already begun.'

The story of our miserable lives on this affair, quipped Kohler to himself.

Christiane hesitantly touched his right arm to get his attention. 'The notes take time to travel,' she said earnestly, 'so you hear them one after another.'

Mein Gott, she was a beautiful creature . . .

'There's counterpoint, the simultaneous singing of two or

more parts.' Genèvieve had touched his left arm. Her fingers lingered.

'Full and half-notes blend,' said Christiane. 'Perfect pitch is required.'

'There's resonance, Inspector. In turn, it produces notes of equal pitch. The pipe of an unplayed organ will resonate suddenly in unison with the note it has been given by one of our voices.'

'Mine, I think,' said Christiane, colouring quickly at the attention Genèvieve was giving him.

'No, mine. A suit of armour or a shield will resonate perfectly in tune with its note. The metal of a cross, a candelabra . . . all such things will do the same.'

'Wash my back, will you?' he said to Christiane, handing her the bar of soap, she to search him out and earnestly say, 'Each object in the hall is capable of picking up the note that suits it and of vibrating at the same pitch.'

His left arm was again hesitantly touched, a reminder Genèvieve gave of her presence. 'Thus each of these objects contributes its echoing note. A fulfilment perhaps.'

A brittleness entered Christiane's voice. 'Hence what you hear are many more sounds than you would normally hear, were we positioned together.'

'Up front, before the audience,' interjected Genèvieve, smiling softly at him. 'Yet all are united. Each voice is totally of its own but dependent on all the others for the life it gives the song.'

Verdammt, but Oona's eyes were just as blue as this one's and she was every bit as tall and beautiful and wouldn't like it one damned bit if she knew he was here alone with them. Giselle neither. 'And totally dependent on the singing master's benevolence,' he said flatly.

'Of course,' confessed Genèvieve.

Christiane began to use the soap on his back but suddenly leaned over to put a cheek next to his, she standing on tiptoes on the edge of the bath. 'Unlike the present day, harmonic systems and chords were not available to medieval composers. Everything had to be built upwards from the *Basso Continuo*.'

'The thorough or continuous bass, Inspector,' acknowledged

Geneviève. 'Very few keys were used and yet . . . and yet such a richness was obtained. It's a totally different way of composing music.'

'And very exciting,' said Christiane, now soaping his neck and leaning over him to do his chest.

'We have not only to *think* as the medievals did, but in some ways to live like them, Inspector. We learn to play their games and to sing their songs.'

And I'm way past my depth, aren't I, thought Kohler ruefully. Louis . . . where the hell was Louis? 'Okay, then let's start with you both and with Brother Matthieu and his postcards.'

The centuries withdrew into themselves in the cellars, thought St-Cyr. Under vaulted ceilings that were low and dank, the refuse of the ages had been left as if forgotten. Crates, old leather trunks, bits of heavy furniture, porcelains and pewter . . . He passed the beam of his torch over them.

Crumbled plaster broke underfoot. Bare limestone was exposed. Mould was everywhere; frost too. Medieval iron rings, black iron hooks and sconces protruded. Water had seeped up through the floor to form sheets of *verglas*, black ice that was often unseen until too late. There were locks upon locks and when, finally, he had found what he was after, racks and racks of wine bottles, some so old the fingers trembled when mould and cobweb were brushed from stained labels.

There were cases, too, *Pernod et fils* having built a distillery at Tarragona in Spain when the production of absinthe had been banned in France on 16 March 1915. Banned not just because it had erroneously been blamed for having caused the drastic drop in the birthrate before and into the Great War, but because, beyond initial feelings of exaltation and abandon, it had excited the central nervous system in ways little understood. Violently antisocial behaviour in the bars and cafés had often culminated in knife fights – its addicts often succumbing to spasmodic fits of delirium, of which, when sober, they had no recollection.

Numbness and passivity had affected other addicts, often

masking a mind tortured by violent hallucinations and delusions. Ringing in the ears – the disease of Van Gogh – had been another side effect, as had feelings of constant anxiety and unquenchable thirst.

'A hundred and thirty-six proof,' he said tartly to himself, examining a bottle upon which there was neither dust nor cobweb. 'Sixty-eight per cent alcohol.'

In this most recent shipment, there were ten wooden cases, 120 bottles, each of a litre. Four bottles had been taken upstairs last night. At least two of those, he knew, had been consumed.

Jammed on to a rusty iron spike that dangerously protruded from the end of a nearby wine rack were bills of lading, all of them written in Spanish no French customs clerk, unless paid off, would ever have seen.

The earliest of the bills dated from 11 June 1941. To enter the country, the shipments would have to cross the *zone interdite*, the Forbidden Zone that extended along all frontiers and seacoasts and inland for a good twenty kilometres. And that meant, of course, with the willing cooperation of the Occupier. A bribe paid, a nod given.

Cast aside, but often gone through in a feverish search for dregs, were empties from Pernod's factory at Montfavet. *L'Extrait d'absinthe*. '1892 . . .' he muttered. Picking up another, '1907 . . .' There were dozens of empties, and several of the labels gave the names of other distilleries in France. Even at the height of its popularity, over 10,000,000 litres a year had been imported from Switzerland alone. The canton of Neufchâtel had been its most important centre of production. But the Swiss had banned absinthe in 1908.

When he looked up, a shadow moved and he suddenly realized he was no longer alone.

They sat on the edge of the bath with legs dangling in the water and the gossamer of their sheaths clinging to them. Kohler could just touch bottom when standing in the middle of the pool facing them, and maybe it really was like it had been back then in 1343 or thereabouts.

181

'Of course we sold photos of our breasts to that shop,' confessed Genèvieve unsmilingly.

'Locks of our hair, too,' offered her playmate.

'Inspector, students always need money. Brother Matthieu and others like him simply stare at the cards and finger the hair in private. What harm is there in our letting them?'

'A kindness, I think,' said Christiane. 'After all, our *gueule cassée* has suffered much and feels deeply that no woman or girl would ever wish to be intimate with him. And he a man of the cloth, we mustn't forget.'

'And Adrienne de Langlade?' asked Kohler, making them both feel uneasy.

'She would never have agreed to such a thing,' said Genèvieve.

'She was too modest,' echoed Christiane.

'But Brother Matthieu wanted a photo of her breasts?'

'Xavier . . .' began the raven-haired one only to be nudged into silence by the blonde who said levelly, 'What she was about to say, Inspector, was that Brother Matthieu had made things very hard for Xavier. Brutally so. Nothing Xavier did was right. The bishop's kennels were never properly cleaned. Night after night we'd find Xavier scrubbing the floors. Control of the hounds when on the hunt was never satisfactory.'

'Nino was always causing trouble, always going off somewhere,' said Christiane earnestly.

'You have to understand how compelling is the desire in Brother Matthieu. But his *fétichisme de cheveux* is never totally satisfying, never complete, *n'est-ce pas*? Not like a man with a woman,' said Genèvieve.

'We would see him averting his gaze every time she entered a room, Inspector. We knew what he desired.'

'He trembled in her presence.'

'He sweated.'

'Inspector, Brother Matthieu put the squeeze on Xavier so hard, we . . . we had to do something,' confessed the blonde.

'Xavier was losing his voice, wasn't he?' asked Kohler.

'Yes, and this was causing trouble enough so we . . . we did what we felt had to be done,' offered the *Alto*, lowering her eyes.

'The picnic in early June.'

'She never knew about the photos. I swear it,' blurted Christiane.

'But she sure as hell discovered she was pregnant, didn't she?'

Herr Kohler wanted them to say Xavier wasn't the only one who had used her, thought Geneviève, nor was that the only time they had got her drunk on absinthe. He wanted to say, How could you have done that to her? But he didn't say any of these things because he was thinking of something else.

'I'm puzzled,' he said. 'You see, you madrigalists do everything as one. You follow orders, too. You have to, right? How else could that *Basso Continuo* of yours and his two pals have avoided the forced labour draft?'

The STO, the *Service de Travail Obligatoire*, a constant threat . . .

Herr Kohler swam up to them, his big, strong arms moving water back and forth to keep him in position. 'Who suggested the picnic?' he asked. 'Was it Madame Simondi?'

When they didn't answer, he said, 'I think you'd better tell me.'

'Before it is too late for us?' blurted Christiane, her dark eyes rapidly moistening.

'I suggested the picnic, Inspector,' said Geneviève levelly. 'Guy had always wanted to see the *mas* César had leased to Mireille's mother. It was a chance, then, for him to do so.'

'But you'd seen it before, hadn't you?'

'Yes.'

'You'd gone out there to see if it would be suitable.'

'*No!* How can you think such a thing? I . . .'

'We . . . we rode out on our bicycles just after Easter, Inspector,' said Christiane, not looking at him but steadily at her friend. 'Mireille was with us. We had a lovely day because when . . . when one was with Mireille, one always shared her love of Provence, of its great beauty and . . . and history.'

'Did she know you would take Adrienne there for a "picnic"?'

The *Alto* bowed her head and, subdued, answered, 'She . . . she thought it a good idea.'

'She trusted you both, didn't she?'

'Yes.'

'She wanted to join us as a full member herself,' said Genèvieve, 'but knew that Adrienne had the better chance.'

'She accepted this,' said Christiane, still not looking up at him. 'Mireille was goodness itself, Inspector. Dedicated always to our success. Praising it, too. Always.'

He began to mount the steps, and when he had stopped on the third one, he was nearest to Christiane, and Genèvieve told herself she knew what he was about to do. He would single Christiane out now, demanding answers only from her.

Be careful, *petite*, she said silently. He cares passionately about those answers and is not distracted in the slightest by our nakedness.

'Tell me about Dédou Favre,' he said and, as she had thought, held a hand up to silence her.

'Dédou must have seen us at the picnic,' confessed Christiane stupidly. 'That . . . that is the only way Mireille could possibly have found out about the . . . the postcards and . . . and Brother Matthieu's little affliction.'

'Then Dédou knew, didn't he, *ma belle*, exactly who had raped Adrienne and, yes, how many of them had gone at her?'

She tried to blink away her tears but they wouldn't stop. 'It was only Xavier, I swear it!' she shrilled. 'We . . . we were all up in the house except . . . except for him.'

'And drunk.'

'Drunk, yes.'

'On absinthe.'

'Yes, damn you! Like last night. Last night . . .' She gripped her mouth.

'Dédou was arrested well before dawn on Monday, wasn't he?'

'Inspector . . .'

'Shut up! Speak only when spoken to.'

Water was trickling slowly down his legs through the hairs. There were other scars, old scars, wounds from shrapnel; from bullets too. 'Xavier said that if it wasn't done, Dédou and Mireille would confront Bishop Rivaille with the matter. The Kommandant might be there – this we didn't know at the time. You must believe me.'

'The audition . . .'

'Yes.'

'So you all agreed to let Xavier turn Dédou in?'

'We are one, Inspector. *One* because we have to be!'

'Then why didn't you share up the reward?'

'What reward? There was no reward.'

'Oh, but there was, *meine kleine Liebling*.'

'Geneviève, what's this he is saying?'

'The hundred thousand francs, I think. That can take time, Inspector. Xavier simply hasn't received it yet.'

He wouldn't tell them, thought Kohler acidly. He'd let them think what they would. As sure as these two had bodies to bring joy to themselves and to others, their young lives were over should the Resistance discover what they'd done. 'Four *maquis* have died because of this,' he said, 'and that's not counting Dédou.'

A great sadness had entered his eyes. 'And what of Adrienne de Langlade?' he asked, seemingly condemning them.

'Brother Matthieu,' grated Geneviève. 'Why not ask it of him? Of *him*! We know nothing of that business. *Nothing*, do you understand? We were away on tour.'

He flicked water at her as he went up the steps. 'Oh but you weren't. You were in Avignon. And what's more, Mireille de Sinéty wrote it all down and hid it away for my partner and I to find.'

They were alone at last, and in the all but silent room the sound of still-lapping bathwater came harshly.

'Is it really true what Herr Kohler said?' asked Christiane in despair.

'That bitch *would* leave things for them to find. I *knew* it!' swore Geneviève, getting up to pull off her sheath and throw it into the water.

'She wrote it down, he said.'

'The *enseignes*, you little fool. The talismans and cabochons – the rebus every young maid wore to tease and taunt the hearts and minds of her admirers.'

185

'Her killers. Those who couldn't have her telling others what had really happened to Adrienne.'

'A bonfire, another "picnic" last October – is that what your loosened tongue will spit out next?' demanded Genèvieve, watching her so closely now she had to shiver uncontrollably and pluck at the sheath that clung to her breasts. She had to say foolishly, 'I must look like a ghost in this.'

We were drunk on absinthe – is that the excuse you'll give if asked, wondered Genèvieve, stepping close to her, so close each hesitant breath the little fool gave was felt.

Slowly the sheath was removed. Christiane would feel it curling up as it came away but when her arms were stretched above her head, it would stop and be held there, binding her by the wrists. 'You had to let him know about Dédou's watching us at the picnic. You weakened, damn you! And don't start crying and begging me to forgive you, Christiane. Not after that!'

The sheath was left for her to remove. Cast into the water, it spread outwards to join the other one and slowly sink, more ghostlike now than before. 'It . . . it looks as if we, too, had been drowned in an *accabussade*. Our screams—'

The slap was hard and fast. Stung by it, Christiane waited.

'We have to think,' grated Genèvieve. 'Mireille must have planned it all. That's why the bishop wanted the sisters to remove things from her body before the detectives found them. He knew what she might do.'

'You hate me now.'

'I don't! I want you to *think*!'

'Then let me tell you exactly what I think!'

'Look, I'm sorry I slapped you.'

But are you really, wondered Christiane. 'Mireille was a Libra, the House of Balance; Dédou was of the Archer, a Sagittarius.'

'And Adrienne?' demanded Genèvieve.

'A Virgo. Carnelian and jade are the stones of her sign. Mine, unless you have forgotten, are agate, the moss variety especially, and chrysoprase, the more golden green the better.'

A Gemini . . . 'And I'm a Pisces, the sign of two back-to-back fishes and the wearer of amethyst. You will never have forgotten that.'

'But Mireille didn't wear her costume when she came to practise with us on Monday afternoon, did she?'

'She needed time to get ready . . . She had hours until the audition.'

'Oh *bien sûr, chérie*, but also she wouldn't have wanted us to see the rebus. It was her insurance the truth would be told should anything untoward happen to her.'

They touched hands. Momentarily they came together to hold each other, then Geneviève hesitantly said, 'After practice, she presented me with a tiny chrysoprase. I . . . I thought nothing of it. Why should I have? The thing was chipped and ancient, a pale and dirty greyish green cameo she had found last summer while rooting around in the garden of that family house she lives in. I didn't want it and told her so.'

'But she made you take it?'

'You saw me do so. Why, then, do you ask?'

And I've wounded you now, haven't I, thought Christiane, but said, 'Because it meant something.'

'What, damn you!'

There were tears now misting those blue eyes that could be, and often were, so warm and compassionate. Tears of anguish and of uncertainty. Of fear. To shrug would only infuriate her, yet the impulse was there and had to be controlled.

'What, *please!*'

'I don't know yet, except to say that it was thought of as a stone neither a Pisces nor a Virgo should ever wear, since it tended to bring misfortune.'

When Geneviève didn't say anything, but turned quickly away in despair, Christiane wanted desperately to reach out to her but hesitated. 'It's over, isn't it, for all of us? We're finished.'

Torn from her silence, Geneviève said harshly, 'César . . . We're going to have to talk to him. It can't be avoided. Not now.'

'They'll kill the detectives, won't they? The Hooded Ones will have to protect themselves. They can't . . .'

Struck twice and then again and again, Christiane fell to her knees to quickly press her face against Genèvieve's bare feet and grip her by the ankles. 'I'm sorry, so sorry,' she wept.

'Then don't you ever say that again! We don't know anything about those people. We're not supposed to know.'

La Cagoule . . .

'*Ispettore, da quando siete quaggiú?*' asked Simondi warily. How long have you been down here?'

'Long enough,' said St-Cyr tensely.

'But what brings you here, *amico mio*? Old bottles? A love of history?'

'Absinthe, I think.'

'Ah! *L'assenzio*.' Simondi tossed a hand. '*La moglie . . . Scusate, Ispettore*, I constantly forget myself even after more than thirty-five years in Provence. The wife. *L'absinthisme* is a disease not seen these days. I understand your concern entirely. It's terrible, isn't it? An intelligent, once beautiful woman . . . But *amico mio*, what is this? You should have come to me. I would have told you everything. To search a man's house without a magistrate's warrant? To wander about in his cellars without permission? *Non siete autorizzato*.' He wagged a reproving finger as he came closer. 'You're not authorized to do that.'

He was right, of course, and unfortunately the bills of lading were now much closer to him and he knew it too.

Simondi unbuttoned the camelhair overcoat with its wide thirties lapels and, finding matches and a cigar, set his torch aside, and took time out to light them. The broad brimmed fedora was of a soft beige velour, the white silk scarf that of a Puccini.

'*La sala delle statue, Ispettore*, the salon of the statues, or better still, let me show you one of my greatest joys. The library. When Marceline and I discovered this house it was in such a state. Old books . . . scattered manuscripts and papers – priceless letters dating from the very days of the cardinals when this and other houses like it were their *livrées*.'

Their palaces, but built on land that had been dedicated to the poor, the servants. Hence the name of *livrée*, and so much for the popular notion that its other meaning of the livery, or stables, applied, thought St-Cyr. 'When, exactly, did you "acquire" the house?'

'I will switch off my torch to conserve the batteries, *Ispettore*, but, really, why don't we go upstairs? It's too cold down here. The flu . . . One has always to watch the health, isn't that so?'

Last winter's flu had been terrible. Too many had died of it in Paris alone, but had the reference to health been a warning? Of course it had! 'The date, please.'

Bastardo, non mi prendere in giro! Don't mess about with me! 'These old houses, Inspector. So few could afford them, but there was always the dream. Marceline had inherited a little money from an uncle she had favoured years ago. Nothing much, you understand, but enough to make the small downpayment its owner was willing to accept.'

'After the house was ransacked?'

'A small matter. A disagreement of some sort. Transients perhaps.'

Hired hoodlums, then.

'The late autumn of 1940,' said Simondi, watching him closely through cigar smoke and Sûreté torchlight. 'Things were in great turmoil, as you will remember. The war had been lost; the country suddenly divided into free and occupied zones. All manner of people flooded into Provence to take refuge from what was going on in the north. We never found out who had caused the trouble.'

'But its owner felt it best to sell up and leave.'

'No, no, it wasn't like that at all. The owner and his family had left the country before the Defeat and decided to remain abroad. America . . . New York, I think. Alberto was handling things for them; small matters of upkeep, taxes, household bills, the wages of a caretaker, gardener, chauffeur, cook and housemaids. He—'

'He cabled them that an offer had been made, and the owner, feeling it prudent, agreed.'

'Yes, yes, that's it exactly.'

Jewish, then, and lucky to have escaped with their lives, thought St-Cyr sadly. 'So, tell me about the disease.'

Ah *bravo, caro Ispettore*, you have come back to what I wanted you to ask! But I must remove the cigar to consider it and give an expression of concern. 'Ever since she came here to live, my wife has yearned to return to the Paris she loves. Surely you can understand such a thing, you who are known to love Paris and to miss it constantly? I did what I could. A little trip now and then, the shopping, the restaurants, but the pressures of work . . . One simply can't give up everything, and increasingly there was what we say in Italian, *le esigenze del successo*, the demands of success.'

'And when the supply of what the former owner had left, and the hoodlums who ransacked the house had missed, had finally run out?'

'I ordered it in from the only place I could.'

'You have friends.'

St-Cyr had already looked at the bills of lading. 'Of course I have "friends". Without them life would be very dull.'

That, too, had been a warning. 'Those bills suggest—'

Simondi blocked the way. 'You don't have to look at them, Inspector. I'm not obliged to let you.'

A bribe, then. 'But we can discuss it, eh?'

No bribe would be accepted. 'As if among friends, yes.'

For the detective to get around him to snatch the most recent bill away would be all but impossible. The nail was sharp and rusty – a dangerous thing. 'Find your murderer, Inspector. Go about your business with that partner of yours. This house and my wife hold nothing for you. She's not well. Now that you've seen so yourself, you must appreciate that even if she did manage to make it to the Palais on the night of the murder, what possible part could she have played in that tragic affair?'

'I don't know yet, Maître, but as in part song, so, too, in murder, each voice carries its own measure. I think you deliberately withheld this latest shipment from your wife. A few days at least before the murder of Mireille de Sinéty.'

Some men would never learn and this was one of them. 'Five days, as you already know,' said Simondi coldly. 'Ask anyone. All will tell you I have repeatedly tried to wean her from that poison.'

'Ah yes, of course, but when in withdrawal, is the absinthe addict not capable of other things? That is the question.'

The sigh he would give this *fottuto di poliziotto* would be long and deep and of a death anticipated. 'Then come upstairs and I will tell you what you want to know.'

8

The singers were hunting for him in earnest now, thought Kohler. One here, one there, but he had no problem, really, in evading them. Simondi's villa was huge.

'Herr Koh . . . ler,' shouted Marius Spaggiari, only to have Christiane's voice anxiously chase the echoes with, 'Inspector . . . where are you?'

YOU . . . YOU . . .

'Please don't do this to us.'

TO US . . .

'*Signore* . . .' cried the housekeeper. 'It is not permissible. You must show yourself at once.' AT ONCE . . . And over to the left, he thought, but these old places. Rooms on rooms, with columned, echoing ambulatories between . . .

'He'll try to question madame,' shouted Geneviève and well to his right, he was certain of it.

'She's awake now,' answered Spaggiari from the head of the staircase.

'She's at her best. She'll say something she shouldn't.' SHOULDN'T, gave back Geneviève.

'He'll find her room!' shrilled Christiane. 'Stop him. We must stop him.'

'Go then, Geneviève. Go!' shouted Spaggiari. 'I'll catch up with you. Christiane, keep looking for him here.'

HERE . . .

The Grand Tinel of the *livrée* seemed to run on for ever beneath a vaulted ceiling that reached to the gods. Repeated patterns of lilies and trumpet vines were interlocked with cameos of saints and cardinals, while far below them large canvases in oils were hung from floor to ceiling, with tapestries between them. Churchy scenes. Popes, nuns and priests. Scenes of the hunt. Murals of the Virgin and Child, the Crucifixion. Peasants flailing their harvest. Life in the mid-fourteenth century. The Palais des Papes, a cardinal on a white mule . . .

A girl in raiment so fine . . .

The painting was large and it made him ask, Had she been a petitioner to the Papal Court? There was a tight circlet of silver brocade around her forehead – there were enamelled blue violets in it. The hair was golden, the eyes were of that softest shade of amber and just like Mireille de Sinéty's. De Sinéty's . . .

There were several rings on each finger. A pendant box hung from her belt, her *girdle*, damn it!

There were tiny silver bells, a sewing kit, a purse for alms – coins!, and a tin of sardines, eh?

The dark green woollen cloak was trimmed with white ermine tails.

It was her, that other Mireille, looking down at him from across the centuries.

Her mantle was of rose madder, her gown of saffron silk, the cote-hardie of cocoa-brown velvet, its bodice of gold brocade and tightly laced up the front. A girl of nineteen. Proud, not haughty; determined, not weak, her lips slightly parted in hesitation as she awaited the verdict of the Court. And *Pater noster, qui es in caelis* . . .

The belt was of very soft suede and studded with an absolute rainbow of stones, replete with *enseignes* and talismans. Helmeted guards with pikes stood ready to take her away.

'I've got to keep moving,' he told himself, but suddenly the *livrée* had gone to silence, suddenly, instead of there being no problem in evading the singers, an ominous feeling had crept in. Had others taken over the hunt? Others . . . *La Cagoule*? He cursed his luck.

Gilded Louis XIV *fauteuils* and sofas lined the hall. A herringbone pattern of brick-red tiles ran to the far end where, across its full width, a floor-to-ceiling arched window let in the sunlight. There were figures down there. Maybe four, maybe five of them and, *Gott im Himmel,* where the hell was Louis when he needed him most?

'*La Danse,*' quavered Christiane Bissert, coming softly upon him to indicate the life-sized marble sculpture at the other end of the hall. Nervous . . . *Mein Gott,* she was afraid.

'Carpeaux . . .' breathed Kohler, stunned by how lifelike the figures appeared. 'The façade of the Paris Opera.'

Hand in hand, buxom naked girls danced madly around a naked boy who held aloft a tambourine. There was laughter, licentiousness, a ribald joy in their expressions. Motion . . .

'Madame Simondi is . . . is so lonely for Paris,' said Christiane, fighting for words and hesitantly having taken him by the hand to lead him away from the painting . . . the painting. 'This copy, found quite by accident in an antiques shop on the rue du Faubourg Saint-Honoré, was one of César's many attempts to appease her desire to return.'

Her voice had climbed but she'd been unaware of it. 'And at the picnic early last June?' he asked. The *Cagoule* . . . where were they?

They would *want* her to answer, to keep him talking, she told herself. Distract him . . . I must distract him. 'We danced. We . . . we often recreate this sculpture for madame. It . . . it's her wish to see us that way and . . . and making love to . . . to each other.'

She swallowed tightly and he knew she was afraid.

'Simondi sent you here last night knowing my partner and I would want to question her. We were to "see" her as she is, weren't we?'

'He . . . he couldn't have known you would come last night.'

'But he didn't take a chance, did he, and now has brought in a little company.'

The Hooded Ones . . . had he already seen them? *Had he?* Somehow she found the will to say, 'She sips constantly. Even now there will be a glass ready for her to begin her day.'

'And if denied her craving?'

'She becomes irritable.'

'Restless?'

'Highly agitated.'

'Aggressive?'

'You're hurting me, Inspector. My hand . . .' She threw an anguished glance over her shoulder.

'Paranoic?' he demanded. 'Bugs crawling all over her? Worms in her guts? Sheer terror? Hatred?'

'Lapses of memory. Blackouts, yes.'

'Vivid hallucinations?'

'Seizures.'

'Jealousy?'

Ah no . . . 'She . . . she thinks things about people that . . . that are not always true. She—'

'Has the urge to kill them? Is that it, eh? Come on, damn it, answer me!'

Answer . . . Answer . . .

Anxiously Christiane looked away again to the opposite end of the Grand Tinel, but no one had come to deal with him. Not yet . . . But he would know now that she had been sent to distract him.

'What really happened Monday night?' he asked, startling her into answering hotly, 'Why must you make trouble for yourself? You don't know what they're like. They'll—'

'Stop at nothing now?'

'*Please!*' she begged. 'Just leave while you can. They'll blame me. They'll hold me responsible for warning you but—'

'Stick closely. Just do as I say and don't bugger about. Hey, you're with the police, eh? The honest ones.'

The fresco was magnificent and a tribute to the villa's former owner who had had it patiently restored, thought St-Cyr. In it, shadows from columns fell across an archway beyond which there was a road that wound downhill through field and farm towards the viewer. In the foreground, to the left, there was a group of six monks and a cardinal. A white mule stood in their midst, they having just arrived on their pilgrimage to the Avignon of the mid-fourteenth century.

To the right, across the gap through which one saw the

archway, there stood a group of maidens, of whom the cardinal was inquiring. Only two of the girls faced him; the one a princess, by the look, the other her lady-in-waiting. All of the others, though just as comely and beautifully dressed, were frivolously discussing the visitors.

The lady-in-waiting had thrown her princess a questioning glance. The princess's long blonde hair was tied behind as befitted an unmarried girl of her day. Her expression was at once one of sincere concern at the travellers' plight, and of innocence.

St-Cyr drew in a breath. 'That's the first Mireille before she was married.'

'Perhaps. One can never really tell with such things, can one?' countered Simondi. 'But I thought you would like to see it.'

'That cardinal is asking if she can provide lodgings. Avignon was very overcrowded at the time of the popes.'

'But did she refuse him the use of her father's house as her lady-in-waiting appears to demand, or did she agree?' asked Simondi.

'Are you suggesting Mireille de Sinéty's judgement of the distant past was perhaps too harsh?'

'Inspector, I'm only making you aware that within the passage of the centuries must exist an element of doubt.'

There'd been no sign of Hermann, thought St-Cyr, though he was certain he had heard his partner's name being called. A worry.

'Come,' said Simondi. 'The library is just this way.'

Verdammt! There must be three of them after him, thought Kohler. Gardener, caretaker . . . what did it matter? They'd be young and agile and everywhere, and they'd damned well know the layout of this pile of stones. They'd make no sound, would move with swiftness. Now from out of a corridor; suddenly from a room . . . Corsicans . . . Retainers . . . '*Cagoulards*,' he breathed.

'You will never know when they'll come up behind you!' shrilled Christiane. He was hustling her along a corridor, was pushing her ahead of him.

'Easy, kid. Take it easy. Where does that staircase lead?'

He wouldn't listen to her! He was still going to try to get free of them and find Madame! 'The roof, I think,' she blurted.

Driven ahead of him, she went up the steep and narrow staircase into darkness. He would have to stop if she stopped. He would bang right into her. And hadn't Préfet de Passe told her to distract him? Hadn't he warned her of what would happen to her if she didn't? 'The door?' she said, catching a breath. 'It'll be locked.'

'Let's try it.'

She could feel him against her. Everything in her said to cry out, to push him back and away from her, to turn and shriek . . . 'I can't. I . . .'

Clinging to him in the darkness, she wept. 'Forgive me. Please forgive me. I'm so afraid.'

The door burst on to a narrow walkway between tiled roof and battlement. The stones were icy, the walkway long. When she fell, she cried out, 'They'll kill me if you don't give yourself up!' and rolled from side to side, gripping herself by the shoulders in despair.

Kohler yanked her to her feet and shook her. 'They killed Adrienne, didn't they?'

Adrienne . . . Adrienne . . .

'Answer me, damn you!'

Christiane blinked several times. The wind came but gently. The air was very cold, the sunlight bright. A perfect morning. 'She . . . she was there with us and . . . and then she wasn't. Please, you must believe me.'

'Where?'

'The . . . the Île de la Barthelasse. César has one of his farms at the northern end of the island. There are reeds, a dock, some punts and an old mill . . . a mill. He and his friends use it as a hunting lodge.'

'Last October?' he demanded harshly and when she didn't answer, shook her hard.

He couldn't see the sunlight burnish the scars on his face as it would glint off the stiletto that would be driven into his back. He couldn't realize that they were about to kill him. Kill him . . . She would throw her arms about his neck, would hug him tightly and let him feel the trembling in her.

'Yes, last October. A . . . another picnic. A bonfire and singing . . . much singing. We . . . we all got very drunk.'

'On absinthe?'

Sunlight flashed as it would have done when cardinals' messages were passed to the Palais. 'Marius had some bottles Madame had given him. She wanted Bishop Rivaille to see what she thought Adrienne was really like. A slut, a little whore. She . . . she made us do it.'

'*Ispettore*,' said Simondi warily to St-Cyr in the library, 'if Mireille de Sinéty thought Adrienne de Langlade was murdered, she was very much mistaken.'

'My partner and I've been led to believe that was why she was silenced.'

'*Dio mio erano molto amici.*' He threw out his hands. '*Lei era molto bella, molto incantevole.* Ah! *Scusate*, I forget myself again. It's so easy to do. My God, they were the best of friends. She was *très belle, très charmante.*'

'An *accabussade.*'

'Ah *pouf*! *Quelle absurdité.*'

'Now calm down or you'll have us shouting at each other.'

'Then you tell me what reason was there for anyone to have murdered her? Adrienne was a mezzo-soprano like few others and the beauty of it was . . . ah, *sì, sì*, she didn't think herself better than the others. She listened. She cooperated. She worked terribly hard. Always there was great attention, the desire to become better and the willingness to subordinate the self so that the voice could develop and blend with the others.'

'She became tractable, is that what you're saying?'

Simondi's dark brown eyes narrowed with suspicion. 'Tractable? Why do you ask? I laboured long and hard writing parts for that girl and adjusting those of the others so that her voice would be what I was convinced it could be. Not just a welcome addition but that which would take our madrigals to even finer heights.'

'How profitable are the concerts?'

The head was tossed as if struck. '*Profit?* You ask of profit and murder in the same breath? *Molto lucroso.*' He shook a hand whose fingertips were pressed together.

'And yet you postdated, by several months, the miserly cheques you gave Mademoiselle de Sinéty in payment for her work.'

'*Bastardo! Fottuto di poliziotto,* how do you know of this, please?'

'Let's just say we are aware of it.'

'Then let me say in return that as a businessman I have many accounts. That's only understandable. Some are overdrawn, others might be and I can't always remember what balance there is in each account, so am cautious.'

Hermann should have heard it! 'You and two of your associates sat in judgement of our victim, Maître. Whether true or not, that girl thought one or all of you either guilty of Adrienne de Langlade's murder, or of trying to cover it up to protect someone.'

It would do no good to argue. This Sûreté, with his holier-than-thou attitude, had convinced himself that something was not right. He had smelled the fish and found it tainted. 'Mireille was a creature of the past, Inspector. Because of what had happened to her namesake six hundred years ago, the girl was overly suspicious of and all too ready to harshly judge the Church. It was *una piccola leggenda* she'd been fed by that mother of hers. *Une petite légende de famille, n'est-ce pas?* With no father there to raise her, the girl grew up under the mother's wing.'

'No father?'

'He lost his nerve when he lost everything in the Great Depression. He killed himself. A hunting "accident" which left the mother and child in near destitution. We did what we could in the years before the war. We Avignonnais are not above helping the less fortunate. You've seen this. In the late autumn of 1940 I was able to buy a small farm that might suit, and the mother agreed to lease it for, I must add, a pittance. So little, *Ispettore*, my associates and I don't even bother to record the rent since it is never collected.'

A saint and a group of them. 'Take me through that evening,

Maître. You and Bishop Rivaille dined with the Kommandant. I gather Frau von Mahler joined you at dinner.'

Merda, what had that woman revealed? '*Ispettore*, I've already told your partner that when the Kommandant refused to be the third judge, I telephoned Albert Renaud who agreed, and that Henri-Baptiste and I then picked him up in the car.'

'The bishop's Bugatti Royale.'

'*Sì*. Henri-Baptiste loves to drive it, but for reasons of prudence, chooses not to do so himself in daylight.'

'That way he can't be blamed for having the privilege of an SP sticker few others could obtain.'

'*Scusate, Ispettore*, but such things as the *Service Public* sticker and the car I myself enjoy also are judged essential by the Occupier, are they not?'

'Of course.'

'*Ispettore* . . .'

'A moment, *mon ami*.' The Sûreté flipped through the pages of his little black notebook. 'Ah yes, here we are. Brother Matthieu gave Mireille de Sinéty his key to the Palais . . .'

'I gave her mine.'

'But Mademoiselle Bissert assured me the girl had been given it by the brother.'

'She was mistaken. She couldn't have known in any case.'

'Then what you claim agrees with what Xavier told me, that Mireille had told him you had given her your key. The only puzzle is . . .'

'Ah *porca vacca*, what now?' Damned cop!

'The girl wondered if the third judge would be your wife, Maître, since Frau von Mahler had told her the Kommandant would be certain to refuse your request at dinner.'

So they were back to that. 'And?'

'You denied your wife the absinthe she had to have and you did so for five days prior to last Monday. *Five* days, Maître!'

And perfect for murder, the one task she was to fulfil – was this what he was thinking? 'All right, I had hoped my Marceline would pull herself together long enough to be with us as the third judge, but this wasn't possible.'

Why hadn't Kohler been brought to the library? wondered Simondi. Had he managed to get to Marceline? '*Ispettore*, my wife was very fond of the girl. While such feelings wouldn't have influenced her judgement – she was once very musical – it might have helped a little with the rough edges. *Il portamento*, the deportment; the stage presence also. I wanted Mireille to join my singers. *Dio mio*, why wouldn't I have? She was my right hand.'

Lies . . . were they all lies? 'She would have fitted in well as mistress of this villa, wouldn't she?'

'*Che cosa dite* – what are you saying?'

'It's obvious, isn't it? One of the finest, if not *the* finest of the remaining *livrées*. A beautiful young girl who understood and appreciated everything here and the madrigals as well. Things your wife has apparently come to hate.'

No response was forthcoming. 'Did that girl come here often, Maître, to search through these old books and manuscripts, the letters you mentioned – letters concerning her family's past perhaps? She did needlework for your wife who gave her things from Hédiard's . . .'

A page of that infernal notebook was sought.

'Yes, here it is. Your wife was generous, but . . .'

'But what, damn you?'

Six Early Renaissance folding chairs were arranged on either side of the table. Simondi sat in the only armchair at the head of it. The table itself was one of the first perhaps to have replaced the trestle design of those early days when most furniture had to be portable. Ivory reliquary boxes held goodly supplies of cigarettes, small cigars and matches.

Lighting his pipe, St-Cyr said, 'Your library, Maître. It has all the appearances of being a medieval boardroom gone modern.'

'I asked you a question, Inspector. Surely I'm due an answer.'

'Ah *bon*! *Mais certainement.* In spite of a rationing system that has never worked and gives increasingly inadequate nourishment, Mireille de Sinéty refused to even sample the delicacies that wife of yours gave her in payment, no doubt, for services rendered.'

'And?'

There was a nod. 'And in spite of knowing others could well use and appreciate the food, she hid the items.'

'The girl was embarrassed. She didn't want others thinking she was privileged.'

'Maître, let's cut to the quick of it. Your wife was, I believe, insanely jealous of that girl and terrified of the threat she posed.'

A former dancer, a drunkard. 'Marceline understands me, Inspector.'

'I'm sure she does, but Mireille de Sinéty would have been perfect for you and for this house. Perfect, Maître, in every way if given time but she knew too much, had too many questions about you and the bishop and the Church, and you couldn't have that, could you?'

Merda! Why had Kohler not been brought to the library?

I could give him a moment, thought St-Cyr, and then ask it of him. Yes, that would be best. 'Why not tell me what really happened after the audition, Maître? We'll only find out. You know it as well as I do.'

St-Cyr and Kohler . . . *bastardi*, both of them. 'The girl failed, that's what happened. This time far worse than ever before. She was nervous. The lines from Marenzio's Petrarchan madrigal which begins with "*Solo e pensoso i più deserti campi*" – Alone, thought-sick, I pace where none has before – were muddled; those from Caccini's *Amarilli mia bella* – Amarilis my beautiful one – were not even in tune and lacked vitality. These were very simple pieces for her to sing, *Ispettore*, but her voice quavered and broke. A *Primo Soprano* can never afford to break or sing out of tune.'

'A *Primo Soprano* . . . but Genèvieve Ravier is your First Soprano.'

To breathe a sigh of relief would not be wise, not yet. 'And you didn't know, did you, *Ispettore*, that Genèvieve was to be replaced?'

'But Xavier is losing his voice. You needed another soprano.'

A reproving finger would be wagged at this Sûreté who thought he had all the answers. 'Both were to be replaced. Why else do you think I would take the trouble to write parts in for a mezzo-soprano last summer? It's an entirely different system of music and not easy, let me tell you. One has to think completely as they did in the fourteenth and fifteenth centuries. Genèvieve was to go. Adrienne was to join us and so, too, I had sincerely hoped, as had Bishop Rivaille and Albert Renaud, would Mireille. We didn't kill either of those girls. We had every reason not to and everything to lose if they were taken from us.'

A saint again. 'Why was Genèvieve Ravier to be dismissed, Maître? Was her voice no longer good enough?'

'You doubt my word? You think I am lying? *Merda*, what is it with you? Constant disbelief? "Good" is never enough. *Squisita* – exquisite – is the word you want, but we Italians would also use its other meanings and give other words to them. *Raffinatezza* – refinement, *e vita* – joy and pleasure. Yes, *gioia e piacere*. A gift from the gods.'

'Then she wasn't to be dismissed because the quality of her voice had lessened?'

Ah *bravo*, now you can feed on the crumbs! 'As happens sometimes in such close quarters, our *Alto* had become too attached to our *Primo Soprano*. Such a thing will inevitably break apart the solidarity a group such as ours demands, and one can't have that.'

'Too familiar sexually? Too possessive, eh?'

It would be best to give a guarded answer. 'That and in other ways, dependent totally.'

'Then why not dismiss the *Alto*?'

Suspicion still lingered. 'Because, *caro Ispettore*, Mireille was to have replaced both Genèvieve *and* Xavier, but could never have replaced Christiane whose voice, among altos, is not just exquisite, but unique.'

'You told Mireille she had failed.'

Bene, they would now settle that business once and for all! 'I did so from the other end of the Palais's Grand Tinel, yes.'

'And what was her reaction? Refresh my memory.'

'She stood as if struck dumb, her head bowed. I tried to be

encouraging. Another time . . . another chance, but she just stood there like that. Beaten, defeated, in tears and ashamed – yes, yes, she was ashamed of her paltry efforts. She *was* good. She could so easily have passed. We had deliberately not asked much of her.'

Good? Hadn't the proper word to use been *squisita*? 'And afterwards, Maître?'

'The three of us left the hall together.'

'A moment, please.'

Note pages were flipped out of the way until St-Cyr had what he wanted.

'A small matter, Maître. It's only that Bishop Rivaille's accounting of those final moments doesn't agree with what you've just said.'

'Not agree? In what way, please?'

'The girl didn't bow her head in shame. On hearing the result, she abruptly turned her back on the three of you and left the hall. Rivaille thought this unforgivable of her.'

'But . . . but that is nothing. A mere moment in time. First she bowed her head as I've said and then, on hearing the result and my attempt to be encouraging, turned her back and abruptly left the hall as Henri-Baptiste has said.'

'You didn't put out the candles?'

'It didn't seem appropriate. Salvatore would do so in any case. I knew he would be there shortly to make his rounds. Even when we reached the entrance, I felt, and I can never forgive myself – *never* – that he would find and escort her safely home, but . . . Why could he not have been a moment earlier? He could have prevented it, could have interrupted things.'

The tears were very real but could hardly be the truth. 'You forgot to mention something,' breathed St-Cyr. 'When you and Albert Renaud were questioned at your flat by my partner, you stated the possibility of your wife's having come to the Palais at the last minute. Renaud then said he was certain there had been someone else present – in the stairwell where he went to get the chairs. A sound, a presence . . . but when he shone his torch around, there was, apparently, no one.'

'Alberto didn't think any more of it at the time and failed entirely to mention it to us, but it was good of him to have come forward wasn't it? And yes, Mireille could well have left the door unlocked behind her when she entered the Palais, but unfortunately none of us will ever know if she did.'

'But let me ask again, Maître, could this other person have been your wife?'

Ah *grazie*! 'Marceline? It's possible, yes . . . but you will get little from her now, I'm afraid.'

'Then one last thing, Maître. When Mireille de Sinéty was found, there was a tin of sardines in her *aumônière*.'

'Sardines?'

'A gift from Frau von Mahler, I believe.'

'Then it's true what the Kommandant thinks. Dédou Favre was there to meet her after the audition but . . . Ah *si*. The boy failed entirely to steal the contents of her purse or to find the nourishment she had denied herself for him, her killer.'

And not the wife – was that it, then? Not Geneviève Ravier, either, or Christiane Bissert? 'But . . . but Dédou couldn't have been there, Maître. Alain de Passe had arrested him early that morning.'

It was freezing up on the walkway that ran alongside the roof of the Grande Chapelle of the villa, thought Christiane, and still the Hooded Ones hadn't come to kill Herr Kohler.

Wet with her tears, the collar of her blouse touched his cheek as she clung to him.

'A *partouse*?' he asked of the picnic last October on the Île de la Barthelasse. An orgy . . . 'We did things,' she wept. 'Scandalous things. Absinthe at first releases one from one's inhibitions, and quickly. It makes one wild. Adrienne we drove crazy in front of them, but . . . but she was pregnant and . . . and some among them noticed this and . . . and took offence.'

Ah *merde*, Rivaille. 'The bishop?' he demanded.

She would swallow and nod, would stand right up on her tiptoes now. He'd be thinking of how enraged Bishop Rivaille had become, of how, when he'd seen them first like that he had coloured rapidly and hadn't been able to take his eyes from Adrienne who was supposed to have been so pure, so virginal, with her belly beginning to swell. Adrienne with Marius and Genèvieve and the others, herself included. She would let Herr Kohler feel her body clinging to him as the stiletto was driven into his back. She would feel him stiffen in shock, would hear his gasp and hold him tightly as he shuddered and coughed blood which would run down her cheek. But he'd be too heavy for her and both of them would collapse.

'Rivaille, de Passe, Renaud, César and . . . and others of their group. The hunters,' she said.

'De Passe heads the *Cagoule*, doesn't he?' breathed Kohler softly and heard her faintly say, 'Yes. Some of those were there, too, with their . . . their women.'

Her arms were still wrapped tightly about his neck. 'What happened?' he asked, so gently she was afraid she would weaken and tell him, but knew the sunlight couldn't be fully in his eyes and that they still must be alone up here, just the three of them. The *three*! No one else would know what she'd done to save the group, not Genèvieve who mattered most, not Marius or Guy or Norman. Not even Herr Kohler's partner. Only Préfet de Passe and the assassin he had sent. The *assassin*!

When she flinched, Kohler threw them both to one side. They hit the tiles and rolled. Several times she shrieked, 'Not me! Not me! Oh God, what have I done?' He shook her hard. He was too heavy for her, too strong, had her by the arms and was forcing her down . . . down . . .

'Where is he?' she spat fiercely and tried to free herself.

The girl ducked her eyes away in doubt and caught a breath. 'Where's who?' he asked.

Sunlight glinted from his scars. She couldn't force herself to look at him. 'One of them. I don't know who, damn you! Antonio, maybe. César's gardener. The one with the . . . the stiletto.'

There'd been no one, thought Kohler. Her imagination had simply run away with her. 'Oh, him. Down below us, I think. Let's have a look, shall we?'

He hauled her up and, holding her by the back of the neck and an arm, forced her to look well over the battlement and far down into the courtyard below.

'Well?' he demanded, the sound of his voice breaking over her.

Pulled back, she fell to a sitting position, couldn't bring herself to look up at him, was so ashamed, so afraid and waiting for his condemnation. 'Please, they're not nice, these men of the *Cagoule*. They can be so very cruel to a girl like me or to Genèvieve. One does what one is told to do, *n'est-ce pas*? One looks the other way and doesn't question. I . . . I thought they . . . they were going to kill you.'

'Things got a little out of hand, didn't they, at that picnic on the Île de la Barthelasse last October?'

'I . . . I can't really remember. I was drunk. Dead drunk! And so were Genèvieve and the others. Absinthe isn't kind, Inspector. It makes some men insane and they do things to a girl they, too, have little or no memory of.'

'And afterwards?' he asked, crouching before her so that she had to face him.

'Adrienne went away to Paris . . . but . . . but couldn't have done so.'

From a covered veranda where, in ancient times, the laundry would have been dried and on summer evenings the cardinal would have taken the air, Kohler looked down into the courtyard. Behind him was the roof that ran at a right angle to that of the Grande Chapelle. Hand in hand, he and the girl had travelled the length of it. Pale and shivering and still very afraid for her life, the *Alto* waited for him to decide what to do next.

'Our friends are in disagreement,' he said of those in the courtyard. 'Apparently there's some argument as to whether they really should put the knife into a member of the Führer's Gestapo.'

Grabbing the girl by the arm, he hustled her to a side door and from there, hurried down a spiral staircase to the floor below.

207

When they reached Madame Simondi's room, he locked them in and let her walk on ahead, only to see her hesitate.

'Madame . . .' she began, only to suddenly lose all faith in herself.

'What have you been saying to him, you little fool!' grated the woman.

'Nothing! He demanded it of me. I . . .'

'Nothing? But if nothing, then what . . . is there . . . for you . . .'

To distress yourself about?

Kohler knew he'd have to fill in the blanks. Madame Simondi had been bathed and dressed. Ear-rings and a three-strand pearl and garnet cameo choker were worn with a dark crimson dress. There were silk stockings, too, and matching high heels. Very much the *Parisienne*, she was languidly stretched out on the divan, propped up by cushions. Her jet black hair had been combed and brushed and was pinned back, her lips and dark eyes were made up.

Drip glass, bottle, bowl of broken sugar, ice bucket and pitcher of water were close to hand. An hour of drinking already, he thought ruefully. Spaggiari and the others must have been told to bugger off long ago.

'My little friends,' she said and fondled the glass when she caught him looking at her side table. 'They keep me . . . going.'

A sip was taken, her lips pursed as it went down, she studying the milky-green liqueur in the glass before adding a touch more water. 'An audition . . .' she said, and then after a long pause, 'at the Palais. I understand two detectives . . .'

Are in my house.

'Did César sleep with you last night, *chérie*?' she asked sharply, acidly. 'Did you let that husband of mine stick that sausage of his into your ass, eh?'

'Madame, one of the detectives is here now!'

Her lips tightened, her eyes became momentarily livid. 'I've seen this *putain de bordel* at it, Inspector. I know what she lets my husband do to her. She and Geneviève are lovers, but . . . César, he . . . He has the use of them both and often together.'

'Madame . . .' tried Christiane.

Kohler moved the girl out of the way. 'Kripo, Paris-Central,' he said firmly.

'At last you've found your voice. Do I . . .'

There was another long pause. 'Shock you, Inspector? A little, perhaps? Ah! You're from Paris. Laperouse . . . Do they still have . . .'

She tried to find the words and pursed her lips. 'Their *cabinets particuliers?*'

Their private little dining cubicles.

Taking a long pull at her glass, she gave him a fleeting smile, half disarming, half knowing. 'I scratched my name . . .'

Again she paused to find the words. 'In one of the mirrors,' she managed. 'The . . . The diamond solitaire César . . .'

Had just given me, said Kohler to himself.

'Silly girl . . . Silly not to have kept my clothes on. I was a fool!' she shrieked and quivered with indignation until the thought left her and she had to hunt for it. 'Now I'm a martyr to this mausoleum of his and he wants to fuck Mireille. *Mireille!* Just as the cardinal wanted her ancestor. Her ancestor.'

Her voice fell back. 'Laperouse . . . Is it still on the quai des Grands-Augustins? On the . . .'

Corner.

'*Numéro cinquante et un?*' she asked coyly. 'The *canard natais* was . . .'

Pure magic.

'The *mousse au chocolat amer* was webbed among the hairs of my little forest. César . . .'

'We get the picture,' said Kohler tartly.

'*Mon cul* . . . I was his *petite nymphe en rhapsodie,* Inspec . . . tor.'

Entreatingly she extended a hand, beckoning him to join her. 'The Galeries Lafayette . . . Do you . . .'

Know it? Tears were now smearing the mascara and eye shadow. One of Paris's giant department stores, the Galeries was a ready-to-wear emporium for shopgirls, housewives, chorus girls and maids of all work. Shoddy goods and bare shelves these days, but he hated to tell her.

Hands shaking, she took a deep pull at her glass, then let her tongue linger lovingly on its rim.

A whining tone crept into her voice. 'Can you still buy the cherries that are dipped in dark chocolate?' And moments later, 'The candied ginger *aussi*?'

Unheard of now, except in certain places.

'Ragueneau's . . . Is it still on the rue Saint-Honoré at *numéro* 202? The tearoom . . .'

When he didn't answer and didn't come to sit beside her, she grated, 'I had my own little place on the ave' Frochot, damn you! Fuck whom I want. Come and go as I please.'

It was just off place Pigalle.

'The Cabaret Pigalle, the Narcisse and then the Alhambra. *Les nus les plus oses du monde, n'est-ce pas?*' she rasped. 'And thousands of men – yes, thousands – wanted me.'

The most daring, most risqué nudes in the world, and oh for sure that was still true, thought Kohler wryly, what with the boys in grey-green lining up night after night! But they were getting nowhere.

'Madame . . .' he began, only to hear her slackly say, 'Les Halles,' while lewdly spreading her legs in an attempt to embarrass him.

Paris's central market was a cavernous shadow of its former self due mainly to the curfew which allowed no one, including the farmers, into the city after 11 p.m., and refused to let anyone leave before 5 a.m. Requisitioning most of the horses and lorries hadn't helped, and neither had the drastic reduction in the availability of gasoline.

'Adrienne de Langlade, madame . . .'

'That whore? César . . . To think that I actually wanted his . . . *child*! Me? Who had never had any brats before but . . .'

She struggled for words, muttered things about Simondi's not wearing riding coats and leaping from the train while the locomotive was still in full power, then said acidly, 'He didn't want to have one with me. He wanted her to have it!'

'Madame, are you saying your husband was the father of that girl's unborn child?'

'Say what you think. Leave me to know the truth.'

Simondi was pounding on the door and crying out her name, but she didn't even realize this.

'Which one do you like?' she asked of the eight or so wrist-watches that were wrapped around her left wrist under the sleeve she had pulled up. 'I can never decide. Each morning I put them on. Xavier . . .'

The shouting continued from the corridor. 'Xavier?' prompted Kohler and saw her smile lewdly and then softly. 'Xavier,' she sighed. 'He brings me little presents. He's always very sweet to me.'

'Madame, we have to talk,' he said and took the glass from her, took away the bottle . . . the bottle . . . '*Those are mine!*' she shrieked and lunged for them. 'You can't take them away. You can't!'

Blows rained on the door. '*Marceline!*' cried Simondi.

With bated breath she waited for Kohler to hand her the glass and when he didn't, tried again to snatch it from him. 'Please!' she begged. 'You don't understand what it's like for me without it. Christiane, tell him!'

'The Palais,' he said, ignoring the shouting.

'An audition . . . Xavier, he . . . *Please!*' she shrieked, and when refused, wept and tore her dress open. 'You want me, don't you?' she wheedled, begging him to have sex with her. 'Xavier, he . . . he said he would help me. He always does.'

When allowed to drink, she drained the glass and for a moment her dark eyes misted. Lost, she looked down at her withered breasts and slowly, deliberately, brushed droplets from them and wondered what was happening to her. 'I tried . . .'

He waited. Simondi cried out her name. 'I tried to be nice to Mireille. I really did,' she wept, 'but César, he was determined to have her and to . . . to get rid of me.'

'You killed her, didn't you?' he sadly breathed and his voice, his words echoed in her head and the pain of them was excruciating.

The pounding had stopped. Her eyes were still open.

'Inspector, she's right out of it now,' said Christiane, buttoning the woman's dress. 'She'll sit like this for hours, sipping a little from time to time, but you'll get nothing further from her today.'

'And you?' asked Kohler. 'What about you?' The girl had sounded relieved.

'I wasn't there. I was at the Villa Marenzio with the others as we all have told you and your partner.'

'*Tesoro, da quando sei qui?*' asked Simondi earnestly. Sweetie, how long have you been here?

'Since early last night, César. You . . .' hazarded Christiane.

He touched her arm in comfort. '*Sì, sì*, I remember now. I asked you and Geneviève and Marius to spend a little time with Marceline. She's all right, isn't she?'

They were gathered in the corridor outside the bedroom.

'She's fine, César. Fine,' said the *Alto*, her dark eyes full of concern for her singing master.

Lightly he kissed her on the cheek and held her a moment. '*Bene.* Try not to dwell on things. Keep the mind and voice clear, eh? We've the concert on the thirtieth and then the tour. Geneviève and you had best spend an hour or two in practice. Verdolet, I think, and Constanzo Festa. *Ispettores*, this is terrible. Ah *Dio mio*, to think that you, Herr Kohler, thought my gardener and others were to assassinate you. *Merda!* How could such a thing have been possible?'

'Maître, my partner and I will find our own way out through your Grand Tinel,' said St-Cyr, ignoring the question. 'There's a portrait of the first Mireille I would very much like to examine more closely.'

'That painting can tell you nothing, Inspector. Nothing!'

'Perhaps, but then . . . ah *mais alors*, perhaps not.'

'*Bastardi*, I'm warning you. Get out of my house this instant!'

'Warn if you like, but unless you wish to prove your innocence after a lengthy incarceration while awaiting trial, I suggest you leave us to do as I wish.'

'I won't forget this.'

'That is of no concern.'

They were in the car now and Hermann was rapidly thumbing cartridges into a spare clip for his Walther P38 while attempting to break open a packet for the old Lebel six shooter this Sûreté would be allowed and nothing else.

'*Verdammt*, Louis, did you have to set Simondi off like that and then hang around like an art student in the Louvre? That girl was totally convinced *cagoulards* would knife me. De Passe must have threatened her with them if she didn't cooperate and distract me.'

'The bishop shows every indication of belonging to the *Comité secret d'action révolutionnaire*.'

'De Passe is head of the *Cagoule, mon enfant*. *That's* why he came running so hard to the villa to call out his boys, but . . . ah *Gott im Himmel*, Boemelburg, Louis. The Chief must have sent us to Avignon hoping those bastards would take care of us once and for all!'

'Calm down. You've been popping too much Benzedrine.'

'I haven't had the time, damn it! *Nom de Jésus-Christ!* Idiot, will you listen to me.'

Kohler told him of the *partouse* on the Île de la Barthelasse last October. Louis found a cigarette and, breaking it in half, lit up and passed him his half. As was their custom at such moments, they began to go quickly through things.

'Our singing master first tries to implicate his wife in the de Sinéty murder, Hermann, as does Albert Renaud – oh *bien sûr*, there's plenty of reason. But when there might be doubt in our believing this, Simondi then confides that Genèvieve Ravier was to have been dismissed.'

'Desperate, was he?'

'The implication being that Christiane Bissert and Genèvieve would have lost everything had Adrienne de Langlade and Mireille replaced the *Primo Soprano* and Xavier.'

'And there's the bishop planting photos of Adrienne for me to find, so as to throw suspicion on to the boy and his mentor, Brother Matthieu.'

'The *fétichiste de cheveux* our shepherd boy felt he might well need to blackmail.'

'Xavier's swift like a fox, Louis. That little *confident* of Madame Simondi's realized he'd be among the fingered and didn't tell the others he had the reward money for turning Dédou in.'

'Ah yes, but a murder, Hermann, that is linked to another which, in turn, is linked to a death six hundred years ago. The brocade, it keeps haunting me.'

'What brocade?'

'The painting Simondi didn't want us to look at.'

'The Papal Court and a bunch of randy old cardinals who had already stripped a girl naked and nearly drowned her!'

'The front of our Mireille de Sinéty's cote-hardie, Hermann, and that of the first Mireille. Did those two look-alikes who were so good with the needle hide something there as well as on their belts? Another rebus?'

A last drag was taken and the butt carelessly extinguished underfoot. 'You tell me. You're the one who had to stall when we should have got the hell out of there and fast!'

Kohler thrust the Lebel at him. 'Use it. Don't hesitate. That's an order.'

Hermann always said such things. 'If one looks closely at that painting, a pattern begins to emerge in slight relief among the gold brocade, but looking closely isn't enough. One really has to think as they did in the Renaissance. They loved the play of light and shadows. Such things had tremendous meaning for them. Stand to the side of that painting as I did, and as light from the end of Simondi's Grand Tinel passes obliquely across the tightly laced bosom, it reinforces that which the artist depicted and one sees that shadows make daggers across her heart. The broad ribbing of the bars of an *accabussade* becomes clearer, Hermann, though still in soft relief and incomplete of form.'

'And?' asked Kohler quietly. Louis sometimes got like this.

'From across the centuries she cries out to us to see that her heart was broken, that the one who loved her had failed to come to her rescue.'

'I thought the husband, the de Sinéty family and her own had been forced into ruin?'

'But would she have been aware of this? A prisoner in the Palais? She hoped and prayed her husband would come, but secretly dreaded he wouldn't and wove that premonition into the brocade.'

'Only to then find herself before the court.'

'Just as our Mireille was before her judges, and in the same Palais, Hermann, the same Grand Tinel.'

'Dédou hadn't shown up but she couldn't have known he'd been arrested. Instead, she must have felt he would weaken and stay away.'

'And having copied exactly the clothing of this earlier Mireille, had woven that premonition into the brocade she herself would wear.'

'An *accabussade*,' breathed Kohler sadly as he slid the gear lever into first. 'Hey, *mon vieux*, I think I can find us one, or at least take us to where it was used and not so long ago.'

They stood alone, the two of them, on either side of the little car, near the flood-damaged northern end of the Île de la Barthelasse. Hermann had pulled up his coat collar and yanked down the brim of his fedora. His breath billowed in the frozen air through which, and all around them it seemed, came the sound of the river.

'A gristmill, Louis. Built to receive grain that had been brought downriver by barge during the height of the Babylonian Captivity.'

He sounded sickened by thoughts of what they might find. The mill was, of course, not nearly so old.

There were boulders of several sizes, uprooted trees, pavements of pebbles, washouts, heaps of sand. But among all this debris, the building stood serenely, its two storeys of soft grey-buff stone and steeply pitched, four-cornered roof with attic dormers catching the winter's light. At the innermost, eastern corner there was a round tower whose spiral staircase would access all floors. Well behind them was the farm, with peach, pear and apricot orchards and fields for artichokes, garlic and melons. There had been severe flood damage there as well, but still . . . 'Our singing master and his associates have an eye for value, Hermann. A real money-earner and a perfect hunting and fishing lodge.'

'Don't get sentimental. I've heard it all before from you.' Louis was always going on about his retirement. *Merde!* What retirement?

215

Three rooks took flight and for a moment they watched them. 'Is it a sign, I wonder?' mused St-Cyr. 'Are their shadows passing over the mill to give warning to us?'

'*Verdammt*, idiot, things are too quiet and you know it! Christ, we could be right back in the fourteenth century.'

The weathered shutters were all closed. There'd been no answer at the *mas*, no tenant farmer-cum-custodian in residence; a worry, to be sure.

'Did they get here before us, Louis? Are they waiting?'

The Hooded Ones.

Beyond the broken forest of poplar, linden and willow, Simondi had laid out a spacious garden through whose grey and vine-tangled broken arbours they had to make their way.

'A regular trysting place, if ever there was one,' snorted Hermann, having read and seen right through his partner's thoughts.

The tower rose straight up beside him from stone steps that led to the door.

'It won't be locked, *dummkopf.*'

'Then let the Sûreté go first, eh? Stay out here and have another cigarette. You still have one, don't you?'

'You took the last of them. Hey, I'd better come with you, just in case.'

Dished and worn, the stone stairs went up and around to small square windows below the heavily timbered roof, but now there was no longer the sound of the river, now, deep from below them, came a constant sucking noise.

'The sluicegates withstood the flood and were fortunately closed before it,' offered the Sûreté.

'End of travelogue, eh?' Hermann had his pistol in hand.

'I'm only trying to ease your mind.'

'Then tell me what that other noise is, *mein brillanter französischer Oberdetektiv.*'

They hesitated. They listened hard. Against the sucking noise something was seesawing gently back and forth. A door, a shutter . . . 'Ah, *merde alors*, Louis!'

'Don't throw up! Tell yourself you're not going to. *Not* this time.'

'I'm going to. Sorry.'

'Go outside! See what you can find but leave this to me!'

Louis was moving now. He wasn't hesitating. At the top of the stairs a door gave into the attic, and all too soon he had disappeared from view.

Kohler could hear him muttering, '*Aïoli*, the sauce, the mayonnaise of Provence. Marinated green beans with sliced sweet red peppers, pickled artichoke hearts *à la grecque*, a *chèvre de crottin* the mice have all but devoured, some black olives, a handful of truffles, good ones, too, and a bottle of grappa . . . The postcards.'

He became very quiet, and Kohler knew his partner must be looking out over the water through the attic portal and down past the hoist beam to where the grain sacks had once been lifted into the loft.

Busying himself, he went below, and when he found the millrace, he found the *accabussade.*

9

The doorway at the base of the mill had all but been choked by cobbles and sand. Beneath its stone arch someone before Hermann had crawled in and had broken through the flood-splintered door but had then carefully replaced the boards.

Immediately inside the cellar there was a drop of about a metre, a crawl space since the flood. Blackened tin lanterns hung from hooks in the worm-eaten timbers. Some of these lanterns were so perforated, they reminded one of vegetable graters, thought St-Cyr. Others were more baroque with many fleurs-de-lis openings.

Gutted of its water wheel years ago, the stone sluice had all but been silted up by the flood. There was barely room to manoeuvre, Hermann's terse, 'It's over there,' revealing he was imagining the screams Adrienne de Langlade must have given, her cries for mercy and gasps for air. An accident . . . would Simondi and the others now try to claim this?

Jammed into the corner and all but buried by sand and silt, the rusty flat iron bars and rectangular, open weave of a man-sized oval cage barely protruded. Dried reeds, moss, algae, bits of twigs and leaves were everywhere, as was the stench of rotting fish.

Kohler took down one of the lanterns and, cleaning it of silt, lit the candle. Immediately a much-dappled light fell over the cage to join shafts of daylight that leaked in from around the foundation. Louis crawled into the corner and, after deliberately fingering the bars, quickly thrust an arm in through the weave to recover something.

'Dried lavender,' he said. 'A small bouquet left as a memorial to what our Mireille had discovered.'

'She took one hell of a chance coming out here!'

'Technically this is not an *accabussade*, Hermann. Those were made of wood.'

Verdammt! Another lecture. 'Then what the hell is it, Herr Professor?'

'The cage in which those who had offended the Papal Court and had remained unrepentant were left until the sun, the wind, the rooks and starvation or thirst had finally finished them. During the Babylonian Captivity this cage would have been suspended from the end of a long pole or tripod that had been mounted atop the Bell Tower of the Palais.'

'In full view of the citizenry,' muttered Kohler sadly. 'Instead, as a consolation, they took it down and used it from the Pont Saint-Bénézet with that first Mireille.'

'But as a threat and a reminder of what was to come should she fail to recant and publicly confess to the harlotry they had accused her of.'

'And after the dunkings in the river?'

'She was taken back to the Bell Tower. This thing must then have been mounted up there when the Pope, the cardinals and the Papal Guard had assembled for her final moment.'

'Dressed in all her finery,' said Kohler, lost to it, 'she chose to beat them, Louis, and leapt to her death.'

'Now show me what else you've found, *mon vieux*, and then I'll take you through the suicide of yet another.'

The bedroom, one of several on the second floor, had been rustically furnished with a curtained *lis clos*, writing table, chairs and one of those gargantuan walnut *armoires* so typical of rural Provence. But what struck the eye, thought St-Cyr, as one looked through the glass of the room's carved and ancient door, was the study in oils that hung on the half-timbered wall.

Dressed only in the thin and transparent gossamer of a bath sheath, a girl of nineteen sat with her back turned towards two much older, tonsured men. Her hand was pressed to her chest in apprehension and she was facing the viewer and caught in the act of listening to what was being said about her.

Of the two men, the one who was tempted and tentatively

reached out to touch her back was dressed in the scarlet robes of a cardinal; the other, in the simple coarse black cassock of a monk.

'I'm certain this is Bishop Rivaille's room when on the hunt or out fishing, Louis. That painting's old, by about six hundred years.'

'The hair is blonde—' began the Sûreté, only to hear Hermann saying, 'There are ends of rope on the back of this door.'

So there were. Cut short, and braided, they were looped about a coat hook that was of greenish bronze and in the shape of an exquisitely formed mermaid, a *sirène* who rose up from the sea with outstretched arms, a salmon caught in her hands by the gills and tail.

'Was Adrienne de Langlade first strung up here, Louis? Did Rivaille have her to himself before she was cut down and put into that cage?'

'Was he in a rage? Was he drunk on absinthe too?'

'Did he beat her first, eh? Scourge her . . .'

'Or flagellate himself with a *martinet*, Hermann, as he stood before her and as has been recorded in Mireille de Sinéty's rebus?'

The girl had been a good four months pregnant. Accepted into the group, she had been living in the Villa Marenzio with the others, but wouldn't have been allowed to continually go on tour, not in her condition, and would have thrown Simondi's plans awry, especially since Genèvieve Ravier was to leave the group. Mireille de Sinéty had been helping the girl to hide things and had written of this in her private ledger. Adrienne had disappeared, had 'gone to Paris'.

'Did Rivaille then make mischief with her, Louis? Did he blame her for tempting him?'

'The hair in that ruby ring . . .'

'He must have really worshipped her, until shown what he came to believe she was really like.'

'He'd have broken his vows. The dream would have been jeopardized . . .'

'Did he rape her, damn it?'

'We shall have to ask him, *mon vieux*, but for now had best get on to other matters. Come and I'll show you what has happened to the monk in that painting.'

The attic was all but barren under a heavily timbered roof but at its northern end, the portal was open.

High above the river the body, dressed simply in a coal-black cassock, swung gently, now turning a little to the left, now turning the other way. Petechiae – blood spots – formed livid blotches on the bald pate. The head was crooked to one side. Rigor had set in. The grizzled, shell-battered face was dark blue in places and puffed. Warts on the prominent nose bulged as did the dark eyes, one of which was still partially closed. Curled-up lips gave a perpetual grimace, the tongue protruding and having all but been bitten through.

A bloodied froth of snot and saliva had drained from the lower corner of the mouth and had frozen fast. He had shat himself and this, too, had been frozen but to his boots.

Brother Matthieu hadn't wasted his time. Having made up his mind to enter the next world, he had found the rope that must have been used to raise and lower the *accabussade*. He had tightened it about his neck and had walked out to the end of the beam, to its hoist pulley, and had simply stepped off.

Cross, rosary, *mégot* tin and wooden-handled Opinel pocket-knife had been laid out for Xavier on a clean white napkin, but the boy hadn't taken the legacy. Instead, Xavier had presented his mentor with the thick twist of Adrienne de Langlade's hair he had taken from her corpse and had no doubt used it as a final warning to blackmail him into killing himself.

This hair was scattered over the montage of well-thumbed postcards that lay near the napkin. There were semen stains on some of them. Old stains, and many of them had been hastily wiped away long ago.

'One wishes for more time, Hermann,' said St-Cyr, ruefully shaking his head. 'A good murder investigation should always be like a fine meal, savoured as each course arrives, the mind appreciatively striving to determine precisely what alchemy the chef has used.'

'How can you talk of food at a time like this? I take it the meeting here was to settle Nino's fate and this other matter. That brother's been dead since yesterday before dusk, *mein Kamerad*. A good twenty hours.'

'And the dog?'

There was no sign of it. 'Hey, I'll take a look around while there's still light.'

'You do that. There's a reedy bay about two hundred metres along the shore. The flood will have buried some things and uncovered others. Look for a place where the dog has been at work.'

'You're getting to sound like me, you know that, don't you? What about Xavier?'

'Will be long gone by now, but clearly has much to answer for.'

Kohler snorted and clenched a fist. 'He'll have been promised his mentor's job. Hell, he'll even have some little unfortunate of his own to boss around and maybe do other things to as well.'

'Two murders and two suicides, Hermann. Each so vastly different from its predecessor, yet bound to it by the centuries. Beyond the lies, there has to be the truth.'

Don't squander patience on this Sûreté, thought Alain de Passe as he stepped into the loft. Put it to St-Cyr and get it over with, but first . . . 'Jean-Louis, where's Kohler?'

Notebook in hand, postcards were being carefully examined but left exactly in place for the police photographer.

'Ah, Préfet, it's good of you to come. Hermann? Gone for help, I think.'

The grey eyes narrowed under their coal-black brows, the cleanly shaven chin stiffened belligerently. '*Imbécile*, don't piss about with me! The car's still here.'

'Then my partner went on foot. The farmhouse, probably.'

'*Couillon*, there hasn't been anyone in that house since last autumn.'

Asshole . . . and he was already shouting at him. 'Last October, Préfet? Right after the party, the "picnic"?'

'*Maudit salaud*, what are you talking about? Parties? Picnics?

When the harvest here is done, the family move on to another. That is the only reason there is no one in that house at present. Come spring, they will return.'

'Then tell me what you make of this.'

'This? A former *transporté*, an *ancien du grand collège*? He killed Mireille de Sinéty, idiot, and took his own life when he felt it prudent. I would have thought it obvious, but then you and that partner of yours never considered it worthwhile to spend a few moments consulting with me at the *préfecture*.'

If not Madame Simondi as the killer, or Genèvieve Ravier or Xavier, then Brother Matthieu. 'A hardened criminal, Préfet? A former resident of the Îles du Salut?'

The Islands of Safety, the penal colony that was just off the coast of French Guiana. More specifically, Île Royale and Île Saint Joseph. Notorious for the tiny triangle they formed with the Île du Diable, Devil's Island, there being no more than 200 metres of shark-infested ocean between each of them and only the immensity of a tractless jungle to tempt escape.

'In 1922 Brother Matthieu violated and murdered a sixteen-year-old farm girl. Oh *mais certainement*, he vehemently denied having done so. He claimed to have come upon her quite by accident and after the fact, had been out collecting morels, and gave her the last rites. But you see, his rosary was found clutched in her fist and he hadn't gone for help, nor had he told anyone about her. He'd been too afraid, he claimed. But with his history of wanting female hair and postcards like those, what was the examining magistrate to think, and then the court? Her blouse, shift and brassiere had been torn away and her throat opened with a pocket-knife not dissimilar to the one he has left on that napkin.'

It gets worse and worse, said St-Cyr to himself, but is it yet another part of the song they must sing?

De Passe took out a cigarette case and offered one and a light, as a chief administrator should to a detective of long standing. 'They gave Brother Matthieu fifteen years, but reduced the sentence to twelve in consideration of his war wounds and his being a man of the cloth. The girl had been seen teasing him about his face and had been known to flaunt herself in front of the boys, but by rights he should have got the guillotine.'

The islands were tiny – the Île du Diable being less than two square kilometres in area and flat under the blistering equatorial sun but, unlike the other two, it had been reserved for the politicals. The penal colony had been closed in 1938 but several had been left to languish, the war having delayed their repatriation indefinitely for all they knew, since no news of its progress would likely have reached them.

'The Church couldn't turn its back on him, Jean-Louis. I myself always felt the bishop too kind. I warned him of repeat offenders. I cautioned prudence, but . . .' He gave a tiny shrug. 'Henri-Baptiste is a true servant of God. He said that it wouldn't be right of us to condemn a man beyond the years of his sentence.'

The cigarettes were American and had, no doubt, been confiscated from a downed airman. 'But why should Brother Matthieu kill Mireille de Sinéty, Préfet? Oh for sure he had a key to the Palais and couldn't be found when the concierge went looking for him, but a girl with the voice and fingers of an angel . . . one whom everybody revered and admired? What possible reason could he have had, since she wasn't sexually interfered with in any way?'

Jean-Louis wasn't going to take the proffered help and leave the matter well enough alone thought de Passe and said, 'You know the de Sinéty girl intended to confront Henri-Baptiste and the other judges with what she mistakenly felt had happened to Adrienne de Langlade.'

It was time to put out the cigarette and to do so carefully. 'And what *did* happen to Adrienne, Préfet?'

Would they now attempt to stare each other down? wondered de Passe. St-Cyr and Kohler had seen the police photographs of the girl's body but had told the clerk not to notify him of this. 'She disappeared.'

Such levelness of tone was all too clear. 'And when, please, did she "disappear"?'

'*Maudit salaud!* Did you think that file deliberately thin – is that it? It *is*! But you . . . you think I'm hiding things from you? Me?' He tapped his chest. 'How could you when I want more than anything to clear this matter up?'

It would be best not to shout as well. 'Thin? There is so little in it, Préfet, Adrienne de Langlade's passing hardly drew breath.'

The bastard! 'Then understand, *mon fin*, that we couldn't pin things down. César came to me on the thirtieth of October last. He couldn't understand her having left without telling anyone. He felt betrayed but thought she could well have paid her parents in Paris a little visit.'

That could have been so easily checked with the Kommandant. 'And did she?'

'Jean-Louis, listen to me. These things . . . You know how they are. A pretty girl goes missing. We wonder what could have happened to her and, yes, we think the worst. Telegrams are sent to the district *préfecture* of the family but . . . Ah! What can one say, but that they revealed she wasn't there.'

There'd be a record of those as well as the Kommandant's issuing of the necessary *laissez-passer* for such a trip, and he could see St-Cyr thinking this but couldn't stop now. 'Nearly three weeks later her body turns up, but the flooding is so extensive we hardly have a moment. There are no signs of violence other than those of the flood. Decay is advanced – you yourself saw the state the corpse was in. What were an overworked, exhausted préfet and his men to have done?'

There'd been the frayed end of a rope tied to her right ankle but he'd leave that for now, thought St-Cyr, and so much for there having been 'no signs of violence'. 'Yet Mireille de Sinéty suspected Brother Matthieu of the killing, Préfet? This is what you're saying.'

Jean-Louis still wasn't going to look the other way. Pride was one thing, stubbornness another, misguided patriotism yet another.

'That girl was mistaken. Tragically so.'

'Then how, please, did Brother Matthieu learn of her intention to accuse him if, as we have been given to understand, she only confided in a very few?'

225

Merde alors, the son of a bitch! 'A few? What few, please?'

Bon! 'For now that information must remain confidential, Préfet. But I can tell you Dédou Favre knew what she intended to do.'

One had best look away and drop the voice. 'The Favre boy. Another tragedy.'

'For which you are not to get off so lightly. You had that boy arrested before dawn last Monday, Préfet. Did you use the coal shovel on him?'

Kohler had still not appeared. Jean-Louis had his back to the portal and was dangerously close to it. A slip . . . A step backwards? wondered de Passe. 'The boy gave us what we wanted.'

'The location of his *maquis*? We know this because you sent the Kommandant out to bring him in, certain he'd bag a few but not the one you had in custody.'

Four steps, possibly five, separated them. 'I did what I had to. These are difficult times. Von Mahler would have been far too soft on the boy.'

'Of course, but you desperately had to find out exactly how much Mireille de Sinéty really knew and then . . . then you had to make certain the girl was silenced.'

'Pardon?'

'You heard me.'

A fist was clenched. Spittle erupted. 'How dare you? *He* killed her. A former resident of the *grand collège*. No examining magistrate will argue with this, Jean-Louis, only with what you and that partner of yours *think* is the truth!'

De Passe had inadvertently stepped on the artichoke hearts. He seemed not to have noticed as he wiped his mouth.

'Then listen to me most carefully, Préfet. Adrienne de Langlade was murdered. You know it, we know it, and so did Mireille de Sinéty, Dédou Favre and the others she confided in.'

'What others? I ask it again, damn you!'

'That's not for you to know yet. You were present here during the picnic at which she was drowned in that iron *accabussade*. You were a part of what happened to her, Préfet. Admit it!'

You fool, said de Passe, silently cursing him. 'I was not present.'

'You *were*! With all the arrogance and stupidity of privileged men who think they can hide what they've done, you and your companions left telltale things.'

'*Nom de Jésus-Christ, bâtard*, what things?'

'Photographs.'

'There are no photographs. None were taken.'

'But then you must have been here, Préfet, and have just admitted it.'

From the crest of a low hill near the eastern shore of the island, Kohler watched as de Passe's car left in one hell of a hurry. Long lines of spindly poplars crossed the *bocage* at regular intervals, hiding the car and there to shield the cropland from the worst of the mistral. Idly he wondered if he could calculate the préfet's speed, given the width of the strips of land between the rows of trees and the time it took to cover five or ten of them.

Mathematics – that kind – he'd had enough of in the Great War. Where more shelter was needed – for melons, strawberries and other tender crops – woven screens of reeds had been used. But the landscape was a tangle. The flood hadn't been kind and Simondi had thought it best to leave well enough alone and not call in the clean-up crews.

Hence the préfet's speed? he wondered, knowing Louis must have said something.

De Passe hit a washout and very nearly left the road. Long before he would have reached the bridge, Kohler had lost sight of him, yet kept on gazing that way.

'*Mein Gott*,' he said. 'How the hell are we to find anything in this?'

The poplars looked bleached and old in the sharp, cold light of the afternoon. Some still had a few dead leaves clinging to their branches and these mirrored the sunlight so that as he looked across the fields, he saw these lights blinking at him.

Longing for a gentler time, he started out towards a tangle of battered, woven screens of reeds. When he found the dog, it was chained to the trunk of one of the poplars and all but hidden among the mats of reeds. Ice was thickly clumped about its paws.

It didn't bark, didn't whine. It just shook hard, was so tired after twenty-four hours or so of trying to break free that it could only raise its sorrowful deep brown eyes to him. Frost clung to its whiskers.

'Nino,' he crooned and grinned like a schoolboy in spite of the state the poor thing was in. 'Hey, you've found a friend. Come on, let me get you out of this.'

Undoing the chain, he lifted the dog and soon had her tucked inside his greatcoat. Freezing, she shivered constantly while he had a little look around.

There was a filthy woollen sock lying on the ground nearby, and in its mended toe a *pétanque* ball. Metal and hard as hell. 'Xavier was to have killed you,' he said, opening his coat a little to comfort her. 'But the one who could finger a *maquis* couldn't bring himself to do it and left you to die all on your own like the coward he is.'

When he got back to the mill, Kohler lit a fire in the kitchen stove and began to warm a saucepan of water. Still there was no sign of Louis and he thought this odd, but the dog had to be cared for. He couldn't leave her yet. 'And you need a little something to eat,' he said.

'Louis,' he called out. 'Hey, Louis, guess what I've found?'

There was no answer. The loft was much as they'd left it. The frugal legacy of the *gueule cassée* was still spread out on its napkin, the humble repast to one side . . .

The grappa was fierce, the view from the portal bleak. Brother Matthieu seesawed gently. 'Louis . . .' he bleated, sickened suddenly by the thought that something untoward must have happened to his partner.

There were no signs of blood in the loft, none of a struggle. Had de Passe had a pistol? He cursed himself for not having sensed trouble and come back sooner. 'But I wouldn't have found you, would I?' he said frantically to Nino.

Man's best friend wolfed the greasy, oil-soaked artichoke hearts and finished up the stray crumbs of the *chèvre* before starting in on the olives.

*

228

The Villa Marenzio had become too quiet, thought Christiane, pausing to listen intently to the house. Marius and the others had stopped arguing and raising their voices over the chances of the singers surviving as a group, but Brother Matthieu *had* hanged himself and now . . . now . . . Were Marius, Norman and Guy whispering to each other about Genèvieve and herself? Were they saying it was all her fault and that each part of the song must live in absolute harmony with the others?

'It's all going to end for us!' she cried. 'St-Cyr and Kohler will find out you were going to be dismissed, Genèvieve, and that César felt we had grown too close.'

Genèvieve didn't hold her. Genèvieve didn't come closer but remained apart and standing just inside the bathroom door.

'You know it's bad luck for a Pisces to possess a stone like this,' said Christiane bitterly. 'Then you tell me why Mireille had to give it to you last Monday after practice? Last Monday, Genèvieve!'

The face, the cameo of the fourteenth-century pin she had been cleaning, looked up at her. Slowly at first, and then more and more as must have happened with Adrienne's body, the flood-waters from the tap began to drag it free and towards the drain. A beautifully carved portrait of a young girl of substance, that other Mireille, the stone no longer a dirty greyish green but a lovely delicate oval of soft yellowish green, the name of the stone combining two words from the Greek. '*Krusos*,' she wept and tried to stop herself. 'Golden, Genèvieve, that's what it means, and *prasos*, their word for the leek. The golden leek – chrysoprase, damn you!'

'Stop it. Stop it now!'

'I can't! I mustn't. I have to say things to you.'

'Then give that thing to me and I'll take care of it!'

'No you won't! It's mine now. With me it's safe.'

A Gemini . . .

Christiane snatched it up and turned swiftly to face her. 'Who really killed Mireille?'

Her slightly parted lips began to tremble as she waited for an answer. She was so tense and afraid, thought Genèvieve. No longer was there any light in her eyes, only suspicion. 'I . . . I don't know. I swear it, *chérie*.'

'I went to bed early that night. You know I did.'

Her voice had climbed. She had to say something. 'There are no secrets between us, Christiane.'

'There can never be any, Geneviève.'

The softness of a smile would be best. 'I wasn't long but you had already fallen asleep when I went in to see you.'

'Liar! You went to the Palais. You were there, Geneviève. Madame came here to get the sickle from the props' room and you . . . you followed her. César wanted Mireille for himself. You know he did but Madame is very jealous. She tolerates you and me only because she knows about us and to her it doesn't matter if César takes either or both of us whenever he feels like it and you . . . Sometimes I think you enjoy it!'

The price they had had to pay, and an honest assessment given by one who could well have gone to the Palais herself. 'But Mireille was different – is this what you're saying?' said Geneviève cautiously.

'You know she was perfect for that *livrée* of his. César would have given her time but would have wanted her as his wife. Nothing less would have satisfied that ego of his. She and Adrienne were to have replaced you and Xavier. I was to stay on.'

'And now . . . now you think I killed her,' said Geneviève.

'You had to!'

'But so did Xavier.'

Christiane ducked her eyes away. 'And . . . and so did Madame,' she said, taking a quick breath. 'I . . . I admit this freely.' Geneviève still hadn't come to her. Geneviève wasn't going to and yet . . . and yet an earnestness had softened the hardness as her lips began to form words – would they be of kindness?

'Then ask yourself, *ma petite*, how could César allow Mireille to destroy everything he and the bishop and the others had put together? César wanted Madame to kill Mireille – he planned it that way. It was that or do it himself. Regrettably he had no other choice. She'd get the guillotine because de Passe and the magistrate would make certain of it. One has to protect one's business associates and fellow *pénitents noirs, n'est-ce pas*? Why else would César have starved her of absinthe for five days, Christiane? You know the state Madame was in by Monday.'

Answers had to be found and one always had to weaken when challenged by Geneviève. 'Xavier is her *confident*. He got her the sickle. He went with her and . . . and let Nino into the Palais to find Mireille when . . . when César and the others had left. Mireille was in tears after the audition and felt she had lost everything. She had stupidly confronted them with the truth about Adrienne but Dédou hadn't come to back her up. She was all alone and . . . and soon left the Grand Tinel.'

And it was very dark in the *Chambre du cerf*, wasn't it? asked Geneviève silently. 'Then Xavier could have killed Mireille for Madame.'

'Yes. Yes, that is so.'

'Then, there, now you know everything. Feel better?' she asked, tenderly enfolding her. 'Cry. Let it all come out, *petite*. I know you didn't mean to say that about me. I know you still love me.'

A hesitant breath was taken. Warm, wet lips were pressed to a cheek as arms were wrapped more tightly about her. Tears flooded.

'When . . . when you came into my room I pretended to be asleep. I . . . I went to your room, Geneviève, but couldn't find you. I looked everywhere and . . . and then I left here and went after you. I had to stop it from happening. I couldn't have you dismissed from the singers and found guilty of Mireille's murder. I couldn't have us parted because of her.'

'You fool. You little fool.'

A few parishioners were scattered about the Cathédrale de Notre-Dame-des-Doms. But the chancel was unattended. No confessions were being heard, the Blessed Sacrament was not being made available.

Alain de Passe cursed the absence and hurried to the left, past the carved white marble throne of a twelfth-century bishop and on into the sacristy, but still there wasn't a sign of any of them. '*Merde*,' he breathed.

They were in the adjacent chapel. 'César . . . Ah *mon Dieu*, at last I've found you.'

'*Un momento, amico mio*. Let us wait until Henri-Baptiste is finished.'

Prostrate in the coarse black cassock of a simple priest, and with his face pressed painfully to the floor and arms outstretched with hands clasped, Bishop Rivaille prayed before the tomb of Pope John XXII.

The reclining stone figure of the pope had been destroyed during the Revolution and later replaced by that of a bishop. Six of the elegant statues which had once adorned the tomb had long ago been removed to decorate the Église de Saint-Pierre which was just to the south-east of the Palais.

'He's begging His Eminence to intercede with the Holy Father on his and our behalf,' confided Simondi wryly.

And so much for stringing up a pregnant naked girl in his room at the mill and thrashing the hell out of himself while standing before her. 'He worshipped that girl even more than he did Mireille de Sinéty. A virgin, he thought,' clucked de Passe and sadly shook his head as if to say, How naive can the clergy get? 'We have to talk, César. St-Cyr didn't believe for a moment that Brother Matthieu had done it, nor that he had killed the *petite lingère*. To him Henri-Baptiste must have violated Adrienne de Langlade while in a drunken rage.'

'And everything we see here suggests that he did,' muttered Simondi sadly. 'The remorse for breaking his vows, the tears of anguish at the threatened loss of the dream, not to mention that of everything else.'

Across the place de Horloge, the swastika flying from the Kommandantur and Hôtel de ville seemed larger than most. In the fast-greying light, the colours were darker, the design sharper, more ominous.

And yet here am I, one of the Occupier, seeking sanctuary, thought Kohler, wishing Louis was with him. But Louis wasn't.

Louis hadn't been in the Café of the Panic-stricken White Mule. He hadn't been at the *préfecture*, he had simply vanished – had he vanished? The river? *Mein Gott*, the river!

Von Mahler was busy at his desk and didn't appreciate the sudden intrusion. Nino barked. Kohler shouted, 'She's with me. She's brought along evidence to match the other shoe she found and good for her, eh, Nino?'

Taking the frayed tennis shoe from her, he patted the dog warmly, then thumped the shoe on the desk. Sand flew up. 'Herr Oberst, my partner's missing.'

'He's at the morgue.'

'And dead! The morgue. I knew it.'

Kohler looked ill. For perhaps ten seconds the detective couldn't seem to move as the colour drained from the scarred and frost-burnished cheeks. Then he yanked at a chair and sat down heavily.

'I need a drink, damn it, and a cigarette!'

Cognac in hand, and doors closed, he stared in silence at his glass before muttering, 'The morgue . . . I always knew it had to end. *Salut*, Jean-Louis. *Salut, mon vieux.* Here's to the best damned partner there ever was.'

Tears fell and he didn't care if he was seen with them. 'You son of a bitch!' he said scathingly. 'You could have stopped this whole thing from happening but oh no, you had to cosy up to those bastards. You had to be seen to get along with them and to tolerate their schemes!'

'Kohler, pull yourself together.'

The closely trimmed, crinkly dark brown hair and good looks of von Mahler only infuriated. 'What's the use of my "pulling" myself together, Colonel? With one down, they have only one more to go and everything will be neat and tidy.'

'Now listen—'

'No, you listen. They drowned Adrienne de Langlade, and when Mireille de Sinéty found out about it, they realized she was about to sing. No matter who used the sickle on that girl, it has to have been done with the sanction of all of them. And don't give me any of that *Quatsch* about the bishop and Simondi worshipping the girl and needing her. To them she was a threat they couldn't tolerate.'

Von Mahler searched for something. A paper-pusher all his life, was that what he'd been? snorted Kohler and said, 'When we first met, Herr Oberst, you told me you had no idea who had replaced you as the third judge. For all you knew, Simondi could have cancelled the audition. Since the concierge hadn't been aware of one, you stated that this must mean there hadn't been one.'

'And?'

Von Mahler's iron-grey eyes met his without a waver. 'Those were all lies, Colonel, and you knew it even then. That concierge was in a cinema that was reserved for your men.'

'The projectionist and usherettes are French. One more would not have mattered.'

'But it *did*, Colonel, and I think you're more than a little aware of this. Salvatore Biron was purposely delayed until after Rivaille and the others had left the Palais – *if* they did leave it, as they claim. He found the body moments too late and heard a sigh that couldn't have been hers.'

'All right. Simondi did ask me to allow Salvatore to watch that film. At the time, I thought it could do no harm.'

'And your wife, Herr Oberst?'

Kohler wasn't going to leave things alone, not now. 'Was at the Palais. It was she who gave the sigh Salvatore heard. I . . . I was merely trying to protect her.'

'From the *Cagoule* or from justice? *Bitte, mein lieber* Oberst, I must ask it.'

'From exposure, then. I couldn't have her forced into facing yours and St-Cyr's questions and then those of an official inquiry.'

'She saw someone.'

'She *thinks* she did, but it was far too dark.'

Von Mahler's expression was firm in resolve, but what the hell . . . 'I'm going to have to speak to her, Colonel. You can't refuse. Maybe you could with my partner, but not with me, my friend. Not with me.'

'Perhaps, then, you had best read this. It's from Gestapo Mueller in Berlin but was forwarded to me via Gestapo Boemelburg in Paris.'

GEHEIME

Achtung. The Avignon murder under investigation by St-Cyr and Kohler is an internal matter for the French to settle. No assistance is to be given.

HEIL HITLER

'Then it's up to them, is it,' asked Kohler, 'and the *Cagoule* they control?'

Some men would never learn. 'Though it will sound lame, and it was myself who requested the two of you, my hands are tied. I'm sorry, but apparently the Reich has far more need of them than it has of you and St-Cyr.'

Kohler sighed heavily at the ways of the Occupation, and for a moment devoted himself entirely to Nino. Then he looked up, took his time, and said, 'At the conclusion of our last investigation, Colonel, my partner and I filled Gestapo Boemel- burg's car with loot we had recovered. All my boss really wants is to make certain he keeps it.'

'And the others? The rest of Gestapo Paris-Central, the SS of the avenue Foch, the French Gestapo of the rue Lauriston, and, yes, Gestapo Mueller?'

'Want an end to us, but obviously they've not heard Louis is no more.'

'No more? But he's at the morgue as I told you. I saw de Passe let him out of the car not two hours ago.'

Alone with the body of Mireille de Sinéty and the things she had worn, St-Cyr tried to concentrate. There was so little time. There was the threat of the *Cagoule* – de Passe and the others would have to put a stop to Hermann and himself. They'd have no other choice, not after what had happened at the mill, and yet . . . and yet time had to be taken. 'You are demanding it of me,' he said to her shrouded corpse. 'You expect me to put my mind back into the very early Renaissance and to think as one would have then, but I have to tell you that that order book you kept with the glyphs as a shorthand is sadly with my partner in the car.'

Spread out on one of the pallets was the jewel-and-*enseigne*-studded belt with its talismans and tiny silver bells. The *aumônière sarrasine* was there but he had emptied the purse and had fanned out its contents.

Taking up the tin of sardines, he asked himself why, if she had known Dédou wasn't to be at the Palais, had she included it? The thing was entirely out of keeping with the rest of her costume, but she must have had a reason. Hope perhaps, that after all, the boy would come. Some reason anyway. Or two, or three, he reminded himself. 'For that was the way of things. The little games one played in those courtly days, but you weren't playing a game, and neither are my partner and I.'

The dirk, the sewing kit, scissors and keys were there and he had to ask himself, as he had when first encountering her body, why had she not used the dirk to defend herself? There really had been virtually no sign of a struggle. Signs of hide and seek, the hunt, the chase, of course; the prayers on her knees also, and in the *Chambre du cerf*, the Pontiff's study, which had direct access to his bedchamber next door . . .

'Ah *nom de Dieu*,' he breathed. 'That first Mireille must have gone to that same chamber late at night to beg His Eminence Clément the Sixth for mercy.'

Unsettled by the thought, for it implied again that history really was repeating itself, he looked at the belt.

'You knew which of them would kill you. It's all here in front of me, isn't it? Bishop Rivaille – was it him? Was it Simondi or that one's wife? Was it one of the singers – Genèvieve Ravier perhaps, or her lover, or Marius Spaggiari? Xavier?' he asked. 'The *Cagoule*?'

High on her left hip she had pinned her own sign, that of the House of Balance in gold, its weighing pans upended as if the hand-held balance had been flung far up into the heavens to hang suspended there for ever. And from its pans had been strewn the cabochons of meaning, the jade and lapis lazuli, moss agate, chrysoprase, amethyst, ruby and malachite – opal, too, and coral and jet. Beautiful things, lovely things, but . . .

The fleurs-de-lis brooches that had fastened her mantle were next to the coins, as were the fine gold neckchain and two of the three rings she had displayed there, since she couldn't have worn any more of them on her fingers. Rings given in friendship or exchanged perhaps to celebrate some event, for people did that sort of thing during the Renaissance. But had the hair in the bishop's ring really matched that of Adrienne de Langlade? Would it ever be possible to lay the two side by side under a microscope?

Rivaille had recovered the pendant box. He practised flagellation and there was the image of a tiny silver *martinet* on her belt and directly above the sign of the Goat, a Capricorn.

Again, as before, he noticed that the Archer's arrow was pointed at this sign, but beyond the goat there was a moonstone cabochon over which was a cluster of pearls, each in the shape of a teardrop.

She couldn't speak, he couldn't seem to put his mind completely into the framework of her own. Anxiety . . . the threat of the *Cagoule* . . . were interfering.

'The keys,' he said when Hermann came to find him. 'I've been the world's biggest fool, *mon vieux*. Keys meant far more to those of the Renaissance than they do to us today.'

'None of those keys would have been a damned bit of use to her, Louis.'

'But that's just it! Keys could and did signify many other things. That the subject's heart was locked up, that her thoughts and loyalties were true, her faith in God still resolute.'

'She wanted others to unlock things,' said Kohler softly. 'She knew she might not survive.'

'I just wish you had brought along her order book. I'm missing something obvious, Hermann. I know I am. She'd have smiled gently at me or laughed, but then . . . ah,' he shrugged. 'She wouldn't have laughed, would she?'

'The sign of the two fishes is often repeated.'

'*Merde*, what an idiot I am! The two fishes . . . The label on the sardine tin. The sign of a Pisces – is this why she had it in her *aumônière*? Not to give to Dédou at all, but to tell us a Pisces had killed her?'

'Geneviève Ravier?' muttered Kohler. 'Hey, the sign of the Virgin, with wheat stalks in hand, is also often repeated.'

'Idiot, that's not just the Virgin; that's the Gleaner, the winnower of facts!'

Kohler pointed to the *martinet*; Louis said, 'The Goat, I think.'

The bishop and Adrienne de Langlade. 'There's a tiny triangle in gold that's formed of letters.'

'C, A, M, A, E, L,' said Louis, 'with the C alone and in the upper corner. That is the name those of the Renaissance would have used for the Angel that rules the planet Mars which, in turn, ruled the House of the Scorpion.'

'Simondi?'

'Or his wife?'

'Why not tell me what happened at the mill with de Passe? You scared the hell out of me. You know that, don't you?'

Louis appeared to pay no heed.

'Her gimmel ring links lapis lazuli with a saffron-yellow topaz, which is one of the stones of the Archer, Hermann. Her gown was of the same shade.'

'Dédou, then. Now quit keeping me in suspense about the mill.'

'Inadvertently de Passe confessed to having been present when Adrienne de Langlade was drowned. He had tried to tell me Brother Matthieu was responsible for both killings.'

'And?' hazarded Kohler.

A hand was tossed at fate, a shrug given. 'He threatened all sorts of things and shouted, "Do you think we will let you and that partner of yours destroy everything we have worked so hard for?" '

They stood in silence, looking down at the rebus, then Kohler found his voice and said, 'Where's Peretti, Louis? Why the hell isn't he here with you?'

It would have to be said. 'Ovid has been sent to Lyon, Hermann. He only had time to give me his report and to release these items into my care. De Passe and the others got to him. He said he was sorry, but . . .'

Louis shrugged again. It was the way of things these days. Someone was always interfering.

Kohler told him of the telex from Mueller. Longing for a cigarette, he found he had none.

'Lies upon lies, Hermann,' said Louis, offering one and a light. 'Always the song they all must sing infuriates the ears of one who once played the euphonium in the police band. But we shall see if, as singing masters to them, we can't improve things.'

Oh-oh. 'You didn't . . .'

It had best be said quickly. 'I told de Passe we would hold an audition in the Palais's Grand Tinel this evening at twenty-two hundred hours. I advised him most strongly to have the singers present as well as the judges and Madame Simondi, though I felt, and still do, that that one would not be "well".'

'*Dummkopf! Verdammt!*'

'Hermann, I really had no other choice. When our préfet told me to pack up and leave immediately or else we'd be lucky to escape with our lives, I had to give him the only answer I could.'

A purist! 'What about Frau von Mahler, eh? You're forgetting her.'

'Not at all. That's why we're going to take these things to her for safe keeping.'

'Idiot, von Mahler won't let you get within shouting distance of that woman!'

'Then we shall have to see that he does.'

Darkness had fallen and with it had come a fresh uneasiness Kohler didn't welcome. Across the place de l'Horloge the Kommandantur was just too busy. Though showing a light from any window or door was *verboten*, repeatedly there were glimpses of the entrance. Armed men in uniform came and went. Two sentries guarded the door and oh *bien sûr* those boys had been there earlier, as they were each and every hour of the day, but now he was going to have to pay particular attention to them. 'Louis, this is crazy. They'll have Schmeissers.'

'Trust me. It's the only way. Just keep the engine running. I won't be long.'

'You're an idiot. You know that, don't you? He'll have you shot.'

'Perhaps but then . . . *mais alors, mon vieux*, perhaps not.'

Louis was gone from the car before anything further could be said. Still keeping his eyes on the entrance, Kohler reached over the back of the seat to Nino for comfort and felt the dog respond immediately. 'You were there at the Palais the night she was killed,' he said.

She licked and nuzzled his hand, got all excited. Was he going to let her out of the car? Were they going for a hike?

'Hey, take it easy. No, stay in the back seat. Stay, Nino. *Stay!*'

The beagle had a mind of her own and found his lap readily enough. Eagerly she licked his face, was all over him. He had completely missed seeing Louis go into the Kommandantur.

'You know all of them,' he said as he patted her head and scratched behind her ears. 'You had this around your neck, didn't you?'

At the sound of the *clochette*, bedlam ensued. Nino barked joyously and tried to get out of the car. It took time to calm her down. 'Who else was there?' he asked. 'Was it Madame Simondi?'

Nino put her head down on his lap and waited to be punished.

'Was it Genèvieve?' he asked and felt her lift her head instantly at the sound of that name.

She got up and looked out into the night. When he said the *Primo Soprano*'s name again, Nino searched the darkness and barked expectantly.

'Good for you,' breathed Kohler. 'Now let's try Mireille. Where's Mireille, Nino?'

The dog returned to his lap and tried to work her muzzle between the buttons and in under his overcoat.

'You loved her, didn't you?' he said. 'Almost as much as you did Xavier. He tidied things up, didn't he? He had to. He couldn't have us knowing that sickle came from the props room. Where'd he hide it, eh? Come on, you can tell me.'

*

Seated at his desk, the mayor of Avignon passed unblinking moist brown eyes over the sudden intruder and let him be. But in that one glance was summed up so much. The humiliation of having to work under the Occupier, the outright willingness now to not see things one should even if it meant an assassination and that the intruder could well be a *résistant*, the knowledge, too, that they were both patriots.

Not one of the *Comité secret* or of its *Cagoule*, not anything but an honest, hard-pressed individual in his mid-fifties, the mayor knew very well who it was and went calmly on with his work beneath the portrait photograph of the Maréchal Pétain that graced every such office. Teleprinters hammered beyond the confining walls of the corridor. Telephones rang. Conversations in French and German incessantly bombarded the ears. Something was said about *Banditen* in the hills, something else about the Reich's need for olive oil and other foodstuffs.

Words went on and on about the *Service de Travail Obligatoire* and February's inauguration of the local detachment of Vichy's newest police force, the *Milice*. Strong-arm boys and men whose job it would be, among other things, to fill the labour quotas – 50,000 a month was demanded – with those plucked from the streets, homes, tramcars, buses and cinemas, remembering always that if such were on a bicycle or in a *gazogène*-powered lorry or auto, or merely carrying home a few hard-won staples for an impoverished larder, these items were an added bonus.

Von Mahler was on the telephone. St-Cyr cursed his luck, for all three doors to the office were open and he was certain one of the secretaries in an adjacent anteroom had seen him. Hermann had been right. This was crazy, but desperate situations require desperate solutions.

'St-Cyr, Sûreté,' he said, softly mouthing the words to the secretary and, putting a hand over hers, pushed the telephone receiver she had been listening in on down until it was back in its cradle. 'Come with me. Please walk in front. I am, as you can see, armed.'

Louis still hadn't returned; he was taking far too long.

'*Verdammt!* What the hell has happened to him, Nino? Christ, I need a cigarette!'

The dog licked hands that trembled. She got up to look out into the darkness as he was now constantly doing. She knew he was anxious and wanted to help.

'You're beautiful,' he said, remembering the souls of dogs long past. 'Giselle and Oona could take you for walks. They'd love you, too, but it isn't healthy for dogs in Paris these days. Count yourself lucky. The citizens here aren't quite so hungry, not yet.'

But give it time, he said sadly to himself and went to open the door, to follow Louis, to . . .

The engine idled. His breath, and that of Nino, were causing frost to build up inside the windscreen. He began to scrape this away. He occupied himself, fought for patience, and asked, 'What really happened in those last few moments before she died? If, as the judges have stated, they left the Palais together, then they left that girl all alone up there in the Grand Tinel. But she wasn't alone – we all know this – and Albert Renaud said he thought he had heard someone in the stairwell when he went to get the chairs.'

Nino put her head down in his lap and felt his hand come to rest, warm and gentle, so gentle.

'Why *did* Renaud come forth with that little bit of info, Nino, unless trying to plant the thought that blame must surely lie with Madame Simondi?'

Mireille would have gone into the Kitchens Tower next to the Latrines to get her overcoat and things, but she hadn't put the coat on, had she?

'She'd have had to take one of the candelabra with her unless she had left a torch with her things. But who put out the other candles, and did that person or persons then call out to her, because sure as hell, she must soon have put out her own light.'

Still desperate for a cigarette, he searched the side pockets of the Renault but found only maps. 'Was it Frau von Mahler who called out a warning to her, Nino? You must have heard it. Xavier had released you by then so that the sound of your *clochette* would lead him to her.'

Had he killed that girl? Had he done so for Madame Simondi?

'*Artemisia absinthium* – that's wormwood to us, Nino. You take the leaves and flowers and pound them in a mortar along with angelica root, sweet flag root, the leaves of dittany of Crête, aniseed, the fruit of the star-anise and other aromatics. You macerate everything – soak it in a high-proof alcohol and let the mixture sit for eight days before distilling, which gives an emerald green liqueur. To this you add more of one of the essential oils; anise most probably – my partner loves it – and *voilà*, you have *l'Extrait d'Absinthe*, the milk of the gods, he'd probably call it. Pure knock-out elixir. How close was Xavier to that woman, Nino? Did she tell him things she'd tell no one else? Did she offer him a job for life as her little companion if only he'd take care of a certain problem, but not like he'd taken care of Adrienne?'

Nino whined and snuggled closer, didn't raise her head.

'Being under the empire of alcohol is no fun, my friend, but as sure as we're sitting here awaiting a disaster, that woman would have been in really bad shape. The shakes like you wouldn't believe. That's why Xavier had to do the killing for her; that's why he took you with him. An accomplice! He played on your loyalty and innocence. He forced you into it.'

'The reed warbler's nest!' he cursed, startling Nino. 'I forgot all about it, didn't I? You and Xavier had been over to the Île de la Barthelasse and were on your way home. That's how it was, and how you came to be in the Palais when it happened. You found the damned door open.'

Again he anxiously searched the darkness for Louis, but there was no sign of him.

Von Mahler looked at the revolver St-Cyr had promptly given up and placed on the desk not nearest to himself but to the one he had intended to kidnap.

'Four things, Colonel, that's all I ask you to listen to.'

'Agreed.'

The door to the office had been closed; the secretary had been told to leave and ordered to remain silent.

'First, your wife planned to kill herself and had purchased a

Belgian FN semiautomatic on the black market, and most probably in Paris on one of her periodic journeys there for medical help. She knew you were very fond of Mireille and that, in her mind at least, the girl would make an ideal replacement for herself.

'Second: two weeks after Adrienne de Langlade's body was freed by the flood, Frau von Mahler took a Cross of Lorraine from beneath the lapel of Mireille's overcoat. This, though she hasn't admitted it, must have made your wife very afraid for your as well as your children's wellbeing. A *résistante*, a frequent visitor and close friend of the family? The Gestapo would most certainly have been interested in such an association should it ever have come to light.'

Was St-Cyr trying to blackmail him? 'And the third thing?'

'Dédou Favre was arrested by Alain de Passe in the early hours of Monday.'

'*Verdammt!* What is this you're saying? De Passe . . . ?'

'Colonel, the reward of one hundred thousand francs was paid. Xavier turned the boy in. It's my belief that he didn't act alone, but was compelled to do so, not out of loyalty to the Reich, but to Bishop Rivaille, Madame Simondi, her husband and the other singers. Like all of them, he didn't want that girl destroying everything they had.'

'And the fourth thing?'

Von Mahler would deal with de Passe in his own sweet time, thought St-Cyr. 'Your wife knew something of what Mireille intended to do. She went to the Palais either to protect or to stop her. She had already told the girl you would refuse to act as the third judge, so was certain in her own mind you wouldn't be there. She has also admitted to having seen someone, Colonel, even if you think it too dark, and hasn't denied being there, but again I must remind you that as well as being a friend, the girl was very much a threat that couldn't be overlooked.'

'And you want me to ignore an order from Gestapo Mueller? You must be mad.'

'Doesn't the Army still believe it's above the Gestapo and the SS, or has it finally come to take orders from them?'

The High Command and upper echelons of the Wehrmacht still distrusted and despised the Gestapo and the SS with a vengeance and were extremely jealous of the Führer's misplaced trust in them. 'How certain are you of this pistol you say she has?'

'Very.'

'Then let us hope she hasn't shot herself because if she has, you will be held responsible.'

10

No sentries stood in the darkness outside the Colonel's house. Unchallenged, Kohler anxiously nudged the Renault as far out of sight as possible. 'Louis, this isn't right. First we have a meeting after curfew on the bridge and von Mahler tells us it never happened, and now he's given his boys time off to warm their toes.'

'And I've been an even bigger fool than I thought. Was he there at the mill when that girl was drowned, Hermann? Isn't this really the reason his wife found it so necessary to go to the Palais on Monday night? Are they both covering things up as well?'

It was a heartfelt plea for answers. Von Mahler had had to get along with the local establishment. And sure he was pissed off about what de Passe had done with Dédou but had also wanted to talk to the boy before anything untoward had happened. Another cover-up, was that it? wondered Kohler.

'It's all in the rebus, Hermann. The Archer points his arrow; two fishes are joined but swim in opposite directions; the sign of the Twins often lies beside them.'

'Geneviève Ravier and Christiane Bissert?'

'The Colonel . . . Was he seen with those two at the picnic?'

'Did he make mischief with them, Louis, and help those bastards drown that girl, or close his mind to it?'

Nino had to pee but her paws were still too sensitive to the cold and Hermann had to help her. Dogs and horses had always been his friends. He had a way with them. A natural. 'Come on,' said St-Cyr gently. 'Let's go in and get this over with. We haven't long until the audition.'

At 2200 hours . . .

*

'In the Middle Ages and the Renaissance,' said Marie-Madeleine hesitantly, 'the five-pointed star, the pentacle, was thought to be the most powerful of talismans and was worn not only to protect one from all enemies but to give long life, peace of mind and harmony. Mireille was convinced of this.'

Frau von Mahler had yet to say a thing. The belt was laid out on a table, the order book and pomander were beside it. Von Mahler was looking decidedly uncomfortable.

'The tiny silver bells were to ward off the devil with their sound,' went on the former nun, her fingers lightly touching them as if in doing so she could bring back her friend. 'This button in which the capital letter I intersects another, has the letters A, G, L, A in the quadrants so formed. *Ate Gebir Leilam Adonai.* Thou art mighty for ever, O Lord. People wore this in the fourteenth century to protect them from fever and . . . and other things.'

'Against lies?' asked Louis sharply. Kohler sat in an armchair with Nino at his feet. Frau von Mahler sat some distance across the room with the Colonel nearby, but the woman had yet to look up. She was composing her thoughts, was deciding on what and what not to say.

'Emerald,' said the former nun, ignoring Louis's question about lies. 'This stone was worn because possessing it allowed one to foresee the future. Its mounting has no backing, and the stone was held up to the light. If clear, as this one is, the seeker immediately saw the truth.'

'The signs of the zodiac, then,' said Louis gently.

The girl looked at him for a moment before taking up the order book to show him the glyphs that were used to denote each house. 'The House of the Fishes is represented by the alchemist's sign for projection, a capital H, but with out-bowed sides,' she said. And then, still holding his gaze with her own, 'Pisces, the twelfth house, is sometimes thought of as the house of one's own undoing. Though Mireille disputed this, she did agree scandal and imprisonment could sometimes dodge those who were born under its sign.'

'Is Genèvieve Ravier the Pisces?' asked Louis.

She gave a slight nod and said quietly, 'Christiane Bissert is the Gemini. The two are often linked because . . . because in life, their lives are almost as one.'

'You spoke with Mireille de Sinéty on the night before the murder.'

'Inspector, Mireille was very afraid. She knew that Bishop Rivaille and Maître Simondi suspected she was about to confront them but swore they couldn't possibly know how damning that confrontation would be.'

'Then Dédou was arrested and they soon learned everything, through no fault of the boy's,' said Louis. 'Most break under torture, mademoiselle. Dédou was not alone in this and shouldn't be condemned.'

'*Merci*,' she said softly, but was so pale and afraid herself. 'You see, Dédou was my brother and though I know it was God's will, I'll miss him terribly. And, yes, in their eyes, especially in those of the bishop, I stand condemned for leaving the Order and for speaking out, but I'll go with you and will confront them as Mireille must have done.'

Very quickly she showed him the rest of the signs. 'The House of the Goat rightly claims the bishop, that of the Scorpion, César Simondi.'

'And Albert Renaud?' he asked.

'The Ram – a bloodstone with blood-red flecks among the dark green. His family outwardly loved and secretly hated the de Sinétys six hundred years ago and Mireille was well aware of this but took it in her stride as she took everything else.'

'And Madame Simondi?'

'A Cancer. For her, Mireille used the cat's-eye which was said to be without equal in bringing success in gambling and in all other games of chance.'

'Could Xavier have killed your friend on orders from her?'

'Xavier . . .'

'Mademoiselle, I regret having to ask, but time is of the essence and we still have much to do.'

'I . . . I really don't know. I wish I did, but . . .'

'What about Christiane Bissert?' asked Louis anxiously.

'Geneviève was to have been replaced, Inspector. Christiane felt this deeply. "Those two," Mireille said, "are the ones I fear the most among the singers because they see me taking away everything they have." '

Then it was true what Simondi had said of Geneviève. 'Was she also afraid of Xavier? Mademoiselle, again I must ask you to set aside feelings I know must be of despair.'

Faintly she smiled through her tears, then said bitterly, 'You're wondering why, if she was so worried about him, did she ask Xavier to contact my brother. It's really quite simple, Inspector, and has as much to do with six hundred years ago as it has to today. Only Xavier can avoid the controls like no one else. Only he could have gone to warn Dédou that morning and not be seen by the préfet's men. I knew it; Mireille knew it, and so did he. When Xavier arrived well before dawn we both saw it as a sign, a supreme test, if you like, of the triumph of good over evil. God wouldn't let Xavier betray my brother. Dédou had to be contacted. What else could she have done?'

So silent had the room become, thought Kohler, not even Nino stirred.

'Xavier is a Leo, and you can see that Mireille has used a sardonyx cameo to represent him. The deep flesh red of its stone is seen through the falsity of the white surplice – the coating that covers its surface. The sins of the flesh, are you wondering? The father of Adrienne's unborn child? Then, yes, Dédou told Mireille what happened last June, and yes she was very upset about it, but couldn't let on.'

'Could she have changed the position of any of these things when told that Dédou wouldn't be coming?' asked St-Cyr.

'It's . . . it's possible but . . . Oh, I can't remember the arrangement. I can't! Madame, I can't!'

Distraught, she turned to Frau von Mahler who still refused to look up or to acknowledge anything.

'Mademoiselle, please try,' urged Louis.

'I *am*!'

'Then tell me why there is nothing here to indicate either Frau von Mahler or the Colonel.'

But was there? wondered Kohler, not liking the thought and bending over to take Nino into his lap.

'Gentlemen,' said von Mahler, 'Mireille was neither afraid of myself nor of my wife. She had no reason to be.'

'Kurt, tell them about the picnic at the mill last October – the "party". Tell them that you were there with Mireille and that, when she asked to leave, you thought it best to . . . to escort her home.'

'I went to the office afterwards, Ingrid. I swear it.'

'You stayed with her. You talked – I know you did because she told me of this. You were "very kind and understanding", she said. *Understanding*, Kurt.'

Nom de Jésus-Christ! swore Kohler silently. Now all the dirty linen comes out.

'The girl was definitely a virgin, madame,' said the Sûreté brusquely. 'Colonel, a little about this "party", please. We gather things got out of hand.'

They'd find out everything. 'Only later, after Mireille and I had left. She saw it coming, as I did, and didn't want to hang around. She tried repeatedly to convince Adrienne to leave with us but the girl refused.'

'Adrienne was a Virgo, Inspector,' said Marie-Madeleine softly. 'She had, unfortunately, both a willingness to admire and to submit to those in power. Bishop Rivaille worshipped the girl and thought her hair matched exactly that of Mary's in his ring. He had great plans for her, but as you can see by this *enseigne* next to his, the devil is allergic to Holy Water. The aspergillum in the friar's hand sprinkles its water over the lead button of the Goat upon which a *martinet* also falls as the Archer aims his arrow.'

'Ah *bon*,' said Louis. 'One thing remains and then we must hurry. Madame?'

Composed at last, Frau von Mahler faced them. They would expect nothing less and suddenly she had to let Kurt know that she would no longer hide this matter or any other.

'I saw someone, and heard things. I was terrified I would be too late. I left the dinner table well before the others but even so was some distance from the Palais. The streets were unfamiliar. I . . .'

'At about what time would you have reached the Palais?' asked Louis gently.

'Nine forty-five, I think. Their car had just arrived. Bishop Rivaille was asking Simondi if the door to the Palais was locked and did he have his key. "It's unlocked," he said. "She must be here already and has left it open for us."'

Madame Simondi would have been able to get into the Palais with no problem, thought Kohler.

Von Mahler took his wife's hand in his and asked, 'What then?'

She gazed steadily at him, no longer afraid of what he'd see and, still doing so, said, 'I waited. I didn't really know the layout of that place. It's so huge and frighteningly empty, Kurt. So cold and cruel, but I thought I must surely hear the judges' steps and I did.'

'They crossed the main courtyard?' asked Louis.

'No. They stayed indoors and went into the Great Audience Chamber and up the main staircase. They had blinkered torches but when they reached the Grand Tinel, César quickly drew the black-out curtains, then helped the bishop find the candles. Suddenly there was light, a beautiful light. Albert Renaud, he . . . he went to get the chairs.'

'They had passed through the *Chambre du cerf* and the Pontiff's bedchamber,' said Louis.

'And the Robing Room, which is just before the Grand Tinel. Monsieur Renaud set up the chairs and they each sat down but . . . but still there was no sign of Mireille. I wondered if she'd come at all, or simply was late, but knew she wouldn't have avoided things or hesitated.'

'And where were you?' asked von Mahler.

Again she would look steadily at Kurt, she told herself, and then she would tell him. 'I wanted to see her and yet not be seen. I . . . I knew there was another tower I could use.'

'The Saint John's Tower,' interjected Marie-Madeleine.

'Yes. It opens off the lower Consistory and the Grand Tinel above. I retraced my steps and . . . and that's when I saw some-one. This person was as startled as I. We had almost collided. She gasped, "Ah *non!*" and retreated swiftly.'

'Was it Geneviève Ravier or her lover, Christiane Bissert?' asked Louis firmly.

'The latter, I think, because she was not so tall, but I really don't know either of them well, only that this one was stooped in haste and wore the heavy black habit and cowl of a monk.'

And there it is, thought Kohler wryly, that clot of black wool Peretti found in the victim's hair, only to hear Louis asking what she, herself, had worn.

'Why, my overcoat, of course,' she hazarded.

'Inspector . . .'

'Colonel, please be patient. Hermann, perhaps Mademoiselle Marie-Madeleine would show it to you.'

They waited in silence, the three of them. Frau von Mahler took to staring at her hands only to suddenly reach for the bowl of fabric remnants and to . . .

She's lost and desperately afraid, said St-Cyr to himself, silently asking, What did you do, madame, when you found that girl alone and on her knees in the *Chambre du cerf*? Did you . . .

'Louis, the overcoat's dark blue and trimmed with lambskin.'

'Ah *bon!*' he said and sighed but didn't look up. Briefly the Colonel's wife glanced at him, then darted her gaze back to the remnants. 'I . . . I didn't go into the Saint John's Tower,' she confessed. 'I went on through the Consistory and up the far staircase – the one that also leads down into Bénédict the Twelfth's Cloisters. Because I had seen someone else in the Palais, I felt it best to . . . to warn Mireille if possible and to . . . to be as close to her as possible.'

'Then you were near the Latrines Tower and in the upper kitchen,' said Louis warily.

'Yes. Her . . . her overcoat and things were lying neatly on one of the stone ledges. Her torch was there on top of everything but . . . but when I switched it on, it . . . it didn't work. The . . . the bulb had been removed. I thought of the girl I'd met – had she done this? I wondered. I searched a little. I did what I could, you understand, but by then Mireille was being told what to sing. Each of the judges was to set her a task. Simondi was the first. "Orazio Vecchi's *L'Amfiparnaso*," he said. "The first seven lines from the fourth, eleventh and thirteenth of the madrigals in this *comedia harmonica.*" '

'But he told us she was only required to sing the simplest of passages!' blurted Louis.

'Ah *non*, they were very difficult but she sang them beautifully. Right from the heart and in defiance of the three of them and what they stood for. Her voice had such clarity and joy. It filled the hall, and I knew then that she sang not only for herself but for that first Mireille and for Dédou too.'

Kohler glanced at his wrist-watch and silently cursed the time. 'The audition, Louis . . .'

'A moment, *mon vieux*. We're almost there.'

'She didn't break down, if that's what you're thinking, Inspector,' said Frau von Mahler. 'She was told what to sing by Renaud and then by Bishop Rivaille and she did so with that same defiant clarity. But . . . but then they gave her their decision. Struck silent by this, she faced them and . . . and cried out, "I know what really happened to Adrienne and I can prove it." '

Ah *merde*, thought Kohler.

'And they said nothing further?' demanded Louis.

'They waited for her to continue and she . . . she told them that if they didn't agree to the demands of the *maquis* for sanctuary and food and warm clothing, she . . . she would go to my husband and . . . and tell him they had drowned the girl.'

The little fool, thought Kohler sadly. Brave but naive and willing to set everything else aside in order to help the cause. Dédou and his friends must've been in really bad shape.

'And then?' asked Louis, using his Sûreté voice.

'Then?' she shot back at him. 'They turned their backs on her as one and left the hall, left her all alone – I couldn't go to her after hearing that, could I? I . . . I was paralysed with shock and fear. She . . . she put out the candles one by one with the snuffer the bishop had placed on the floor beside his chair. And only when it was dark did I hear her weeping. It . . . it was then that I called out to her – I had to, don't you understand? "Madame," she cried. "Madame, you must leave here at once! There are others in the hall." Others I couldn't see at first. My torch was blinkered.'

'How many?' asked Louis sadly.

'Three, maybe four. I couldn't be sure because all of them wore those same black cassocks with their hoods pulled up and my light touched only bits of them until . . . until knocked from my hand.'

Verdammt! The singers. Spaggiari, Rochon and Genèvieve, Norman Galiteau as well. 'Louis . . . Louis, we have to leave.'

'I'll come with you, Inspectors. I must. For her sake as well as for my own.'

'As will I,' said Marie-Madeleine.

It was von Mahler who swore under his breath and said, 'Ingrid, you mustn't. If Berlin were to find out, Gestapo Mueller would see that I was shot for insubordination or sent to the Russian Front.'

No truer statement had been made, thought Kohler ruefully. Mueller would have the Führer screaming with outrage and von Mahler had known this only too well. 'He's right. Why chance it?'

She would face right up to Herr Kohler, would tell him how it was. 'Because I must. Because even though, at the end, she had turned against the Reich, that girl meant a lot to me.'

'*Liebchen*, I'm asking,' entreated von Mahler only to hear her say, 'And I'm telling you, Kurt.'

He gave a sigh. 'Then you leave me no other choice but to join you and defy Berlin.' He unbuttoned his tunic and removed it. 'A sweater . . .' he said. 'Give me a moment.'

'Colonel, might I suggest you ask your wife to take along her pistol?' said Louis. 'Just in case. And you your own. Hermann, can we all fit into the Renault? They'll have men watching for it. If you pull right up to the entrance staircase, and we stay close together, they may think there are fewer of us.'

'And Nino, Louis. I'm not leaving her behind. Not tonight.'

Alone, the blue-blinkered beam of von Mahler's torch sought out the floor plans of the Palais that hung in the former guardroom, now the ticket office. It came to rest on each of the ten, massive stone towers that formed the square corners between which had been built the long and vaulted reception halls and chapels, with subordinate rooms.

'Each tower has four or five levels,' he said, not liking the look of things. 'Access within each is by narrow staircases that were built into the walls. Since it was a fortress first, a treasury second and a palace and administrative centre lastly, all of the upper levels of the towers were and still remain sealed off for defensive purposes, except for those same narrow staircases.'

'And below the Papal Bedchamber?' hazarded Louis.

'The Chamberlain's room, the lower treasury and, below that, the wine cellar.'

Only in those lower levels, from the Papal Bedchamber down, was there access to the rest of the Palais.

The *Chambre du cerf* was in the Wardrobe Tower which abutted the Angels Tower and had, again, free access only on its lower levels, most particularly through the Papal Bedchamber which adjoined it.

Mireille de Sinéty had thus been able to move from the Kitchens Tower, which was near the northernmost corner of the Palais, far to the south through the length of the Grand Tinel, passing by, on her left and midway, the Saint John's Tower before entering first the dressing room, then the bedchamber and finally the *Chambre du cerf*. She had, no doubt, been heading for the Clementine Chapel and the main staircase which would have taken her down into the Great Audience Chamber. Somehow she had realized the way to freedom had been blocked and that she could no longer flee.

On her knees, she had begun to pray and had been killed while doing so, but by whom? Had it really been the singers? Xavier, eh? demanded Kohler of himself, wishing it was so but finding he had also to ask, Rivaille, Simondi or Renaud? Any or all of whom could so easily have turned back to ruthlessly hunt her down and silence her.

Nino fidgeted. Tied to a long leash, she began to bark. Unfortunately it was a sound that was bound to carry. 'Come on, then,' he said. 'Find it for me. There's a good girl.'

Marie-Madeleine stayed close to Frau von Mahler, but neither of them had said a thing since leaving the house, and Kohler really didn't know why the former nun was crowding the woman. Comfort maybe, or something else, something she knew that she hadn't let on. Louis and the Colonel brought up the rear. Their torches winking, all hurried because Nino hurried. All passed quickly under the high and vaulted ceiling of the Great Audience Chamber and went up the main staircase, the sound of their steps harsh in the cold darkness. Another and far narrower staircase soon followed. This the dog raced up, Kohler following as best he could.

Nino didn't hesitate in the *Chambre du cerf*. With her muzzle close to the floor, she went on into the Papal Bedchamber and from there up yet another of the steep and narrow flights of stairs. She was panting, was anxious.

They were now in what had once been the upper treasury and directly above the bedchamber. Polychrome timber beams in the ceiling were all that remained of the original decoration but even here, bits of wood and plaster had been plundered and sold off when the Palais had been a barracks.

All of the glazed ceramic tiles were gone, those with their pale green and brown doves, their bounding hares and hunting hawks.

Nino stood rigidly pointing at one of the flagstones in the floor.

'What is it?' asked Kohler. The dog gave three short, sharp barks and began to worry the flag.

Prised from the floor, it revealed its hidey-hole. Where once a bag or two of silver and one of gold, or vessels of the same, had been hidden, there were now, at the bottom, both the sickle and the *martinet*, whose short, black leather thongs lay over the blade of the other.

'Good girl,' sighed Kohler, fondling her head. 'I knew you could do it.'

The blade of the sickle was dark with age and smeared with dried blood. Bits of lavender and winter grass still clung to the wooden haft which had been bound with baling wire. 'Xavier, Louis.'

'But why the *martinet*, Hermann, unless he wanted us to blame Rivaille?'

'And get free of blame himself. He'd have had to bring it from the mill.'

Louis got down on his hands and knees, and using his handkerchief, gingerly pulled away the thongs to look more closely at the blade. 'It's perfect, Hermann,' he sighed, 'and exactly as I'd imagined.'

'Ingrid? My wife . . .' began von Mahler, only to realize she had slipped away.

'Sister . . .' began Louis.

'I'm not a sister, not any more.'

'Where has Frau von Mahler gone?'

There were tears she couldn't stop, and Marie-Madeleine knew she must appear very pale and shaken under the blue light from their torches. 'I . . . I don't know. Honestly, I don't.'

Voices rose to fill the Grand Tinel and filter out to rooms and halls and staircases, the song now racing like the wind. '*Alla caccia . . . alla caccia . . .*' To the hunt . . . the hunt . . . '*Subito . . . Subito . . .*' Hurry . . . Hurry . . . '*Di qua . . . qua . . . qua . . .*' Over here . . . here . . . here . . . '*Venite volontieri . . .*' Come gladly . . . gladly . . . '*Chiamatie li bracchi . . . bracchi . . .*' Call the hounds . . . the hounds . . .

Deep in the cellar of the Wardrobe Tower and still searching frantically for Frau von Mahler, Kohler let Nino go. Joyously she raced away and soon he could hear her barking high above him in the Grand Tinel.

But then the singing stopped, and for a time he could hear nothing. He shook his torch, cursed the unreliability especially of Gestapo Paris's batteries these days, and got the thing going again.

A discoloured seepage had frozen to the ancient stone walls, the room square and seemingly vast but also a forest of stout octagonal stone pillars that rose to the arches they supported.

Verdammt! Where the hell had that woman got to? Why had she felt it so necessary to leave? She'd been present during the murder – had she lied about what had happened? If so, others would know of it. Others.

257

Switching off his torch, he strained to listen but could hear nothing definitive and then . . .

When he heard a breath escape, he thought it must be her, but moved aside and made no sound. The breath had come from behind one of the pillars – off to his left, he thought, and asked again, Why had she slipped away, if not because she still had things to hide? Had she killed the girl? Had she been able to lie so well until faced with their finding the sickle?

Kohler moved among the pillars until his foot came against, and sought out further, a stone ledge. Something was resting on the damned thing. Something tall and round and of cold metal that was evenly coated with chalky dust.

The thing stood on a low platform, and it was huge but still he couldn't figure out what it was, knew only that he wasn't alone.

Feeling always the fine coating of dust, he began to move forward. The walls were at least six centimetres in thickness and it was definitely round. Three stone steps led up the side and stopped him from continuing.

Hearing the breathing again, Kohler turned and waited, and to the feel of the dust on the rim, came the touch of a coarse woollen cassock. A sleeve . . .

Silently he stepped off the ledge and moved away. The voices of the singers started up and began again to filter throughout the tower. They soared, they raced away, chasing after one another, shifting . . . constantly shifting, the song in Spanish and about three Moorish girls who had stolen someone's heart.

Suddenly they stopped, and he strained to hear them.

When he switched on the torch, its ghostly pale blue and slit-eyed white light fell on the Pontiff's lead bathtub that had defied the centuries.

There was no sign of the cassock, and he knew then that it could well be that others were also hunting for Frau von Mahler.

Lute, recorder, shawm and tambourine were in hand, the tableau the singers presented like a painting of Caravaggio's, thought St-Cyr. Beatific, pastoral, their costumes magnificent and full of vibrant colours and the play of candlelight, they looked so at ease with one another and their music. Banishing everything else from their minds, as only the truly professional can do, they sang not only for the sheer joy of it but for the group as a whole, as one and immensely proud of it. Their expressions were keen to every nuance, one smiling, another listening attentively for a note or passage which would rise above the others even as their voices chased after it, the centuries retreating from that of the mid-sixteenth to that of the mid-fourteenth.

The Grand Tinel filled and echoed with the sound of them and the echoes themselves were used to chase after or run before a part or two or three, the sound superb in every way . . . but murder . . . Murder . . .

Genèvieve Ravier sat central to them and at the back, with the warm tone of a lute cradled in her sky blue, silken lap. Christiane Bissert sat below her and to the right, the outspread knee of the one touching the green velvet shoulder of the other in comfort . . . would it be in comfort or as a warning, a threat? he wondered, entranced by it all.

Guy Rochon, the tenor, was to the *Alto*'s left and also just below Genèvieve. Then came Norman Galiteau with shawm in hand, and opposite him, Marius Spaggiari, and finally, Xavier.

All looked so innocent. The madrigal came to an abrupt and racing conclusion. 'Disperse,' cried out Simondi, as if they had to do this, had to show this Sûreté what would be lost if one or all of them were found guilty.

They took up positions widely spaced about the hall and from each other . . . 'Orlando di Lasso's, *Bonjour: et puis, quelles nouvelles*,' called out the singing master. Good morning. So now, what news have we?

A madrigal about a pretty maid who drew water from a well followed, their voices coming from each and every part of the hall. Echoing, ringing with bell-like tone, chasing as the maid would chase, first one and then another of the village boys, racing in joyous abandon, all united, all as one . . . One . . .

'*Quando ritrova*,' sang out Simondi. 'It's from the masterpieces of Constanzo Festa, *Ispettore*.'

A song about a shepherdess in a meadow, at a murder inquiry!

A sickle . . . Another *faucille?* wondered St-Cyr, suddenly sickened by the thought of his throat being cut . . . *Cut!*

At the opposite end of the hall, and where the judges would have been seated on the night of the murder, Simondi sat to one side of Rivaille, Albert Renaud to the other. And the business suits those two wore were not at odds with the white-and-gold robes of the bishop who aspired to have the Papacy returned to Avignon in this 'new and even brighter Renaissance'.

Grim-faced, and wearing the ruby ring only and on the third finger of the right hand as it would have been worn back then when given in marriage to God or to a woman, Rivaille gazed coldly at one of the singers . . . Which one? wondered St-Cyr.

The Kommandant had still not joined them, nor had his wife and Hermann . . . Hermann. Only Marie-Madeleine was with him, a worry to be sure, for he couldn't guarantee her safety here.

It was not good. No it wasn't.

Nino wandered in and out of the window alcoves and far in behind their black-out curtains. She searched for and followed one scent while Xavier patently tried to ignore his former friend.

Ten candelabra, each with five candles, had been placed at intervals about the hall. *Fifty* candles had had to be extinguished before Mireille de Sinéty could be killed.

'Gesualdo's *Moro lasso,*' sang out Simondi, his voice firmly in command. '*Ispettore,* in 1590 Gesualdo arranged for the murders of his wife and her lover, but he was one of the finest composers of his time and far in advance of most. Flamboyant, daring, a man of the world and of varied tastes and many, many love affairs, a master of the contrapuntal whose music still lives while the dead wife quickly slipped into obscurity.'

Like your own might well have done? wondered St-Cyr, frantically looking about the hall for Hermann. Where the hell was Hermann?

The singers sang the madrigal and then, at a curt nod from Rivaille, an instantly subdued and suddenly tearful Christiane Bissert stepped dutifully forward. She looked so fragile now, so lost and afraid. Setting her recorder carefully down on the floor beside her, and kneeling, she crossed herself while facing her judges and then, her lips moving in silent prayer, bowed her head and, with hands clasped devoutly, awaited their sentence.

'There is your murderess, Inspector,' said Rivaille scathingly. 'Let it not be said that the Church ever failed to uphold justice and truth. She is mighty, as God is mighty. Let no man question it. This court is now adjourned.'

'A moment, Bishop. Forgive a humble Sûreté, but . . .'

'Don't be a fool! Haven't we provided you with the answer you so demanded and at great cost? That girl was here and has confessed! What more could you possibly want?'

'The absolute truth, Bishop. A few small questions. Nothing . . .'

'Don't you dare taunt me with that rubbish you people from Paris pack around with you! Here we do things in our own way.'

'The maître's wife, Bishop? Might it not please the court to tell me where she was on the night of the murder and why, please, she's not with us as specifically requested?'

The bastard!

'*Ispettore*,' began Simondi, gesturing apologetically. 'My Marceline couldn't have been here, either then, or now. She wasn't well. Both you and Herr Kohler, and the members of this court, my singers also, know how ashamed I am of her repeatedly disgracing herself in front of others. I do what I can, isn't that so? but . . .' He shrugged. 'What is a loving husband to do with such a one?'

Kill her, was that it, eh? The hypocrite! To lie like that and to think one could get away with it!

Marie-Madeleine had now gone to join Christiane on her knees, but with her back to the judges at the far end of the hall and all but hiding the girl from them. Looking pale and badly shaken and ready to bolt and run, Geneviève Ravier stood next to the curtained entrance of the Saint John's Tower.

The hall grew quiet except for Nino's constant comings and goings. Not a one among them could fail to realize the dog was retracing the final steps of Mireille de Sinéty. Nino would pause to lift her head and look at the judges as if to say, Aren't you going to follow me like you did on that night?

Silently Rivaille cursed Xavier for not having killed the hound and so did Simondi and Renaud, but where, really, was Hermann and why, please, had de Passe not come? De Passe . . . Ah *merde* . . .

The match was struck but broke and all Frau von Mahler could think about was the acrid smoke it gave. In panic, she dropped her torch, couldn't seem to move, couldn't even cry out.

Another match was found and she heard the grating sound it made on the sandpaper of the packet. Sparks flew up. Flame burst suddenly – hot, so very hot it became a roaring inferno in her mind. Showers of sparks landed in her hair, on her clothes, down her back . . . her skin . . . her skin . . .

The match went out and for a long, long time she couldn't move yet knew she must. She must.

Another match was struck. This time the flame wavered in his hand and she saw the faces of the past leap out at her from the wall behind him. The faces of women in soft, pale blue and chalky-pink gowns. Some were staring impassively at her, others at each other or looking away. Some wore a bit of white lace over their plaited golden tresses, others did not or had their hair completely covered. Some were old, most were young and with these last, their lips were not wide in smiles of grins but compressed in judgement – *judgement* – their eyebrows plucked into perfect arches to frame the eyes. The eyes . . .

Tentatively she felt her own eyebrows, exploring where they'd once been before hesitantly covering her mouth to stop herself from being sick.

Again the match went out. *I'm in the Saint John's Tower, the lower chapel,* she cried out silently to herself and tried desperately to find her torch.

This time the flame revealed him to her and she saw him against the fresco. He had removed the leather greatcoat, military cap and gloves. These were nowhere near him.

The knitted pullover he wore was of coarse black wool but frayed and worn completely through at the elbows and she wondered why he had chosen to wear it, not just because she had made it for him years ago, but because . . . because . . .

'*Liebchen*, it's only me,' he said in *deutsch*. 'My torch doesn't seem to be working.'

'Nor mine,' she quavered and said silently to herself, I thought I knew you, Kurt; asked again, Why has he worn that sweater?

Neither of them moved to comfort the other. Darkness came swiftly. Kohler waited for his eyes to adjust, waited, too, for something else, and when the Hooded One followed the couple, he followed him.

The cote-hardie was of emerald green velvet whose sheen rippled softly in the candlelight. The laced-up bodice was of white silk with gold piping and brocade. There were jagged slashes of burnt sienna, an undersheath of rose madder.

St-Cyr took in everything, the cinematographer within him alert to the slightest change, the detective keyed up. Nino had ceased prowling and now stood rigidly pointing at the curtained entrance to the Saint John's Tower and upper chapel as if she had heard or seen something.

Genèvieve Ravier was hesitant but pleaded with her eyes as she looked towards her friend and lover, and Christiane Bissert faced her from the far end of the hall.

At the opposite end, Rivaille's expression remained grim and unyielding in its condemnation of the girl, he seated smugly with the others. In turn, Simondi and Renaud also waited for the accused to confess.

'Inspector . . .' began the girl, only to falter and to look again at Genèvieve, imploring her to understand. '*Chérie*,' she begged, 'I have to tell them. I must!'

'You promised not to! You said you wouldn't!' WOULDN'T . . . WOULDN'T . . .

'I know, but . . .'

'Mademoiselle Bissert,' said St-Cyr sternly. 'At the *livrée* this morning you felt someone would kill my partner. You attempted to distract Herr Kohler. Please state the reason for this clearly.'

Still just within the stairwell and surrounded by stone walls,

Kohler could hear Louis well enough but had to shut him out of his mind, was close . . . so close to the Hooded One.

'I . . . I had been told to do so, Inspector,' she confessed with eyes lowered.

'By whom?' demanded Louis sharply.

'César . . . César, must I say it here? *Here* and . . . and now!'

'Little one, you'd best.'

She swallowed hard and stood with fists clenched, was pale and shaken and in tears no comforting Marie-Madeleine could give would stop.

'Maître . . . Maître de Passe, had come to the *livrée* to help César. He found me in one of the corridors and . . . and told me what to do.'

There, she had condemned both Geneviève and herself, she cried inwardly and begged God to forgive her, only to hear the Sûreté asking gently, so gently, 'Or else what would happen to you, mademoiselle?'

'Or else I would suffer and . . . and so would Geneviève. The *accabussade* for us both. Me first so that Geneviève could watch what was happening to me, and then . . . then her, too, but . . . but after I was no more.'

'Ah *bon*,' said Louis. 'Now we can return to the murder of Mireille de Sinéty and to the night of Monday last. Your lover was to have been dismissed, mademoiselle.'

He had moved nearer to Geneviève but was on the opposite side of the hall from her and the entrance to the Saint John's Tower.

'To save herself,' he said, and his voice carried and was full and robust and without fear, 'your lover instigated what happened to Adrienne de Langlade, both at the *mas* of Mademoiselle de Sinéty's mother and then at the mill on the Île de la Barthelasse. She egged the rest of you on, didn't she, but with Xavier's help and under instructions from Madame Simondi?'

'I'm sorry, Geneviève. I know you will hate me but yes. And *yes*, I helped her, Inspector. I did! And . . . and may God forgive me.'

'And as an accessory to that first murder, mademoiselle . . .'

'*Ispettore*, I object! Adrienne de Langlade drowned.'

'An accident,' spat Rivaille. He'd had just about enough of this upstart from Paris.

'An accident, Bishop, to which we will return,' countered the Sûreté. 'But first, mademoiselle, to the murder here. You had to intervene, didn't you?'

'I knew what you planned to do to Mireille, Geneviève. I couldn't let it happen.'

'Happen . . .' sang out Marius Spaggiari.

'Happen . . .' echoed Norman Galiteau.

'She took a black robe . . .' continued the tenor, Guy Rochon.

'A black robe from our props r—' Xavier's voice broke. Shattered, the song fell apart, and for a moment Christiane glared hurtfully at each of them, then angrily wiped her eyes and blurted, 'Damn you, yes!'

'The sickle also, mademoiselle,' said the Sûreté, his voice carrying into the stairwell. 'The main entrance to the Palais wasn't locked.'

NOT LOCKED . . . NOT LOCKED . . .

'The door was wide open!' she cried in despair. 'Geneviève, I had to do it for you. I had to!'

Marie-Madeleine had reached out to the girl to grip her by the shoulders. 'Quite by accident you ran into Frau von Mahler,' she said accusingly. 'You turned around and left her, didn't you? Well, didn't you?'

It was no use. The Inspector must know everything, thought Christiane. He was watching Geneviève closely, was afraid she would try to make a break for it. He was watching Xavier and the others, even Nino too.

She gave a nod and said hollowly, 'They . . . they had come into the Jesus' Room through the entrance that gives out on to the Main Courtyard. They . . . they were all wearing cassocks and hoods as black as mine, but . . . but I didn't see this until later.'

So silent had the hall become, she felt she could hear the candles.

'There were four of them, weren't there?' sighed Louis, his voice carrying and causing Kohler to wince at its intrusion into the Tower.

The girl must have swallowed tightly and nodded, was probably still trying to beg her lover to understand and forgive . . .

'One of them took the sickle from you,' sang out Louis. She was heard to answer faintly, 'Yes.'

'And one of them killed Mireille de Sinéty,' he continued. 'It wasn't Genèvieve Ravier because she hadn't been able to get to the Palais.'

'*Ispettore*, what is this you are saying?' demanded Simondi.

'Only that Genèvieve failed to reach the Palais.'

'Then where was she?' demanded Renaud, his glasses winking in the candlelight.

'With Madame,' said Genèvieve bitterly. 'Madame had made it as far as the Villa Marenzio. She was frantic, incoherent, highly agitated and shaking like crazy. Like *crazy*! *Chérie*, that is why you couldn't find me when you went to my room after I had found you "asleep".'

'Ah no. No!'

'And now you've told the Inspector that you were here with them, *petite*. With *them*!' said Genèvieve in tears.

The echoes ran. They seemed to chase one another and for a time no one moved in the upper chapel and in the narrow staircase that led to it.

Cautiously Kohler let the fingers of his left hand explore the rough stone wall ahead of him, and when he touched the cassock again, he waited once more.

It was Louis who said clearly and sharply, 'Four men, Mademoiselle Bissert, but were our three judges and Alain de Passe those four? That is the question. *Bien sûr*, they each know who did the killing, but did those who judged her so harshly not leave the Palais as claimed after the audition? Did they not turn their backs on that girl and let others do the task they wanted?'

WANTED . . . WANTED . . . 'Who really killed Mireille de Sinéty?' he sang out suddenly.

DE SINÉTY . . . DE SINÉTY . . .

In the pitch darkness of the upper chapel, one name was said softly but urgently by Frau von Mahler. 'Kurt . . .'

And then, 'Ingrid, I tried to warn you that I couldn't countermand an order from Berlin. We weren't supposed to be here. It was all to have been left up to them.'

'But Mireille . . .'

'Was a terrorist, *eine Banditin*, was she not?'

Ah nom de Jésus-Christ! swore Kohler silently.

But then the point of a stiletto dug itself in under his chin and the gun in his hand was teased away. Others were behind him. Others had come up the staircase so silently.

'Go on up, Inspector. The time for all such singing is now over.'

The Grand Tinel had grown so silent, even Nino cringed at Hermann's feet. Von Mahler, furious with what had happened, had been forced to relinquish his pistol. He'd objected coldly and with threats that were far from hollow, but Alain de Passe, who had been the last to arrive, was totally in command. Berlin would understand. Berlin.

The one in the black cassock stood out, with hood thrown back, but not a monk, by the look, not one of the brothers. Tough, grim-faced and in his mid-thirties, had he been the killer? wondered St-Cyr. Marie-Madeleine had glimpsed him only once and that had been enough for her. Terrified now, her lips moved silently in prayer, for she knew only too well what was going to happen to them and to herself.

But this one alone wore black. On both sides of the hall, and at equally spaced intervals with glowing candelabra between them, some sixty of the Hooded Ones stood in two long lines facing each other. They blocked all exits. No weapons showed – they didn't need those to strike terror into their victims. And the white hoods they wore hid their faces except for the eye, nose and mouth holes. And on the left breast of each white robe, each shroud, was the silvery dark blue brocade of a fleur-de-lis with gold piping.

Mireille de Sinéty had had to make these 'costumes' and would have known only too well what she and Dédou and the rest of his *maquis* had been up against.

Only the turn-ups of stiff, coal-black trousers showed beneath the hems of these robes, and then . . . then the black leather, hobnailed boots Vichy must have given them. The *Milice?* wondered St-Cyr and glanced at Hermann, only to see his partner grimacing with distaste and know the stomach was tightening at the thought of Vichy's newest police force playing dress-up as *cagoulards.* Ah *nom de Dieu,* to be kicked to death by those boots – and they would be; he could tell Hermann was thinking this – would not be nice.

Strong hands, perpetually tanned by generations and generations of Mediterranean sun, were there, but so, too, were those of the fairer. Peasants, small businessmen, shop clerks and bankers, the extreme far right, the *Comité secret d'action révolutionnaire.*

Here, at last, was its Action Squad and its leader, Préfet de Passe.

'Your revolver, Jean-Louis,' said de Passe, and though his voice hadn't been raised in the slightest, it was heard throughout the hall.

Kohler could see Louis hesitate. Those big, dark brown ox-eyes watered. The moustache that had been grown long before the Führer ever thought of wearing such a thing was twitched, a sure sign the former *pugiliste* and champion of the Police Academy was furious.

The singers were clustered, but not about Christiane Bissert who stood alone, dejected, lost and terribly afraid.

Marie-Madeleine had gone quickly to join Frau von Mahler and to take the woman by the hand.

Von Mahler waited by the entrance to the Saint John's Tower but was defiantly blocked from entering it.

The judges were standing beside their chairs, each of them looking on with bated breath.

'Don't be foolish,' breathed de Passe to Louis. 'Just hand it over. You and Kohler can do nothing.'

'Then that's it, is it?' demanded the Sûreté coldly.

'You know it is. Why argue?'

Louis tossed a gesturing hand in defiance. 'At least allow us to settle this matter so that all may go their separate ways knowing the truth.'

Verdammt! Don't push your luck, *mon vieux*, thought Kohler. Stall for time – *ja, ja*, of course, but watch out.

The Lebel was taken. 'Proceed,' taunted de Passe acidly. 'Please let us have the benefit of your "truth", knowing well that you ignored the warning I sent you.'

Louis indicated that he wished, at least, to enjoy his pipe and tobacco, only to remember Frau von Mahler, to look at her with concern and empathy, and say, 'Forgive me, madame.'

She nodded tightly. She watched him closely. *Mein Gott*, the strain in that woman's expression, thought Kohler. The grief, the anger, the tension . . .

'Ah *bon*,' acknowledged the Sûreté, tossing his head a little. 'Now let us begin. Mireille de Sinéty thought as one would have done in the fourteenth century. Bishop, you of all of us know this best. You lingered over her body while giving the last rites. You tried desperately to read the rebus you knew she must have left for others like us to find, but until now I didn't fully comprehend how deeply she felt and lived that century, nor how complete was her foretelling of this affair.'

He began to walk about, cupping that cold pipe in his left hand and gesturing with it now and then. 'She had laid it all out for us, hadn't she, Bishop? The Cross of Saint Bénédict, the tiny silver bells, the pentacle and others were there to tell us she knew she was in great peril. The keys were to signify that something was locked up – a secret. But she knew you could and would quite probably read and perhaps even remove a part or all of the rebus, so lost among the coins she included a maze you might not see if in haste. That maze, Bishop, and the tin of sardines were there for people like myself and my partner to divine.'

'Get on with it,' shouted Rivaille angrily.

'Of course. She named you, Bishop. To her you were at the heart of the matter because as God's emissary you should have been sitting at His right hand and not caught up in your own dreams and aspirations. You're the Capricorn at whose sign Dédou Favre points the Archer's arrow. But, please, Préfet, be so good as to tell us what sign you were born under. Was the moonstone yours?'

'What moonstone?'

'The one that was pinned next to the friar who sprinkled holy water on the devil of the Goat!'

'Enough!' shouted Rivaille. 'Alain, stop him this instant!'

INSTANT . . . INSTANT . . . came the echoes, to be chased by ENOUGH!

Get to the point, Louis, swore Kohler silently as he tried to edge his way closer to Frau von Mahler, but Nino . . . Nino was sensitive to the slightest move and would questioningly lift her head and look at him with sorrowful eyes.

'Then let us accept,' continued Louis, 'that all present will find themselves spelled out in the comet's tail that trailed so beautifully and mysteriously across that young woman's belt from the sign she wore high on her left hip, the sign of herself.'

It was coming now, thought Christiane, her heart sinking further at the thought of what awaited them. Geneviève was ashen and had sensed it too, and when the Chief Inspector said, 'But what, really, was the answer to the rebus? We know now that the killer couldn't have been born under the sign of the Fishes or that of the Twins. Xavier could well have done it, but she had worn an emerald, a beautiful deep green, crystal-clear stone to signify that she had seen well into the future. And when you called out to her through the darkness of this tragic place, Frau von Mahler, she told you to leave at once because by then she had realized exactly how true that emerald's voice had been.'

'Jean-Louis, this is all hearsay, a figment of that girl's imagination no magistrate or judge would accept. We gave you a suspect—'

'As you tried to give us Brother Matthieu, Préfet? That girl's comet's tail ended with a moonstone over which fell a rain of pearls.'

'Pearls?'

'Tears, then, for that is what they represented in the Renaissance. The assembled. Your *cagoulards*.'

Louis gave them a moment, and then, like the judge he had

become, said sadly, 'Which of you ordered them to kill her, Bishop? Was the choice drawn by lots as when a new Pope is elected?'

'By lots,' said Rivaille condescendingly. 'And in the old way, as during the Babylonian Captivity.'

'The Second Babylon,' acknowledged the Sûreté with a curt nod. 'You drew the white slip, Bishop. That girl had even foreseen this. A single pearl was pinned next to your leaden Goat, and on the right hand.'

'I did not kill her.'

'Of course you didn't. Your kind never do, not when you have cowards like these at your beck and call. They wore black, not white, those assassins you sent. They swiftly entered via the Jesus' Room and we know the rest, Bishop. Xavier, coming back from a night of poaching rabbits on the Île de la Barthelasse, found the door to the Palais open and let Nino loose. He knew what was to happen, didn't you, boy?'

'I knew,' taunted Xavier.

'And may God forgive you for what you did to Dédou,' said Louis. 'The *Résistance* won't. I'll make certain of it. Believe me, *mon fin, La belle France* will be well rid of you.'

The candles flickered, throwing soft shadows over the Hooded Ones. And why did he have to emphasize his patriotism? wondered Kohler. A last taunt, was that it? Had he completely forgotten what awaited them?

Nino fidgeted. Unnoticed by the others, von Mahler had somehow moved much closer to his wife.

'Last October,' said Louis, 'your little friend led you to Adrienne de Langlade's body, to where these four and others had hidden it underwater. You took some of her hair, Xavier. You might never know if it would be needed but, just as in your hiding of the sickle and the *martinet*, it would give you such a hold over Bishop Rivaille. You rejoiced, I think, in your good fortune.'

'What if I did?' sang out the boy. 'It means nothing now to you.' YOU . . . YOU . . .

'Keeping silent about a murder is punishable by a stiff sentence!' shouted Louis.

'One I'll never see!' SEE . . . SEE . . .

Frau von Mahler and Marie-Madeleine had somehow moved themselves a little away from the Colonel. What the hell was going on? wondered Kohler. *Verdammt!* How were they ever going to get out of this?

Louis wanted desperately to light that pipe of his, even to taking out his matchbox, only to acknowledge the mistake. 'Of course, you'll never see prison,' he went on. 'We've other plans. But let us finish with you so that we can taste the Châteauneuf-du-pape of this whole affair. Everything you do, Xavier, is done first to protect yourself and gain the upper hand, and secondly to keep the bishop content. Adrienne de Langlade's hair was presented to Brother Matthieu as a parting gesture of contempt. You told that poor unfortunate he had best do as the bishop had instructed and put an end to himself.'

'You raped Adrienne de Langlade,' said Kohler. 'She was as much of a threat to you early last June as she was to your *Primo Soprano.*'

'I wasn't the only one.'

'I didn't think you were, did you, Louis?'

'Norman had a go at her twice,' said the boy, 'to prove himself capable of being a man.'

'You little bastard!' shrieked the cherub. BASTARD . . . BASTARD . . .

'Enough!' shrieked de Passe. 'Take these two from Paris and dispose of them. The river, but first the garrotte and the knife.'

The Hooded Ones began to converge on them. Hastily Louis stuffed that precious pipe of his away.

Kohler . . .

'Stop! Don't any of you move!' shrilled Frau von Mahler. 'Let . . . let him finish.'

The Belgian FN was in her hands. De Passe was so taken aback, he frantically looked to Rivaille for help and was signalled caution.

She motioned to the *cagoulards* to retreat to their former positions. 'Please continue, Inspector. Let us have the benefit of your analysis. Kurt, stay where you are.'

'Madame,' said Louis, still standing some distance from her and therefore not able to get that gun from her, thought Kohler ruefully. 'Madame, we know Bishop Rivaille, in a drunken rage, had Adrienne de Langlade brought to his room at the mill. We believe he did things to that girl, perhaps after first purging himself with the *martinet* for being so foolish as to think her "pure", and that he forgot his vows and then blamed her for encouraging him.'

'Alain, tell him it wasn't so! She refused to name the father of her bastard, damn you! I . . . I repeatedly asked her.'

'But she couldn't! She didn't know, Bishop, and no one, not one among those she was to join and call her friends and associates, would tell her because they didn't want her with them. "She didn't work out." And for her "sins", Bishop, you sentenced her to the *accabussade*. What happened, Maître Simondi? You've listened to all I've said and known it was the truth, yet have said so little.'

'It was an accident. That infernal cage was far too heavy and awkward. The rope broke and we . . . we couldn't raise her in time.'

No one moved. Frau von Mahler glanced apprehensively from one to another of them, and to the long lines of *cagoulards* who waited as before.

Far from sure of herself, did she really know where to go next? wondered Kohler sadly.

'Ah *bon*,' said Louis with that little toss of his head his partner had come to know so well. 'But then, Maître, the four of you had a problem on your hands, one that Mireille de Sinéty refused to let you hide. Dédou wanted her to use the information to gain the *maquis* a small reprieve, but couldn't be here to back her up. Instead, she had to face you all alone.'

'She wouldn't listen! She defied the Mother Church!' seethed Rivaille.

'No, Bishop, she defied the four of you, one of whom, I'm certain, deliberately detained the concierge until the deed was done.'

'Messieurs,' quavered Frau von Mahler, and there were tears she had yet to realize. 'You robbed me and my family of a light when it was most needed. Did you not think of this?' THIS . . . THIS . . .

'Louis . . .' began Kohler, only to see the Sûreté raise a cautionary hand.

'Robbed?' said Renaud, deeply puzzled.

They faced her, the four of them. They still didn't know quite what to make of her. To a man, the Hooded Ones waited, the singers also.

Von Mahler started towards her, only to find himself held back by Marie-Madeleine.

'*Dio mio*, do something, Alain,' breathed Simondi. Renaud just stared at her as if he couldn't yet comprehend her intentions. De Passe took a step toward her, saying, 'Frau von . . .'

'Don't come near me!' she shrilled. 'I'm warning you!'

Rivaille hastily crossed himself and went down on his knees, his hands clasped in prayer.

'Now give me the name of her assassin. Call it out to me, Préfet.'

Merde alors, she wouldn't really use that gun, would she? demanded de Passe of himself. 'Duverger . . . Vincent,' he sang out.

DUVERGER . . . DUVERGER . . . 'Remove the hood,' she shrilled. 'Let me see your face.' YOUR FACE . . .

He was not old, nor young, nor anything but ordinary and when she shot him, he simply collapsed as the sound of the gun boomed and echoed all around them. Other shots quickly followed it. One by one, and without hesitation. De Passe tried to get to her. Renaud turned away to run and was hit in the back. Simondi begged her not to kill him, but she wouldn't listen.

'Ingrid!' cried out von Mahler, but her hand refused to shake and she still didn't listen.

Rivaille looked up at and beyond her to his God as she fired. 'It was the only way, Kurt! The only way!' she cried, and walking among the fallen, fired once more into each of them.

Leaderless, the Hooded Ones had vanished.

*

It was freezing in Orange, some twenty-five kilometres to the north, when they got to the station, the night so pitch black, the hour so small, it was uncomfortable. Von Mahler's driver simply lifted their bags out of the boot and dropped them on the pavement.

Then he was gone and they were left alone. Hustled out of Avignon without a moment to lose, they stood listening to the tourer's rapidly dwindling sound.

No one else was around. No one.

'*Verdammt*, Louis. How the hell did you know that woman would do a thing like that?' muttered Kohler, still shaking.

It was tempting to call up a further *enseigne* but Hermann was just not himself. 'A pistol without a safety? And fully loaded? She had to have had some training to have known at least enough to leave the firing chamber empty until needed.'

Frau von Mahler had risked her life to save those of two police officers. It would be claimed not by them, but by her husband, that she had suffered from a severe psychotic trauma. The courts would be lenient – *bien sûr* – and she would probably be confined to a private clinic in Paris for a while to satisfy the Vichy authorities and the Occupier.

'The singers will be sent into forced labour,' said Kohler emptily, for always at the end of a case, especially a difficult one – and when were they never difficult? – there was this tremendous sense of loss.

'Even so, Christiane and Geneviève will be separated. Will they find each other, Hermann, after this war is over?'

Louis worried about such things and was of too forgiving a nature. He'd wanted stiff prison sentences but had had to defer to the Kommandant's express wishes, seeing as *cagoulards* could well be skulking in the streets and magistrates, especially those in the provinces, were tardy at best. 'Madame Simondi will find her way back to Paris, once she dries out. It would have been too hard to pin anything on her. Forget her, *mon vieux*. Remember that you can't always win all battles.'

Hermann invariably said things like that, and one nearly always let him. 'Marie-Madeleine will move into Mireille's flat to take up where her friend left off.'

'Yes . . . yes, she'll do that, Louis. A nice kid. Thérèse and she'll get along okay. They'll pay Madame de Sinéty a little visit and break the news as gently as they can.'

'And us?' asked the Sûreté, still looking off into the cold black emptiness.

Kohler searched his pockets desperately for a forgotten cigarette to share. 'We'll just have to stay out of Provence. *Mein Gott*, it'll be a relief! No more talk of your finding a little farm down here and retiring to raise melons and strawberries without me around to tell you how to do it!'

They were still arguing when the *sous-chef de gare* found them and, passing her blinkered torchlight over them, said haltingly, 'Messieurs, there is a telegram for whichever of you will agree to pay the fifty-seven francs that are due.'

Louis snatched the flimsy tissue from her, Kohler the light.

' "Beekeeper", Louis.'

'*Merde alors*, let me read it will you? "Body of Beekeeper found in apiary near Père Lachaise Cemetery requires your immediate and urgent attention. *Heil Hitler*." '

'Boemelburg's still mad at us for not letting the *Cagoule* put us down, but is willing to momentarily kiss and make up. But isn't it a little cold to be worrying about bees?'

'Perhaps, but then . . . ah *mais alors, alors*, Hermann, in Paris anything is possible, especially when under the Occupier.'

As if he didn't already know it!

Kohler thought to add a word but was too tired. And anyway, Louis deserved to have the last one. 'Come on, *mon vieux*. Hey, I'll even let you ride second-class if you want.'

'*Merci*. And while you're up there in front with others of the Occupier, please think about his use of "urgent", Hermann. That suggests trouble.'